MERCY'S REFUGE

MERCY'S REFUGE

RITA GERLACH

Dusk to Dawn Books

MERCY'S REFUGE

'Come out from among them, and be ye separate.'
Corinthians 6:17

Endorsements

'Rita Gerlach never disappoints. All of her well-researched historical novels promise to take readers on exciting voyages and introduce them to courageous characters, and *Mercy's Refuge* is no exception. You'll fall in love with her characters and feel as if you're right there with them, watching history unfold. Make room on your 'keepers shelf' for this one, because you're going to want to read this thrilling story time and again.'

—Loree Lough, USA Today Bestselling author of 123 award-winning books, including *50 Hours and Home to Stay.*

❀❀❀

Mercy's Refuge is indisputably Rita Gerlach's finest historical novel yet. Unlike many romantic novels, Rita brings her stories to life through her deep immersion into the history and culture of the period. This time, she has written the gripping tale of a young woman fleeing dangerous enemies to join the other passengers aboard the *Mayflower*.

Rita never strays from historical accuracy, so readers can be assured they will experience the true difficulties and challenges the Puritans faced on the ship and while carving out a home in the New World. This is a story that will stay with you and one you will want to read again and again. I believe Rita Gerlach is one of our finest authors today in the category of inspirational historical novels.'

—Editor Barbara Scott, author of *Dreams of My Heart.*

Author's Note

More than 400 years ago a group of humble believers in Christ and the Bible, left England for a new life in Holland. For twelve years, they lived amongst the Dutch. When they feared their children would grow up to live as the Dutch in a more liberal view of life and God, they decided to risk the voyage to begin a new life in America, and be free from religious persecution by King James VI.

While researching their story, I read William Bradford's missive 'Of Plymouth Plantation'. It is a moving account of the dangers and trials they faced. I've included some of the incidents Bradford wrote about, and fictionalized these events by including the romance between Caleb Treymayne and Mercy McCrea, two people brought together through dire circumstance.

One of the persons I grew a fondness for is Dorothy Bradford. There is no telling everything she must have felt leaving her son behind with her parents with the hope of seeing him again. She had to be a courageous woman, and one of virtue and faith. There are debates about her falling off the ship and drowning, whether it was an accident or that she threw herself over. No one will ever know, but I'd like to think it were the former, even if Dorothy was sad, weary, and fearful.

If you put yourself into the shoes of the other women, it is hard to imagine what life was like for them aboard a tiny ship tossed about in the ocean for eight weeks, landing in a place not planned, and staying aboard for four months in the dead of winter. Out of the eighteen women who sailed on the *Mayflower*, five were alive after the first winter. Four were left by the time they had a thanksgiving feast for the bountiful harvest they shared with the Wampanoag Indians.

Chapter 1

Ipswich, England, March 1620

Mercy McCrea stood on a wooden platform above a crowd of faceless people. Her feet and limbs were bare and her hands bound behind her back. A hard wind blew her hair forward, stinging her face like the whipping of nettles. Something coarse and heavy fell over her head, down her neck, and tightened.

A street vendor's cry below her window startled her awake. She gasped. Her heart raced. A nightmarish dream lingered although her eyes had opened. "It was a dream," she breathed. "It means nothing." It had no prophetic meaning, yet she struggled to put it from her mind.

"Mercy, time to rise." A voice called from downstairs. "Make haste, child."

'Twas Nan Patience's voice calling. Throwing back the tattered blanket, Mercy sat up and ran her hands over her face. Gripping the front of her shift, she swung her legs over the side of the cot and rubbed her eyes.

"Do you hear me, Mercy?" Nan Patience shouted up the staircase.

"I do, Nan. I shant be long."

"Mark the time. You do not want to lose your place."

A drop of water plopped on her shoulder and she looked up. Last night's rain seeped through the roof, down to the upper floor of the house and stained the cracks in the plaster. She frowned. Eventually the cracks would widen and bring the century-old ceiling down on top of her. Too poor to pack up her belongings and

1

find a safer place for her and her grandparents, she had to take her chances. She looked at dawn coming through the window. Its rosy pearl color caused her mouth to lift into a slight smile. The vendor called out again, his voice like a song on the daybreak air. She pulled at the edge of her blanket and tucked it under her chin. The coolness of dawn chilled her bare feet when the blanket slipped away.

Dragging off her cap, her hair fell down her back in a mass of loose curls. Setting her feet on the freezing floor, she shivered and hurried to a small trunk kept against the wall. From it, she snatched out a pair of wool stockings Nan Patience had knitted. Her fingers were numb with cold. She quickly slid them over her legs and up to her knees.

Plink!

She turned. Freeing the window latch, she placed her hand against the mullions and pushed. The window screeched open, and she looked down to the street. Her friend Martin Flagg stood below. His youthful smile came from a boy who'd been infatuated with her since the first day they met, when he moved into a small room across the street.

"Good morning, Mercy." He raised his hat and slapped it against his chest.

"What time is it?"

"Time for you to hurry down, otherwise you'll be late."

Her shift slipped over her right shoulder and she hiked it up. She saw him blush and look away. "Wait for me, Martin. I'll be disappointed if you go on without me."

"I must be away to the docks. So make haste, will you?" He shoved his hands into his pockets and leaned against the wall.

Mercy closed the window. Hunger gnawed at her belly. If she rushed to dress, she might have time for a bowl of porridge. After slipping on her gray petticoat and bodice, she pinned her hair and placed a coif over it. She poured icy water from a chipped pitcher into a plain white washbowl, touched the water with her fingertips and shivered. She craved to hurry back under her blanket, frayed as it was, and sink her head into the soft goose down pillow. Awe the warmth—to sleep in a daze far away from life. Then again, the dream might come back.

She dipped a towel into the bowl and rubbed it over her skin. If she could afford tallow and lye, she would make her own cakes of soap. Use of a washbowl was not the same as a soaking tub. Mercy relished the thought of a hot bath by the fire, with lather and scent dripping over her skin. She heard the Elizabethans did not believe in bathing, that they never swam in the Thames or the sea, let alone take a bath in a tub. The new Scottish King, James Stuart, probably had the same aversion to soap and water. Mercy shook her head as she imagined the King walking about his gilded halls in expensive doublets, breeches, and funnel boots, smelling the same as his unwashed subjects.

"One day, I'll marry high, and have a bath every week in a bright copper tub of my own," she said aloud, "with lavender and rose blossoms and soap bought from a London shop."

Was it wrong to dream, to long for an easier life? Certainly, the want for something feminine could not be a sin—could it? She bit her lower lip and set the towel aside. After strapping on her shoes, she turned to leave, but paused to look in the broken mirror on the wall. She found it one day walking along the River Orwell. Its size was enough for her to see her eyes and nose. She turned her head and frowned at the freckle on her right cheek. At least her eyes were blue as the day she'd been born, so she was told. She turned away and went down the narrow staircase to the first floor of the small brick row house. Nan Patience and Grandpapa Jonah were at the kitchen table near the hearth. Charred wood burned bright within the gray ash.

"Good morn." She leaned down and kissed their cheeks. "I must be away."

"Have a bit of porridge, child." Nan slid a bowl toward her.

"I haven't time to eat, and Martin is waiting for me."

Grandpapa glowered. "You must eat, Mercy. Waste not your grandmother's cooking."

"Worry not." She picked up a spoon, and to appease him shoveled a heaping spoonful into her mouth. "I'll break the rest of my fast at the inn."

"But it is an expense, is it not?"

Mercy shrugged. "There is more than enough without having to pay."

Truth be told, what the innkeeper provided sustained her just enough to get her through the day. Bread and root vegetables in broth. If patrons left scrapes on their plates, her employer would allow the staff to have it after he gave bits to the stray cats outside the back door. He needed to keep them close in order to keep the mice and rats at bay.

3

Nan Patience looked concerned. "Eat the rest. Otherwise you'll faint on the street from hunger."

"I'll not faint. I'll be punished if I'm late." From a hook beside the door, Mercy grabbed her cloak and swung it over her shoulders. "I am owed wages today, so I'll buy flour, apples, and the cheapest meat I can find at the market."

"We can do without meat," Nan said. Mercy took out the last of her coins and looked at them. If anything Nan had taught her it was to be patient—a reflection of the name given Nan once she passed the first year of her birth. She said little, voiced even less in opinion, and bowed her hoary head in thanks at meals even if it were a bowl of pottage bland and simple.

Seated across from Nan, Grandpapa Jonah set his pewter mug on the table. "You're worth more than what he pays you." He sounded bitter, and she knew why. He'd grown old, unable to support his family as he once did. The chess pieces he carved and sold to the upper class helped keep the wolf from the door. Still, the wolf stood outside it waiting for a moment to leap inside, teeth barred and growling. Mercy saw concern in his face every time he packed the chess pieces into a box to sell. He wondered if it were to be his last, and if so what would happen to his wife and granddaughter if he were gone. He was a dutiful man, and carved from the time he rose to the time he slept. Mercy hoped one day, she could ease his burdens and give his last years peace of mind.

A fist pounded on the door and drew her away. She tucked the coins back in her pocket, and hurried to the front of the house. Martin glared when she opened the door. "If you don't come now, I must leave you to walk alone. I fear it, Mercy, but I cannot lose my place because of your tardiness."

She stepped out onto the stoop. "You know you do not have to do this every day, Martin. I am capable of walking on my own."

He huffed and slapped on his hat. "I'm sure you are. Still, I'll do it for your protection."

Martin's limbs were lanky. His arms thin as the reeds along the soggy banks of ponds. The doublet he wore hung loose around his waist. Mercy looked it over as she pulled the door closed and stepped into the street. "I can tailor your doublet. It is a cast off, is it not?"

Martin wiped his hands along the frayed edge and frowned. "Aye, what else would it be? I cannot afford anything new."

"I can make it look close to new." Mercy tugged at Martin's waist. She let go of him and stood back with her hands on her hips. "Have you lost weight?"

Martin threw back his shoulders. "Nay, Mercy. The doublet is too large for my frame."

"I would say so."

"I've always been lean."

She gave him a sympathetic look. "Have you been going hungry?"

"Been stuffing myself with bread and fish. I may be thin, but I'm fast on my feet and quick with my fists."

"I have yet to see you in a brawl, Martin, and I'm glad for it. I would not want you hurt."

"You care that much for me, Mercy?"

"We are friends, and friends always care."

Martin made a fist and punched the air. "I'd whip any man who tried to lay a hand on you."

Mercy smiled. "No doubt you would make a good attempt at it."

"Aye I would. I'd do anything to protect you. Even suffer a black eye."

She slipped her arm through his. "Come, Martin. There will be no black eyes or brawls today. Work awaits us both and we should hurry."

Her words changed Martin's mood. He picked up his step and kicked a loose stone across the street. Cookery scented the air and smoke rose from the chimneys of houses. A woman across the way swept her porch and shooed away a cat with her broom. Men left for their trades and tawny-headed children peered from upstairs windows. Merchants hawked their goods and tipped their broad hats, for all knew Mercy McCrea the craftsman's granddaughter, the lass with glorious auburn hair and sapphire-blue eyes.

Hurrying along, she heard a raspy voice say, "Such a woman ne'er looks at a man unless he is a rich one. She's naught but a dreamer."

The cobblestones beneath Mercy's feet were worn so smooth she slipped and moved to the walkway closer to the buildings. She pulled her cloak closer while Martin rambled on. He gave her a nudge and a nervous smile.

"You're not listening." He stared at her and she gave him a quick smile to acknowledge his attention.

"I'm sorry. Must we talk? I'm in a rush."

"I was saying I worry about you walking alone."

"It is nice of you to show concern for my wellbeing, Martin."

"Ipswich streets can be unpleasant." He kept pace beside her "There're all sorts of lowlifes around here."

"You do not need to keep telling me about you protecting me, Martin. I am well aware of the risks. With you, I do not think anyone will bother me."

Mercy paused in the street, leaned against the boyish imp and tickled his ribs. Martin gasped and jumped back, his face red with shame.

Mercy drew her hand away. "I shouldn't have done that."

Martin shot her a stern look. "No you shouldn't have…here…in public on the street."

"I was playing, you know, like a sister would with a brother."

Martin tugged at his doublet, took Mercy by the elbow and strode on. "I'll not deny your touch was pleasurable," he said. "I'd not complain it if you would marry me."

"Not today, Martin."

"Must you tease me?"

"Your feelings are on a razor's edge. Why?"

"Is it any wonder? You know how I feel."

"So you have told me many times, and I have told you mine."

"Aye and I'll be an older man in a few years with money in my pocket. You'll see. Maybe then, you'll change your mind."

"I think Temperance Glasken is better suited for you. You told me once you thought her pretty. She's a modest girl, and lives out her faith, making me think she'd be the perfect wife."

"Temperance is a fine girl, but I'm not in love with her—not like I am with you."

Mercy sighed. "Infatuation is temporary. Over time it vanishes."

Mercy knew how much she disappointed young Martin. He groaned and his hand eased its grip on her arm. She regretted his hurt feelings, but she wanted to be truthful. She was not for him, and he was definitely not for her. She loved him but only in a sisterly way.

"Is not Temperance a virtuous young woman?" she asked, her tone turning to sympathy.

Martin rubbed his temple. "She is, but if you'll not have me, you'll never see me again."

"I hardly think so."

"Think what you will, but I can go if I want to."

"Running away won't make you happy, Martin."

"I'll never marry anyone but you. Temperance is not at all like you. You have a lively spirit and a smart brain. She does not."

Mercy raised her chin to defend the poor girl. She'd seen her eye Martin from her church pew. "But Martin, if you romanced her, you'd quicken that lively spirit within her in no time."

Martin rolled his eyes. "No amount of romancing will do that."

"You could be content with her ways and keep your disagreements with the Church of England to yourself."

"In the same manner as you, I suppose. I've tried, and it has proven hard, Mercy. One day, I'll have enough courage to leave Ipswich and join a fellowship of saints in Holland."

Mercy shook her head. "The Crown jails their leaders. A sorrow for many."

"I shant be a leader. Just a follower."

They neared the River Orwell. From a distance, the river looked calm as clear ice. Blue water flowed above a soft clay bottom. Tall sailing ships moved like clouds over the current alongside small fishing vessels and leisure boats. A pair of swans swam near the bank, and boys with fishing poles set their lines into the water.

Martin swung his arm in front of Mercy and held her back from an oncoming coach. It rolled closer in gleaming black, the horses gray as the clouds overhead. The driver pulled on the reins, and the horses threw up their heads and twisted against them. A crest upon the door caught Mercy's eye. Such a carriage had to belong to a wealthy lord or lady. Gilding outlined chevrons flanked by a pair of dragons. Each held in their claws clusters of wheat and rye. Too dark to see who sat within, and having no reason to see the person, Mercy pulled her skirt away from the wheels and moved on.

"I suppose you hope for a rich man like the one who owns that coach," Martin said.

"No. Rich men are prone to wander from their wives. I want to be the only woman my husband loves. And if he wants to give me a soaking tub that would be alright." She held up her hand the moment he started to reply. "Never a mistress or a jilted wife shall I be."

They turned a corner. Martin squared his shoulders and looked at Mercy. "You should be careful what you say. England's churchmen do not like that kind of talk. Women are not to have such hopes and desires, but accept their lot."

"I'm certain Separatists men agree women are their equals. My father had hopes. My mother too. Grandpapa told me so."

"Hush. Such words would cause you to be shamed."

"I'd rather be a Separatists if that is all there was. Why shouldn't I say what I want?"

Martin leaned closer. "Because a loose tongue will get you into trouble. You cannot say everything that pops into your head. You have to think first."

Ahead, one of England's ancient churches morphed all other buildings. It cast a deep shadow over the street. Mercy looked at the tall tower with its arched window. The stones glinted in the dull light. Stone upon stone, she marveled at its age, wondered how many people had passed through its doors and worshiped under the nave.

"It is sad, Martin. One day, centuries from now, those stones will crumble."

"You confuse me, Mercy. That church has stood for centuries."

They walked on. "Nothing of this world lasts forever. Grandpapa told me how the Separatists meet in their homes, that their fellowship at Scooby was uplifting to all."

Martin's eyes darted around at the people on the street. "Again I warn you," he whispered. Someone will hear you, and you'll be scolded."

Mercy lowered her eyes. "I am not ashamed. Nor afraid of what people might say."

"You do not fear imprisonment."

"My father and mother did not."

"Patience and Jonah could suffer for your loose tongue."

Mercy set her mouth and narrowed her eyes. "My parents were watched day and night, hunted down and persecuted. My grandparents dare not speak of their faith outside their door."

"You should follow their example. Otherwise go to Holland and take them with you."

A roughly clad man pushed between Mercy and Martin. Others followed. Before Mercy could comprehend what was afoot, a dozen or more men gathered in a huddle and started making bets.

Mercy stopped short. "We must find another way."

Martin stepped ahead. "Come, Mercy. They'll pay you no mind." He held his hand out to her. "I'll make sure of it."

Through the roar and tumult of the crowd, Mercy was carried away crushed against human bodies rabid for what was ahead. Drawn apart from Martin she resisted the mob. They moved her closer to the spectacle that drew their attention, the press suffocating her. With a cry, she reached for Martin. He shouldered through the crowd and flung his arm around her waist.

Two shirtless men in leather breeches swung their fists and struck blows into one another's faces and chests. They spit blood and saliva, wrestled and grabbed. Parting they circled and raised their arms and fisted hands. Mercy gasped and turned into Martin's shoulder. She looked back and gore poured from the nose of one man. He staggered and the crowd pushed him back at his opponent. He fell, bloodied, writhing, and shamed. His opponent raised his arms high, and the crowd cheered.

"How can men take pleasure in doing such things?" she said. "Fights should be banned."

Martin moved Mercy to the other side of the street. "Only on Sundays, Mercy. Today is Thursday."

Mercy looked back at the crowd. "They do harm, and men profit from it. I can say what I think, can I not?"

"Not without having horse dung thrown at you."

Determined to prove a point, she rushed into the crowd. The fighters stood apart and stared. Mercy narrowed her eyes and thrust her hands over her hips. "For shame all of you. Such barbarity. Do you think our Lord approves? There are women and children in the street and you make a spectacle out of beating one another." She eyed the men standing around her. "And for shame you who bet money and neglect your wives and children by doing so. With what you gamble away you could put food on your tables and shoes on your babes' feet."

Before she could rebuke them further, a clump of horse dung struck her smack in her stomach. She gasped and looked down at the front of her cloak. Tears sprang into her eyes. Men laughed. Humiliated, she raised her skirts and hurried back to Martin.

"Ruined. And now I smell like...well you know."

Martin shoved his hands into his pockets. "I tried to warn you."

"You did, and I should have listened. A bolt of lightning would not change their minds." She wiped the tears away, pressed her lips together and stepped out onto the street. Rounding a corner, the inn came into view. Made of stone blocks and a slate roof, blue wooden frames lined mullioned windows. A matching door, deep and shadowed, flanked a shingle that read *The Blue Heron.*

Mercy turned to Martin. "Thank you for seeing me safely here. I must be such a trial for you. I haven't made much sense out of anything this morning, have I?"

"Not really. Listen. If there are no ships to unload, I'll be here early." He glanced at her cloak. "You don't smell bad."

Drawing off the soiled cloak, she laid it across a barrel in the alleyway beside the door. She bid him goodbye, turned the handle, and stepped inside. Before shutting out the noise of the street, she watched Martin wipe the sweat from his forehead and swagger away.

Chapter 2

Mr. Ely, the innkeeper, burst through the kitchen entry. "Mercy! You're late."

Mercy locked eyes with him. "Not so, sir. By a hair perhaps, but I'm on time." In attempt to pay him no further heed, she gathered a mixing bowl in her arms and walked toward the larder. He called out to her again in his cold, menacing voice.

"Do not ignore me, girl. You should have been here closer to the hour, not after it."

There was nothing for her to do than turn and face him. "I promise to make up for it by staying late." She gave him a coy smile. "Pardon me, sir?"

Ely screwed up his sweaty face. "Bah. What excuse do you have?"

"None, sir, except there was a crowd in the street and they held me up."

"I care not for what held you up. I should toss you out on your ear."

"My family would suffer if you did." She did not reply meekly, but spoke in a manner that caused some of the staff to gasp. "Surely you would not want people to know you let a family starve by firing a wretched girl like me who was blocked in the street. Would you?"

"Awe, the poor suffering family tale. I've heard it dozens of times from a dozen girls like you. Being late shows laziness, and I'll not have lazy workers in my establishment."

"Indeed you should not." She waved her hand toward the door. "Do you wish me to go now? Today is Thursday, and we usually have a large crowd on Thursdays."

The others stared and Mercy glanced at them hoping someone would speak up. They turned their eyes away. She had to face this on her own. Ely narrowed his eyes and bit his lower lip. "Stay, but if you're late again there will be consequences. Understand?"

She tossed up her chin at him. "Most emphatically I do."

His jaw jerked. "What's that you say?"

"I understand your warning, Mr. Ely."

"Good. Don't be late again."

"No, sir, and I'd love to chat further with you, but the vegetables will spoil if I do not attend them." She whirled around. He stopped her.

"Look you. Show me the respect that is due me. I am your master."

Master? More like slave driver. She made a short courtesy, even though she knew she had pushed the man a bit too far, and risked changing his mind about sacking her.

Ely turned to the head cook Martha. "Yesterday, we served mutton pottage to a man who told me he's coming back today noon sharp. The dish is a favorite of his and he wants it hot and ready when he arrives." He turned to leave, but whirled around on his buckled shoes. "Mercy is to make the pottage."

She looked at him. "Me, Mr. Ely? Martha always makes the mutton pottage."

"Martha has enough to do. Let's see if you can do this in proper time."

"I'll start right away." She found a stirring spoon on the table. "I promise I'll not disappoint the gentleman."

"We'll see." He watched her every movement. She could tell, by the gleam in his eyes, he had other ideas in mind. He crooked his finger at her. "Come here."

Taking in a breath, Mercy wiped her hands along her apron and stepped up to him. He took her by the elbow and drew her out into the hallway. "Do you know what puts off consequences?"

She narrowed her eyes and pulled her arm away. "I think so."

"You could soften my anger, Mercy." He fingered the edge of her collar. "Well?"

"Is your wife downstairs this morning, Mr. Ely? Perhaps I should ask her how."

He pushed her away. "Get to work. And remember what I said."

Back at the butcher-block table, Mercy picked up a peeled onion and plunged a knife into it. Martha threw her hand over her mouth and laughed.

"What is so funny?" Mercy asked.

"I laugh because you gave Mr. Ely a taste of his own medicine."

"He deserved it," Mercy said. "The menu?"

Martha set a pottage pot on the table and stood beside Mercy. "A miracle if ever I saw. Do you know how hard it is for a girl to find work in this town?"

"Yes, honest work. I'll never stoop to the other kind."

Martha unfolded the cloth from a shank of mutton. "Cut it into bite-sized pieces. Then flour it and brown it in butter. It will be tender and give the sauce a nice brown color."

Mercy took a handful of parsley from the basket of herbs. "Thank you, Martha. I'll do as you say."

"Cut the turnips small. Soak them in water and salt while you sauté the rest. They'll cook faster when you add them in. But mind you drain them, and take care how much salt you use."

Salt. A luxury for most. When was the last time she'd bought some at the market?

Martha opened the door to the clay oven and took out a pan of bread. The aroma filled the air. Hungry, Mercy eyed the loaf and the pot of butter and honey on the table.

Martha cut off the heel from the loaf. "Had you enough to eat this morn, Mercy?"

"No need to worry about me." She sliced carrots and tossed the tops into a bucket.

"Here." Martha handed the heel to Mercy. "You may have some butter and honey with it."

Mercy took the bread from Martha's hand. "I'm grateful, Martha. How did you manage this? You know how stingy Mr. Ely can be."

Martha leaned forward. "Either you are hungry or you are not."

She bit into the edge. It tasted sweet and soothed her empty stomach. "Ah, but this is good. You make the best bread."

Martha shook her head. "No need to flatter me, my girl." She opened the back door and threw fish bones out to the strays. She wrinkled her nose and lifted Mercy's cloak from the barrel. "Why is this in the ally?"

13

Mercy went to her, took the cloak in hand and set it back. "I'm too embarrassed to say. It is best I leave it outside."

"I'd say so." Martha closed the door and went back to the table. "Those scraps could be made into a broth. Take them home. It is sinful to waste food." Martha snatched a canvas sack used to hold potatoes, dumped the scraps into it and held it out to Mercy. "Afraid to take it? You think Mr. Ely will care?"

Mercy hesitated. "I...."

"Not good enough for you? Food for pigs is it?"

Ashamed, Mercy looked at the floor. "It is too good for me, I suppose. I cannot recall the last time I had vegetables to make broth. I did not mean to appear haughty."

Martha came around the table and patted Mercy's shoulder. "Of course you didn't. Excuse what I said." She opened the door and set the sack under the soiled cloak. "Let me know how it turns out."

On the strike of the clock, one of the serving girls came through the door into the kitchen. "Someone is asking for you in the dining room, Mercy. He says you're to stop what you're doing and come at once."

With haste, Mercy untied her apron and set it aside. The dining benches were crowded with people eating and drinking. She scanned the room. An older man huddled over his bowl of pottage at a corner table near the fireplace. He swiped a handkerchief across his lips, and shifted his eyes to hers. He raised his hand and motioned for her to come over.

By the look of his clothes, he was of the servant class, dressed in drab brown with a white linen collar over his shoulders. His gray hair streaked with the black of younger days brushed along his ears, and a thin mustache spread above a wide flushed mouth.

Mercy grasped her hands and went to him. "You wish to speak to me, sir?"

"Yes." He extended his hand across the table. "Please, sit."

"I beg your pardon, sir, but we are forbidden to sit with customers."

"I'll deal with your employer if he complains, though I doubt he will."

Hesitant, Mercy lowered into the seat across from him. She kept her hands in her lap, uncertain what he wanted, yet it pleased her to see the bowl empty and mopped clean with bread. "What is it you wish, sir?"

He inspected her face and did not immediately answer. It made her nervous and she glanced away. "I'm told you are the one who made the pottage. Is that so?"

She nodded her reply. He had to be the man Mr. Ely had spoken of earlier.

"You're too young to be so fine a cook."

"I've a good teacher. Martha, our head cook, deserves all the credit. She made the pottage yesterday."

"Nevertheless, yours was better. How old may you be?"

"Twenty and one as of the New Year."

"Your name?"

"Mercy McCrea, sir."

He slid a card across the table in front of her. She stared down at the name and the crest upon it. "The crest is not mine," he said. "It belongs to Lord Glenmont. I am his butler Charlton."

"I see. How do you do, sir?"

"As well to be expected for a man my age."

"Prithee, who is Lord Glenmont?"

"Charlton raised his eyebrows. "You have not heard of him?"

"I have little experience of those in his class to know him," Mercy said.

"He's the fifth earl of Glenmont, one of the richest gentlemen in England."

"And you are employed by him?"

"Happily so. He has a fine house in town, another in the country. Lady Irene, his wife, inherited her family estate in Plymouth." He glanced at the door leading to the kitchen, and leaned across the table. "Do you like your position here?"

Mercy swallowed. Where was this leading? "I am grateful, sir."

"I wager it is not enough to keep your purse full."

"I cannot complain. Work is scarce."

"Women have other skills which pay far more."

Mercy shot him a stern look. Offers of the most insidious kind had been tossed at her before, and if this were the like, she would pour the last of his ale in his lap. "I think not, sir."

"Mercy McCrea," Charlton lightly laughed. "You mistake my words."

"Do I?" She moved to the edge of the bench.

15

He held out his hand and implored her not to leave. "I wish to make you an honest offer," he said. "You may not ever have another one like this."

"Honest, sir?" She looked down at his hand and he lifted it away. "Speak and I'll tell you whether it is or not."

"Lord and Lady Glenmont are in need of an under cook in their home here in Ipswich. They've given me the task of finding one. The wage is fair if you are interested."

Mercy studied the kind face and eyes. "You are in earnest, sir?"

Charlton placed his hand over his heart. "As God is my judge, I am most earnest."

"You say an under cook? In Lord Glenmont's house?"

He nodded. "That is what I said."

She could not believe what she was hearing. The chances of employment in a lord's house were slim to none. She paused to think, then lifted her eyes back at Charlton. "What is expected of an under cook in a lord's house?"

"Politeness. Cleanliness. Keep to your place and do not engage his lordship in conversation unless he speaks to you. You must work alongside his cook and do as she bids. If you prove yourself, which I have no doubt you will, after a week your wage shall be doubled."

Mercy's mouth fell open. "Double? That is most generous."

Charlton pulled on his gloves. "You must arrive first thing in the morning. Do you agree to the terms?"

Again, Mercy stared at the card. She looked at Charlton and saw in the soft gray eyes sincerity. Yet, caution held her back from giving him a quick answer. "We are taught, sir, honesty is pleasing to the Lord. I asked you if you are in earnest and you answered. But are you honest, sir?"

"I do not blame you for doubting the offer. Still, I assure you, I am honest as the day is long. What is here to hold you?"

"In comparison to your offer nothing."

Charlton smiled. "Then give the innkeeper your notice. I promise you will not regret it."

Mercy stood with him and followed him to the door. "From his lordship." Charlton dropped a coin in her hand and closed her fingers over it.

Shocked when she looked at it, Mercy handed it back. "I cannot take this, sir."

"Why, is it too little?" he said with a hint of sarcasm.

"No, Mr. Charlton. 'Tis too much, and I haven't worked for his lordship yet. You are too trusting, sir."

"You are right. I am. What girl would reject such an offer, and a token such as this?"

"Very few, I imagine." Mercy worried she had insulted Charlton, thereby insulting Lord Glenmont.

"His lordship instructed me that if you were to decide later to refuse the position, you are to keep the coin. It is his way." Charlton tipped his hat. "First thing in the morning, mind you, eight o'clock." He smiled and exited the door.

Stunned, Mercy looked at the shiny coin in her palm. She stared at the stamped image of King James I seated on a throne wearing a crown, and holding a scepter. She turned it over. An inscription in Latin circled the royal shield. Mercy could not read Latin, but had been told what this meant by Grandpapa Jonah. *This is the Lord's doing and it is marvelous in our eyes.* She paused to think—could this offer be the Lord's doing?

The serving girl drew up beside her. Empty tankards dangled from her overworked fingers. "What did he give you, Mercy?"

Mercy smiled. "The chance for a new start." She headed back to the kitchen, her steps light. She had to allow all this to sink in. She went through the door and the heat from the hearth caressed her. She laid her hand over them, felt the warmth, and imagined it came from the blessing that had occurred.

"Ah, you're back, but you took too long, Mercy." Martha tossed a lump of bread dough into a greased wooden trencher. "I don't care if it was the King, you should not have spent so much time with a patron. I peeked out and saw you sitting at his table." Martha clicked her tongue. "I hope Mr. Ely did not see you."

"It does not matter if he did. Is there anything else you need me to do, Martha?"

"I can find plenty for you to do."

"Anything urgent? I would not want to leave you with work undone."

Martha flung her hands over her hips. "Leave me? You're acting strange. What happened in the dining room?"

"Promise you'll not be angry."

Martha squinted. "What do you mean? What did that person want?"

Mercy opened her hand and showed Martha the coin. "He offered me a position in Lord Glenmont's kitchen with twice the pay."

"Twice the pay?" Martha sighed. "I won't say I'm glad to see you go, for I shall miss you. But oh, I wish you well."

Mr. Ely stormed into the kitchen. "What is this I hear you sat at a table with a customer? Sitting with customers is strictly against the rules."

"You would be pleased. He said the pottage was the best he's tasted. He wished to talk to me and so he bid me to sit with him."

"Who's he that he would tell you to do such a thing? You should have refused."

"I did at first but he insisted." She approached the back door and put her hand on the latch.

Mr. Ely pinched his brows. "Where do you think you're going? There's work to be done."

"Not for me, sir. I'm done slaving in your hot kitchen."

He choked. "You're quitting?"

"I am, Mr. Ely. Good day to you, sir." Smiling she stepped outside, picked up her cloak and bag of scraps, and walked away.

With the coin in the small leather bag she kept tied to her waist, Mercy walked along the row of merchant carts and stands. She stared at oranges and apples set in neat rows in a stall. The merchant peddled his wares and fastened his eyes on her.

"Care to try one? They arrived today all the way from the south coast of Spain."

"Do they grow oranges in Spain?" she asked.

"They do. Come, I'll give you a sample."

He lifted one from the counter, sliced it into quarters, and handed her a piece. Mercy bit into the fruit and sighed. "Oh, so sweet."

"Heavenly, ain't it?"

"Oh, yes. I'll buy two. How much?"

He skimmed his hand over the lot, pulled out two large oranges, and placed them in the basket Mercy carried. "For you, a half penny."

"Indeed you are kind, sir." After counting the coins, she handed him the money. "I'll remember you in my prayers tonight."

He thanked her, and as she passed by, another merchant called out. Plump rabbits hung from his stall. "I can knock a little off the price if you'd give me a kiss." The merchant grinned. His apron, smeared with grime, matched the blotches on his face. He touched her arm with his grubby forefinger and she slapped his hand away.

"You should be ashamed of yourself."

His mouth turned downward. "Ouch!"

"Does your wife know how you treat young women in the market?" Mercy raised her voice loud enough for those close by to hear. People in the crowd stared.

"Is this fellow bothering you, Mercy?"

She turned to see Martin. His clothes were smudged and his hair lank about his face.

"I've taken care of it." She glared at the merchant and walked away with Martin.

"I went to the inn and they said you quit. Is that true?"

"Yes, and I'm sorry I forgot you were going to walk me home. I was anxious to get to the market."

"You're forgiven." Martin tipped his hat. "I missed you by a few minutes."

"After today you won't have to walk me home."

Martin raised his brows. "That snipe of an innkeeper abused you, didn't he? Is that what happened? Did they lie to me about you quitting?"

"It is no lie. I've been offered another position. Come along. I'll tell you all about it."

As they made their way home, the sun dipped below the horizon, the lamps in the streets grew brighter, and the windows of the houses and shops darkened. Martin was silent all the way, even when he left her at the door. Had the news convinced him, he would not win her? Her life was moving on—without any man that could not give her more than what she would get for herself.

Inside the house, a gentle fire burned in the small brick hearth. Mercy found Grandpapa Jonah stirring the ashes. The kitchen seemed warmer than usual. Everything seemed better as she drew off her cloak and laid it aside. Nan Patience shuffled down the narrow hallway from the kitchen. Mercy saw her in the dim light, and pitied the small frame, aged and thin, that walked with a slight bend in the knees and hip.

"Look what I've brought home." Mercy held out the basket. "An orange for each of you."

Nan Patience looked into the basket. "How did you afford oranges? We have no money for such luxury."

"It is nothing to worry over, Nan. Take one."

With nimble hands, she chose one from the basket and held it under her nose. She drew in the sweet scent and sighed. "It is nice to know there're generous folk among the merchants. If you see him again, give him our thanks. I'll say a prayer for him tonight."

"I told him we all would." Mercy stepped toward the kitchen. "Oranges will go well with bread for our evening meal. Don't you think?"

"Indeed, and I made a cabbage pottage," Nan Patience said. "I know you would prefer to make it yourself, but you toil hard and must be bone-weary."

Mercy kissed Nan's cheek. "I worry about you lifting that heavy kettle."

"The Lord has kept me strong, and I must do something during the day. Otherwise, I'll feel worthless. I'll wither away faster than I should."

"I'll not let you, Nan."

"Wither? Oh, child, it is not to be avoided."

Setting the basket aside, Mercy put her arms around her grandmother. "You and Grandpapa will live to be a hundred."

Grandpapa Jonah drew his pipe out from between his teeth. "That shall never be. Who would want to live long in this world?"

"I would."

"You think? I prefer Heaven to this wicked place. It grows worse by the day. Men doing evil to others, stealing, cheating, lying. Their hearts have grown cold. They have no fear of God in their eyes. Even the King has made himself a god with his ways. He will be judged for how he has persecuted believers."

Nan Patience lifted a spoon from a drawer. "Settle your nerves, my dear. You must let Mercy inspect my pottage." She handed Mercy the spoon. "Taste it and tell me if I've done all the right things."

Mercy lifted the kettle to the table. "It smells good." She dipped in the spoon. Lacking salt, she knew if she said anything, it would disappoint Nan. She took down a bowl from the oak hutch and held it out in front of her. "I'm starved. Please, ladle me a good helping."

It was enough to make Nan smile and dip a ladle into the kettle. The pottage steamed, and the scent of the cabbage raised Mercy's desire for it. She moved Nan to the table and took Grandpapa Jonah

20

by the elbow. She led him to the head of the table where he always sat. Then she scooped out their portions and sat across from them.

Grandpapa Jonah folded his hands. "It is humble a meal that shall keep us humble."

"Amen, and to be humble is pleasing to the Lord." Nan lifted her spoon. "True, Mercy?"

"Yes, Nan."

"It is better to be humble and live humbly than to have riches?"

Mercy looked up from her bowl. "Ah, a warning? There is naught for you to fear. I am plenty humble."

Nan Patience shook her head. "These oranges are riches."

"And the means to have them a blessing, dear Nan. You know of scurry. Oranges are good for the body."

Nan shifted happily in her chair. "I never wanted to be rich for I wish to enter the Kingdom someday." She tasted the pottage. "Needs salt."

Nan Patience never passed up the chance to remind Mercy of the scriptures. Had the Lord made lords and ladies rich in money and land? Or had man through greed and pride made it so? "Nan, did not the Lord say it is by His hand a man is made rich? Perhaps the scriptures mean a different kind of richness. Health, love, and having babies."

"It is to dwell on, Mercy."

"For instance, I was offered a new position today."

Both grandparents set their spoons down and looked at her. "You are leaving the inn?" Nan said. "We thought you were content there."

"I have left, yes."

Grandpapa Jonah's eyes wrinkled with concern. "You took this position without speaking to me first, child? Why would you do that?"

"It happened so fast, Grandpapa, and I needed to give an answer. I've prayed hard for a change, and God answered my prayers. Our prayers." She reached inside her sleeve and drew out a card. "Here is the address."

Grandpapa Jonah poked his finger at the coat of arms. "Glenmont's home along the river?"

"I'll serve as an under cook, and there's the chance I could move up to a head cook or even a lady's companion." Charlton never said such a thing, but Mercy let her imagination run.

"You're best suited for the kitchen, Mercy." Grandpapa Jonah set the card down and frowned.

21

"Cooking is my passion. But would it not be grand if I did rise higher?"

"You should not aspire greater than you should. Lord Glenmont might try to take advantage of you, you being so pretty."

"There is nothing to fear on that score."

"I should forbid you."

"But you won't, because you love me."

"Harmful entanglements with the world must be severed."

"And you think a better position for me is harmful? How?"

Grandpapa Jonah drew in a long breath. Mercy knew she frustrated him by his pursed lips and silence. She leaned forward and kissed his cheek. "I must go in the morning."

"You're as stubborn as you are beautiful. It is hard to deny you anything."

Mercy smiled. "Then you approve? You'll at least let me try?"

"You must pray, Mercy, to be sure this is God's will."

"I have for a long time. God does not want me to stay at the inn the rest of my days, not with its licentious owner and low wages. I've never said how it was for me there, customers putting their hands on me and saying things they should not. I'll be safe. So please do not worry."

"Show me one grandfather who does not." Grandpapa Jonah broke open the orange.

Mercy took out the coin and showed it to him. "Here," she said.

Nan stood and leaned over to look at it. Grandpapa Jonah's mouth fell open. "You have saved this much?"

"It is from his lordship to start me out."

"'Tis a bribe, I should think."

Mercy shook her head. "No, Grandpapa. It is a sign of better days to come. Read the inscription on the back and you will be convinced."

Chapter 3

Hours ago, Mercy's future seemed grim, one with no other prospects other than that of a kitchen maid. She had toiled until her body wore down and her mind crumbled under the weight of despair and poverty. A position in Lord Glenmont's household was so unexpected—so amazing. She tossed and turned all night with her heart beating with hope. When dawn broke, she scrubbed her body, brushed her locks until they were sleek, and dusted oat flour on her skin. She stepped out into the dismal hallway and glanced at the door to her grandparents' room. It disturbed her, the worry in Grandpapa's eyes and the last words Nan said before going to bed.

"Perhaps you'll never meet Lord Glenmont, but if you do be cautious of his carnal ways. Do not allow him to corrupt you."

She wished she could relieve her grandparents' anxiety. Servants were not allowed upstairs and the chances of her meeting Lord Glenmont were slim, unless she was elevated to an upstairs servant or her ladyship's companion. No matter, she would not allow any man to debase her.

The familiar desire to rise above poverty hurried over her. They seldom had meat on the table and ate mush every day. She imagined ginger jars in rows on the hutch filled with herbs and spices, salt and peppercorns. The honey crock would be filled. The box of kindling full.

She stepped outside the front door and looked up at the haze above her. Smoke coiled from chimneys and mingled in the damp weather. Soft drizzle fell with soot the size of snowflakes. A murky gray mist mingled with it, borne by hundreds of hearth fires.

Gliding her hood over her hair, Mercy looked out into the crowded street. A servant walking a pair of wolfhounds wished her a good morn and passed her. A woman and child stood in a doorway, stretching out dirty hands to passersbys. She had nothing to give. Not yet.

Chimneysweeps carried their brooms over their shoulders. Peddlers hawked their wares. A flower woman handed a winter posy to a gentleman. He placed a coin in her hand. Aristocrats hid within shadowy sedan chairs carried by smartly dressed footmen, untouched by the grime of the city and the site of those less fortunate.

The River Orwell was glazed in mist. A musty scent of rot floated from it and wound its way into the city. Mercy imagined the marshes and farms adjoining Ipswich were deep in fog, and the lowing of milking cows louder than the grind of carriage wheels and horses' hooves. She pressed a handkerchief to her nose and thought how pleasant it would be to live in a country house away from the muck and mire of town. It frightened her, a little, to be alone—not with pickpockets and thieves lurking in dark corners. Lord Glenmont's home was inland from the docks, too far a distance for Martin to escort her and keep his position.

She raised her chin with a brave spirit and continued down the street. The closer she came to Lord Glenmont's home the more upper class homes she passed. Porters sweated under their burdens, and tradesmen called out to the rich to buy their wares. Shop owners opened their doors offering fabrics, rosette ribbons, and lace. Tailors displayed embroidered doublets and breeches, women's gowns in various somber colors. Cobblers sold boots and ladies' satin slippers. Yet none attracted Mercy, for her mind fixed on her new duty and the filling of empty stomachs in her household.

She turned a corner that led onto a rural road. An iron gate stood open, and she went through it. Slowing her pace, in awe of the mansion at the end of a sandy lane. Lattice windows graced three stories, and boxwoods hugged the exterior. If she were a lady, a footman would welcome her through the front door, to a tiled foyer into a room with velvet couches and chairs. A fire would crackle in a granite fireplace. A clock on the mantle would tick away as she waited to be greeted by Lord and Lady Glenmont.

Her daydream vanished when she remembered Nan's words. Slowly she walked on beyond a fountain of carved cherubs. She had never seen one before, and looking around, she stepped back and dipped her finger into the water. Around the back of the building, she found the lowly servant's entrance. Swallowing her nerves, she knocked. A buxom woman in a white apron and coif answered. "Yes? What is it?"

"Good morn." Mercy made a slight dip. "My name is Mercy McCrea."

The woman looked her up and down. "Hmm, so you're the one Charlton raved about. He praised you for *one* dish. What does he know? It will not compare to mine. One dish indeed."

Already, by first impression, she'd been judged inferior. Inwardly, she grew tense by the distrustful look in the woman's eyes. Her complexion reminded Mercy of rye flour, neither stark nor dusky. Her eyes were large with folds beneath them and brown as the dress she wore.

"Well don't stand there staring. Come inside." The woman glided the door open and Mercy followed her down a narrow hallway. There were rooms to pass, a scullery, laundry, and pantry to name a few. The walls were whitewashed and spotless.

"Prithee, by what name should I call you?" Mercy asked.

"Penance."

"A strong Puritan name."

"I suppose," Penance shrugged. "You'll be meeting with Mrs. Dunmore later. She runs his lordship's house—top to bottom. She'll be inspecting you."

Nervous, Mercy glanced down at her clothes. "Am I poorly dressed?"

"Not really. Just remember all girls working here must be clean and presentable at all times. Put your best foot forward."

Mercy smiled. "'Nay, but make haste; the better foot before.'"

Turning, Penance bent her brows. "What's that you say?"

"Forgive me. I did not mean to sound pretentious. 'Tis a quote from William Shakespeare's play 'King John'."

"Putting on airs, are we? How does a lowborn girl like you know such things?"

"I heard a street performer read out the part once," replied Mercy. "It was a small portion, so he said. The saying stayed with me for reasons I know not."

Penance turned back and headed down the hallway. "I never go to plays and do not read books. I read recipes."

"The only book in my house is a small Bible left to me by my mother."

"A great comfort to you, eh, Mercy?"

"Yes, Penance."

"I suppose you don't think going to plays and reading is sinful?"

"Some Puritans believe it to be. Would it not depend on what they are about?"

Penance sighed. "Help us, Lord. Mr. Charlton has brought a Separatist into the house."

Mercy decided not to reply to such a remark. This woman knew her not, and it were best to avoid a debate especially on her first day. She followed Penance into a kitchen larger than the inn's. She imagined it would be dark within, but the windows to the east let in the morning sun. It spread over copper pots and pans, teakettles and dippers, across the oak floor and tables.

The woman tapped Mercy's shoulder. "Not awake yet?"

"Forgive me. I was admiring the kitchen."

"Not what you're accustomed to?"

"The kitchen at the inn is much smaller, and the cookware old." She reached up and touched the bottom of one of the copper pots. "These are so bright."

"Costly too. His lord and ladyship will only have the best." Penance jerked her head toward a table. "I'll have you begin by baking. Does that suit you?"

"I'll do any task you ask of me," Mercy replied. The aroma of English sausages reminded her of how hungry she was. Kitchen maids were spooning food into covered serving bowls. A smart-looking footman picked up a tray and left the kitchen. None spoke to her.

"His lordship likes his breakfast in the small dining room." Penance handed Mercy an apron. "You should see the evening dining room. It's grand. The table alone can seat fourteen."

Mercy tied the apron around her waist. "I suppose I can only imagine them, seeing I'll be working down here."

"True." Penance went around to the other side of a worktable. "All you need is here. I want you to make a dozen cherry tarts."

Mercy set to work measuring out flour, lard, and a bit of salt. Once she made the dough and rolled it out, Penance leaned forward to inspect her talent. Mercy looked away after noticing the mole on Penance's chin. A single gray hair perturbed from it. She would never dare mention it, for Penance had a disposition not to be offended, and Mercy endeavored to be kind.

"Um. It is quite good, Mercy. Maybe not as tasty as mine, but good."

After the morning fare was complete, the staff sat at a long oak table for breakfast. It seemed unusual to Mercy, having heard of other houses allowing servants to eat in the large hall. In Lord Glenmont's house, things were apparently different. After they gave thanks, there would be no talking. She wondered why but was happy to comply. Yet, she could not wait to speak to the other servants to find out more about her employer.

The afternoon came and wore on. The smell of beef roasting on the spit, and the rattling of pots and pans, overwhelmed Mercy's senses. It would be a blessing if she had a handful of beef to carry home. A roast would be occasion for a feast, and would last days. Penance put her to work churning butter. She paused and set her hand on her forehead.

Penance stepped over to her. "Is the work too hard, Mercy?"

"I'm in the habit of hard work. I must say I'm amazed by the amount of food for one man. That roast would serve an entire room of patrons at the inn."

Penance wiggled her head. "You think it's all for his lordship? He will eat what he wishes and the rest is for guests. They're always coming and going. You'll have a chance to taste the beef, and it will melt in your mouth. I know the value of herbs and butter, you see?"

"We weren't allowed to eat at the inn unless we paid."

"Well, you're not there anymore. No one goes hungry in this house."

She pointed to the golden pastries cooling on a kitchen cloth. "I've finished the tarts."

"Well, let me see." Penance examined each one, taking in a whiff of the sweet scents and tapping her finger on the crusts. "Nicely done. Set these aside for the servants. These others are for Lord Glenmont. They have the best looking crusts." She dug a spoon into one and popped the bit into her mouth. "Not bad."

Relieved, Mercy thanked her.

"Well, we'll see how you do with making your mutton pottage we hear so much about."

Mercy's nerves quivered. "Surely a pottage is not a meal for a lord."

"He asked for it."

Mercy swallowed the lump in her throat. "Are you sure? It seems below a lord's table."

Penance held up a finger. "One rule here. Do not question your orders. Do what you're told. How hard can mutton pottage be?"

Put in her place, Mercy lowered her eyes. "Yes, Penance."

"Today is a test, so before you get on with that pottage of yours, you're to make the fish."

Two dishes thrown at her at once seemed unreasonable. Ely never required it of her. However, things were different in such a house, and she knew if she wanted to stay, she must be obedient and keep her grievances to herself.

She laid trout in a baking dish, made an almond paste with butter and spread it over the skin. She whipped together white wine with a bit of ginger and poured it over top. Dates and currants were added into the pan. Taking the corners of her apron, Mercy lifted the pan and set it in the brick oven beside the hearth. Soon the skin crisped and the meat flaked. She drew out the pan and called Penance over.

Penance waved the steam toward her nose. She tasted a morsel of white flesh and her brows arched. She dipped a spoon into the sauce and tasted it. "Yes, this suits."

Reassured, Mercy smiled. "I'm glad."

"We'll see if his lordship approves." Penance's eyes shifted over to the doorway, and Mercy followed her glance. Dressed in black, his lordship leaned against the doorjamb. At first, everyone froze. His lordship took a step forward. The women curtsied and the men bowed. Mercy followed their lead. She looked up and fastened her eyes on Lord Glenmont, but looked away the moment his met hers. His were rich brown, nearly black in color. Most surprising of all was his figure. She expected him to be portly with the amount of food prepared for him daily. Yet he had a slim figure at middle height, without a hint of over indulgence.

"Good day, my lord." Penance smiled and spoke cheerfully. "This is an unexpected pleasure. Is there something I can do for you?"

"I could not resist coming downstairs."

Mercy's heart fluttered at the tone of his voice, but not out of awe. His speech overpowered any noise in the room, and his mien seemed dark and shadowy. His doublet was of the latest fashion, embroidered with green vines and a long white collar edged in fine lace.

"I caught the most delectable fragrance coming from the kitchen. Can you imagine, Penance, all the way from here to there?" He pointed to the ceiling.

Penance curtsied. "We're honored, my lord."

He craned his head toward the table and stepped beside Mercy. Her nerves tightened having him so close. She watched him look into the dish of trout and wave his hand up toward his face to catch the aroma.

"This is what I smell." He picked up a spoon and dipped it into the fish. "Is this for my midday meal?"

"If you wish, my lord," Penance replied.

"Hmm, it is delicious."

"We're glad you are pleased."

"We?"

"Yes, my new kitchen maid and I. I chose the dish and she prepared it."

Setting the spoon down, his lordship turned on his heel to Mercy. "Would that be you, girl?"

Mercy lowered her eyes and curtsied. "Yes, my lord."

"Charlton spoke to me about you, said you were an exceptional cook."

"It was kind of him, my lord."

"My servants do not need to be kind, just truthful."

"If I may say, my lord. Kindness and truth can complement each other."

His lordship picked up a grape from a platter and placed it in his mouth. "A philosopher and a cook. Well, philosopher. What duties are in store for you today?"

"Penance has me making your evening repast, my lord."

Once he lifted her chin, her eyes engaged his. He leaned in and whispered. "I'm sure you have many specialties for me to test."

Heat flooded her face. She'd known that look in a man's eyes, the way they trolled over a woman's face and spoke what could not be spoken aloud. Even though he was rich with his mansion and elegant clothes, he lacked in courtesy, and she despised his gaze.

His lordship stepped back. "I wonder if I can wait for midday. I feel ravenous now."

He walked out of the kitchen, and Penance turned to Mercy. "You take care, my girl."

Mercy set her palms on the table. "He's jesting. I'm below him."

Penance thrust her whipping spoon into a bowl of cream. "Class differences never forbade him before."

"I'm not worried. I can take care of myself."

"Even if it means your position?"

"I won't give in to any man I'm not wedded to."

She remembered Grandpapa Jonah's counsel. Her mind drifted back to a drizzly, cold October day when her parents were laid to rest in a small churchyard cluttered with gray stones. He lifted her on his shoulder to take her home, eased her confusion of where Mama and Papa had gone. She should heed his warnings, without any doubts.

The clock moved forward. She'd stayed with her pottage, and when done, Penance ladled it into a tureen and handed it to a footman to take upstairs. Night fell and she returned to the hovel she called home. Exhausted, she left for the peace and solitude of her room. She untied the purse tied around her waist and took out her last penny. She'd be paid at the end of the week. She thought of the gold piece Charlton gave her from Lord Glenmont. Turning the lowly penny over in the candlelight, she frowned.

Had his lordship's uninvited comments made any amount of money worthwhile?

Chapter 4

The following afternoon dense fog weaved through the streets and alleyways of Ipswich. The moisture clung to everything, making windows glaze over and lantern light feeble. It descended upon the town like a winter's storm, blocked the light of day, and hid the sun in a bleak veil. Mercy looked out the kitchen window set below the street. She had put in a hard day's labor beginning shortly after dawn, and her body ached. Pulling her shawl over her shoulders, she shivered when the fog drew colder. She sighed thinking how quick a fortnight passed since she first came to this place. She'd grown accustomed to the staff and the daily schedule. Yet the longing to be elsewhere stirred deep within her.

Penance ordered a serving boy to put more kindling on the fire. A box the size of a traveler's trunk brimmed with tinder and logs. Mercy tried to imagine how much was used in his lordship's house over the course of a day—each fireplace in occupied rooms had to be lit during the cold months and kept going around the clock. She counted the bedrooms on her fingers. Twelve there were, six on the second floor, six on the third, and servants quarters in the attic. Why did anyone need so many rooms, and why had Lord Glenmont housed his servants at the top of the house instead of below?

The kitchen hearth required large amounts of kindling bought in from a country woodsman, for he did not trust the locals to provide the best cedar and oak. The scents were pleasant, a relief from the disgusting peat smoke that permeated Ipswich.

She moved across the floor to the worktable and filled a teapot with hot water. "Has her ladyship gotten in the habit of tea drinking?" she asked Penance.

"I do not know. She's hardly ever here. I can tell you one thing. Tea leaves are expensive, and that's the reason I reuse the leaves. It is weak, but a treat nonetheless. His lordship does not seem to care." Penance bid her to sit across from her. "Have a cup before you leave, Mercy. It'll do you well."

"My thanks Penance, but I long for home and my bed."

Penance patted the seat near her. "I'd like it if you were to sit with me a moment. We don't have many chances to talk, do we?"

"We are too busy." Mercy poured the tea into Penance's cup.

"We've a wee bit of time now. The house is quiet and the chores done." Penance folded a napkin and set it on the stack with the others. "You know, you should consider moving into the servants' quarters."

"I cannot. I have my grandparents to look after."

"An upright girl, you are. Some people abandon their elders and leave them to fend for themselves."

"Not I. Have you any family, Penance?"

"None at all." Penance lifted her cup. "Now sit down."

Mercy lowered into the chair and glanced at the pair of well-worn hands. They were red and rough with raised veins. And although her fingers were plump, Penance's hands looked older than her age of forty and two.

"Have you always worked for his lordship?" Mercy asked.

"Yes, and with too many years to count."

"The inn was a fair place, but the innkeeper was a harsh man." She put her hands tight around the mug. "I am glad to be rid of him."

"Did he mistreat you?" Penance slouched forward. "Some girls are, you know, and their lives are ruined by it."

Mercy stirred suddenly in her chair. "He was harsh in his manner, like I said, but I never allowed him to strike me."

"I bet he was angry you left. Good cooks are hard to come by." Penance lifted the edge of her apron and dabbed her eyes. "I got my husband Peter, God rest his soul, because of my cooking. He got fat as a hog, though still as loveable as ever a man could be."

Pondering how Penance loved her husband, Mercy hoped she would do the same one day. It seemed impossible to accept a man as he was and tolerate his peculiarities. Yet she'd seen Nan Patience bear without complaint Grandpapa's shortcomings, few as they were.

"What kind of work did your husband do? Was he a tradesman or craftsman?"

A sad smile crossed Penance's face. "He was his lordship's tailor. He never made anything fashionable for himself, but wore simple clothes." She pushed her cup aside and folded her hands in her lap. "Some men can win a woman with sweet words—even persuade the gullible ones to please him. Lord Glenmont is no exception. He expects gratitude."

"I am grateful, and have said so."

"Don't you realize his lordship thinks he owns you?"

"No one owns me." Uneasy by this remark, Mercy paused to drink the last of the weak tea. Mr. Ely came to mind. He had been as Penance described. Forward and domineering. Too free with his words and hands. When Mercy had first begun working at the inn, he would complement her sweetly, but when she did not respond in the way he hoped, he chastised her in front of the staff for the smallest of things. Surely, Lord Glenmont could not be compared to a common innkeeper—could he?

"You may say he does not own you if you wish, Mercy, but he believes he does."

"Well, he is wrong. I do not care who he is. He may be free with his glances and makes comments he should not, but surely he is faithful to Lady Irene his wife."

Penance chuckled. "You're naïve to be sure."

"Perhaps, but I would rather think better of my master."

"You go right ahead. Do not tell me I did not warn you."

Penance's meaning sunk into Mercy. She had not seen Lord Glenmont in several days. Still the way he stared at her made her nervous. He had the blackest eyes she had ever seen in a man—and she admitted they were attractive. She would look away, but never was able to escape the sense of them. She stood and reached for her cloak. "It is time I head home. My grandparents will worry."

Penance stood from the table and placed her hands on Mercy's shoulders. Eyes that had once looked at Mercy with authority, were now staring at her with worry. "Promise me, you'll avoid his lordship. If he makes advances toward you, you must find a way to put him off."

"You worry for naught, Penance. I will avoid him as you say."

"You will even if he offers you special favors?"

Mercy gave Penance a reassuring nod. "If he does have designs on me, he'll know I cannot be persuaded."

A candle flickered in the front window of the McCrea house. Since the first day, Mercy had gone to work for Lord Glenmont, Nan had placed it there every evening when shadows lengthened and the sun was setting. Mercy went inside and drew off her cloak. Then she hung it on a hook beside two others. One belonged to Grandpapa Jonah, many a year faded from black to mellow gray. The other belonged to Nan. Mercy touched it, thinking it had been lovely at one time. As soon as she saved enough, she would buy them new ones.

After removing her shoes, she tiptoed barefooted up the staircase and peeked inside the small bedroom at the top of the landing. Grandpapa and Nan appeared to be fast asleep, and she would not disturb them. As she moved away, she heard Nan's whisper. "You are home, Mercy?"

Mercy went quietly in. "Yes, Nan. Go back to sleep."

"We were worried."

"I stayed late talking with Penance." Grandpapa Jonah snored and rolled over. Mercy smiled in the darkness. "Worrying did not keep Grandpapa awake. I am to bed."

Nan squeezed Mercy's hand. "I love you, child."

"I love you as well, Nan…more than I can say."

"Life is hard, Mercy. Wherever you are led, have faith."

Mercy nodded. "You have taught me to do so, and I will."

She bent down and kissed her grandmother's cheek, then left silent and thoughtful. The curtains were open in her room, and the moonlight came through. She laid her palm against her heart and felt it beat. More than once, she'd been warned about the path she treaded on, where it would lead, and what she would need to do. *Have faith.* The words rolled over in her mind.

She crossed the floor to the window and peered outside. The fog had lifted. A full moon glimmered above rooftops. A multitude of stars graced the sky. She leaned on the windowsill and set her chin in her hand. Could it be possible, somewhere a man longed for her? How he would find her, she could not imagine. Who was he and what kind of face had he? Would he love her to the point he'd lay his life down for her? She could not see into the future. Yet she fell in love with the idea of him.

She looked over at her modest bed, with its humble stuffed pillow and tattered blanket. Too small for two, she settled down on her side and drew the blanket close. Sleep did not come easy, for she could not forget Penance's warning. Lord Glenmont said nice things from time to time but his stare made her uncomfortable. He must have noticed the blush in her cheeks and the uneasy look in her eyes. Were those the reasons he would laugh and saunter from the room?

Eventually, she fell asleep and woke at dawn to a cockerel's crow. Swinging her legs over the side of the cot, a troubled feeling stirred within her. She tried to soothe herself by thinking she may not even see his lordship today, and if she did, she would go on with her work and ignore any attention he might give her.

After dressing and giving Nan ease by eating a slice of toasted bread, Mercy made her way through town. When she reached Lord Glenmont's manor, she walked through the back door into the kitchen. The heat from the hearth oven flushed her face as she reached for an apron. Penance was giving instructions to one of the scullery maid. "We have a busy day ahead. The earlier we start the better. So get busy and clean those pots."

Mercy adjusted her apron. She felt a bit sorry for the scullery maid, a petite girl of fifteen whose face had been marred by smallpox. Mercy smiled at her. "I'll help if you need me."

Penance turned. "Your work is here with me, Mercy. His lordship is having guests for dinner this evening. I went over a menu with him. He wants fowl. See what you can do."

Mercy tied her apron string into a knot. "Chicken, goose, or pheasant?"

"Chicken is too humble."

"I've roasted goose before."

Penance slanted her eyes. "It takes skill to roast a proper goose. Are you sure?"

"I am. I'll make it with a plum sauce and chestnut bread pudding."

Smacking her hands together, Penance smiled. "I think his lordship and his guests shall be pleased. I'll send a boy for a fresh one." She took coins from her pocket and grabbed one of the boys as he passed her. "You, take this." She placed the coins in his hand. "Go to the butcher and acquire a fat goose. Tell him it is for Lord Glenmont."

The boy nodded and, slapping on his hat, raced out the door.

For the remaining hours, the kitchen buzzed with activity. Puddings, pies, and cakes were prepared. The aroma of Mercy's goose filled the room. When she drew it out of the clay oven, servants sighed and stood by the table where she placed the copper pan.

Clicking her tongue, Penance looked at her wide-eyed crew. "I can see your mouths are watering. We'll have a hearty soup from whatever is left…though I doubt there will be much meat." She arranged sprigs of parsley on the platter, and nodded to his lordship's footman to carry the tray up to the dining room.

The others returned to their duties, while Mercy wiped down the table. Penance put her hand on her arm. "Come with me."

"Where are we going?"

"Upstairs to spy on his lordship and his company," Penance whispered.

Mercy shook her head. "I do not know if that is wise, Penance."

"Wouldn't you like to see their reaction to your goose?"

"Well, of course but…"

Penance took hold of Mercy's upper arm and led her out into the hallway to the other side of the scullery. An exit led into a winding wooden staircase scared and discolored from years of use. Penance moved Mercy inside where there were no windows, no light to guide them up the steps. Mercy followed Penance, lifting their skirts and stepping quietly. At the top of the staircase was a door. Penance set her hand over an old brass latch and moved the door in enough to hear voices on the other side. The only sound Mercy heard were footsteps exiting the room.

"They have not come in yet," Penance said. "Go on. Look inside. Tell me if you've ever seen a more beautiful room."

Mercy leaned forward and peaked through the opening. The room had the brightness of a July garden. A Turkish carpet of burgundy, golden amber, and muted jade lay beneath the table. The table sparkled with crystal goblets and water glasses. Lit candles threw their light into the diamond shapes of the drinkware and over a wine bottle in the shape of a large onion.

"See that condiment set?" Penance pointed. "Her ladyship ordered it from an Italian glassmaker in Florence. Have you ever seen anything so elegant?"

Mercy perused the table. Envy washed over her. "I have not," she replied to Penance. She supposed she'd never own such a thing, which only caused her to admire it even more. 'Twas a sin to covet those things belonging to another, and she'd been taught not to desire things of little importance or need, but to be thankful for what she had.

She could not resist in asking, "What is within the bottles?"

"Olive oil and grape vinegar, also from Italy," Penance replied. "Lady Irene insists on having them at every meal, even when she is not here. Look beside the plates. His lordship had forks specially made also from Italy. They are very popular with the wealthy these days." Penance nudged Mercy. "I wager you'd like to try one. I'll see what I can do downstairs."

Intrigued, Mercy stared at the one she could see closest to her. "Have you tried one?"

"Not I…Not yet anyway."

"Clergy are against forks, but I am not. Shall I go in and get one? I'll bring it back for us to look at and then return it."

A giggle passed through Penance lips. "Oh, Mercy. You are a bold girl. I do not advise it. You might get caught."

The dining room door swung open, and the footman stepped inside the room, held the door for his lordship and guests without meeting their eyes. A gentleman in an embroidered blue doublet walked in with a fair-haired lady. The gown she wore revealed the breadth of her white throat. A collar of Belgium lace fell over her shoulders along expensive taffeta, the color muted into mellow yellow by way of the candlelight. The lady giggled and tapped her fingers over the gentleman's hand after he seated her. He sat next to her, snatched them up and kissed each one.

At the head of the table sat Lord Glenmont. His long dark hair brushed along the collar of his doublet. He lifted his beringed hand, and his footman came forward and poured wine into the glasses. Mercy watched his lordship lift his glass to his lips, his dark eyes fixed on the woman.

The footman laid the first course, a bisque soup, followed by salmon delicate and pink. The lady raised a two-pronged fork. "I daresay, my lord, this melts on one's tongue."

"I'm pleased you like it," he said. "There are more pleasures to come."

Mercy's goose came next, served on a platter of winter squash and onions, and the parsley Penance had added. The footmen held the platter to each guest. They ate with gusto, and when she saw Lord Glenmont taste the succulent meat with his fingers, she waited to see his reaction. He leaned back and dabbed his mouth with a linen napkin. Another luxury reserved for the wealthy.

"I acquired a new girl." He stabbed the goose with his knife and slapped a piece of meat on his plate, dragging it through the plum sauce. "She made this dish. I doubt your cook could compete with her. It's delicious, is it not?"

The gentleman smacked his lips. "I think you're right. If I can, I might steal her from you."

His lordship laughed lightly. "Try it and you'll meet the tip of my sword, sir. This one I mean to keep."

The gentleman set his elbows on the table and leaned forward. "Is she young and pretty? A virgin I wager." Then he straightened up. "Call her. Bring her forward and let us have a look at the wretch."

Appalled, Mercy drew back. Penance set her hand on her shoulder and held her finger to her lips for quiet.

"I do not think we need to see her. She must be poor and simply dressed and lacking in elegance," the lady drawled.

"Yes, but she is beautiful," Glenmont said. "I've no aversion to the dress of the lower class. In fact, I find it alluring. Satins are slippery, my lady. Broadcloths and wool are not."

"Is she a faithful Puritan?"

"I hope not."

Mercy frowned. Whatever did his reply mean? 'Twas an awful thing to say.

"Or is she one of those law-breaking Separatist?"

His lordship laughed. "How am I to know?"

The man laughed back. "Oh, there are ways."

"I should be pleased to see her dressed like you, Blanche."

The woman gasped and threw her hand over her strand of pearls. "But you said you prefer broadcloth and wool, my lord. You are of a double mind."

"I suppose I am. One day I may like one and the next day the other."

"Why not make her your lady's companion? Then you could feast your eyes on her often."

"An interesting thought."

"By the by. Where is Lady Irene?"

"At her country house in Plymouth."

"So far away?"

"Yes—she'll be joining me soon."

"Best to keep Lady Irene in the country. Otherwise she'll get in the way of all your fun," the gentleman said, his tone sly. "Female servants are stimulating to pursue, and when caught—willing."

Mercy wanted to burst through the door and let them have a good look at her, a poor lowborn girl upright and gifted unlike them. She wanted to confront their opinion of her, rebuke them for speaking of her so casually as if she were without feelings and ideas of her own. The moment she set her hand on the door, Penance grabbed her sleeve, and pulled her away back down the staircase.

As the sun lowered over the roofs of Ipswich, Mercy stepped out into the crisp night air and wearily tucked her hair back into her coif. Reaching home, she stepped up to the door and laid her hand over the knob. Nan met her in the hallway. Through the gloom, her face appeared etched with age, thin, yellowed, and haggard. "Grandpapa wishes to speak to you, Mercy. He's been worried. Only you can ease his mind."

Immediately, Mercy went into the sitting room. Grandpapa fixed his eyes on her. A sterner look rose as he set his mouth. Usually he would greet her warmly, allow her to kiss his cheek, but when Mercy leaned up, he turned away.

"You're late tonight. Why must you cause us to worry?"

Mercy tried to calm him with a touch of her hand and a soft word. "Lord Glenmont entertained guests and I had to cook the main course. It took longer than usual."

A package on the table beneath the window drew her eyes away. "Who is the package for?"

"You, Mercy. It came moments ago. I had no coin to give the delivery boy, and he looked at me most disappointed."

Grandpapa Jonah sunk into his chair and lit his clay pipe. A sheet of moonlight fell through the window and settled over his face. His deep wrinkles faded with the pale dusting, something Mercy liked and caused her to imagine how he looked in his younger days.

"I see we need tinder," she said picking up the package. "I'll take care of it tomorrow."

Rita Gerlach

"Do not ask Glenmont for it. I'll not be taking charity from the likes of him." Grandpapa Jonah turned to the fire. Nan stared at the floor.

"Why not, Grandpapa? You should be obliged to Lord Glenmont for giving me work and paying me a fair wage." She hurried beside Nan Patience. "You agree, don't you, Nan?"

Glassy eyes gazed at Mercy. "I do not know him one whit, Mercy. How am I to judge a man I do not know? Who am I to judge at all?"

"You cannot and should not," Mercy said.

"Except by what the Lord said, 'you will know them by their fruit'." Grandpapa Jonah spit out the words in such a way that they made Mercy shiver. He drew his pipe from his mouth and pointed the stem at her. "You are young and gullible. You are a stubborn girl for not heeding to what I said. You should not have gone there. Now that you have, you must face whatever comes your way—or walk away from it."

Mercy frowned. She opened her mouth to question him. The look on his face, so drawn and grim, caused her to bite her tongue.

"Let us change the subject," Nan said. "Open your package instead."

Mercy pulled away the string and paper and opened a blue velvet box with a note attached.

Here is a token of my appreciation for the fine goose you prepared. You have brought much notoriety to my house. I hope to see you wear this gift.

Lord Glenmont

She folded the note, tucked it into her sleeve, and raised the lid to the box. Upon a piece of white cotton, a teardrop pearl dangled from a silver ribbon. "Oh, my," she sighed.

"You must return it," said Nan. "It is improper for you to keep it."

"But it is so beautiful."

"What have you?" Grandpapa Jonah snatched Mercy's hand and scowled at the trinket. "Who sent this?"

"Lord Glenmont in appreciation of the work I've done. Is he not generous?"

"Patience is right. You must give it back." Grandpapa Jonah took the box from her and held it out. "Put it back."

Disappointment flooded Mercy, and she wanted to challenge him, her being of age, but held her tongue with respect to the man

40

who had taken her under his wing. She would use soft words or no words at all to calm him. It worked in the past. Surely, they would work now. She laid the pearl inside the box.

"Did you hear me, child? It is no gift, but a bribe."

The sternness in which he spoke rattled and hurt her. He'd always been kind, like her father, and given her almost everything she asked for. Something gripped her—something rebellious.

"Yea, I heard you, Grandpapa." She stared down at the box from under frowning brows.

"First thing in the morning you will return it to Lord Glenmont. He should know better than to give a young girl such a thing."

She could not look him in the eyes, knowing his anger mounted. "I will do as you say."

"A pious woman does not wear such things."

"Noble women do."

"You are not a noble woman."

She looked up at him. "I might be one day. What would you have me do then?"

"You'll never be anything but lowborn. Your defiance proves it."

"One day I *will* rise above my birth, and when I do, Grandpapa, you'll be glad for it."

"Not if you rise above your station in this way. Being bought and paid for by a libertine."

She paused once hearing the last word. Her grandparents were much wiser than she, and had experienced the world. Her respect for them had faltered a moment, and then she realized her mistake. "I will obey you, Grandpapa. But it may cost me my position." She clutched the box to her breast, lifted her skirts, and headed upstairs.

Mercy closed her bedroom door and set her lip between her teeth. She stared at the box in her hand and opened it. She held the pearl up to the window so she could see it in the moonlight. It heightened its shades of white and pink. The silver ribbon glimmered. The candle in the windowsill flickered, and Mercy turned her eyes to it. The tallow burned down to a stub and melted over the pewter socket. Any moment, the flame would die and darkness would engulf her room. The candle was her last, for they were expensive. Instead of a necklace, a box of tapers would have been a more appropriate gift. Perhaps it would have caused Grandpapa Jonah to think better of Lord Glenmont.

The floorboards creaked outside her door. She listened to the distinct shuffle of Grandpapa's feet passing by and descending the stairs. She coiled her shawl over her shoulders, opened the door and stepped down the staircase. Grandpapa Jonah sat by the fireside warming his hands by way of the low burning coals behind the grate. His visage meditative in the feeble light. Her feet pattered over the floor without disturbing him. Her shadow reached the floor in front of the grate and he looked at her. Then she rested her hands on his shoulders and moved him away from the fireplace to his chair.

"The clock struck midnight a moment ago, Grandpapa. You should be abed."

"Sleep escapes me." Not once had he looked at her.

"As it does me. Let me fix a warm brick for your bed."

"I do not suffer from the cold."

"But you are ill. I heard the coughing."

"It is nothing."

"I'll fetch Nan's elderberry syrup."

"I do not want it."

Mercy lowered in front of Grandpapa's chair. "You are troubled over me, aren't you?"

"Yes, and so is your grandmother."

"Prithee, don't be." She touched his aged hand and knelt in front of him. "I promise I'll keep my virtue and not fall into the ways of transgressors."

Grandpapa Jonah clasped Mercy's hand. "You must understand it is in our nature to be watchful. We want the best for you, and as long as you keep to your place and obey the Lord's commandments, all will be well."

She lowered her eyes. "You should not doubt I will."

"Have we not guided you wisely?"

"You have."

"Being rich takes away hunger, but it is not what makes for a happy life."

She looked at him. "You think I want riches?"

"It is not you I doubt, child, but those who might influence you to follow a path not pleasing to God."

"You have taught me right from wrong, and I've given you my promise."

Grandpapa Jonah kissed the top of Mercy's head. "Explain to his lordship and his lady it is not our way. They will understand. Now, get thee to bed. I'll sit here awhile and pray."

Rising from the floor, Mercy left the room humbled, determined to keep her promise. She would return to Lord Glenmont's kitchen and do her duty to a wealthy married man—and as far as she knew not one to live a good life.

Chapter 5

Mercy woke early, slipped on her woolen stockings and dress, and tiptoed down the staircase. She had no way of knowing when Grandpapa Jonah made it upstairs to bed, and did not want to wake him or Nan. Inside her cloak pocket, she put the box containing the pearl. She spied out the path before her and hoped no thief would accost her along the way to steal it. If one did, the she-wolf would rise in her to defend herself and what was hers—hers at least for the time being.

After walking alone through town and out to the road leading to the mansion, she paused at the gate before going on. It could be the last day she'd enter, the last day she'd walk over the graveled walk and dip her fingertips into the Glenmont fountain. She walked on, and hurried through the backdoor of the kitchen.

The footmen were seated at the table eating their breakfast.

"You look fetching today, Mercy," one said.

"Not I. I did not sleep well last night." She pointed to the circles under her eyes. "It shows, does it not?"

"Someone keeps you awake?" All three footmen laughed and Mercy glared.

"You think it's a joke? You'll not speak to me again in this manner or…"

"Or what?" the footman snapped back.

"Or—I'll tell Mr. Charlton."

Penance shook her stirring spoon at the group. "Leave her be, or I'll smack the lot of you, and *I'll* do the reporting to Mr. Charlton. He'll not have you teasing the female staff."

Robert the footman gave her no answer, but pushed away from the table and left the room.

"You're a tad late this morning, Mercy." Penance glanced at the clock on the mantle. "By twenty minutes I'd reckon."

"I am sorry, Penance."

"Never mind. Measure out the flour for the day's bread, will you?"

Mercy's hand shook as she scooped out the flour and emptied it into a bowl. She brushed her hand over her cheek to stop an inch, and when she looked over at the pots hanging in front of her, she saw a distorted reflection. Lifting her apron, she wiped the flour away, and turned when Lord Glenmont entered the room. She stood back and curtsied along with the rest of the female staff.

"Penance, I wish to speak to you privately."

"Yes, my lord." Penance lowered her head and dipped. Her knees wobbled as she drew up and untied her apron. His lordship fastened his eyes on Mercy, lifted a corner of his mouth, and walked through the open doorway. He looked back at Mercy, smiled and touched his cheek. Embarrassed, she wiped the flour off her face with lowered eyes.

She returned to her flour mixture, her gaze steadfast on the doorway. Shortly Penance returned. "He wishes to see you upstairs in the library."

Mercy punched the dough. "Have I done something wrong?"

"He saw you coming down the drive from his upstairs window and wonders why you arrived late. He's concerned something may be amiss."

Frowning, Mercy dusted off her hands. "Is it a rule his lordship could not ask me, but instead spoke to you about it?"

Penance shook her head. "He spoke of the day's menu. The rest was in passing."

A stern warning gripped Mercy. She dabbed her hands on her apron, removed it, and headed up the steps to the upper floor. An obscure door set in shadow for servants stood off to the side of the grand staircase. Mercy opened it and peered into the foyer. She slipped out, her shoes touching an elaborate tiled floor. With her eyes wide, she glanced around at the opulent furnishings, the tapestries and paintings, the enormous vaulted ceiling.

A servant in red livery stood in front of a double door. He did not meet her eyes but opened it as if he were more machine than man. He need not speak, for this gave her signal to enter. A fire blazed in a marble fireplace. Along the mantle were statuettes of animals and pairs of lovers. Floor to ceiling shelves made of carved mahogany were crammed with books. Various paintings covered the walls. Mercy's gaze drifted upward to a painting of one of his lordship's ancestors. The same chiseled face and the same austere eyes stared down at her, and deepened her dislike of arrogance.

"Don't stand in the shadows. Step inside where I can see you." Lord Glenmont looked up from his writing desk. The sleeves of his pointed doublet were decorated with blue piping, and accented by a sheer white collar. He set his quill down, thrust out his gray bucket-top boots, and leaned back to look at her. For a moment, he did not speak, but his eyes betrayed his thoughts.

Mercy curtsied. "You wish to see me, my lord?"

He turned the ring on his finger. "Did you like my gift?"

"It was generous of you but…"

"It was too expensive for your taste, or should I say situation?"

"Yes, my lord. Forgive me for being so bold, but you are a married man and this is something you should give Lady Glenmont, not a kitchen maid." She drew the box from her pocket and held it out. "I must return it."

Lord Glenmont stood. "You do not like it?"

She held the box out to him. "It is not right of me to accept your gift. Please, take it back."

Lord Glenmont set his hand against the breast of his doublet. "You insult me, Mercy. You wound me."

"It is not my intention, my lord. Please, you must take it back."

He drew closer with practiced ease. "For no other reason other than I am a married man and you a kitchen wretch?"

"In part, my lord. My grandfather insists I return."

"Hmm, he does not approve?"

"He does not, my lord. Neither does my grandmother."

"Interesting. Some people would have you sell it." He took the box from her and set it on his desk. "Well, I'll keep it for the day when you no longer listen to an old man's objections."

"He's objections are valid, my lord."

He huffed. "Are they? Certainly he would not object to you doing whatever I ask."

She shook her head. "I'll serve you as my position dictates—nothing more."

He pulled away from the desk, stood in front of her, and lifted her chin for her to look at him. She gasped and the lace on his cuff brushed over her throat. She stood back, and Lord Glenmont turned on his heels and leaned against the desk.

"I planned to increase your wage. You did so well with dinner the other night, my guests asked to return when Lady Irene arrives home."

"Thank you, my lord. The rest of the staff worked as hard as I. May I go?"

A smile curled his lips. "You're awfully opinionate and audacious for a servant."

She could say nothing in return. Servants were to be silent before their masters, take what was given them, accept what was taken away, and be sight unseen.

"It is a fault of mine. I apologize."

"I see a flush in your cheeks. Am I that fierce? Am I ugly to look at? Do you not trust me?"

Mercy looked aside wanting to run away if she could. "I do not know, my lord."

"You do not know?" He snickered. "You've heard rumors, I'm certain. Do you fear me?"

She raised her eyes. "I do not, my lord."

"Why not?"

"You've given me no reason. I do respect you though, my lord."

At the inn, Mercy fended off the attentions of lascivious men, but this was different. He was her master, the one who provided a means to have a roof over the McCrea's heads and food on the table. His gaze soaked into hers, glided down her eyes to her lips.

"You know my housekeeper?"

"I do, my lord. Mrs. Dunmore."

"Dunmore told me you declined living in the staff quarters. Is there a reason for this?"

"My grandparents need me at home, my lord."

"They will be better off without you under their roof. With your new wages, they will not suffer." From his desk, his lordship took up a jeweled dagger and examined it. "You should not have been born into poverty. Why God chose you to live such a life, I question."

She gripped her hands tight. "I'm content with my lot, my lord."

"Even when you've gone hungry?"

Rita Gerlach

"There are times when I've been hungry. Yet, I'm living."

Lord Glenmont laughed and spread out his hands decked in Venetian lace. "Don't you see?" he said, with his eyes wide. "I'm God's instrument to keep you that way." He set the knife down and circled around her. She grew nervous feeling his eyes, and stood stark still not knowing what to do. "You should be traveling in a grand coach, not walking on foot every day."

"Such things do not bring happiness, my lord."

"Neither does poverty." He lifted her hand, leaned over and kissed it with so much ease her feet froze to the floor. She drew back.

"You look confused. There's no reason to fear a kiss on the hand. It is what gentlemen do. It is a harmless gesture."

"Not to me, my lord."

"You should feel honored. It's my way of showing gratitude for a job well done."

She shook her head. "Lords are not required to show servants any kind of gratitude."

"Nevertheless, a *thank you* would be in order from you."

"I am thankful, my lord."

"Then you must find a way to show it. Deeds speak louder than words, they say."

"I thought I had shown it, my lord."

His eyes gleamed with a light frightening to Mercy. Then he glided away from her, looking triumphant, and sat down at his desk. "I want you to leave the kitchen."

Stunned, she looked at him with a plea. "Please, do not let me go. I need this position."

"I suppose you do."

"It has kept my family from starving, my lord."

"You do not like the pangs of hunger and want?"

"No, my lord. No one does."

"I've never felt such pangs. Do they hurt?"

Her eyes filled. "Yes, my lord."

He settled back against his desk again and crossed his arms. "I'm inclined to spare a cook, decent as you are."

"But that is what I know. Please do not dismiss me."

He raised his hand to stop her. "That I shall not do. What I want is for you to be my wife's lady's maid."

"But I have no experience."

"You'll learn."

48

Mercy looked down at the floor mystified. Is this not what she had hoped for, to rise above a kitchen maid?

"You'll begin when my wife returns home. I received a letter from her days ago. Plymouth can be a bore, but you wouldn't know, would you? Exactly when she is due to arrive, I am uncertain. Perhaps in a day or two, or a fortnight with the way the roads are." He shuffled a stack of papers on his desk, and silence came between them for a moment. "In the meantime, Dunmore will train you. Believe me; you will be happy as my wife's companion, instead of sweating in a kitchen all day."

Mercy swallowed and took a small step forward. "What if her ladyship does not like me? Will I go back to the kitchen?"

"Do not think of her not liking you." His lordship thrust his boots up on his desk. "As my servants do, so does my lady. Whatever I wish, she accepts."

He tossed the box with the pearl in his hand, opened a drawer and threw it in. He stood and pointed at it. "I shan't lock it. However, if you want it back, all you have to do is take it. It wouldn't be stealing. I gave it to you. It is still yours." He walked around the desk and stood in front of her. "I will show it to my wife, and if she approves and wishes you to wear it, you will not refuse. Do you understand?"

Mercy nodded. The scent of lavender water made Mercy shrink back. "You must dress well," he went on. "Not in those shabby things you wear." He flicked her simple collar with his fingers.

Mercy glanced at her clothing. There were no stains or tears, no faded cloth. Needle in hand, she repaired tiny flaws and restrung her bodice with new strings. Her shoes were a bit worn, but wearable. She knew they were not suitable for a lady's companion, and to please her ladyship she would wear what was required of her. The idea of new clothes ran through her mind. She had wondered what expensive cloth would feel like against her skin. Now, she would find out.

"May I go, my lord?"

"You're anxious to leave me. Why?"

"I've much work to do."

"What if I want you to stay with me the rest of the day?"

"Do you, my lord?"

"It would depend on my mood."

"Yes, my lord, but I'd fall behind in my duties, and since you like my cooking, you'd be disappointed. You hired me to assist Penance, not to be shadow you through the day."

He laughed. "I had not expected such wit from you. You may go in a moment. I've one more thing to require of you."

She turned her gaze to the shadows crossing over the eastern rug she stood on. How she wished he would give her leave to go. His lordship moved around to his chair, sat, and with a flurry of his lace cuffs took out paper from a side drawer. Dipping his quill into an inkwell, he held it above the paper and then began to write.

"As my lady's companion, you're to live in the house," he said.

Mercy's eyes widened. She had not expected such a demand, and it caused a sinking feeling to pass through her. "Oh no, my lord."

He arched one black brow and continued to write. "No? Then to the inn, you'll return—if the proprietor wants you back. I'm willing to write to him." He tapped the quill against his chin. "The Blue Heron was it? Ah, yes. I've heard it to be a very rough place. But if that is what you wish…"

Mercy gripped her hands and tried to think. What answer could she give him without losing her position? What could she say that would sway his wishes? He was lord and master here. Not she.

"The Blue Heron is the last place I want to go, my lord."

"I'm glad to hear it. I'm sure your family will agree."

"Yes, my lord, and I'll assure them their lives will be better for it."

The idea of leaving her grandparents saddened her. In the back of her mind, she heard their warnings. Worry would be with them always no matter where she went or what position she held. Grandpapa told her, it was in their nature to worry.

"You'll have one day off during the week. That way you can see your family. Sundays are for church with her ladyship."

He drew away and stood in front of one of the large windows that faced his back garden. The light grew pale, reached his figure, and faded. It changed the color of his coat and the darkness of his hair. "I'm aware there are whispers my lady and I do not get along. Our relationship will be difficult for you to comprehend, but I assure you, my lady is the picture of grace and dignity. She is a dutiful wife."

"I have heard she is both gracious and beautiful, my lord."

"Beautiful? Beauty is but in the eyes of the beholder."

He pulled the bell cord. The door opened and Dunmore, his housekeeper, entered the room. A ring of keys dangled from a cord around her waist. She wore a coif with sidepieces falling to her shoulders, and a gray dress made of broadcloth. Her modest dress made a sweeping sound as she crossed the floor, her height dwarfed by Lord Glenmont.

Dunmore curtsied. "Yes, my lord?"

"I'm taking on Mercy as Lady Irene's companion. My carriage will take her to collect her belongings. You must accompany her."

Dunmore blinked. "Mercy her ladyship's companion, my lord?"

His face stiffened. "Don't look surprised, Dunmore."

"I am, my lord. She only knows kitchen work."

"Then you must teacher her, mustn't you?"

The color in Dunmore's face pinked. She gripped her skirts and bowed her head. "Yes, my lord. As you wish."

"Have Penance pack a basket of food. Plenty of bread and jams, and whatever else she thinks will comfort an elderly couple."

How kind. Was there a soft side to Lord Glenmont Mercy overlooked?

"Where shall I put this girl upon our return, my lord?" Dunmore asked.

"Use your head, woman. Put her in the room next to her ladyship's."

Dunmore's eyes enlarged. "Not in the servants' quarters, my lord?"

"Are you hard of hearing? The same room used for the last lady's companion."

Dunmore swallowed. "Of course, my lord."

"Take her to the shops her ladyship prefers and buy whatever she needs. I do not care how much it costs. She needs appropriate clothing."

Dunmore glanced at Mercy, and made a face. "Of course, my lord." Then with a lift of her head, Dunmore held her hand out to Mercy for her to follow.

Astonished at what had just occurred Mercy trailed behind Dunmore up the grand staircase. It hugged the east wall where an old tapestry hung, adding to the gloomy look on the woman's face. At the end of the hallway, she unlocked a door and stepped inside.

Dunmore went straight to the windows and threw the curtains back. Sighing, she then opened the double doors to the armoire. "These are the gowns the previous lady's maid wore. His lordship forbade her from taking them with her to Lady Irene's country house, which was strange indeed." She pulled out several pieces and laid them across the bed. "You cannot speak, Mercy? I suppose this is overwhelming for someone like you."

"How can it not be?" Mercy touched one of the dresses with her fingertips. She disliked the bland charcoal color, which was too close a shade to her best dress. "I thought a lady's companion wore more cheerful colors."

Dunmore turned swift on her heels and huffed. "You have a lot to learn, my girl. You must never dress equal to or above her ladyship. You're to be obscure, yet refined. You are expected to dress modestly and simply."

Mercy had seen ladies' companions before, always a few steps behind their mistresses, dressed humbly yet in quality clothes. They were demure, silent, assisting whenever possible. This would be her lot and she needed to learn fast how to hold her tongue and keep her opinions private if she wanted to succeed.

She took a moment to look around the softly lit room. The bed was much larger than her tiny one at home. A white linen spread covered the mattress. On the side table was a brass candlestick, and an unused candle. An embroidered chair, a dressing table and washstand, made up the remainder of the furniture. Green flocked wallpaper added to the beauty of the room. Pink roses and delicate vines decorated the glossy surface of a hand painted porcelain pitcher and bowl. A fresh bar of soap sat in a matching dish. Mercy smelled the lavender within it and smiled.

"What is this symbol?" She admired the marking on the bar.

Dunmore leaned over to look. "Lord Glenmont's coat of arms. All soaps in the house are stamped with it."

Fascinated, Mercy touched the cake of soap. "It is pretty. It would seem a shame to rub it away."

"Your finger might rub it off touching it. Leave it be." Dunmore hung the dresses back in the armoire and closed the doors. "I hope you are grateful. Not every girl of your station has an opportunity like this."

"I've never been more indebted in my life," Mercy said. "I hope to please her ladyship."

"She's an understanding person." Dunmore stepped ahead of Mercy and they left the room for Lady Irene's bedchamber. The drapes were drawn, but for some reason unknown to Mercy, Dunmore did not open them. A Turkish carpet covered the floor. A canopy bed with brocade curtains matched a crimson spread stitched in gold thread. The dressing table stood in front of a large window. Upon it were scent flasks, pomade boxes, a silver horsehair brush, and a tortoiseshell comb.

"Her ladyship's room is beautiful." Mercy sighed.

"It is the best in the house." Dunmore stood a foot inside the door and went no farther, as if the room were some sacred, hallowed place.

Mercy turned. "Will you not open the windows and air the room?"

"When the time is proper, I shall. Too much sunlight will fade my lady's bedcover."

"You must think poorly of me. I'm not a lady's companion, and did nothing to earn it."

"You must have, otherwise his lordship would not have elevated you so high." A hint of sarcasm soured her words. "His lordship might regret it in the end."

Mercy closed her mouth and bent her brows. If she displeased her ladyship, would Lord Glenmont regret his choice? Would he send her back to the kitchen, or straight out the door?

Dunmore picked up a scent bottle and with her apron polished it. "Your duties are to care for her ladyship's wardrobe, assist her at her toilette, draw her bath, lay out her clothes, and dress her. You're to keep her room tidy. You're not to clean, nor are you to make the bed. That is the duty of the chambermaid. You'll go abroad with her ladyship, accompany her to church, to the shops, and to wherever she may require you. You'll sit with her in the evenings, read to her, but never engage in conversation of a personal nature. You can read, can you not?"

"I can. I especially like Shakespeare and the Bible."

"Well, no doubt that will please her ladyship."

"Will she be arriving soon? His lordship said it could be any day now, or a fortnight."

"His lordship sent for her. That's all I know. She may come alone or with an entourage of friends from the country. We must be prepared for every contingency.

Dunmore handed a gown made of maroon linen to Mercy. "We begin immediately."

Chapter 6

From a discreet side door, Mercy stepped toward the stairs. Dressed in the maroon gown, her hair fixed modestly beneath a new coif, she caught her reflection in a pane of window glass. Was that her true self? Her grandparents and Martin would not recognize her. The color of her gown, the dressing of her hair and the sheer linen cap, were after all *serious* and subdued colors in Puritan circles. This gown had not a show of repair, not a frayed hem or faded sleeve.

A horse whinnied and she looked out the window. A pair of grays pawed the ground and shook their manes anxious to pull his lordship's coach. In the coachman's seat a man in a dark blue coat, gold braid, and broad-brimmed hat steadied the reins. Mercy held up her hem and rushed down the staircase. Dunmore met her at the door, and together they climbed inside the coach. The seats were purple velvet and the shades made of damask rose. Mercy placed her hand over her heart.

"Dear me. What ails you?" Dunmore said from the seat across from Mercy.

"My heart. It is beating so fast."

"You best calm it. I'll not have you fainting."

"I worry what my grandparents will say."

"They should be glad. It's not every day a girl of your rank becomes a lady's companion."

The coach rolled on, out the gates and into Ipswich. Mercy looked out at the shoeless children running alongside. The carriageways were littered with horse dung and slop from chamber pots. The children's legs covered in tatter breeches were caked with filth.

"I wish more people could rise above there situations," she said, glancing down at her clean hands.

Dunmore pursed her lips. "Class never changes."

Dunmore spoke the truth. The chances of moving from a kitchen wretch to a lady's companion caught Mercy by surprise, though she had dreamed of it. An answered prayer? A miracle—or a test of her convictions? Nothing had really changed in regards to her station. Even if she were wed to a lord, she'd still be Mercy McCrea born on a poor street in a house of lowborn Separatists.

She brushed her hand over the velvet seat. The din of the city grew louder. A group of boys ran alongside close to the wheels. Mercy leaned from the window and looked up at the coachman. "Please, be careful with the children." He slowed the horses to a walk and shouted at the boys to stay away. The gangly group halted when the wheels splashed through a puddle. Mercy heard them shout something she dare not repeat.

"Unruly urchins," Dunmore grumbled. "They need a rod across their backs."

"No need to beat them," Mercy replied. "They've had the misfortune of poverty and a lack of guidance from their fathers."

Dunmore huffed. "Their drunkard fathers you mean, if they have fathers."

"Have you children?"

"If I did, they wouldn't be running after coaches and putting out their dirty hands for a shilling. Their parents should be flogged or put in stocks for breeding those little scoundrels."

"They are poor, Mrs. Dunmore. Poor and hungry. Have some compassion."

Dunmore pursed her lips. "You think me harsh?"

"Only your words."

"You presume too much. You don't know me at all, and never will."

The coach drew near the McCrea's door. Mercy tapped the roof and the driver pulled the horses to a halt. The windows were dark and the house bleak in the mist and fog.

Dunmore looked out and wrinkled her nose. "This is the place?"

"Yes," replied Mercy. "It may look poorly to you, but it is my home."

"Poorly does not describe it. Oh, such lowly conditions."

Mercy scooted over to the coach door. "It is not four walls that make a home, but the love abiding within it. Believe me, there has always been plenty of love here."

The footman jumped down to hand Mercy out. Grandpapa Jonah opened the front door and widened his eyes. Nan Patience stood beside him and put her hand over her mouth.

"Child? What is this? You've come to see us in a coach?" Grandpapa Jonah said.

"And why are you dressed in such a way?" said Nan Patience.

Mercy smiled. "Let us go inside and I'll tell you."

Grandpapa Jonah moved the pair inside and shut the door. With purpose, he stepped into the sitting room. "No doubt you've come in his lordship's coach?"

Mercy set her hood back on her shoulders. "It is a kindness on his part, Grandpapa. The streets are dark, and his housekeeper has accompanied me."

He drew back his shoulders. "She will not step foot in our humble home?"

"It is best she stay where she is."

"You haven't been long at your work, Mercy, and here you are. I pray you haven't come to tell us ill news."

"Not ill, but good, Grandpapa."

"There is only one reason a lowborn girl would be clothed as you are, and travel in a lord's coach. I pray it not be so, Mercy, for we warned you…"

"It is the way I must dress from now on. I've been chosen to be Lady Irene's companion."

Nan Patience's eyes widened. "You, Mercy?"

"Is it not wonderful? I'll buy you a new shawl and a warm nightshift, Nan. And for you, Grandpapa, a new set of clothes and a pipe."

Grandpapa Jonah thrust out his arm. "I've no need for a new set of clothes. I like what I have."

"Oh, Jonah. Mercy only means to be charitable." Nan Patience's gray eyes looked proudly at Mercy. "No more slaving in a hot kitchen, Granddaughter?"

"No more slaving, Nan."

Grandpapa Jonah drew his wife away and made her sit down. "I am not content to think this is a worthy thing like you, Patience."

She looked at him blinking her eyes. "If it makes her happy, Jonah, we should be pleased. It is her life and we have no right to question the path God has put her on."

"Has God done this, or perhaps another force? Use discernment, Patience, and guide the girl. You know how I feel."

Nan Patience looked at Mercy. "It is true, Mercy. You must honor your grandfather and heed his wishes—no matter what I think."

"What is it you want me to do, Grandpapa?" Mercy said frustrated.

"Live rightly."

"How is being a lady's companion not?"

Jonah stared at her, and did not answer.

"I thought you would be pleased. I thought you would be happy we've been lifted out of poverty."

"By Lord Glenmont's hand…"

"Yes, and I have obeyed you. I gave back the pearl. I made it clear I will not accept gifts or special treatment. He understood, and you must trust me. Would you rather I go back to the inn? There is no lack of ungodly men at Mr. Ely's." She moved near the window, hands clasped. "I have been told Lady Irene is a kind woman, and a Christian. The housekeeper says her ladyship is generous to a fault, not given to wine or offensive behavior. I will be attending church with her on Sundays, so we will see each other there and…"

Grandpapa Jonah's eyes softened. "Do what you wish, Mercy. I have misjudged you. It was wrong of me to think you would give in to the ways of the wealthy. After describing her ladyship, I know you will be alright."

Nan sat forward. "Mercy will learn many good things from her ladyship. Won't you, Mercy?"

Mercy nodded and crossed the threshold into the hallway, paused and turned. The next bit of news needed to be told. She knew they'd be saddened by it, but it could not be helped. "Lady Irene requires me to live at the manor with her. I must gather a few things."

Nan stood. "You're leaving us? We knew this day would come. But so soon?"

"I won't be apart from you. Think of me here, just not sleeping in my bed. We will see each other at church, and I have one day a week free. I will come and be with you on those days."

Grandpapa Jonah stayed at the window. Nan Patience wiped her eyes. "This house shan't be the same. We will be lonely without you."

Mercy went to her and grasped the aged hands. "I'll save my wages and move you to a better house closer to me."

"We won't leave." Grandpapa Jonah crossed his arms.

"Not if you do not wish to."

"I do not, child. We shall remain here."

"I love you, Grandpapa. Will you forgive me for the worry I've caused?"

He turned and as she beheld his face, it softened. "Forgive my tight hold upon you. It is time I let you go. But we shall not be estranged."

Mercy held his hand, felt the raised veins and the hard callouses from years of hard work. She pressed it to her lips. "No, not ever."

His eyes watered, and Nan Patience drew beside him. "We shall look forward to the days you visit, and we shall pray for you."

It troubled Mercy to see how worried they looked—so sad she was leaving. Grandpapa Jonah gathered his wife into his arm. "If you should need us, if anything should go wrong, you'll come back to us won't you?"

"I promise. Next time I visit, I will bring a basket of good things to eat." She smiled. "Only Nan must make the tea."

With a heavy heart, Mercy lifted her skirts and headed up the creaky staircase.

"Shall I come with you, child?" Nan Patience called up to her.

Mercy set her hand on the rail. "I should like a moment alone, Nan."

She went on to her room. When she opened the door, it seemed airless compared to the room given her at the mansion. She had left it clean and swept, her bedding folded and her washbowl emptied. Her window faced west and let in less light than before. Her chest beside it had not been moved in years. She knelt in front of it and opened the lid. On top of the folded garments lay a pair of wool stockings Nan Patience had knitted. Picking them up, Mercy clutched them in her hands and put them into her bag. She quit the room and glanced back at the rustic door. The cracked mirror, the pallet that made up her bed, the small window that let the moonlight in, she bid goodbye. Nan waited at the bottom of the stairs.

"Look, Mercy. A letter has arrived from your Uncle Silas." Her gray eyes glimmered. "I haven't heard from him in so long. Read it

59

to us before you go. You know my eyes are poorly. I'm afraid I'll skip over words."

Mercy came down the stairs. The letter looked tattered, for it had come across the English Channel from Holland, to their little Ipswich house. Mercy broke the seal and unfolded it. "He says he is in excellent health. The farm has done well, and he has learned to make cheese. Can you imagine Uncle Silas a cheese maker?"

"I can, for anything my brother sets his mind to do he does well. Go on."

She then read the rest, which mentioned the Separatists were considering leaving Holland and how torn he was whether to go with them. Virginia was far away and formidable for a man his age. "He says 'life is pleasant in Leyden, except the fellowship cannot abide the culture, and they fear their children are growing up Dutch'."

Grandpapa Jonah stood in the sitting room doorway. "No different than the fears of them growing up in England."

Mercy shook her head at him. "Grandpapa."

"I know what you're thinking, Mercy. I have proper reason to stay Church of England. Your grandmother and I are too old to be hounded for being anything but what the King wishes."

"If Uncle Silas makes the voyage it may be a good thing. Virginia colony would be a refuge where Separatists can be left in peace."

Nan Patience laid her hand across her forehead. "Oh, but so far away. Much farther than Holland. I have not seen my brother in twelve long years. 'Twas bad enough when we lost your father and mother. Now you're leaving, and Silas might go too."

Without knocking, the footman entered through the front door. "The hour is growing late, and we needed to be on our way."

Mercy kissed Nan's cheek. "I must go. I will see you at Sunday church."

"You did not forget your wool stockings did you?"

Mercy smiled. "I could not leave them behind. You made them especially for me."

"Then be sure to wear them on cold nights."

"I will, and when I do I will think of you and Grandpapa." She looked over at him and gave him that childlike smile he liked. He held his arms out to her and she embraced him. Before exiting the house, she stood silent in the doorway and glanced over the dull walls.

Never again would she live so poorly.

In the foyer, Mercy waited beside Mrs. Dunmore. She donned a gown of forest green for the occasion, and stood perfectly still hoping her appearance would please the mistress of the manor. Lady Irene's coach stopped out front and when her ladyship entered, Charlton welcomed her home and eased her cloak from her shoulders. Soft ermine fringe bordered the hood and the deep blue velvet of the garment. Lady Irene struck an imperious figure, even though her looks were hardly what one would say beautiful. Her ladyship's large green eyes, and full red mouth, were youthful. Light came through the window near her and Mercy drew amazement from the bright colors of red and burnt orange that made up her hair. Tall and slim, she wore it in spirals that cascaded down her shoulders. Dressed elegantly in a traveling costume, an emerald hung around her neck to match its color. Her skin looked light and pure like the lace at her throat.

The study doors flung open, and Lord Glenmont walked out. "Home at last."

With her chin high, Lady Irene held her hand out to him. He bent over and kissed it. It did not take long for Mercy to see affection did not bode between them.

"Welcome home, my dear."

"It has been a long time, Simon," her ladyship replied. Mercy thought her voice pleasing and refined. "Home is my country manor, or have you forgotten? I have little use for anywhere else."

"Yet you came anyway."

"Of course I did. You are my husband after all, and we must keep up appearances."

She handed Lord Glenmont her Papillion. The dog yelped, and he held it out and set it down with a sneer. Lady Irene turned from her husband and looked ahead. "Ah, Dunmore, how good to see you again. Is my room ready?"

Dunmore stepped forward and curtsied. "It is, my lady."

"Good, I'm so weary."

"Was your journey dreadful?" Lord Glenmont shooed the dog off with the tip of his boot.

"The roads were unbearable. I doubt I shall get over being tossed around like a rag doll. You must have the coach springs looked at, Simon."

His lordship set his hands on his hips. "If it is my wife's wish, I might. You have circles under your eyes, Irene. Go upstairs and rest, but before you do, you must meet your new companion."

Mercy feared she would not be able to speak. Would she stumble over her words? She kept her back straight and her breathing even, hoping her ladyship would not notice how nervous she grew.

"My lady," Dunmore said. "This is Mercy McCrea, your new lady's companion."

Mercy curtsied in the manner in which Dunmore taught her. Low and gracious.

Lady Irene took a step closer. "Look at me, girl. No need to be nervous."

Mercy raised her eyes. Her ladyship turned to her husband. "You always employ the prettiest girls, Simon."

He looked bored studying the ceiling. "I had not noticed. Mercy worked at an inn before coming to us. I let Penance have her downstairs in the kitchen for a time. I felt she'd make an even better lady's companion to you, my dear."

Her ladyship turned toward the staircase. "Come unpack my trunk, Mercy. I should like us to get better acquainted."

At once Mercy followed, but Dunmore set her hand over her arm. "You must wait. If her ladyship wishes to leave a room, you must follow at a distance."

With Lady Irene several steps ahead, Lord Glenmont stomped out the front door. His horse, held by a servant, shifted when he thrust his boot into the stirrup and climbed into the saddle. Dunmore narrowed her eyes and watched through the open doorway with Mercy. He dug his heels into the horse's ribs and rode off. "He always leaves like this when Lady Irene arrives," Dunmore said. "We should linger no longer."

Together, Mercy and Mistress Dunmore went up the staircase. The balustrade felt cold to the touch when Mercy gripped it. The carpet silenced each footstep. Dunmore leaned toward Mercy and whispered. "You caught on they do not love each other?"

"I am not to say."

Dunmore paused on the step. "Very good, Mercy. You spoke rightly. It is not your place to say what your eyes behold when it comes to his lordship and lady. Do not speak of it, but remember it, for her ladyship may confide in you, and when she does listen, and only speak when she asks you a question. I've seen her ignore his lordship's dalliances on more than one occasion. A woman can only hold back what her heart feels for so long before it bursts."

That night, when the candles sparkled and the house grew quiet, Mercy brushed out Lady Irene's hair. It reached her hips, fine as silk and adorned with curls. How could his lordship not love Lady Irene? Kind and soft-spoken, she possessed natural grace.

Her ladyship shut her eyes as Mercy dragged the brush through her hair. "We shall get along very well, Mercy. You seem competent, and you have a sweet disposition."

"I'll try my best, my lady. You have lovely hair."

Lady Irene sighed. "You bush it much gentler than my last girl. She hurt me several times."

"I'll take great care not to, my lady. I imagine his lordship admires it."

"He has never said."

Her ladyship reached back and dragged her hair forward. Mercy set the brush down and took out a linen handkerchief from the dressing table drawer. "Here, my lady. So you may dry your eyes."

Lady Irene dashed her hands over her cheeks. "I have no need for it, Mercy. My eyes do water from time to time. Are you concerned these were tears?"

"Yes, my lady."

"Because of what I said about my husband?"

"I've been told men have difficulty complimenting their wives," Mercy said, in an effort to console her ladyship. "They say compliments are reserved for courtship."

"And after the wedding night, they end." Lady Irene tossed the handkerchief on her dressing table. "He tells me, he needn't compliment me. I should know without him saying."

Lady Irene stood and Mercy helped her undress. "I expected to have a good marriage. I came to Simon and he quickly let me know I was not, nor ever would be, the only woman in his life. We have no children, and with no heir to give him, he has resented me. I believe his affairs are meant to punish me for disappointing him."

"These are private matters not for my ears, my lady."

Lady Irene turned. "Oh but they are for your ears, Mercy. You are the only one I can speak to freely. I trust our private conversations shall go no farther than this room."

"You can ask anyone who knows me. I never repeat what I'm told in private. Besides, the Lord would not approve of such a betrayal."

Lady Irene touched Mercy's chin. "Thank you. You are a fine girl."

Mercy smiled and helped her ladyship into a robe. As the room darkened, she replaced the waning candle on the dressing table with another. "Shall I read to you, my lady?"

"Not tonight, Mercy. Concern for you weighs on my mind. You must know by now my husband has a fondness for pretty girls. Has he made advances toward you? Has he given you gifts?"

Mercy could not speak. How was she to answer? Would her ladyship send her away?

"Speak freely," her ladyship said.

"He has been kind—that is all, my lady."

"Resist him. If he threatens to throw you out, come to me. I assure you, I'll not allow it."

Her ladyship slipped into bed and settled back against the pillows. "I am so tired," she said closing her eyes.

Softly Mercy stepped over to the windows and drew the curtains across them. The colors in the room dulled, except for what sat close to the candle's flame. Closing the bedchamber door, she stepped out into the gloomy hallway. As she released the handle, she furrowed her brow, her mind troubled with all Lady Irene had revealed to her. Then she turned toward her bedchamber. A shadow crossed in front of her, darker than the night that swallowed the hallway. Lord Glenmont leaned against the wall watching her.

"My lord," she curtsied. She passed him and hurried to her room, knowing he followed her with his eyes.

Chapter 7

When Sunday arrived, the day began surprisingly sunny. The nighttime fog dissipated, and the sound of church bells echoed throughout the city. After stepping out of doors and looking up at the empty blue sky, Mercy followed Lady Irene to the coach and climbed in after her. Her ladyship barely spoke a word that morn. Instead, she fiddled with the tassels on her reticule and sighed several times as the coach rolled out of the drive and into the lane leading into Ipswich.

"Are you feeling unwell, my lady?" Mercy asked.

"I do every Sunday while in Ipswich," her lady answered. "It should be a day for rejoicing and meditation. Without Lord Glenmont at my side, it gives me cause to feel disquieted." She pulled at one of her gloves. "When I am asked about him, I make excuses he is in some way indisposed."

"I did not see his lordship this morning. Perhaps he is indisposed."

"This time he told me he felt a cold coming on." Her ladyship sighed. "I suppose people are accustomed to seeing us apart and it no longer matters. Just the same, I am saddened by his lack of interest in spiritual matters." She reached over and gripped Mercy's hand. "At least I have you with me. And that gives me comfort."

Mercy was surprise by Lady Irene's openness and said not a word. The journey did not take long, and before the bells had stopped ringing, she found herself stepping out of the coach behind Lady Irene. Arched windows and the white stone tower of Saint

Margaret's Church loomed over her. Imposing and daunting, the church threw a long shadow over the street. The doors stood open to worshipers, and as Lady Irene walked ahead of Mercy, men doffed their hats and bowed, and ladies bent their heads in greeting. Inside the nave, she glanced through the crowd to see her grandparents. Grandpapa Jonah and Nan attend the Church of England services. Each Sunday, Jonah's face tightened at the sermons that poured from the minister's pulpit regarding King and Country, how Devine appointments were to be obeyed without question, and decenters punished. In his heart, he followed the Separatist beliefs. Believers should not have church connected to political powers, but should freely worship God in fellowship with one another. In public, he kept silent in order to safeguard what remained of his family.

Lady Irene drew down into a front pew and bid Mercy to sit beside her. Mercy hesitated. "No one will object, Mercy. It is expected."

When her ladyship took her seat, a gentleman in Puritan black turned to her. "Good morn, my lady. It has been some time since we've seen you in church."

A graceful smile crossed Lady Irene's lips. "I've been away at our country house, sir."

"Ah. And his lordship?"

Lady Irene touched her nose. "A cold."

The gentleman nodded. "I see," he whispered. "I will say a prayer for him, my lady."

"I thank you," she answered. "His lordship is in need of prayers."

Mercy glanced around at the aristocrats and upper class people nearby in their Sabbath attire. She looked over her shoulder to where the lower class sat apart from their betters. When she saw Grandpapa Jonah and Nan Patience moving into a pew, she longed to raise her hand to them. Soon they caught her eye and exchanged smiles.

The service commenced, and it came time for the minister to preach. He stepped up to the podium with his head high, his gray hair brushing along his shoulders. He wore a black cassock and had a most imposing face and eyes. The moment he gripped the sides of the lectern, silence fell—so hard one could have heard a mouse scurry across the floor between the pews.

"And, behold," he read, "one came and said unto him, Good Master, what good thing shall I do, that I may inherit eternal life?"

Mercy raised her eyes.

"And he said unto him, 'Why callest thou me good? There is none good but one, that is God. But if thou wilt enter into life, keep the commandments.'"

The minister went on reading Christ's words and the rich man's responses. Then causing her to pity Lord Glenmont, she heard, "'Tis easier for a camel to go through the eye of a needle, than for a rich man to enter into the Kingdom of God.'"

The minister pointed at the ceiling one finger. He glared at the congregation and exclaimed, "Examine yourselves, oh ye rich. Can ye be saved? Will you repent and give to the poor? If you turn your eyes to the places in which they sit, you will see many."

Wealthy men shifted in their seats. Had the minister's words made them uncomfortable? Were their hearts uneasy? These were the words of the Savior, meant to turn a rich man's eyes to greater things, eternal things, and not the want for worldly gain. She pondered the Scripture and did as the minister bade to examine her heart. She'd gone up in the world, and thanked God she would go no farther.

When the service ended, she bade Lady Irene to pause and allow her to speak to her grandparents. Permission was enthusiastically granted on the condition Mercy introduce them. She curtsied and hurried to Grandpapa Jonah and Nan Patience. They were gladdened to see her, but in public, a show of affection would not be permitted. Mercy informed them firstly that her health was in good order, and that Lady Glenmont wished to meet them. Grandpapa swept off his hat and clutched it. Nan brushed down the front of her dress and positioned her cap. She drew them away, and over to her ladyship. Nan's hand trembled in Mercy's.

"My lady, may I introduce my grandparents, Jonah and Patience McCrea?"

Her ladyship looked at them kindly and inclined her head. Grandpapa Jonah, hat in hand bowed, while Nan attempted to curtsy.

"Oh, no, Mrs. McCrea." Lady Irene took hold of Nan's arms and helped her rise. Nan looked astonished. "At your age there is no need to curtsy to me. You are in good health, I hope, save for your knees?"

Nan straightened up. "Yes, my lady, as much as the years afford, God be praised."

"And did you approve of the minister's sermon, Mr. McCrea?"

"Dare I speak my opinion is this holy place, my lady?" he replied.

"I am forever interested in hearing the opinion of others."

Grandpapa moved on his feet. "Certainly my opinion on the scriptures is not…"

"The scriptures are for all, Mr. McCrea."

"Indeed, my lady."

"I am thankful for the upbringing you've given Mercy. She has become a constant comfort to me. I would hate for anything to change that. She has told me of your concerns that she lives apart from you. Rest assured she will be safe in my charge."

"Then she is doing her duty well, my lady?" Grandpapa Jonah asked.

"She is, Mr. McCrea. Mercy is as amiable as they come."

"Well, my lady. My wife and I are pleased to hear it. I cannot deny we were cautious at first, but you have set our minds at ease."

"I am glad for it." Lady Irene smiled. "We must be on our way. Mercy will see you on Thursday."

Lady Irene walked down the aisle and out the church doors ahead of Mercy and her family. Alone with them, after her ladyship entered her coach, Mercy kissed their cheeks. The footman, patient as he could be, cleared his throat. Mercy climbed in and leaned to the window. Grandpapa and Nan walked on hand in hand, through the lingering crowd of congregants. She wished she could have carried them to their door in the Glenmont coach. Home was a distance away, especially for Nan. Each stepped seemed an effort.

As the coach rolled on, clouds gathered overhead, and the scent of rain moved through the air while the light of truth rose within her.

That evening a cheerless wind blew up from the south and battered Mercy's bedchamber window. There were no clouds that night. A wintery moon shone through the sheers. She sat at a writing table, candle burning, to pen a letter to Martha, her old friend at the inn. She held the tip of the quill above the paper and hesitated. What care would Martha have to know how she got along? Besides a letter from her could spark jealousy, and unwanted gossip that she had become full of pride over her elevation in life.

She set the quill down. A sudden silence fell, as if the wind had changed course instead of laying low. She let her hands fall idly on her lap. She raised her eyes as though her thoughts had been carried outside the four walls of the room by the light passing through the window. The silence broke. Her thoughts returned to the present. A coach drew up outside, the wheels grinding over the gravel drive, the sound of bridles jingling from the horses' necks. She went to the window and peered out between the curtains. Lord and Lady Glenmont had dined at the home of a prominent family in the city. At the stroke of midnight, they arrived home.

Mercy dressed and slipped her feet into her shoes. Then she hurried to her ladyship's bedchamber to make it ready. The downstairs door closed. The sound echoed to the upper floor of the house. Voices too were heard, and Mercy recognized the opening and closing of the sitting room door. Her ladyship most like delayed coming upstairs for a cup of chocolate before sleeping. It was her habit to sit with his lordship for a short time before bed, as long as his mood favored to do so.

Inside the room, she lit the bedside candle and placed the glass dome over it. The flickering light spread as far as the bedcover and dressing table. Lady Irene's jewelry box caught her eye. It sat open, and Mercy went to close it. Open, it would be a temptation to the chambermaid to examine the contents. She studied the brilliant blue French enamel, the scrolling gold mounts and legs. Tiny gilded ivy and blue forget-me-nots decorated the edges with raised rubies no bigger than the top of a pin. Mottled turquoise enamel glazed the inside. How anyone could make such a splendid object amazed Mercy, and to own one was beyond her imagining. A gold pendant beside it caught her eye. She picked it up to put it into the box, but waited when she saw that the silk cord that held it had tangled. She sat down and she worked to undo it.

The chamber door creaked. "Put it back."

Her breath snatched in her throat and she spun around. Lord Glenmont stood inside the doorway. He scowled. A muscle in his cheek jerked.

"My lord." Quickly she stood. "I was tidying up her ladyship's table. I always do before she goes to bed. Was the evening pleasant? I imagine she is very tired. Is she coming upstairs soon?"

He stepped forward. "What have you got in your hand?"

Slowly, she unfolded her fingers. "Her ladyship's necklace was knotted and I was trying to…"

"Steal it?"

"My lord. I would never take anything of Lady Irene's."

"You're lying. Isn't it against one of the rules you follow?"

She stared. "Yes, my lord, it is one of the Commandments. I…"

"Stealing and lying, am I right?"

Mercy nodded and set the necklace in the box and closed the lid. "I had not thought of you as knowing much of the Bible, my lord. I was wrong."

He stepped up to her. "Perhaps wrong on many accounts." He took her arm and pulled her close. "There is one way for you to prove what you say is true."

"My word is enough, my lord."

"Deeds declare truth more than words."

"Deeds? Do they show what is in a man's mind to do?"

His eyes narrowed and he looked at her intently. "Then…you realize how much I want you?"

Mercy jerked away and turned back to the dressing table. She sought the words to say. "You do not speak of love, my lord. Even if you did, I would not accept you."

He lifted a corner of his mouth into a cynical grin. "Oh, I see. You think Irene is in the house. She is not. She decided to stay over and will not be home until tomorrow. So, you see, Mercy. You and I are alone. Just the way I want it." He touched her cheek. "Obedience has its rewards."

"Obedience to God—not to you."

"What do you wish?"

"To be left alone. For you to never speak to me the way you have."

He paced the room. He stopped and looked at her, then paced again. "Is this what I receive for having been so good to you? I don't understand why you are not honored by my desire for you. Are you so blind you cannot see how heated my blood becomes in your presence? I want you, and I will go mad if I do not have you."

Mercy swallowed. "I do not have the same feelings, my lord." She spoke softly to him, hoping it would cool his anger. "Perhaps you've had too much wine tonight, and do not know what you are saying. Allow me to call Charlton so he may help you to bed. You will see things differently in the morning…when Lady Irene returns."

"It isn't the wine," he said with clenched fists and teeth.

She turned to face him. "Let me go or I shall call for help."

He set his mouth so firm the blood rushed from his lips. "Fine. Leave me to suffer. Go!"

Unsure if he meant it, but having no other choice, Mercy hurried out. Inside her room, she shut the door and braced her hands against it. When she heard footsteps, she stood back. Fear rippled over her skin. The lock clicked.

Lord Glenmont stood on the other side of the door. Mercy sensed the pressure of his hand against it. "You will feel the consequences of your rejection of me."

Mercy gasped. Lord Glenmont's footsteps faded. She knew, for all her tears, he would not change his mind. She rushed to the window. It was too high to climb out and too far to reach Lady Irene's terrace. She rushed back to the door, seized the handle and shook it. She slapped it and called out. No one answered. No one came to free her.

She backed away and slipped down to the floor against the bed. Without a fire in the hearth and no way to light her candle, she curled up in the darkness and begged Heaven for help. She pulled the bedcover down over her, wrapped inside it for warmth. She dare not crawl into bed and cry to sleep. He might come back, wake her, and force her to him.

The wind moaned through the gaps in the window casement. Shadows moved across the walls and Mercy stared at them with frightened, watery eyes. The rays from the moon slipped away, as clouds passed over it.

Mercy could not sleep. She kept her eyes on the door, and glanced at the clock on the mantle. Before the hands could reach the hour, someone knocked gently on the door and whispered through it. "Mercy, it is I."

"Penance!" Mercy scrambled up. "His lordship has locked me in."

"Not to worry. I have a key."

The lock clicked and Penance slipped inside. She held a candle, and the vague light passed over her worried face. "Oh, you poor girl, I wish you had never come to this house. You've brought sorrow upon your head."

Mercy wiped her eyes. "His lordship wanted to…"

"No need to say more. I understand." Penance set the candle on the table beside the door. "I was in the hallway and heard everything. When the door opened, I hid around the corner and waited."

"You don't believe him, do you?"

"Would I be here if I did? Would I take the risk? You wouldn't steal a crust of bread if you were hungry."

"I wish Lady Irene were here." Mercy lowered her head. "What am I to do?"

"You must get away." Flinging the armoire doors open, Penance pulled out Mercy's old cloak. "Hurry, girl. You're in danger of being arrested."

Mercy's chest heaved. "Arrested? I have done nothing."

"Glenmont has sent Charlton for the constable. Everyone below stairs knows." Penance turned and put her hands on Mercy's shoulders. "You understand. The sheriff will believe his lordship over you, and the magistrate hasn't a merciful bone in his body when it comes to lowborn girls."

"If I flee, it might make things worse."

"Not if you go somewhere safe where they cannot find you. Get your cloak. You must take the risk."

"You'll be in trouble if his lordship finds out you helped me."

"His lordship will have no proof I did anything."

Mercy threw her cloak over her shoulders. "Why are you helping me?"

"You've become dear to me, Mercy, and I hate how Lord Glenmont has treated you. Now hurry, child. You're wasting time."

Penance stepped into the hallway ahead of Mercy and took her down the servants' staircase to the lower floor. She shoved her key into the back entry and opened it. With no other word spoken between them, she turned Mercy out into the dark and shut the door.

Mercy's heart raced as she made her way down a dirt path to the next street over. She slipped around a corner in the fog. The fog acted as a cloak over her, blending her into the darkness. She stopped and looked up and down the street, her eyes wide and frightened. *How can I run away without seeing Grandpapa and Nan? They'll tell me what to do, where to go, whom to trust.*

Her eyes darted about the street as she hung in the shadows. When she saw the rustic dwelling that had been her home since she were a small child, she ran toward it. Rushing in she raced up the stairs. Nan and Jonah shot up in bed.

"Mercy!" Grandpapa said.

Nan donned her robe. "Something is wrong, Jonah."

Trembling, she hurried into her grandmother's arms. "I'm in trouble." Tears sprang into her eyes. "I do not know what to do."

"You've done right in coming to us, child. Surely it cannot be all that bad."

She looked into Nan's grave face. "But it is, and I'm terribly afraid."

Mercy looked at Jonah's face. He stood barefoot in his nightshirt, and in the dark, his eyes shone fear and anger. "I'll tell you what it is, Patience. Glenmont has shamed our girl. Well, he won't get away with it." He set Mercy back and took his clothes down from the peg. Nan Patience grabbed him.

"No, Jonah. You'll not go. Confront him you must not until we know what has happened. Even then, you must do no violence to the man."

"Look at our girl. She is shaking, and it isn't from the cold." Grandpapa Jonah narrowed his eyes. "I'll get it out of him, whatever the cost."

"And risk your life? He's a powerful man, and would be sure to punish you...worse shoot you the moment you come near his door."

"It is true, Grandpapa." Mercy held her hands out to him and pleaded. "Don't go."

"What has he done? Is it you that have made this trouble? Are you with child?"

"No, Grandpapa," she gasped. "I swear it."

Through her sobs, Mercy explained how she was preparing her ladyship's room as she did every night, how he came in and saw her holding the necklace. "He has accused me of wanting to steal it, and then..." She lifted her eyes. "He wanted me to lay with him. I refused and he locked me in. One of his servants heard it all, and let me out. She said he has summoned the sheriff." She stepped forward. Her eyes and heart were equally desperate. "I have come to you, and shamed you both."

"You have not shamed us, child."

"Oh, but I have. You warned me, and I did not listen." She covered her face in her hands.

Grandpapa Jonah stood stiff. "The law will do Lord Glenmont's bidding and come looking for you. You know that, do you not?"

Mercy shook her head. "If I hide, they will not find me."

"Here is the first place they will look. They will search every inch of this house."

"I will hide elsewhere. I'll go to the inn. Mrs. Ely will help me. She was always kind to me."

"Mr. Ely will turn you over. You'll be dragged before a magistrate and thrown into prison. Anyone you trust will be implicated. You'll be condemned, Mercy. Condemned to hang."

Mercy broke into tears. Grandpapa Jonah pulled her into his arms. "We will find a way, and it must be swift." He turned to Nan as he pulled on his clothes. "You are to bolt the door behind us."

"You mean to leave me here alone?"

"You cannot come."

"But I must…"

He ignored her pleas. "Wife, obey me. You cannot hurry, as we must. You barely are able to walk as it is. If anyone comes do not answer. If they break in the door stay where you are and tell them I am working, and that you have not seen Mercy. They wouldn't dare harm an old woman."

"You cannot let her go, husband." Nan grasped his hands. "She'll be in worst danger on the road, with no food or money, or a man to protect her."

"We are wasting time."

"Hide her!"

"See sense, Patience."

"She is my girl and I cannot let her go."

"You must. If they find Mercy here, they will take her. She could be hung, do you understand?" He squeezed Nan's shoulders. "Which is worse? Hanging or having her far away and alive?"

Nan shuddered. "Alive, my husband." Just as quick as she had begun to cry, she stopped and blinked at Grandpapa Jonah with a look of knowing in her eyes. "Oh, Jonah. I've an idea. Send her to my brother in Holland. Yes," she nodded. "Send her to Silas."

He patted her cheek. "Dear woman, it is a wise idea. With the number of ships coming in, there's sure to be one going to Holland."

Mercy gasped. "Holland? Away from you?"

"Yes, Mercy." Grandpapa Jonah set his finger against his temple. "It will make no difference what passage. It should not be hard to get to Leyden. His farm is just outside the town."

"I do not want to go," she said.

"You will do as I tell you and live."

"But will Uncle Silas accept me? I'm practically a stranger to him, and when he hears my story, he might…"

Nan stepped closer. "Silas will not turn you away. He's loved you since the day you were born. In his last letter, he asked about you. Remember when you read it to me. You left out that part. You were in a hurry. I looked at it again, and he told me how he prays for you and has hopes of seeing you again. I will have much comfort, Mercy, knowing you are with him."

Mercy hung her head. Grandpapa Jonah took a key from his pocket and unlocked a drawer in the chest beneath the window. From it, he took out a leather moneybag. He opened it and took out the coins within it. He set them in Mercy's hand. "I promised to keep your coin safe. Now is the time when you need it most. Take the rest. It is not much, but it is enough to get you to your uncle."

"God bless you, Grandpapa." Tears fell along Mercy's cheeks.

"Dry thy tears, child, and rally your courage."

She threw her arms around his neck and embraced him. "I am afraid."

He put his hands over her shoulders. "You must trust in the Lord and be strong. Now kiss your grandmother goodbye. We must leave and waste no more time."

The three went down the stairs. Upon reach of the last of the steps, they paused. Nan Patience threw her arms around Mercy and wept. Her arms grew tighter and Mercy held Nan close. Her tiny frame seemed weaker than usual, as if her bones could break in Mercy's embrace.

A quiet rap fell three times on the door, and an equally quiet voice followed. "It is I, Martin. Let me in."

Grandpapa Jonah moved the latch and opened the door. "Martin?"

"Forgive me, sir. The hour is late, but I saw from my window Mercy coming through your door, and my instincts plague me that she is in some kind of trouble."

Grandpapa Jonah hesitated, but the look on Martin's face said he could be trusted. "Your instincts are right, Martin. Come inside."

Martin drew off his hat and stared at Mercy. "I saw you below, Mercy. You were hurried. Are you in trouble?"

"I am, Martin, but you must not tell anyone."

He drew up, his gaze resolute. "I won't. If you want me to stand guard outside, I will. If you want me to arm myself, I'll do that too."

His loyalty caused a weak smile to cross her lips. "You must go home."

Martin gave Grandpapa Jonah a sidelong glance. "You granddaughter hasn't your wisdom, sir. Her troubles muddle her head."

Grandpapa put his hand on Martin's shoulder. "You know the ships that are in?"

"I do, sir. I know their comings and goings. Why?"

"Can you help us find a ship sailing for Holland? You're sure to know the safest among them."

"Yes, sir. I can do that."

"Mercy must be put on one of those ships. She must go to her uncle in Leyden."

"But Mercy cannot go alone. Not without a protector. I'll go with her. I'm sick of this place, and," he grinned, "I'm in the mood for some adventure while I'm still young."

"You would do that for me, Martin?" Mercy asked. "I cannot let you."

Martin shrugged. "Why not?" He turned to the McCreas. "Sir, put your hat aside. I will take Mercy. It'll be safer for your sakes. I know back ways you do not, and I can easily steal her away if any soldiers are near. Trust me."

Grandpapa Jonah thrust out his hand and the two men shook. "Godspeed, and thank you." Blinking back tears, Nan kissed Mercy's cheeks. Mercy embraced Nan, felt the frailness of her shoulders under her tattered shawl.

"Be brave, child," Grandpapa said. He drew her into his arms, and then set her back. "Have Silas write to us when you are safely with him."

Martin whispered, "We must hurry."

Grandpapa Jonah cautiously opened the door and peered out. He drew back sharply. "It's the magistrate and his men," he said. He closed the door and bolted it. The sound of boots marching over the street grew louder. They stopped. A fist hammered the door. "Open up in the name of the King."

"Hurry," Jonah ordered, and moved the pair through the hall. More pounding. "Patience, see to it they are out, then lock the door." Jonah looked at Mercy and turned back. The front door opened and there were voices. "She is not here, Captain. She lives in Lord Glenmont's home. Ask him. My wife and I are abed."

Nan kissed Mercy's cheek. "Go, child. God be with you."

Martin went out first, looked around, turned and grabbed Mercy by the hand. "I cannot leave them," she said.

"Jonah knows what to do," Martin whispered. "No need to fear for them. They'll be all right." He yanked her forward. "Now come on."

Drawing her hood over her head, she dashed out into the night fog with Martin leading her away.

Part Two

I prize thy love more than whole mines of gold,
Or all the riches that the East doth hold.
My love is such that rivers cannot quench,
Nor ought but love from thee give recompense.

Anne Bradstreet – Puritan Poet of the American Colonies

Chapter 8

A young man with an unhurried gait, made his way toward Colchester where he had been born. He strode along, free of the stifling uniform of the King's Navy. Over his shoulder, he carried a sack containing a few worldly possessions—one set of clothes, a bone-handled knife, and a few shillings to get him by.

Tired from walking all day, he longed for a place to lay his head. Soon the sun would set and darkness would grow deep in this place. He would have to sleep rough, off the roadside if he failed to reach Colchester before nightfall, before the frigid air passed through his doublet to his bones.

Behind him, carriage wheels grated over dirt and stone. Caleb turned. Four dapple-greys were headed right for him at a furious pace. With flying manes and tails, the steeds pounded the road as the coachman cracked his lash above their heads. Upon seeing Caleb, the coachman jerked the reins and pulled the horses to a stop. They whinnied and reared, shook their heads, stomped the road, and laid large eyes upon the stranger.

"Out of the way, you fool. Else I'll land this whip across your back," the driver warned. The horses groaned and blew from their nostrils.

"I'm standing off the road. Are you blind?"

"I clearly saw you on the road and would have run you over if not for my conscience."

Caleb stepped up to the lead horse. He ran his hand down the beast's nose to calm him. It shook its mane and snorted. "Drive your horses at an easier pace and you wouldn't need to use your conscience."

The coachman eyed him. "You roguish devil. Move away."

Caleb grinned. "Your employer should buy you a pair of spectacles."

"For goodness sakes, why have we stopped? You caused me to roll out of my seat." A middle-aged woman poked her head outside the window. When her eyes caught Caleb's in the fading light, she let out a little cry, a chirp of panic like a startled bird—or a squeal of excitement. "Oh dear. A highwayman. He'll rob me if you do not carry on."

The driver fumbled with his whip and the pistol he kept tucked inside his baldric.

Still in front of the horses, Caleb raised his hands. "I'm no highwayman."

"Then who are you, and what do you want?" the woman asked.

"I want nothing. I'm traveling home." He stepped to the side of the carriage and there he saw her more clearly. She had to be fifty if it were a day, heavily wigged in gray ringlets and curls, and her shoulders shrouded in a fur cloak. The plume on her hat fluttered in front of her face and she blew it back with a puff of her cheeks. Her eyes fixed on Caleb, and a coy smile crept over her lips. What game she meant to play, Caleb could not tell, but he knew it to be a game nonetheless. He decided to go along with it for a few moments and then carry on his trek without further interference.

"You are a traveler, you say?"

He bowed. "Yes, my lady."

"Don't you mean to rob me?"

"I've no interest in robbing anyone."

She leaned from the window. "My virtue then? My money or my honor?"

Caleb laughed. "Hardly, my lady. I'm a gentleman, though not a nobleman."

"Anyone can be a highway robber. I have many friends that have been held up, and one is the lady of a duke. She is a good friend, and made me swear not to tell anyone. She told me he took her jewels and then…ravished her. I have read her account."

"Have you?"

"Indeed, I have. She gave it to me written in her own hand. She said he caused her to faint away in her carriage—unlike her husband whose advances she avoids."

"An unfortunate lady on both counts."

The woman tapped her chin with her finger. "Oh, I cannot be sure."

"Was he arrested, hung, drawn, and quartered?"

"I do not know. But his name was Falstaff, dressed in black and in a mask."

"Falstaff?"

"Yes. Have you a name?"

"Treymayne, my lady. It is *lady* is it not?"

She raised her chin. Dear laud, she had a large mole growing on it. "Lady Winifred Dewitt." She held her hand out to him, and glanced at the top, a signal she wanted him to kiss it."

Caleb reluctantly obliged. She giggled. "As I recall," he said, "Shakespeare wrote several plays that have a character named Falstaff, a robber with no other purpose than to take pleasure in holding up ladies such as you."

"Surely a coincident. Or he chose that name as a disguise."

"It has been said to happen." Caleb put his hat on. "I must leave you now. I've kept you too long."

But it was she who had held him up. From the window, she handed him some coins. "Take these. They mean nothing to me. My virtue is everything. If you demand I step down into the highroad, I shant." She said all this with a saucy smile.

Baffled, Caleb stared at her palm. "I've no need of your money, my lady."

She flattered him with her eyes—at least she tried to. Seeing the attempt did her no good, she went on to ask, "Is there something else you want? I can have my driver pull off to the side of the road and walk off."

Caleb stood back and frowned. "Your implication is insulting, my lady."

Her mouth fell open. "What?"

"You heard me. Shame on you, you a lady and married no doubt."

"I am a widow," she countered.

"Dead or alive, your husband would disapprove, and so would the Almighty."

Her face reddened and she spluttered so loud, one of the horses turned its head. Caleb bid her a good eve and picked up his satchel. He walked on, humored by the whole affair, and sorry the lady seemed so desperate for some kind of romantic adventure with a stranger.

The lady cried out. "Shoot him, James. He meant to do me a mischief."

Caleb looked back. The coachman leveled his pistol and fired. The bullet grazed Caleb's sleeve. Burns marred the edges of the gash, but thank the Lord the man missed his mark. Dumbfounded, he clapped his hand over his sleeve. "What do you mean by shooting at me? I'm no highwayman. Yet you try to murder me where I stand."

The coachman fumbled with the pistol. The horses rolled the coach forward and backward. The lady squealed for her driver to steady the horses, then to drive on. Caleb stepped away, pounding the ground with his boots. "Have people gone mad since I left?" He kept his hand over his shoulder. "On my word, this hurts."

Caleb headed into a plowed field and trudged over uneven earth. After a short distance, he stopped to examine his sleeve. He pushed his finger through the hole to his skin. Just a scratch of little consequence. Still, it smarted like the sting of a bee.

Coming over a crest, he saw a village nestled in a plane of grass. Bells were ringing in the church. Dogs barked at the moon as it rose. Candles twinkled in a few windows. He hurried on anxious to have a meal at an inn, sleep in a feathered bed, and bandage his wretched scratch.

Once he reached the village, his hopes dashed when four men on horseback surrounded him, drew their flintlocks, and aimed. Caleb froze and looked up at a man in a scarlet doublet and plumed hat. He realized he faced one of Essex's constables.

"Stay where you are," the constable ordered.

Caleb raised his hands. "No doubt I will with pistols pointed at me."

"You're to come with us."

"May I ask why?"

"For highway robbery, that's why."

Caleb laughed short. Lady Winifred wasted no time. He hadn't realized how greatly he had offended her. Shoot him dead, or have him arrested. Obviously a woman not to be toyed with.

"Good, sir. Having been recently relieved from His Majesty's Navy, I'm making my way home. I have my papers in my bag to prove it." He moved to get them.

"Keep your arms raised. What name do you go by?"

"The one my mother gave me. Caleb."

"No one threatens Lady Winifred Dewitt and walks away."

"I made no threat, sir. In fact, it was the contrary."

"Her word is as good as the law here."

"I will not oblige her want for revenge. No doubt you are familiar with her inclinations."

Before he could say more, they roughly fastened his hands. He struggled, but when a pistol dug into his ribs, he stood motionless. His jaw tightened and he clenched his teeth. "You are arresting an innocent man."

The constable's horse sidestepped. "The magistrate will determine your guilt or innocence." He reached down and snatched at Caleb's doublet. "Look at that sleeve. The coachman said you were such a menace he shot you. You're lucky he did not take your life—although a hangman may."

The constable turned his horse and walked it ahead.

After a dreadful night in the village gaol, Caleb was brought before a magistrate. The man, elderly in years, stared down at Caleb from his seat above the floor. His eyes were severe and speckled, his face heavily lined. Vague light passed through the dirty windows behind him—gray and dingy as the hairs of his head.

Men and women gathered in the gallery above and the seats below to watch the morning's proceedings—or more aptly their entertainment for the day. A man stepped in front of the bench and announced, "His Honor, Sir Geoffrey Longwood. Court is in order."

In a black cassock, Sir Geoffrey sat down. He moaned when bending his knees. He adjusted his spectacles and looked down his nose. He grunted, opened a silver snuffbox, and pinched some snuff between his fingers. After sniffing it into his nostrils, he sneezed and people jumped in their seats. "Do you know what you're accused of?"

"I do. A mistake, for I have done nothing wrong."

The crowd stirred. Sir Geoffrey hammered his gavel. "Silence!" The crowd settled and he looked back at Caleb. "You say you've done no harm to any person?"

"It is the truth."

"State your name."

"Caleb Treymayne recently released from the King's Navy on my way home. My father was Jonathan Treymayne, a well-known carpenter in Colchester. I have come back to pick up his business, and..."

"Enough," moaned Sir Geoffrey. "We do not need a history of your life. Whether you are a veteran of His Majesty's Navy or the son of a respected citizen is of no consequence to this court. Her ladyship," and he turned to look at the woman, "and her coachman have identified you as the highwayman that held them up yesterday on the main road. Do you deny the charge?"

"I do."

Sir Geoffrey's eyes shifted again to the lady seated several feet away in a box reserved for the elite. Caleb followed his eyes and when his met the lady's, she snapped open her fan and batted it before her face. Dressed in a russet gown and a hat so large it made her head look the size of a small child's, she set her fan on her lap and held a handkerchief to her nose. Her prideful eyes and the sternness of her mouth attempted to persuade Sir Geoffrey. Her expression was one of nobility, the kind that insisted she must have her way.

She wore a great deal of powder to hide the flaws on her face. Dangling from her sagging neck, were a handsome string of pearls. As she removed the handkerchief from her nose, she raised her head in imperious fashion, and her eyes fell upon Caleb.

Sir Geoffrey coughed to signal her attention. "Lady Dewitt..."

He was immediately interrupted by the lady. "First name, please. Dewitt is a silly name."

"Lady Winifred," Sir Geoffrey sighed. "Is this the man who held up your coach?"

A woman stood in the balcony and shouted, "I wouldn't mind bein' held up by such a handsome fellow. His voice makes my knees turn to wa'er."

The crowded laughed. Again, Sir Geoffrey pounded his gavel. "Ladies in the audience, please rein in your remarks. Save them for outside the courtroom if you please. Otherwise I'll have you escorted out."

A pin could have dropped on the floor and echo off the four walls after such a threat.

"Lady Winifred, I must impose upon you once more. Is this the man? Remember his fate is in your hands."

Lady Winifred proudly stared. "His face is as I remember— handsome yet devious. My coachman halted when he leapt from the bushes and planted his feet in front of my coach."

"He had no horse? Highwaymen ride."

"I know not what he did with his horse, perhaps he hid it."

The crowd murmured at her comment. Sir Geoffrey leaned forward. "Your coachman testifies this person had no horse, and he had to intervene on your behalf."

"If he could have, he would have laid his whip across this man's shoulders and taught him a lesson. Instead he drew out his pistol, which he carries every time we go out and wounded him."

"Was this man threatening you with a pistol?"

"Alas, I saw no pistol."

"And your coachman fired at an unarmed man?"

"Surely not."

Sir Geoffrey spoke to his clerk. "Ask him to put forth his arm to show the mark in his doublet."

The clerk did so, and Caleb put out his arm. There upon his sleeve lay the charred tear the bullet had made. "I was fortunate he missed. He ruined my doublet though, which cost me plenty. I ask to be compensated."

Lady Winifred smacked her hands on the railing in front of her. "How dare you ask anything of me, you rogue?"

"A fair request, my lady," said Sir Geoffrey.

"But my coachman was defending me."

Caleb gave her an impertinent smile and bowed short. "I was no threat to you, my lady, other than being a man who might have stolen your heart." Lady Winifred's face flushed. Caleb glanced up at the women in the balcony, smiled and winked. Swoons made their rounds. Hands fluttered handkerchiefs.

Lady Winifred snapped open her fan and beat the air in front of her face. "You'll receive no compensation."

Sir Geoffrey sighed. "This court will not order compensation, my lady." He looked down at Caleb. "Did you threaten the lady either of her wealth or person?"

"No, my lord. I shouted at her coachman to slow my lady's horses. If I had been in the road and not off to the side, he would have run me down."

Lady Winifred huffed and set her mouth. "He lies! My coachman feared for my virtue."

"He approached you directly, my lady?"

She placed her hand over her heart and heaved a breath. "I did greatly fear him."

"Stand coachman." The man stood. He turned his hat within his hands and looked at Sir Geoffrey sheepishly. Sir Geoffrey leaned forward. "So the accused had neither horse nor a pistol."

The coachman blinked. "No horse, but I think he carried a pistol."

Sir Geoffrey glowered. "Everyone *thinks* he carried a pistol. Did he or not have one? Did you see him draw it?"

"No."

"He wore no mask?"

"None. He's bold as you can see by the look he gave me."

"Did he tell you to stand and deliver?"

"Ah...no."

"So you shot an unarmed man you thought to be a highwayman, who had no horse, no pistol, no mask, but only asked you slow the horses in order to save those on the road from being trampled?"

"I only meant to scare the fellow."

Before he could go on, Lady Winifred stood. The room fell silent and all eyes were turned upon her. No doubt, she held a high position in the community, but by the looks on the villagers' faces, she was not well respected no matter how powerful she was.

"You cannot release him. Ladies everywhere are in grave danger. I insist you pass sentence."

Her words roused the courtroom to a murmur, and the constable who had arrested Caleb stood amid the crowd. "This man was armed. We confiscated a knife."

"Why had you not reported this earlier?"

"I thought I had."

"Ah, I see. How much money did he carry?"

"I cannot recall, but it was written down.."

After stifling a sneeze, Sir Geoffrey looked down at Caleb. "How did you acquire money?"

Caleb set his hands on the rail. "Through my service to His Majesty, my lord. It was honest money saved. I have the scares to prove it—if you wish to see them to know I am no liar."

Sir Geoffrey leaned closely to inspect Caleb's claim. "I see no scars."

"Of course not, sir. They are beneath my clothing." A burst of laughter ignited in the gallery.

Sir Geoffrey's cheeks puffed out and his face turned red. "Silence," he shouted. He continued. "Her ladyship states you demanded money. Is that where you got it?"

"No."

"He smiled as he came toward me," cried Lady Winifred.

Sir Geoffrey sighed heavily. "There is no law against smiling, my lady."

"You are letting him go free?"

Sir Geoffrey peered over the rim of his spectacles at Lady Winifred. "This case is most befuddling."

"Befuddling? Not in the least is it befuddling," said Lady Winifred. "Either you take my word or his." She pointed her finger straight at Sir Geoffrey. "You know the consequences if you call me a liar. At least put him in the stocks and whip him."

Once more, silence fell in the courtroom. Lady Winifred continued to stare at Sir Geoffrey. He cleared his throat, fingered some papers, and looked at the Constable. "Constable, have you anything else to say on this case?"

"Yes, my lord," he grinned. "He was found stalking across her ladyship's fields."

At that point, Sir Geoffrey put on his judgment cap. "Caleb Treymayne, I sentence you to four months imprisonment for the crime of trespassing. You are to be transported to Tyburn at noon tomorrow."

Shocked, Caleb's mouth fell open. The crowd jeered. Ladies gasped and some wept in their handkerchiefs. Sir Geoffrey gave way to Lady Winifred's warning, and waved his hand to his bailiffs. "Take him away."

Caleb sat against the wall in a mucky cell. Sweat beaded on his forehead and his soul trembled at the idea of days spent in an even worse place—Tyburn. He begged God for mercy, and when the gaoler came in with a bottle of ale beneath his arm, the thought crossed his mind his petition was about to be answered.

"Sorry it ain't more." The gaoler handed him a bowl.

Caleb took it and looked at the white pasty gruel within it. He lifted it to his nose and wrinkled his nose at the starch smell.

The gaoler shoved him on his shoulder and grinned. "Eat it, man. It'll fill your stomach."

"It smells terrible."

"Aye, it always does." The gaoler crouched down. A scrappy cat had entered the cell and rubbed up against the man's legs. "This here is our gaol cat. He ain't got a proper name, but he is good at keepin' mice away. Better eat up, or he'll eat it for you."

Caleb tasted the mush. He wanted to spit it out but his stomach growled. "Is there anything besides water to wash down this slop? I would welcome a mug of ale if you have it."

"I'm not supposed to have ale in here, let alone give it to a prisoner." His eyes shifted. "But, I'll make an exception. It's the least I can do for a wretched soul unfortunate enough to fall into the hands of the village carbuncle—Lady Winifred Dewitt."

Caleb thanked him. The jailer sat across from Caleb with the clay bottle. "You promise not to attempt escape?"

"How can I? You have the key."

The jailer wiggled his mouth. "It wouldn't be easy, I can tell you. Nevertheless, I welcome a bit of ale with another fellow. It doesn't happen often."

"This is your own ale?"

"Aye it is."

"It's good of you to share it with an innocent man in anguish."

"What terrible luck." The jailer pulled the cork from the jug and took a swig. Smacking his lips, he handed it to Caleb.

"Terrible indeed." Caleb handed the jug back. "I'm innocent down to the last breath of my body."

"Or your last kick, as the case may be if the magistrate changes his mind. He's done it before. I've seen it enough times to know."

A chill rushed over Caleb. "Have you?"

"Aye." The jailer took another swig. "Ah, don't worry, lad. It is unlikely. He'd have all the women in the village in an uproar. There's lots of talk goin' round about you."

"Talk? Your meaning, sir?"

"The women hereabout like to gossip." He paused, his eyes staring as if he were trying to remember something. "I almost forgot.

Two of those hussies sent this." He reached inside his doublet and drew out a sack. "A bit of dry venison and a pasty."

Starving for real food, Caleb grabbed the sack. "Why did you hold this back? Instead you give me slop."

"I forgot. You're the lucky one. First time the village ladies ever brought food to the gaol. They find you handsome and some even say fearsome."

"I do not know why. I'm ordinary," Caleb said, biting into the pasty. "Have you a woman?"

The jailer leaned in. "Nay. The lasses round here are frightened of my ugly mug. Smallpox as a child, you see. It left me marked and my right eye is milky. Jailing is the only job I could get. None of the farmers would hire me for fear I might frighten their cattle."

He felt sorry for the man to be cast aside due to the pox and an eye that none saw too well.

The jailer swallowed down more ale and leaned over. "Ever see Tyburn Prison?"

"I have not."

"You will soon, and let me tell you, it's enough to make a man wish for death. Rats the size of cats. A stench so bad it'd knock over a horse. Food so poor and foul to make your stomach turn to putty, but enough to keep a body alive. I know, 'cause I visited my brother there. He stole some bread and ended up eating moldy crusts crawlin' with weevils. Cells crammed with people—dirty people, lice infested people—fleas to make you go mad. And those rats be the only meat you'd get if you're lucky enough to catch one."

"Is that so?" Caleb tasted the ale. Bitter he spit it out.

"Aye and you'd have to eat it raw. They don't have fireplaces in those cells." Then the gaoler cocked his head. "I hear some prisoners make pets out of 'hem." The jug dry, he began to slur his speech and went on to talk nonsense. It did not take long before he leaned against the wall and fell asleep. With his chin on his chest, he snored so loud he chased the cat from the cell. Slowly Caleb stood. The key dangled from the gaoler's finger. Careful, he slid it off and silently slipped out the cell door. He pressed his back against the wall and looked out into the other room. No one was in sight. He stepped aside and stole out into the darkness. He traversed the field outside the village with a full moon above him. Frosted grass crunched under his soles, and the chilled air touched his face. He glanced up at the stars to mark his course. The North Star sparkled gloriously in the heavens.

Reaching the road, he crossed over into the woodland on the other side. From there he made his way east, where the sea met the land and the hope of freedom called.

Chapter 9

The journey across the English Channel caused Mercy's nerves to grow taut with each wave that struck the hull of the boat. She hated the nausea of the rocking ship, and the aggravating slowness of the voyage when no wind blew. When the ship's skiff came ashore with a half-dozen sailors pulling at the oars, Mercy held her bag tight. Beside her, Martin shivered in the frigid wind. His large brown eyes searched the shoreline, and Mercy turned hers to see what held his attention. Tall stucco houses and shops lined the waterway. Ships, with their masts furled, were moored along the docks. Seagulls whirled like kites above them. Holland and the river Nieuwe Maas fascinated her.

Her friend certainly sacrificed much to accompany her. Mercy was thankful beyond words for Martin's chivalry. What she was to do with him now, she did not know. She hoped Uncle Silas would give some guidance on the matter, whether he should stay or go back to England. On the ship, Martin talked incessantly about the Separatists who lived in Leyden, their courage and faith. The King's men hounded them, throwing their leaders into prison, and calling them heretics for separating from the Church of England. The persecution grew to unbearable proportions and a large number fled England for Holland.

As Mercy pondered these facts, her anticipation to see Uncle Silas grew. Yes, she fled to escape arrest and possibly hanging, but he of all people would understand why she ran and welcome her warmly into his home. She was, after all, his niece.

A sailor jumped up to the wharf and reached down. He spoke Dutch, and once she understood, Mercy took his hand and he pulled her up leaving Martin to do for himself. The town of Deftshaven bustled with activity. How she would get by without knowing the language caused Mercy to worry. She spotted a woman selling apples from a fruit cart. Lifting her bag, she hurried over.

"Good day," she said. "Leyden. Can you tell us the way?" The woman polished an apple on her apron and handed it to Mercy "I have no money to spare," Mercy told her.

The woman smiled and placed the apple in Mercy's hand. "*Engelsen* in Leyden. *Je* English?"

Mercy rummaged through her bag for a coin. "Yes, we are both *Engelsen*—English."

The woman understood and offered Mercy another apple. "A present."

"You are kind, madam. *Dunk u.*"

After repeating Leyden to several passersbys, Mercy and Martin made their way through the town confident in the direction they took. They walked along a road headed north to the town where the Separatists had made their home for the last twelve years. There were no clouds in the sky. The sun shone bright and the land had begun to bloom with wildflowers and tulips. Farmers had planted their fields with wheat, and one could see green shoots sprouting from the rich soil. Giant windmills turned in the soft breeze. Birds sang along the hedgerows and in the trees, and Mercy's heart sang along with them.

As she strode along, a sense of safety filled her. Gravely dirt crunched beneath her shoes, and her hem brushed against a patch of daisies growing wild along the roadside. A man leading a pair of oxen approached and tipped his hat. He spoke to her in Dutch. She smiled and he moved on with the lumbering beasts.

"We need to learn the language," she said to Martin. "Could you understand him?"

"I think he gave us a greeting. These are strange people. We'll find comfort among the Separatists." He smiled. "They speak English."

Mercy grew quiet. She paused in the road and looked up at the sky. "I wish I had listened to Grandpapa."

"About?"

"Not working for Lord Glenmont."

"What happened is not your fault. But yes, it would have been wise to have listened to Jonah when he first warned you."

"It cost me too much, and now I am separated from the people I love and have to live as a fugitive."

Martin tossed his apple into the air and caught it with the other hand. "It was the right thing to do."

"You think they'll be all right?"

"Sure I do."

"I feel such regret. I abandoned them."

"That's not true, Mercy. Think what it would be like if you'd been caught."

She set her hand over his arm. "I know I said it the night we left, but thank you again for helping me, Martin. You have been a true friend."

Martin crossed into the grass and sat under a tree. "Let's rest."

Mercy sat beside him and put her chin in her hand. She attempted to put her worries out of her mind. She gazed at the scene around her. There were miles of green pastures interlaced with ribbons of streams and banks of trees. Lambs huddled close to ewes, and flocks of snow-white geese waddled toward small ponds. The farmhouses were made of stone and heavy slates, some with bright colors painted over the window frames and doors. "Holland is different than Ipswich."

Martin wrinkled his nose. "Aye and it doesn't smell."

Mercy stretched her neck and looked across the road. "Look over there. You see those twin windmills?"

"How could I miss them? Those bright red spokes are enough to pain my eyes."

"We're not far from my uncle's farm. He wrote about them in a letter."

Martin yawned. "I'm weary of traveling."

"So am I."

"Mercy?"

"Yes, Martin?"

"Do you think your Uncle Silas will let me stay a while? I'm a hard worker, you know."

"I'm sure he will."

Martin leaned back against a tree. "Maybe I'll like Holland and stay. I can fellowship with the Separatists. I admire them, you know."

"Yes, I know. It is all you talked about on the voyage over."

"They're a courageous group to do what they have done, leave home for a strange country in order to freely worship God."

"Nan had me read his last letter to her. They plan to go to the New World."

"They're braver than I thought."

"Or very unwise."

"Others have done it."

"Yes, and barely survived. No one knows what happened on Roanoke Island."

They strolled on, and Martin skipped in front of Mercy. "The New World, eh? Now that would be an adventure. Just think to go to an unsettled land, build a house and farm. I should like to meet an Indian."

"I would fear them."

"They'll teach the Separatists much, and I pray to God they live in peace with each other."

"You are in a daring frame of mind. What changed you?"

He shook his head. "I was never happy, and I thought being in love with you was the answer to all my troubles. I found out it was not. I still love you, Mercy. Just not in the same way I did before."

Intrigued, Mercy smiled. Had Martin finally grown up and come to his senses? "What do you mean?"

"Well, you are more like a sister. I know you don't love me enough to be my wife, and I have accepted your feelings. You're older and wiser. Still, I'll always be here for you if you need me." He tossed his apple core into a bush, grabbed Mercy's hand and pulled her up. "Come on," he said. "I'm anxious to meet this Uncle Silas of yours."

Hidden in a blanket of mist coming in from the sea, Caleb reached the River Colne. A ferryman with a cragged face and bushy eyebrows brought him across to the other side. He followed a narrow path to a stone bridge over Ray Creek and walked the rest of the way to the shores of the North Sea. He knew the area well, having been there on several occasions as a boy. As he stood on the beach a crisp sea wind blew back his hair. Should he head north to Scotland or leave England all together.

Sunrays splintered the clouds, and the sea turned deep sapphire. Caleb set his hand above his eyes and looked across the water. A ship weighed out in the distance, and a skiff bounded over the whitecaps toward the beach. Oarsmen lifted the oars and the boat slid over the sand. The men within it jumped out, each wearing headscarves. One stout man, dressed differently than the others, looked at Caleb, placed his hands on his hips and set his feet wide apart. His hair, a mass of black curls, reached his shoulders and brushed against his beard in the salty breeze. He lifted a wide-brimmed hat. The scarlet plume rippled in the wind.

"Come down, good sir," he called.

With nothing to lose, Caleb headed down the stretch of sand toward a line of shells and weeds and met the man.

"Such timing is to be admired." The man made a quick gesture of his hand to his men and they began to unload their burden. "But you come empty-handed. Where are the casts you promised?"

"I think you have me mixed up with someone else, sir." Caleb glanced at the flintlock pistols with brass fixtures tucked inside the leader's belt. He stepped back to go on.

"Then you're not the merchant I'm to deal with?"

Caleb looked back. "Merchant? Not I."

"Who might ye be?"

"A poor sojourner, sir."

"Steelworthy is the name, Master of the *Seajack*. Where are you headed?"

"Scotland I think."

Steelworthy threw his hands over his hips and laughed. "You're on the run, aren't you?" He strode up to Caleb, his teeth white as oyster shells, his boots sinking up to the top of their heels in the sand. "We're comrades in that regard. I've faced the King's men on a few occasions. What crime did you commit?"

"None, sir. It was a matter of a mistaken profession."

"Just the same, they declared you guilty."

"Only to appease a person of high rank. Four months in prison."

"A light sentence really."

"Not for me."

"Come with us and have an adventure."

Caleb gave the man a sidelong glance. "Piracy?"

"No piracy. Trade. Unless you have a lass waiting for you in Scotland, why not come along?"

"Thank you just the same."

"Only a fool would turn down the chance. Ask my men. They'll be rich by year's end."

Caleb glanced at the masts of the tall ship. "I'm a carpenter, and I can earn a living."

Steelworthy laughed. "Fear the gibbet, lad. You know what they do, don't you? They leave your body for the crows, and after those devils have picked your bones clean, what is left stays for months. Without being buried in hallowed ground, a soul wanders these parts for all eternity."

The man's words haunted Caleb. He looked out at the sea, unsure whether he should trust the old salt. He heard of men tricked aboard ships and taken to the West Indies and sold into slavery, or beaten and robbed for whatever their pockets possessed.

He set his mouth firm. "I cannot pay you. I have no money."

The seafarer placed his thumbs inside his belt. "But I can pay you and take you to Holland. Sometimes we go to France, but on this run, we sail to Holland. You look like you have a strong back and a robust pair of arms. I could use your help to load and unload goods."

"Break the law, you mean? I don't know. I'm already in enough trouble as it is."

"It'll take three days in a fair wind to get there. By then you can decide whether you want to stay with us or in Holland or return if enough time has passed for them to forget you."

Cold and hungry, without a coin in his pocket, Caleb contemplated the offer. Could he be caught? If so, he'd suffered through Tyburn and be hung. Had he been a fool? Should he have stayed in the gaol and faced an unjust sentence? Could he have survived months in the dank and dark cell where disease and despair were more than punishment, where most did not live to see their executions or freedom? One thing was certain; he'd never let the King's men take him alive.

Chapter 10

From the top of a hill, Mercy looked down at the town of Leyden, a shining city with spires that reached into the clouds. There were no billows of hearth smoke, no soot upon the roofs of buildings. Excitement filled her to hurry there and explore, but dread gripped her at how foreign she will be to the people there.

"Look." Martin drew in a deep breath. "It is a fair looking place, is it not, Mercy?"

"Indeed. I can see why the Separatist chose to live here." She hugged her meager bag of belongings. "Will they welcome us, you think?"

"Surely they will."

"I have little memory of them when my parents were living."

"Why should that matter?"

"I suppose it should not."

"They'll like you, Mercy. You worry too much."

"And you have naught to worry about either. You're smile and good nature will win anyone over."

"God looks on the heart. You believe it is true, don't you, Mercy?"

She smiled. "Come. My uncle's farm is this way."

All around were small granges and broad fields. Herdsmen with their dogs were corralling milking cows toward their barns. It did not take long to find her uncle's home, the one with two large pear trees out front and a windmill near the barn. She paused in the middle of the road and stared at the house. Sunlight burnished the thatched roof golden-brown. Hens strutted in the yard and a shaggy gray dog lay across the flagstone stoop and raised its head.

Mercy stepped forward with Martin. The dog stood forward and barked. Martin held Mercy back. "Watch out. He might bite."

She bent down and held her hand out to the hairy beast. He quieted, sniffed her fingers and allowed her to stroke his ears. "Why he is as gentle as a lamb."

"A lamb but I bet there is a wolf beneath that fur."

Mercy put her hand under the dog's chin. "I've come to see your master. No need to fear us." She straightened up, knocked on the door, and moved beside Martin. Suddenly her palms sweated, and she clutched them. Would Uncle Silas be shocked to see her? Would he accept her warmly, or would he not want another mouth to feed and send her away?

The door swung in. A man met her eyes. "Can I help you?" he said in Dutch.

"I'm sorry, but I do not speak Dutch. I hope you can understand me. Is your master at home?"

He laughed. "I am my own master, young woman," he answered in English. "I'm Silas…."

Mercy hurried forward. "Uncle Silas, I am Mercy McCrea your niece. Grandpapa and Nan have sent me."

His eyes widened. "Mercy!" He threw a pair of massive arms around her. Heaving a breath, he held her at arm's length and looked her up and down. He was not at all, what she expected. She imagined he'd be short in stature, thin as a reed, and for some reason bowed at the legs. Before her stood an aged man with handsome features, one who stood a head taller than Martin, and who's built was muscular. His eyes were like Nan's, large and hazel. His shock of hair showed signs of turning silver and brushed over his shoulders.

"Is it true?" he said. "You were small the last time I saw you. You're a grown woman now, and so pretty like your mother."

"I have never forgotten you, Uncle."

"I was young then." He winked. "I could tell by the look on your face you were unsure who I was."

His comment made her smile. "True."

"I made you doubly unsure by speaking Dutch when I answered the door, did I not?"

"Yes, you did, Uncle."

Uncle Silas eased her inside. "Let us not stand outside all day. You and your companion come inside. I bet you are both weary and quite hungry from your journey."

"I hope we haven't disturbed you by coming unannounced."

"I admit it troubles me. Has something happened to your grandparents?"

"Both are still living, Uncle. I must talk to you about why I've come."

"I'm anxious to hear it. Did I not say in my letters if you should ever need me come to Holland?"

"You did." She looked at Martin who lingered in the doorway. "Uncle Silas, this is my friend Martin Flagg. He lived across from our house. I've much to be thankful for when it comes to Martin. He watched over me our entire journey."

Uncle Silas hurried to him with an outstretched hand. "You have my thanks, young lad."

Martin's stomach rumbled and everyone heard it. His cheeks blushed. "I beg for your pardon."

Uncle Silas raised his brows. "I said you were famished, and you just proved it to be so.

We were about to have supper, Jasper and I. Come to the table."

"Jasper?" said Mercy.

"He's the friendly dog you met coming in." Silas held out his hand and the dog scampered over. "He's been my companion these many years. He'll be ten come December."

Mercy rubbed Jasper's ears. "He is healthy for an old dog."

"Holland has good air, and Jasper runs through my fields all day. You'll meet my barn cats eventually. They come and go as they please...from the barn to the house and back again." He turned to Martin. "I hope you like cats, Mr. Flagg. You'll have to sleep in the loft."

"I do not mind, sir. I'm thankful for a mound of hay to sleep in, cats or no cats."

Excitedly, Silas took down two more pewter plates from a shelf above the mantle. "I hope you like my cooking."

Mercy moved to his oak table. "I have no doubt I will, Uncle."

With heads bowed, they gave thanks. "And thank you, Lord, for the safe arrival of my niece and her friend. Give them comfort and peace among your saints here in Holland."

Mercy remained standing. "Allow me to serve, Uncle." The men took their seats, and Mercy lifted the lid to the cast iron pot. She dipped the ladle into the pottage and drew in the scent of onions and herbs. "My, it smells good."

"Mercy is an excellent cook, sir." Martin eyed the food.

"Is she? Will you cook for me, dear niece?"

"I will with a glad heart, Uncle."

"So, tell me what has brought you to me?"

Mercy slipped into the chair. "I'm unsure where to begin."

"Eat first and then we will sit by the fire and talk."

Mercy dipped her spoon into the pottage. Tears welled in her eyes and she tried to forbid them from falling. One slipped down her cheek and she brushed it away. Uncle Silas reached over and gripped her hand. "All will be well, niece. There is no reason to fear. Eat your food in comfort and peace, and thank the Lord above for his mercy."

Three days later, Caleb stood at the ship's bulwarks and made out the shoreline of Holland in the moonlight. A starry sky danced upon the water and the sea breeze blew crisp as the sails plunged the ship onward. Without a village, or even a single house, there were no lights. The land looked desolate without habitation. Yet moon and starlight dispelled the grim darkness.

The voyage gave him false hope he had escaped peril and he would eventually be forgotten. Someday he could return to England, perhaps the Cornish coast and begin again. But as the waves lifted the ship, he doubted his thoughts and questioned his decision to join Steelworthy. The voyage across the Channel had been ruckus. Sailors drank and brawled. He kept to himself, but with a watchful eye.

The anchor dropped with a great splash into the sea. Sailors climbed the shrouds to furl the sails. Steelworthy turned on his heels, shoved his hands on his hips and shouted orders. "You men, start hauling up the merchandise to be loaded." He gave Caleb a gentle nudge on his shoulder. "You'll get your pay when the job is done."

Bothered by Steelworthy's tone of voice, Caleb went below halfhearted, and joined the others. They lifted the barrels onto their shoulders and climbed back up the ladder. Free of their burdens, the men descended back into the hold for the crates that remained. Whatever was in them, Caleb did not know. It did not matter. All he wanted was to get ashore with money in his pocket, find work, and a place to sleep. Three days tossed around in a rugged sea had been all he could stand.

When he started up, the hatch crashed above his head. "What goes on there," he shouted. "There are four of us left down here." He slapped his hand against the rungs.

Steelworthy peered down. His first mate held up a lantern beside him. His teeth shone white against his black beard as he grinned down at Caleb. "Why are you shouting, Treymayne?"

"Your sailor shut us in."

"He did upon my orders."

"Your orders? Have him open up and let us out."

"You'll be safe under hatches, you and the rest. The sea can get rough."

One of the four men clapped his hand on Caleb's shoulder. "We've been hoodwinked. What'll we do?" One and all, they stared at the man in black and silver, clenched their fists and uttered their wish to clasp their hands around his throat.

Caleb scowled. "Upon your word, we're to go ashore."

Steelworthy slapped his hands over his belly and cackled. "I do not recall my word to set you upon Holland's shores." In a measured step, he set his boot upon the hatch.

"You gave your word." Caleb smacked the rungs of the hatch.

"I dispute your claim. Did you sign an article of agreement to make you part of the crew, or take an oath of allegiance?"

Caleb spat. "A pirate's agreement."

"Aye, you could say that."

"With these bars between us, you think you have nothing to fear?"

"I fear no man. You'll be feed. I wouldn't want to sell sickly men, now would I? The heartier you are, the more you're worth."

"You won't sell us. I'll have you by the throat before you do."

Steelworthy bent down. "Silence. You'll not see the sky until we arrive."

One of the poor souls drew up beside Caleb. "Where are you taking us?" he called up to Steelworthy.

"Why the islands of course."

The trickster slapped his hands over his hips and stalked away. Caleb's blood boiled. He balled his fist and struck it against the hatch

Mercy stirred the hot coals in the hearth. They were expecting guests, for Uncle Silas sent word to the Separatist leaders his niece had arrived along with young Martin. She set the poker back in its place, stood, and hoped they would not ask her too many questions. Uncle Silas waited in his rocking chair smoking his long-stemmed pipe. Jasper curled at his feet and laid his head between his paws. Martin sat by the window reading Uncle Silas's Bible. Mercy glanced at him, and noticed how engaged he was. His eyes were riveted to the page, hungry for every word. A knock on the door made them lift away.

Uncle Silas drew his pipe out from between his teeth. "You may answer it, Mercy."

Hurrying to the door, Mercy's heart raced. When she opened it, two men stood outside in English clothes and broad-brimmed hats. The first one drew his off and laid it against his chest. "Mercy McCrea, I presume?"

She curtsied short. "Yes, sir."

"I am John Robinson. This gentleman is William Bradford. May we come in?"

"Yes, please. My uncle hoped you'd come." She stepped aside. Both men brought a reverent presence into the house. They carried an air of dignity, absent of smugness. Their eyes were humble. Their expressions kind. Mercy led them into the sitting room. Silas greeted them with cheerfulness and introduced Martin. "Pastor Robinson. Mr. Bradford. How kind of you to come." Uncle Silas's greetings were many and full of cheer, as if he'd been visited by brothers long absent.

Robinson extended his hand. "Elder Brewster would have come, but his wife is ill."

"I'm sorry to hear it," Silas said.

"She will survive. It is a mild malaise."

"I've been anxious for you to meet my niece." Silas moved her to his side. "I never thought to see her again, but here she is—my dear sister's grandchild Mercy."

Each man spoke in turn how glad he was to meet her. She was struck how at ease they were, not like the stiff minister she had listened to in St. Margaret's Church. It was as if a light shone from each—a graciousness and forbearance.

John Robinson was by far the most beloved and respected member of the Separatist group. A man of distinction, and one of the oldest men among the elders, he had been a student of divinity at

Cambridge, and raised a stir in Great Britain with his radical sermons. Despite his gentle spirit, he had been too outspoken and eventually resigned from the Church of England. From what Mercy's grandparents told her, Robinson was an eager sensitive man who questioned the established doctrine founded by the old plagued King of England.

As for William Bradford, he met her eyes only once, but in a friendly manner. He was the son of a prosperous man, admired by all. He had spent an unhappy childhood suffering sickness and ill health, but by the age of twelve, he was as deep in the Scriptures as most grown men were. On the Sabbath, he walked eight miles to Scoopy, the little village were the saints gathered. Under the gentle and knowing hand of William Brewster, he left England zealous to spread the Gospel.

Earlier in the day, Silas told Mercy about Bradford and his wife Dorothy. He kindly suggested she get to know Mrs. Bradford, she being a devout young woman and eager for friendship.

"How is Mrs. Bradford?" she asked.

"Very well, thank you. I should like for you to meet her, when the time is convenient."

Mercy smiled. "I'd be delighted."

"I knew your parents," Pastor Robinson said.

Mercy looked at him elated and smiled gently. "Then you knew me as well, sir, for they took me to meetings. I was so small then, and remember little."

"Yes, I do recall seeing you on your mother's knee and falling asleep during Pastor Clifton's sermons."

Mercy lowered her eyes. "Oh, yes, I have a faint recollection of Pastor Clifton. Was he the gentleman with the great white beard, sir?"

"Indeed he was. He passed away four years since. Tell me. Are your grandparents in good health?"

"They are faring, sir."

"Surely it grieved them for you to leave England. At least they have been comforted knowing you are with your uncle and among friends."

"My grandparents wished it. I needed to escape the ire of a wicked man. Martin came with me as my protector." Her gaze grew desperate. "Prithee, believe me, sirs. I am a woman who would not have been believed over a lord."

103

Bradford leaned forward. "We understand persecution. You are safe with us."

"You ask no more of me?"

"There is no reason and no purpose in knowing any further details."

"I thank you, sirs." She made a short curtsey.

"No need. We are glad to see you are with your uncle," Bradford said. "I too was sent to live with my uncle, although at an age younger than yours."

At his words, a great swelling filled her heart. What had she done to deserve acceptance? And why had a dream come to her in the night where a masculine hand lifted hers and held it fast? Facing the window, she watched a spear of sunlight cross its length. A quiet voice whispered. Someone faced trouble, and his deliverance depended on her.

Chapter 11

Caleb stood beneath the grate clamped against him and four others. When he heard one man groan, he turned and went to him. The man's face was heavily lined, and his eyes blinked with the misery he felt. "Why did I believe Steelworthy?" He put his face in his hands. "I'll never see my dear wife again. She'll never know what happened to me." His face disfigured with desperation, he grabbed Caleb's arm. "She'll think I abandoned her."

"Be calm, my friend. We'll get out somehow." Caleb glanced back at the grate, and anger filled him. To settle his rage, he breathed deeply. "If I have to claw my way out, I'll do it, and we'll all get off this wretched ship."

"How? The crew is armed," the man said.

The others drew close. "What do you say, men?" Caleb asked. "Are you willing to fight your way out?"

"I'd rather die trying than rot in this hulk."

"Or be sold like an animal."

Overhead, boots trampled over the deck, causing each man to jerk and look up at the hatch. Caleb peered through the grates. Shadows moved rapidly back and forth. Voices, along with the baritone voice of Steelworthy, grew heated. "They're quarrelling." The men hurried under the grate to listen.

A croaky voice called across the deck. "Steelworthy. We never agreed to smuggle human beings. If we're caught, it's the gallows for us."

"You dare to accuse me of putting my crew in danger?" Steelworthy rebuked the man speaking. "I'll have you tied to the shrouds and whipped; not only for questioning me, but for the slop you serve."

"No you won't, not when you have us against you."

"I've enough loyal men to throw you blackguards into the briny."

"Not if we throw you overboard first." A murmur followed, then a moment of silence. Were they staring one another down? Had pistols and swords been drawn?

Springing up the ladder, Caleb slammed the rungs with his fist. "Let us out. We'll join you."

Suddenly the chain that held the hatch closed, rattled and broke free. The hatch opened and faces appeared in the moonlight. "Come on up, lads. We're takin' the ship."

Caleb turned to the men beside him. Smiles broke out on their faces and they hurried up the ladder to the deck. With some hesitation of what he might face, Caleb followed. When he came topside, he saw Steelworthy standing on the break of the deck with his hands on his hips. His eyes darkened with a readiness to fight— and to murder the mutineers. The tip of his beard fluttered in the breeze, and when his eyes met Caleb's he laughed. Indeed, it was as Caleb suspected. Pistols had been drawn and pointed at Steelworthy.

Steelworthy swung his fist. "This is mutiny."

"We'll not hang because of you."

Steelworthy's eyes ebbed between anger and fear. A few of his crew hung back behind him. Unwashed and sunburnt, their faces were dark and indistinct in the flicker of ships torches.

"Hand over your weapons," demanded the leader of mutineers. A corner of Caleb's mouth curved into a smile. The cook was the least person he'd have guessed to lead. He had spoken only to him once—once when he filled his bowl with fish stew.

"Don't listen to these fools." Steelworthy set his hand on the hilt of his pistol. "You'll have gold aplenty in your pockets when the job is done." Steelworthy spread out his hands. "All will be forgiven if you end this folly."

"He's only thinking of his money."

"He wants to cross the ocean to do the unthinkable."

A few stepped forward and joined the mutineers. Steelworthy set his teeth. "Stand with me, and you'll taste the pleasures of the islands, where native women bath naked in pools of clear water, where they treat a man like a king. Why, you'll pick gold straight off the ground."

The band of seafarers loyal to their captain rushed forward at his command. Gold lured them. Lust captivated their flesh. One man jutted out his chin. "What our captain speaks of is true. Gold and jewels on the beaches and three women to every man."

Caleb stepped forward. "Lies. I was in the King's Navy, and I can tell you, you'll find nothing but shells on those beaches, and pirates to rob you of your money, women to snatch your purse right out of your hand and give you sickness. You're taking a mighty risk, gentlemen. You're outnumbered. Think what you are about to do. You'd risk your lives for a tall tale and false promises?"

Steelworthy narrowed his eyes. "You're calling me a deceiver?"

"I am, and cheat."

Steelworthy drew his pistol, aimed and fired. The shot whizzed past Caleb's head and missed him by a hair. Caleb sprang forward and slammed his fist into Steelworthy's face, causing him to stumble back against the capstan. Steelworthy, being a hulk of a man regained his footing and drew his cutlass. Caleb jerked to the right and the cutlass met wood and rope. Clenching his teeth, Steelworthy swung the blade again and cut into the sleeve of Caleb's doublet. He grabbed Steelworthy's wrist and squeezed. The cutlass clamored to the deck. Steelworthy cursed and reached for Caleb. His eyes blazed and he laughed. Then he thrust his hands around Caleb's neck. Caleb dug his hands between his flesh and Steelworthy's fingers. He could not breathe. He felt the blood flooding his face. He pried free and kicked Steelworthy back with his boot. Steelworthy stumbled. The man's strength was relentless. He swung his arms around Caleb's waist and lifted him off the deck. "Can you swim, Treymayne? I'm anxious to find out."

Grinning, Steelworthy carried Caleb over to the rail and threw him over the side. Plunged into the sea, the water sharp and cold, Caleb was sucked down.

Mercy looked out the upstairs bedroom window and watched the evening clouds form along the horizon. Sunrays fell through them and crossed the fields. Searching the temperate shades of blue, she swallowed hard, and threw back her shoulders. "Lord Glenmont will never find me here. I'm as safe as safe can be in this place."

Out in the barn, the cow lowed. She needed milking. Mercy laced up her boots and headed outside with a pail. She crossed the yard, her skirts swooshing away hens and chicks. She glanced up at the open window in the hayloft and thought of Martin. It seemed strange not having him near, that he had gone on to Leyden to meet a doctor named Fuller who was in need of a male servant. If he had stayed at the farm, his old feelings for her might have rekindled—his heart to be pained again.

The hinges on the barn door squeaked when she pushed it in. Rock doves fluttered from a rafter, settled on another and cooed. Mercy looked up at them and smiled. How peaceful and gentle they seemed. They stared back at her and ruffled their feathers. "You hope I've brought you something, don't you."

She reached inside her apron pocket, took out a bit of bread and crumpled it. Tossing it from her hand onto the ground, the birds flew down and pecked at the morsels. The barn smelled of fresh hay. Dusty light streamed through the cracks in the thatched roof. She drew up beside Uncle Silas's milking cow. Setting her hands on the animal softly she pulled the udders. Milk shot into the pail and the barn cats came running. Then—the barn door swung open.

"I'm about finished, Uncle." When there was no reply, she paused and laid her hand on the cow's belly. She stood from the stool and met a stranger's eyes. His clothes were English with a rip in one sleeve and stains on his doublet. He smelled of seawater and sweat. His hair hung limp around his shoulders, the color blending with the hay in the stalls.

Instinctively, she set her hand against her thigh where she once kept a small dagger for protection. Since coming to Holland, she had forgone the practice, believing she were safe without it. "Who are you? What do you want?"

He raised his hand. "I'll not hurt you."

"How do I know?" she countered with a boldness that made the man stare.

"You speak English."

He took a step toward her and Mercy moved back. "I'll cry out if you come any closer."

"Forgive me. I've been walking a long time and when I saw this barn, I thought to risk it and take shelter here. If you don't mind, may I rest a moment? Rest is all I want and a bit of bread if you have it to spare." He looked at the doves pecking the crumbs.

Mercy made a quick study of him, taking notice of his clothes and unwashed appearance. The sun fell through a crack in the roof and rested over his shoulders. Although he was in dire need of bathing, of his hair being combed and his doublet and breeches cleaned, he looked handsomer than any man she had yet to behold. How could such a man, a thorough stranger, cause her heart to flutter like a butterfly's wings? Such feelings never happened before, and they confused her. His gaze returned to hers, and she swallowed the heightened emotion in her throat, one hand resting on a post beside the cow pen.

"You haven't said who you are."

He set his hand over his chest and bowed. "Caleb Treymayne, at your service."

"You are English too."

"That should be obvious by my voice."

"Are you a Separatist? They are the only English I know in Holland."

"No, but I am curious."

"My uncle is a Separatist. This is his home."

"I'm glad to hear it. Separatists are peaceful folk and kind. He won't shoot me."

"Do not be so sure. He would defend me to the death."

He continued to stare. "By your clothes, I would say you were a Separatist as well."

"I'm persuaded in that way."

"Where is your husband? Can I speak to him?"

"I have no husband. But that doesn't mean I cannot protect myself until my uncle comes."

Caleb spread out his arms. "I'm unarmed."

Mercy shrugged. "You carry no pistol, no dirk?"

"They took my pistol."

"Robbers? Or was it the law?"

"You guested right with the latter."

She gasped with wide eyes. "God help me, you're an escaped criminal."

Caleb stepped in front of her, his face grave, his hands outstretched. "I'm an innocent man seeking refuge who was wrongly accused. And yes, I escaped. I did it in order to save my life. For what judge in England believes the word of a lowborn man over the word of a lady of the upper class?"

"Or a lowborn girl over the word of a lord."

109

"I suppose that is equally true," he replied.

"Convince me you are speaking the truth and intend no harm to me or my uncle. Harm being robbery, of which you'd find we have no money to give. I am poor, and so is my uncle." She looked at the cow. "But if you must, take a quart of milk. That should sustain you."

He sat on a stool and picked up a piece of straw from the ground. "I am not going to rob you."

"Then what *are* you going to do?"

"Drink a quart of milk. I'm hungry."

Mercy picked up her pale, filled a tin and handed it to him. "You may now tell me your story," she said, spreading her skirts and sitting on a barrel opposite Caleb.

"I was on my way to Colchester when a coach came barreling full sped straight for me. I stopped it, spoke a firm word to the driver, had a brief encounter with a lady old enough to be my mother, and soon after was accused of being a highwayman."

"A highwayman? You do not look the part."

"Hmm, so you noticed."

"What happened then?"

"I was dragged before a magistrate, and I insisted upon my innocence. But her ladyship wheeled her power over him and I was put in the gaol. I escaped, made my way down to the sea and fell prey to a band of smugglers."

Mercy hugged her knees. Could it be true? "You're story sounds like the makings of a tall tale."

"To be considered," he said, drinking the last of the milk. "The master of the ship gave his word he would bring me to Holland, where I could lay low. I should have listened to my conscious and gone on to Scotland. Some of us were destined for the West Indies to be sold into slavery. There was a mutiny. I struggled with the fiend, but he being a large man got the best of me."

"How?" she asked intrigued.

"He threw me overboard."

"Into the sea?"

"In the black of night. I swam to shore, traveled a ways, and here I am. I do not know what happened to the other men on that ship."

"Indeed this is a tall tale, sir. Give me one reason I should believe you."

"I cannot think of one."

"Not a single one?"

"I've been told some women can read an honest face. Can't you read mine?"

"Your face tells me nothing."

"I see." He stood. "I have no way of proving what I've told you. I'll go."

She understood how it felt to be falsely accused, to know if caught she would have possibly hung. She knew how painful it was to leave loved ones. Did this man have family back home—perhaps a sweetheart or wife? Here they were together, both in similar predicaments.

"I would like to believe you," she said. "But no one should be so trusting in these times."

"I have nothing to give but my word," Caleb told her. "Before God Almighty, what I told you is the truth."

Nodding to her, he walked out into the yard. Chicks scattered and the hens flapped their wings away from the storming of his boots. Mercy picked up her pale of milk and followed. Clearly, he had been through a misfortune by the look of him. Could she go by sight alone?

"Wait. I noticed you have a tear on your doublet."

Caleb looked down at the rip. "That deceiver of a captain did this."

"Are you wounded?"

"A scratch." He set his hand over it, and when he moved it away, there was blood on his fingers.

"Do not go, sir," Mercy said, rushing forward. "It still bleeds."

He gave her a short bow. "I do not wish to trouble you any further than I already have."

"It would be no trouble. Besides, you are hungry as well, are you not?"

He hesitated, but had to admit what his body told him. "I am."

"We have bread and eggs."

"I'll work for my food." Again, he gave her a slight bow, his hand over the breast of his doublet. "I'm a carpenter by trade."

"You've well-bred manners, sir," she told him.

"Are you not deserving of them?"

Dismayed, Mercy blinked. "I? It is not expected."

"I cannot help but expected it of myself." He put his shoulders back. "What must I do to pay for a meal?"

"You can carry this pail of milk." She handed it over, a bit sloshing over the lip. Caleb winched. "A mere scratch is it?" Mercy said. "You need to have your wound cleaned and dressed. Stay here."

He switched hands to hold the pail. "It is nothing."

She frowned. "It could be enough to cause infection, take your arm and possibly your life."

He frowned and looked down at his boots. "You've uncovered my pride. I have seen enough in my life to know you are right."

Mercy's smile came lightly, astonished the man could swallow his ego in front of a woman. "I suppose you would welcome our fire in the sitting room."

"I would indeed."

"I must ask my uncle first."

Caleb nodded without meeting her eyes. "I'll wait, and if I'm not welcomed inside, I understand. I must smell like a fish market or worse."

Mercy laughed. "Indeed you do, sir. But that can be remedied too."

Mercy hurried across the straw-laden yard and called to Uncle Silas. Casually he lifted his head and waved. She had not been completely won over by Caleb, and looked back to see if he followed her. He had not. Moving away from the sheep pen, Silas walked toward her.

"Is something wrong?" Uncle Silas said. "You are flushed, Mercy."

"What do Separatists teach about helping a stranger?" she asked catching her breath.

Silas rubbed his jaw. "The scriptures are clear. Remember the parable of the good Samaritan?"

"Yes, I remember."

"Why do you ask if you know the parable? Has a wanderer come to our door?"

"There is an injured man in the yard. He came upon me while I was milking Buttercup."

Uncle Silas's brows wrinkled and he eyes fixed on the yard ahead. "Did he frighten you, threaten to harm you?"

Mercy went to him and placed her arm through his. "He surprised me but did me no harm. He says he fled England to save his life."

"And you believe this vagrant?"

"After hearing his story—I hope to. He is waiting for an answer whether he is welcomed."

"What is he accused of?"

"Of being a highwayman. He claims he was falsely accused."

"Is that so? Well, we can only take the man at his word and hope he is speaking the truth. I'll meet with him."

"He will work for a meal."

"And so shall we give it, and willingly. But If I sense danger, I'll give him food and send him on his way."

Mercy looked ahead. Caleb sat on the crude wooden bench near the troth. His head was down and his arms resting over his knees. Uncle Silas cleared his throat, and Caleb stood.

"Good day, sir," said Silas. "Hungry?"

Caleb nodded. "If I have intruded, I'll go."

"I never turn away a hungry person."

Upon her uncle's words, Mercy headed for the kitchen, down the narrow hallway to where the fire in the hearth burned down to red coals. She spooned hot porridge into a pewter bowl, fried four eggs in grease, and buttered a slice of bread. She glanced at her reflection in the window, checked her face for smudges, and her clothes. She frowned at the freckle on her cheek. The dress Dorothy Bradford sent up to the farm, fit her to perfection, plain and simple as it were.

She laid the food, a spoon, and a pitcher of milk on a tray, and went out into the hallway. The men's voices were amiable and made her smile. When she stepped out the door, Uncle Silas turned and frowned. "You intend our guest to eat outside, Mercy?"

Caleb shook his head. "I am hardly presentable, sir, to sit at your table."

"Nonsense, Mr. Treymayne. You will eat at our table with us."

Mercy gripped the tray and glanced at Caleb. His eyes were softer, his mouth relaxed, and his doublet buttoned. Looking away, she headed back inside the house. The two men continued to speak as they came through the entrance. Mercy made haste setting the table, and when she finished, she stood back and folded her hands over her apron.

Uncle Silas gave thanks and took his seat at the head of the table. "Sit down, Mr. Treymayne. We've had unusually chilly weather for this time of the year. Is the fire warm enough?"

"I welcome it, sir."

Mercy lifted her eyes. Why did Caleb hesitate? If he were starving as he claimed, wouldn't he dive it to the food? "Is something wrong?" she asked. "Is the food not to your liking?"

"It is very much to my liking. I'm not accustomed to such generous hospitality."

Lifting the basket of bread slices, she handed it to him. "Please, take what is given you, but say Amen first."

He straddled the chair and did as she bid, but silently with his lips moving. Mercy glanced at Uncle Silas whose eyes were upon the newcomer. With the look of a battle-worn soldier, Caleb opened his eyes and pressed his back to the chair. "You must forgive me. I have never been asked to pray in front of anyone."

"Not even your family?" Silas asked.

"I have none, but when I did, that was the duty of my father."

"As it were mine. We all end with an Amen though." Silas took a slice and laid it on his plate. "Eat up, sir."

Caleb finished his plate of food, and Mercy offered him more. He looked content, yet tired.

Uncle Silas handed down a slice of bread to Jasper. "I feed him what meat I can spare, Mr. Treymayne. Yet he has a fondness for my niece's bread."

"I can understand why, sir."

"Would you not say she is an excellent cook?"

"By far, sir."

"She'll make a fine wife someday for the right man." Uncle Silas gave Mercy a wink, and she felt her face flush scarlet. Embarrassed she got up and began clearing away the dishes. It was the first time Uncle Silas said anything about her marrying. Mercy had abandoned that thought months ago, but now to glance at the man seated across from her uncle, she wondered if it were possible to find happiness with another.

"Fetch a blanket for our guest, Mercy, so he may sleep comfortably in our hayloft."

"Yes, Uncle."

"And the salve you made when I cut my hand. Bring it too and dress Mr. Treymayne's wound."

Mr. Treymayne's wound. She wondered how many more there were, and if they could be healed. Or was he the kind of man that wounding did not come easy to. Hurriedly he stood and took the tray from her hands. "Let me," he said.

Chapter 12

Caleb sat beneath a large oak near Silas's barn with his back against the rough bark. He ran a sharpening tool over the prongs of a hayfork and watched the sunset. Its soft colors and tranquil mood made him think of the girl he could see behind the kitchen window. Such a true beauty with a kind heart. She hummed as she cleaned pewter plates and cups, and pushed back her hair from her forehead with the back of her hand. He could not help but watch her.

How long should he stay in Holland? Might it depend on Mercy? Should he join the Separatists, or be the man he always had been—a man without fellowship, but believing? Silas could only pay him in food and a hayloft bed, and the list of repairs to the house and barn were about over. If he stayed in this situation, he would never have a penny to his name. If he left Holland, he could sail to Scotland and lose himself in the highlands among his mother's people. However, to part from the lovely Mercy greatly vexed him.

How can I be anything to her? What have I to offer?

He studied her profile. He explored the contour of her jaw. He noticed how the rosy light shown over her cheek and painted her lips. He wanted to toss the hayfork aside, go to the window, lean in, and speak to her. To control his feelings, he looked away, and when he stood, he saw Pastor Robinson coming down the lane toward the farmhouse.

It was late in the day, near to the sun setting. Robinson's

arrival surprised him. Shouldn't he be at home with his wife and children? Did he want to convert him to the movement? He had not told anyone, not even Mercy, he had dedicated his life to God after his mother came through an illness her physician thought fatal. Suddenly, he felt ashamed he lacked the courage to make a confession of faith publicly. Was not his relationship with God a private one? Unsure of the answer, he walked a few yards ahead until he and Robinson met.

"Good day, Caleb. You're looking better since the last time I saw you. Has your wound healed?"

"It has, thanks to Mercy."

Robinson smiled. "I have known women who would make the best of doctors given the chance."

"I believe Mercy would indeed, sir. I take it you're looking for Silas."

"I've been gone most of the day on business and thought I would stop for a quick visit."

"Business, sir? I imagine it has to do with leaving Holland for the New World."

Robinson wrinkled his brow. "Silas told you about our plans?"

"Aye." Caleb walked with him as far as the door. "Such a voyage will take courage."

"My family and I will remain behind to serve those that stay," Robinson said. "I admit it saddens us we cannot return home to England. We Separatists are a loving, peaceful people. Yet we are persecuted on every side, and the King has proclaimed he will harass us until not one of us is left."

"There is no shame in fleeing danger."

"Indeed that is true. We Separatists know it all too well."

"I would like to hear you preach."

"You are welcome to, Caleb. Come and pray with us."

Caleb dug the heel of his boot into the ground. "What is my prayer that God Almighty would hear anything I might utter to Him? I am a sinner, sir."

Robinson smiled, the way a wise man would. "We are all sinners. God hears you as much as any other. He requires earnest faith the size of a mustard seed—that's all."

"Faith I understand. But what things a man's heart is allowed to desire I'm unsure of." He turned and set his eyes on the window. "I confess the desire for a woman is what I've come to know. Am I in the wrong, Pastor?"

"Love for a woman, God placed in man. But beware of lust. It is a sin. Desire for spiritual things is different. It is divine. It glorifies God so that He may reign in our hearts and keep us from sin."

"No one can be kept from sin."

"That is true. But to be kept is to be guarded."

Caleb nodded, soberly amazed at Robinson's wisdom. Jasper barked and bounded around one of the barn cat's kittens. The little one hissed and arched its back. The mother cat raced out from the barn and swatted poor Jasper on the nose who, upon her stern rebuke, sat back on his haunches.

Robinson nudged Caleb on the shoulder. "There is your answer."

Caleb smiled and shook his head amazed. "I think you are right. 'Tis something for me to ponder."

Jasper cantered over to Caleb. He rubbed the dog's shaggy ears until he trotted off. The milking cow lowed. She needed milking, a chore of Mercy's. Earlier in the morning, he watched her gentle way with the docile Guernsey, how she squirted milk to the barn cats and laughed. Her glee came like music to his ears. Would she object if he asked to sit with her by the fire tonight?

"I have wondered if Mercy will leave." He spoke in a quiet tone, grim and searching for an answer from the kind pastor.

"I do believe Silas will remain here due to his old age. Mercy will stay so to care for him."

"I hope she will tell me."

"Her choice is important to you?"

"It is. Her decision will determine mine."

Mercy appeared in the doorway. She wiped her hands in her apron and glanced at Caleb. The tips of her hair fell across her shoulders from beneath her cap, touched by the golden light falling over the land. He filled his lungs with the soft breeze and fixed his eyes on hers—those shimmering eyes that captivated him.

"Pastor Robinson, you're in time for supper," Mercy said. "Come join us."

"Thank you, Mercy, but I cannot," replied Robinson. "I was on my way home. Bridget will fret if I fail to show up for our evening repast." He leaned forward and smiled. "With as many children as we have, and James being a baby, my dear wife needs my firm hand to keep order at the table."

Mercy put her hand over her mouth and giggled. "I imagine it
is a site to behold. Perhaps another day, you and Mrs. Robinson
could visit. Bring the children, for my uncle adores little ones as
much as I do."

Robinson squashed on his hat. "Indeed, we will. Tell your
uncle I stopped by but needed to be on my way."

As Robinson strode off, Caleb wished he could be half the
man Robinson was. With an air of manly confidence, his stride
was strong as he passed over the hill. Mercy drew beside Caleb.
The closeness of her caused his pulse to race and a gripping of the
heart to rise.

"I like what you did to the barn doors. They are pretty. Most
doors barely have a smidgen of paint on them. Did Pastor
Robinson mention the color? I would think he would. Red is such
a bright color."

She seemed to be rambling. Was she as nervous in his
presence as he was in hers? He looked at his work and thought
little of it. Still, it pleased him she appreciated his skill. He had
scraped the rust off the old hinges and painted them black. For the
doors, he removed the rotted planks and replaced them with new
ones, and finished with paint. "You approve, do you not?"

"I do." She turned her eyes from his and looked at the doors.
"Look. The sun is setting and changes the color."

"Your face is the prettiest I have yet to see."

She heard him speak, but did not make out the words. "I'm
sorry. What did you say?"

"Nothing," Caleb said.

Mercy gathered her skirts and turned to go inside. "Be sure to
wash your hands, and wipe your boots before coming inside, Mr.
Treymayne."

He did as she bid him, and walked inside behind her. "Have
you promised yourself to anyone?"

Mercy stopped short and looked at him. "Such a personal
question, Caleb Treymayne."

"What about this fellow Martin Flagg?"

"He's a boy."

"Then you do not love him?"

"Not enough to be his wife. He's a child to me." She moved
on, reaching the table. Setting her hands on the cloth that covered
it, she smoothed it out. Caleb stood in the doorway. "Is there

something else?" she asked.

"Yes. What would it take for you to pledge yourself?"

"I would have to love him, and he would have to be trustworthy."

"And you doubt I am a good and honest man?"

"I don't know you well enough to say, but...I'm hopeful."

Jasper raced up behind Mercy and she jumped. "He wants me to feed him." Mercy drew away. She caught Caleb's eyes as she passed him. He lingered, and her imagination took hold of her. She thought she heard Caleb say Jasper had to wait. She went on with the hound trotting ahead.

"Mercy," said Caleb.

She turned. "If you intend to say another word about pledges, I do not wish to hear it."

He frowned. "You can read minds?"

"Of course I cannot. Can you?"

"No, but I'm good at reading expressions and yours tells me you think I'm hinting at making you an offer. But mind this. I'm not good enough for you, Mercy. I've no means of support, and I've many faults."

Jasper whined and jumped up on Mercy. "Down, Jasper. Mr. Treymayne, there isn't a man alive that does not have faults."

"Some have more than others. One of mine is allowing myself to love you."

"But you don't." She walked away, leaving him alone in the vanishing light of the hallway.

Chapter 13

By the end of the week, the sky turned bright blue and sunny. Mercy passed through the yard and sauntered down a narrow path to the main road. The fields were lush with spring grass and wildflowers. Birds sang clear and sweet, and through the breaks in the trees, the sun showered gold and silver motes. Windmills turned in the breeze, and sheep grazed in the meadows.

Mercy drew in the fresh air. The countryside soothed her soul and gave her the urge to skip down the road. Instead, she held her skirts above her latchet shoes so the dew-drenched grass might not brush over them. A row of newly bloomed day lilies grew on a bank, and she stopped to gather some. With a bundle in her hand, she turned to see Uncle Silas driving his cart pulled by Buttercup his milking cow. Dressed in his olive green doublet and brown leather breeches, he hailed her. Mercy stopped at the side of the road.

"So you found them," he said, pausing Buttercup.

"Just where you told me they'd be." She held them out to him. "I hope they don't wilt."

"I see you chose to wear your waistcoat with the buttons Caleb carved for you. You were quick to replace the old."

She climbed up beside him. "Is it so wrong, Uncle? Buttons are hardly a fancy adornment."

He smiled. "They might evoke jealousy, even envy, among the women."

"Shame if they have such feelings." Mercy fiddled with the flowers. Uncle Silas moved Buttercup on. "Caleb did not wait for us? Do you know the reason?"

"Perhaps he does not like to be seen with me."

Uncle Silas replied by telling her how she was indisputably wrong, and that from his observations knew how very much Caleb liked her.

"Like me?" she retorted. "He avoids looking me in the eyes, and says little to me." She dare not tell him of the conversation they had in the house when he were not present. It would only solidify his observations further.

They were silent the rest of the way. The town clock chimed the ninth hour as Silas drew the cart to a halt in front of a large brick dwelling. Located in the heart of Leyden, in front of Pieterskerk Plaza and the garden grounds of the University, it housed John Robinson and his family, and was a place of worship. Inside, sunshine flowed through the windows in broad misty shafts. The scents of spring lingered though no flowers adorned the interior. When Mercy took her seat beside Uncle Silas, she spotted Caleb.

"Finally, he's decided to attended services," Silas whispered to her. "Are you pleased?"

"He should not be here to please me, Uncle."

Silas drew up his shoulders and looked forward. "I doubt that to be the reason, Mercy."

She looked down at Uncle Silas's hands. They were trembling in his lap. She reached over and laid hers gently over them. He gripped her fingers and held tight. The quaking did not end. What was wrong? What troubled him so greatly?

Pastor Robinson stood and moved in front of the people. He spoke plainly of Christ's sacrifice, and upon his final word, Silas released Mercy's hand. Placing his hat on, he withdrew with the men and the elders to a separate room. Dorothy Bradford sat beneath one of the windows in the rear with her son on her lap. She spoke to the boy, and when his large eyes looked up at his mother's face, she kissed his cheek. Mercy drew beside her.

"He behaves so well, Dorothy. He'll grow into a fine man."

Dorothy brushed her hand over her boy's hair. "I pray I'll live long enough to see that day."

"Is something troubling you? You look unhappy."

"I know what they are discussing. They want to leave Holland."

"Yes—I believe you are right."

121

"I wish you were going with us. I would feel braver if you did. There will be storms at sea, and there will be no shelters and not enough food on land. We will be among *strangers*."

Mercy touched Dorothy's hand. "You must catch your breath."

Dorothy shut her eyes. "I have so much unease—too much to bear."

"Be at peace, Dorothy. There are English in Virginia, and they have built houses. Don't you see? You'll be greeted warmly. You'll not starve."

"William tells me to pray and I'll find peace. I have prayed until my throat is dry and I've cried until I have no tears left. I do not know if God hears me."

Mercy looked at the sunlight streaming through the window. At a loss of words to ease her poor friend, she drew her arm through Dorothy's and set her mind to comfort her. She would not lie, for what Dorothy said about the dangers of crossing the ocean and arriving in a stranger's land, were true.

Other women remained behind waiting for their husbands, holding babies in their laps, some scolding their children for running about and making too much noise. They were smiling, and laughter seemed so common among them. Mercy watched Dorothy's eyes drift over to the others. "As you see, I'm not like them. They seem so sure." She looked at Mercy. "If you were going, would you be afraid? Or would you be like them, laughing and smiling."

"Dorothy…"

"The worst of it is leaving John behind with my mother and father. He is but three years." Tears came into Dorothy's eyes.

"I'm sure William is thinking of your son's comfort. When you are settled, and a house built, you can send for him to come on the second voyage."

"Yes, Mother and Papa plan to."

"So there—you can have peace about the future. Think of the hardships your child would endure if you took him on the voyage, and for him to be in Virginia with no roof over his head. You are only torturing yourself by doubting your decision."

"You don't understand, Mercy. You are not a mother."

"But I do believe I will be."

"I hope William and I have more. One is not enough."

"We will stay close and encourage each other. Years from now, when we are old and gray, we will have many stories to tell our grandchildren."

With silence falling between them, Mercy fastened the buckles on her shoe that had come loose. Dorothy stared at her hands, turning them over in her lap. She gathered her shawl over her shoulders and went to her husband as soon as he came through the door. Mercy sat alone to gather her thoughts, and oh what turbulent thoughts they were—crashing over her like a boiling sea the moment Caleb walked out and looked at her.

Mercy stirred a small fire in the hearth and drew off Uncle Silas's shoes. "There," she said. "Warm your feet, Uncle."

He sighed. "Lately they are always cold. 'Tis too hot for you to have a fire, Mercy."

"It is but a small one. Would you like another pair of socks?"

He shook his head. "No need. How I ever lived without you, I know not."

Sitting on the floor, she drew up her knees. "You did very well without me, and you had Jasper to keep you company."

He flexed his stockinged feet. "Aye, that is true." He drew his clay pipe from his mouth. His hand shook as he held it by the bowl.

Mercy sat up on her hunches. "Uncle, what worries you?" She took his pipe and set it aside. Then she picked up his hands and held them fast. "You tremble so."

"Age is catching up with me. That's all…"

She studied his face. Though the creases were deep and long, they had a softness about them that caused her to appreciate him even more. She scooted closer to his chair and drew a wool blanket over his lap. The clock on the mantle chimed.

"It is late. Would you like me to help you to bed?"

"It is too early. I'll toss and turn. Talk of going to the New World is troubling, is it not?"

"Dorothy Bradford has told me as much, and I have to agree with her."

"I pray the Lord will give her comfort."

She laid her head on his lap. "Why can't Mr. Bradford let her stay with her parents and little John Bradford? They can sail on the next ship in a year."

"A decision between husband and wife, so I do not have an answer to give you."

Mercy frowned. "It is so difficult."

"What of Caleb?"

She looked up. "What of him?"

"What are your feelings toward the man?"

The question was unexpected. She twisted a loose thread hanging from the blanket around her finger. "I hardly know."

"Oh, I think you do. You haven't seemed the same since he told us he is leaving."

"There does not seem…to be anything keeping him here. And why should he stay? Leaving is the right thing to do."

"But you are saddened by it."

"Am I that obvious?"

He nudged her chin. "As obvious as Caleb."

Footsteps came to their hearing. They grew louder and someone knocked on the door. When Mercy opened it, she found Martin standing outside. He dragged off his hat and inclined his head. "Good eve, Mercy."

"Martin, come inside." She shut the door, but not after throwing a glance at the small window in the barn loft. "We've eaten supper, but there's some left if you are hungry."

"My thanks, Mercy, but I've had my meal." He set his hat on the table. "Good eve, sir."

"There's a brisk wind tonight, lad. What brings you by?"

"I've come to tell Mercy about my decision. I'm going to go to America with the others." He looked at her, and she could not help but notice the gratification in his eyes. "I doubt you are surprised, eh, Mercy?"

She smiled. "You've always been the adventurous sort. Uncle and I are staying." She set her hand over his. "You'll be in my prayers every night."

"That gives me comfort. I feel as if I'm leaving my family, and I suppose I am. Knowing you will pray for me will keep us together though an ocean apart."

Mercy leaned toward the window to open the curtains wide. A full moon rose above the roof of the barn. The red doors opened and out stepped Caleb. This would be the last night he would spend in the loft. The last night, she'd see that small diamond of a flame flicker in the window.

He stepped up to the troth, dipped his hands into the water and splashed it over his face. She looked away, but only for a moment. She scolded her attraction to him, chastised her riveted gaze as he ran his hand across his neck.

"What are you watching, Mercy?" Martin inquired.

"Oh, nothing." Her tone rang with disinterest, but her heart beat in a different rhythm.

Martin leaped from his chair and drew beside her. He threw open the sash and called out to Caleb. Mercy's pulse raced when he looked up from the troth and pushed back his wet hair.

"Grab the lantern and come inside," said Martin.

When he came through the front door, he held his hand out to Martin and they shook. Mercy bid them to sit. She sat beside her uncle and folded her hands in her lap. "Your hair is damp, Mr. Treymayne."

He gave her a sly smile. "When I move to town, I'll have a proper bath."

Silas leaned back in his chair. "There's the stream below the hill, Mr. Treymayne. You'd have better luck there than in town."

Caleb leaned closer to Mercy. "Is it true, Mercy? Have you tried the stream?"

The heat rose in her cheeks. "You should not ask such questions." She crossed the room and sat in a chair away from the hearth. "The fire is too hot, I believe."

Caleb crouched in front of the hearth and worked to bring down the fire. The firelight danced over the contours of his face, sparkled in his eyes. "Is that better?" he asked looking at Mercy.

She nodded. Martin went on speaking, and when she heard her uncle snore in his chair, they all smiled.

"Don't leave," she said when they went to rise. "My uncle is only dozing. Besides, I'm interested in what you speak of, Martin."

"Are you?" Martin turned to Caleb. "Mr. Treymayne, are you interested?"

"Such a journey will not be safe," Caleb said.

"Dr. Fuller is going with his wife, so I must go too. He has been good to me. We know there will be challenges, but our leaders will guide us through."

Caleb crossed his booted legs. Happy to see no mud caked on them, Mercy lightly smiled.

"Are you doubtful?" Martin asked Caleb.

"I'm merely cautious. Jamestown and Roanoke were not so fortunate and should be a lesson to us all."

"That is true, but they went for the sole purpose of finding gold, of which there were none. And they were ill prepared. We're not going there to seek our fortunes."

Silas opened his eyes. "I dozed off. Anything important I missed?"

Mercy helped her uncle up. "No, Uncle. Now, you need to be abed. Come, I'll help you upstairs."

Silas shuffled from the room with Mercy aiding him. As they climbed the creaky staircase, Mercy heard Martin and Caleb talking. The thought of him leaving, and never seeing him again, stirred a troubled feeling in her. She kept her uncle's arm through hers, intent on helping him but with her ears keen to listen to the two men speaking. Silas hand gripped the banister. It shook violently and he gasped.

"You must let me send for Dr. Fuller, Uncle. I'm worried how you shake so."

Silas paused. "Believe me, it is naught but old age, my girl. No need to worry. I will sleep well, and then I'll be better in the morning. I've much work to do with the sheep and our little vegetable patch needs attention."

When they reached the bedroom, Mercy helped her uncle into bed. She drew the coverlet over him, tucking it around his body. "Are you cold?"

"This will do, Mercy. Let me sleep. Go back to your friends. Call Jasper upstairs. I want him to lie on the floor next to me."

She went to the door and called the hound. He scampered up the staircase, jumped up on the bed, and settled at his master's feet. "No, Jasper. Onto the floor."

"Let him stay, Mercy. I do feel a bit chilled, and Jasper will keep me warm." Silas closed his eyes. "It is a good dog that comforts his master."

Mercy stroked Silas's brow. "There now, you lay quiet and go to sleep."

"Yes, sleep. I am tired." He opened his eyes and looked up at her. "But not tired of you, Mercy. Just tired of living, I suppose."

"It is the hard day talking. You've toiled too much for a man your age. Go to sleep. You'll feel better in the morning."

"Mercy. Open the curtains, please. I'd like to see the moonlight come through the window."

She got up from the bedside and pushed them apart. The moon glowed in a cloudless night sky, and the fields were a misty blue with its light. For a moment, she gazed at it, soaking in its glory and that of the stars. ""Tis a beautiful moon. I wonder. Has God set his Word among the stars?"

When she turned, Silas drew in a breath, held it, and released a long exhale. Silence followed. Jasper whimpered and pawed at the bedding. Mercy made no motion to hurry forward but stood looking at Silas. Jasper edged closer to Silas. "Do not wake him, Jasper. He is asleep." Stunned, she knew he was not. No breath. No heaving of his chest. Open eyes staring into the dark. Tears springing in her eyes. Her heart went up into her throat, and when he did not answer, she walked back to the bedside and touched his hand. With a strong shudder, she looked at his face, white and still, softly composed to the darkening night and to the moonlight calmly shining through the window.

Silas was gone.

Chapter 14

On the day Mercy laid Uncle Silas to rest, she stood at the grave wrapped in her cloak and tried not to cry. Heartbroken, she stared at the brown mound of earth near her shoes and listened to the wind sigh through the trees. It crossed the sickled grass around gray tombstones and shook off petals from a row of red tulips. His burial, as with all Puritans, was a silent affair. The people gathered and the body solemnly carried to the grave. All stood by solemn and hushed as his earthly vessel was given back to the Earth.

Caleb took Mercy's hand to lead her away. Martin stepped up to them and swept off his hat. "Forgive me, Mercy," he said, his brows deeply creased. "It is a sad day and I do not wish to add to your grief with a letter from your old neighbor, my landlady. I hesitate, but it would be wrong to keep it from you, unless you want to wait."

"News from home, Martin? How could that add to my grief?" Mercy took the letter and opened it. She scanned the handwriting. "She addresses you. Perhaps I should not read this?" She held it out to him.

He gently pushed the letter toward her. "No, Mercy. It is for you to read. It concerns Jonah and Patience."

Mercy read Nan and Grandpapa Jonah explained to the widow Brynes why Martin had suddenly disappeared, where he had gone and why. She was grateful, for she had been worried something terrible had happened to him, and was angry he had not told her he was leaving.

Mercy looked at Martin empathically. He lowered his eyes. "We were in haste." Then he lifted his eyes. "I wrote to her after we arrived here. You see there in the letter she has forgiven me."

Mercy returned to the missive. Indeed widow Brynes told Martin she had, and that she was proud of his willingness to see Mercy safely to Holland. Not a soldier or magistrate's men had come to her door, and it were all good except—. She paused and swallowed. "What is it?" Caleb said.

"A malignant fever has taken them…a day apart…" She dropped her hand and the letter fluttered from her fingers. "This cannot be."

The blow came down hard. Her knees buckled and met the ground. Tears came fast as she gasped for air.

Caleb hurried to lift her. "My poor girl," he said.

"Do not tell me God willed it. I cannot hear it. I won't hear it!"

"I'll not say it, Mercy."

She rocked in his arms. "Have no one say it."

"Hush now."

Martin turned his hat in his hands and sorrow flooded his face. "I'm sorry. I shouldn't have given it to you. I should have waited."

"I could have gotten medicines and nursed them. Instead, I ran away like a coward."

Caleb drew closer to her. "You are no coward. Grief is speaking."

"Yes, Caleb, grief *is* speaking." She put her hands over her ears. "I wish I could block it out, but I cannot. I have lost my grandparents and uncle at the same time. It is not fair."

Caleb kept his arms around her. "Come. Let us leave this sad place."

Mercy rested her head against Caleb's shoulder. A light drizzle of rain fell. If not for the strength of Caleb's arms, she would have fallen to her knees, thrown herself across the mound of dirt and wept. Moving away from the grave, he guided her over the grass to a path leading down to the road. Together with Martin, they walked back to the farm where Separatists leaders and their wives had gathered.

The place that had been Silas's dwelling for many a year, seemed strangely quiet to Mercy when she stepped through the door. Dorothy Bradford came through to the hallway and drew Mercy aside. Caleb went into the sitting room with Martin and joined the gentlemen.

"The landlord is here," Dorothy said. "He waits in the other room to speak to you."

For a moment, Mercy did not answer Dorothy. "I do not want to see him."

"I doubt he will go away so easily."

"I've lost my grandparents, Dorothy, and just buried my uncle. My heart is too heavy to bear more bad news, for I have no doubt he brings it. He will tell me to leave."

Creasing her brows, Dorothy laid her hand on Mercy's arm. "Perhaps not, but if he does, you have naught to worry. We will look after you."

"Why are people here? I did not expect it?"

"Martin sent us word earlier regarding your grandparents. That is why some of us have come. Indeed this is a heavy weight to bear."

With every ounce of strength Mercy had, she wiped her eyes and lifted her head. "But one I must carry. And I will carry, God help me."

"Do you wish me to send the gentleman away? He should understand, considering the circumstances."

"It is alright. I will speak to him." She drew off her cloak and handed it to Dorothy. "It is best I get it over with."

Gathering her resolve, Mercy went into the room where cedar fires had burned softly on cold days. A tall gentleman in a rusty-brown doublet stood by the fireplace with his hands behind his back. He swept off his hat and bowed, his blond hair brushing along his linen collar.

"Mr. Andersen. I had not expected you today." Mercy turned to pull the double doors closed.

"You must excuse my coming on such a sad occasion. I'm deeply sorry for your loss. Silas was a good man, and the best tenant I ever had."

Mercy lowered her eyes. "Thank you, sir. I have also learned this day of my grandparents passing."

Andersen frowned sympathetically, but did not offer to leave and come back another day as Mercy had hoped. "I'm sorry to hear it. You've had a mighty blow."

"I do not lack for comfort among my friends."

"Indeed, for I saw them as I came in. Mrs. Bradford was exceptionally gracious to allow me to wait."

"You are welcome to join us if you like, otherwise quickly say your mind."

"The latter I'll do." He drew from his doublet a paper and unfolded it. "As you see, this is the agreement Silas signed when he became my tenant. Everything on the farm belongs to me. I furnished the place and purchased the livestock. Silas was happy for it, for all his needs were in place when he moved in."

"So you owned the sheep? Did he not keep the money from the sale of their wool?"

"It was agreed he would do so."

"And my uncle's milking cow?"

"I bought her at auction."

"I see." She held her lower lip between her teeth a moment. "My uncle's dog—Jasper? What will happen to him?"

"I cannot imagine you taking him. What good would a dog do you?"

"I have grown attached."

"He is an excellent sheep dog from what I was told."

"But you could buy another, couldn't you?"

"Yes, indeed I could, but Jasper is accustomed to the farm. It would be unwise to take him to town. He'd be unhappy."

"My uncle would not want him to be."

Andersen smiled. "I'll not deny it. Let him stay. I promise we shall take good care of him."

"Thank you, sir."

"My boys have a dog of their own—a fine little terrier. He will serve me well on the farm. Catches rats, you know. I'm sure he'd be useless at herding sheep."

The man could not have been more generous. After all, Mercy owned nothing except for the clothes she wore and a cedar trunk Uncle Silas gave her. "Is there anything else, Mr. Andersen?"

"As a matter of fact there is. It grieves me to say it, but I wish you to vacate as soon as possible. Say within a day or two." He stepped forward. "As soon as I heard the news, I sent for my wife and children in Amsterdam. We will set up our home here. It has always been my intention once I had the leisure to close my business in the city and retire. It is ideal for my children, and the country air will benefit my wife."

Mercy folded her hands. "I understand."

"Have you a place to go?"

"I'll find one. Surely there are households in Leyden in need of a servant."

"I would hire you myself, but my wife has a maid, and I've hired a man to…"

Mercy held up her hand. "Please, sir. You do not need to explain."

"But I think I do, so to ease the troubled feelings you may have toward me."

She met his eyes. "I have none, sir."

"You do not despise me for this?

Mercy shook her head. "I do not dislike you if that is what you mean."

He drew up. "Yes, that is what I mean."

"What I do dislike is the loss, sir. It will take time for me to adjust, especially leaving what has been my home these months is added to my sorrow."

"I'm sorry," Andersen said. "It was my wife that was insistent."

Mercy gave him a weak smile. "I'll have no trouble find lodging and work." She spread the doors open, and gave him a slight curtsy. "I wish you well, sir, and bid you a good day."

Andersen picked up his hat. "Again, my sympathies." He bowed and passed into the hallway. For a moment, Mercy leaned against the door. The ridges of the crude planks against her back reminded her all was never well in the world. Footsteps came down the hallway, and Caleb stopped outside the door. She looked at him.

"What did that man want?"

"He was my uncle's landlord."

"He wishes you gone?"

"Indeed he does, and it is his right."

"The others have brought food and drink." He held out his hand and she took it. There was a table beneath the window. The women had laid out food. Fowl, fruit, cakes, and bread. Their gesture touched Mercy, for the custom was on days such as this, families left for home in silence.

Dorothy stood from a chair and hurried over to Mercy. "Come sit near me," she said. "Look at the table, Mercy. There is plenty of food. Let me get you something. I imagine you haven't had a thing to eat all day."

"Some food would help, eh Mercy?" Caleb said.

Mercy shook her head. "I want nothing." She wished they would not pamper her. Instead, she wished everyone would leave for their homes and let her spend the rest of the day by herself. Except for Caleb. If only she were his wife, she could be alone with him through the lonely hours ahead. She'd sleep in his arms and feel the comforting beat of his heart with her head on his chest. The want to cry her eyes out overwhelmed her. Yet, she would not in front of others. A glistening of tears was enough. To let them fall she feared they'd think her weak. No, to be alone in the quiet dark was all she wanted. Caleb was all she needed.

Jasper lay on the rug in front of Uncle Silas's chair. "Mr. Andersen owns everything, down to the last bit of string in a drawer."

Caleb frowned. "You are not staying here?"

She looked at him. "He wishes me gone. It is his right."

Dorothy set her hand on Mercy's "It grows late and you are tired. I'll tell the others to go." She got up and went over to her husband. The remaining leaders and their wives quietly left with their faces somber in the growing dusk. The front door closed, and Mercy watched William Bradford linger in the hallway with Dorothy.

"Now the world will know I'm cast out," Mercy said to Caleb. "Dorothy is telling William I'm to leave, and he will have sympathy." She lowered her head. "I do not want pity or charity."

Caleb sat next to her. "You are considered a sister among these people. Would you expect anything other than love and compassion from them? You think they'd leave you to find a way on your own?"

"I'm sorry. I did not mean to sound ungrateful."

"You can stay with one of the families.

tender eyes.

"You give me ease." She clicked her fingers and Jasper stretched his legs and came to her. She stroked his ears and he set his head on her knee. Caleb leaned in. "If we married, I'd take care of you for my heart is full as you should know."

Mercy looked at her hands and smiled. "A proposal at a time as this, Caleb Treymayne?"

"I admit it is the least romantic time to give one."

"Perhaps you could ask me again—when I'm not so sad."

His eyes glowed. "I'll ask again, but I'll take your comment for a *yes*."

"But I did not say…"

She broke off when the Bradfords approached. "Come with us, Mercy," Dorothy said. "It is unwise for you to stay here alone."

Glancing at the staircase, she knew her to be right, although her feelings were of the contrary. The steps were set to the left beyond the fireplace, and coiled to the upper floor. The reminiscence of helping Uncle Silas up them deepened her sorrow along with the memory of seeing her grandparents bidding her farewell at their door in the dark and gloom.

"Mercy?" Caleb said. "Would you like Dorothy to help you pack your clothes?"

She tore her eyes away from the staircase and looked at him. "Forgive me. The stairs. I'll never see him or my grandparents again."

"It is not so," Caleb said. "Your separation from them is only for a moment in time."

"God willing I should go to Heaven." She lowered her head.

William Bradford leaned down. "We offer our home to you, Mercy. You cannot stay here."

Mercy sighed. "I would be another mouth to feed."

"Nonsense. My wife and I have food aplenty to share."

"We have an extra bedroom, Mercy," said Dorothy. "Please come."

Mercy nodded. "It is good of you...too good, but..."

"William and I will wait outside," Dorothy said. "Think a little, but do not be too long." She leaned down to Caleb. "Help her see sense, will you?"

He stood with her and went upstairs. She pointed at the chest. "I hope it is not too heavy," she said to him. "All my clothes are in there."

"It is a small thing. At least it is not filled with books." He smiled at her, and his look caused a small smile to sweep over her lips. She grabbed the covering off Uncle Silas's chair. "I made this, so 'tis mine to keep. Perhaps I can show Dorothy how to make one like it. Uncle Silas kept it over his knees."

"I fear for that woman," Caleb said. "Her moods are quick to sink."

"I believe that is why men have a difficult time understanding us. Do you think I am weak?"

"I think you are foolish—at the moment. You're going to the Bradford's. If I must, I will carry you there. "

He took Mercy by the elbow and led her to the staircase.

"Where are we going?" she said.

"Upstairs for you to pack."

Mercy paused, her hands pressing against the banister. Sunlight was fading and the hallway on the upper floor grew dark. She turned away. "I fear if you do not leave, I will break into tears in front of you." She moved to Caleb and looked into his eyes. "But you'll not leave me, will you?"

"Not I, Mercy McCrea. Not on my life's blood."

Days passed with golden sunrises and magenta sunsets. Yet Mercy's eyes could not comprehend their beauty. She settled into a spare room in the Bradford house, and scrubbed every inch of the floor until her hands were chapped from the harsh lye soap. She heard a man's voice outside the window and hurried to it. Pushing the pane out, she looked into the street. She hoped it were Caleb. He'd been to see her every day, he too settling into a cheap dwelling in the city.

Disappointed, she pulled away from the window.

"Mercy." Dorothy appeared in the doorway with a bright smile. "Look what I've made. It's for your hands."

Mercy took the jar from Dorothy and opened it. "I'm delighted. You have my thanks."

"It's made of beeswax and oils. It will soothe your hands. You've been working hard, and must have some relief. I never wanted you to live with us to clean my house."

"I cannot abide to be idle."

"Nor can I. I have dough rising, but I've made a mess of it. Will you help me?"

Mercy smiled. "A chance to bake bread has always been a distraction to my woes." She hurried out the door and Dorothy rushed beside her.

"Do not be shocked by the amount of flour on the floor. It is my fault for spilling a measure full," Dorothy said as they hurried down the staircase.

"You have it on your cheek as well as the floor."

Dorothy rubbed her face. Once inside the kitchen, Mercy looked at its condition. She grabbed a broom. Dorothy patted the dough with flour.

"We are taught not to gossip, but there are some who do not obey that rule."

Mercy swept the spilled flour out the door. "Why have you brought that up?"

"Oh, no reason, except…"

"Except what?"

"Well, I will not say who, for I do not wish them to be caught, but there are a few women who say you have become too close to Caleb." Dorothy dusted her hands with more flour. Then she cut the dough into halves and handed some to Mercy. "Here, I know you like to knead."

Mercy smiled and pushed her half of the dough across the floured board. "Whoever they are, they must dislike me very much. Why else would they speak against me?"

"Jealousy makes them speak so."

"You should not feel ashamed of your feelings for Caleb."

"Or his for me?"

"Or his for you, Mercy."

"I suppose those women forget their own feelings for their men."

Dorothy shoved her half of the dough across the floured board. "Caleb is a good man. You should wed him."

Mercy sighed. "He has not asked me."

"It is evident how he feels. Sooner or later, he will fight it no more and ask you to be his wife." Leaning forward, Dorothy set her palms against the table. "Would you accept?"

"I would."

"You should help him along. Give him smiles and warm gazes."

"I'm amazed at you."

"You don't think I know how to win a man's heart? I won William's didn't I?" Dorothy punched the lump of dough. "Once I knew he loved me, everything changed."

"You love him still?"

"More than ever. I can tell you miss Caleb."

"Can you? How?"

"By the look on your face every time I mention his name." Dorothy giggled. "It lights up, especially your eyes."

Mercy smiled. Caleb and William were on their way to Delfshaven. She wondered. Would they be speaking of her the way she and Dorothy spoke of Caleb? Dorothy ran her hands along her apron and sighed. "These men. They know nothing of seafaring, and I fear they may get talked into a ship not seaworthy."

"Since Caleb is a carpenter, I think he will be able to tell. He was in the King's Navy. And your William is wise when it comes to business."

Young John Bradford tottered into the kitchen whimpering and holding his stomach. His cheeks were flushed and his eyes squeezed shut. Dorothy rushed to him and picked him up. "My darling. What is the matter?" She brought him over to Mercy. "Is he not hot, Mercy?" Panic grew in her voice. "He has a fever."

Mercy set her palm over the boy's forehead. His skin was cool to her touch and he pulled away. "He woke from his nap. It is the cause." She touched Dorothy on the shoulder. "You've nothing to fear."

Dorothy shook her head and ran her hand over her boy's hair. "I did cover him warmly with too many blankets." She set the boy down. "Do you feel poorly, John?"

He looked up with eyes Mercy found charming, and then tugged on his mother's apron. "I'm hungry, *Moeder*."

Dorothy set her hands on his shoulders. "Mama, John. You must call me Mama."

"He's so little to speak Dutch. Indeed he is a smart lad." Mercy said. "You must admit, he sounds sweet the way he calls you 'mother'."

Dorothy set John at the table and went back to her dough. She kneaded it hard, and tossed flour over it. "I don't want him to speak Dutch. He's English, and English he must speak."

Mercy buttered a slice of bread and handed it to the boy. "Yes, of course." She could have said more, but bit her tongue. Young John was not her child. She had no rights to advise Dorothy or speak her mind on the raising of him. She had no child of her own to know from experience what to do, only a slight intuition on what was right or wrong.

The Separatist had a growing concern their children were growing up Dutch, and their group would fade into obscurity. For Mercy, Holland proved to be a momentary refuge, but nothing more.

Chapter 15

In the town square, crowds mingled around merchant stands, haggling prices and amounts. Chickens and ducks squawked inside wooden cages, and children watched intently a puppeteer. Mercy hurried through the street and turned a corner. Overhung second stories shadowed the cobbles. Women shook out rugs and blankets from the windows.

Dorothy had run out of flour, having wasted plenty spilling it on the floor. Mercy hugged her basket close, and search for a merchant among fruit and vegetable carts. As she walked by, a flower cart caught her senses. Red and white striped tulips, white and yellows, drew her eyes away from the crowds. They would look pretty in the window. A patient matron stood on the other side of the cart and smiled.

"These please." Mercy pointed to a grouping of colors.

The woman nodded and handed them to her. Mercy counted out the coins and paid the woman. Reaching a stand with barrels of rye, wheat, and barley flours, she lent the merchant her basket, and saw from the corner of her eye a group of Separatist girls staring at her. They were maidens in burgundy and powder gray dresses fit snug about their waists. Simple white caps covered their hair and untied strings dangled over their shoulders.

After she paid the vendor, Mercy strode over to girls. "You are engaged in lively conversation this morn."

Their faces blushed. The oldest among them spoke up. "Prithee, Mercy, we did not mean to stare. It's just that we were…"

"Were what?"

"Do you not know?"

"I am at a loss. If you have something to say, say it."

"Caleb is working as a carpenter for a Mr. Jorgenson, a builder here in Leyden."

"Yes I know. I'm glad he found work in his trade."

"We are as well, but we've been hearing rumors."

Mercy narrowed her eyes. She didn't like this kind of thing, not from young ladies taught not to gossip. "You should not listen to them," she said. "Rumors end up badly."

"But a woman has been seen visiting his quarters," said a younger girl, who upon the last word slapped her hand over her mouth.

The older girl shoved the other. "You were not supposed to say. You've upset Mercy."

"It is nothing more than a malicious rumor," Mercy said. "You should know better. I'll go to your fathers if I hear you speak of it again."

The girls lowered their eyes, except for the younger. "But we all care about you, Mercy. None wish to see you hurt."

Mercy lightly laughed. "It is good of you to care, but a rumor shall not hurt me."

"Unless it is the truth."

"Is gossip ever the truth?"

"'Tis wrong to gossip, but it could be."

"You best tell me what it is you're worried about. Get it off your minds, before it builds into something worse."

"It is believed the woman is the kind we dare not speak of or speak to."

Mercy raised her brows. "You mean a prostitute?" Their faces colored, appalled at the word. "As I recall our Lord ministered to prostitutes and sinners."

"But that was the Lord. A woman like her could be the downfall of a man," one said.

"You're his friend," said another. "You should warn him before he's led further astray."

"Yes," said a younger. "He should repent and marry within our church."

Mercy's tolerant nature toward girls of this age, shown in her face, a smile that disarmed them. She meant to open their eyes, hoping they would see the folly of their over imaginative minds.

"Hmm, and most likely he should wed one of you, I suppose. If what you say is true, tell one of the elders. But beware of spreading a rumor you might regret."

"Perhaps the elders already know, Mercy."

"If they did, they would have spoken to him by now. Haven't you ever heard, 'he who brings a tale takes two away'?"

Speechless, the girls set their mouths firm. As they walked away, Mercy went on with her tasks. The idea Caleb would be so unwise to take up with such a woman was ludicrous. Yet—he was a man, and men had passions difficult to control if a woman was willing to fulfill them.

She stopped in the street, bit her lip, and scolded her thoughts. Pushing the idea from her mind of him being unfaithful and fallen, she went on at a slower pace. She saw the girls up ahead, gathered at a booth were a merchant sold bolts of silk. If they did not heed her, their gossip could lead to vicious lies, and vicious lies to broken trust. Mercy needed to warn Caleb and put out this fire before it grew into an inferno.

The Bradford's tabby leaped at Mercy when she walked through the kitchen door. She managed to steady her basket as the feline rushed between her feet and jumped into the chair beside the door. "Why are you not out chasing mice?"

Dorothy looked up from her chair near the fireplace. On an iron hook simmered a pot of stew. The ashes glowed beneath it. "Are you all right?" Dorothy asked.

"I'm perfectly fine. It was the cat that startled me." Setting the basket down, she picked up the kitten and rubbed her cheek against it. The cat mewed and Mercy set her on the floor. She grabbed a cloth and lifted the lid off the pot.

"Smells delicious, Dorothy. Your William will be pleased."

"I'm sorry about my kitten. She's always leaping at people. I will set her outside."

"She's just being playful. My, the day is warm. Are my cheeks as red as they feel?"

"I do not think so." Dorothy picked up a basket of turnips and sat back down. She began peeling them with her paring knife and humming. Then she said, "Going to the market does wear one out though, no matter the weather. Perhaps you need to lie down?"

"An afternoon rest will not solve anything." Mercy wiped her face and sat at the table. Her thoughts jumbled over Caleb and the rumor, she cupped her chin in her hand.

"A moment's rest works for me," Dorothy said.

Mercy chose an apple from the basket and inspected it. "I'm not tired. I'm worried."

"About a problem you have?"

"There's a rumor Caleb is seeing a woman, the kind men pay for."

Dorothy laughed. "Where did you hear that?"

"Some of the girls in our congregation were in the market."

"I hope you paid them no mind."

"I fear they will keep tattling. People might start to believe it."

"The elders will hear of it soon enough. Allow them to deal with it." Dorothy tossed a turnip into a bowl and set it on the floor beside her chair.

Mercy pressed her brows. "You mean they might believe these girls?"

"I do not know. There is an understanding it takes time to overcome obstacles in our lives once we confess Christ. Caleb may need guidance."

Mercy set her palms on the table. "Then it could be true. He might have another."

"Mercy, this may be for naught. Caleb is a decent man. Speak to him. You have that right."

"I suppose it would set my mind at ease. But I don't want him to think I do not trust him."

"For all you know, the woman could be a good person and not what they imply."

Mercy's heart gripped. "If that is so, I'll be glad. If she is one who would take his love from me, I'll not be happy. I'll be full of sorrow."

Setting the apple back, she stood. She would not waste time. She needed clear answers. The conversation with the girls and Dorothy confused her. She could not tell whom Dorothy sided with, since one moment she spoke highly of Caleb. The next she implied he needed guidance.

"I'm going to him," Mercy said. "I do not know how long I will be, so excuse me from supper."

Dorothy set the turnips aside. She wrapped a loaf of bread in cheesecloth and set it and a pot of jam in Mercy's basket. "Take him this. You made enough for the rest of us. Men enjoy a good loaf of rye."

Mercy looked up at the sunny sky and headed west down a cobbled street. She turned a corner where houses were made into flats along one of Leyden's canals. Women swept their steps. Children ran in the street playing games. A man and a woman conversed in Dutch in front of a door painted bright blue. The man tipped his hat, and walked away. Mercy met the woman's eyes.

"Excuse me," she said. "Do you know if this is where Mr. Caleb Treymayne lives? He's an Englishman."

"*Boven*," the woman replied.

Mercy did not understand and repeated the word back to the woman.

"Ya, *boven*." The woman pointed to the ceiling. "Upstairs."

A smile lifted Mercy's mouth. "Oh, I understand now. Thank you."

She stepped past the woman into a darkened hallway and climbed the staircase. It creaked under her feet, and she found herself feeling sorry Caleb had come to such a place. Cramped and airless, a musty smell lingered in the air. The plastered walls were murky yellow, the windows few and small. No doubt, the rent was cheap. How could he afford anything else?

At the landing, she moved back to allow a woman and her children to pass. Carrying an infant in her arm, the mother corralled the children down the stairs, their flaxen curls bouncing about their angelic faces. Squeezing by, Mercy realized she had not asked which door. She glanced down the corridor and took a step, when suddenly one opened and Caleb appeared. Over his shoulder, he carried his tool sack and swung it forward when he saw her.

"Mercy?" he said. "What are you doing here?"

"I…" She found herself tongue-tied. "Well, to see you, Caleb."

"Is everything all right?"

She shook her head and her curls slipped out of her cap. "Yes, everything is fine. I'm sorry if I shocked you."

He walked toward her. "I'm glad. I've wanted to call at the Bradford's but I've been busy with work. I hope you can forgive my neglect."

Mercy lowered her eyes.

"You miss him, don't you? You miss Silas."

All she could do was nod, her grief still raw.

"He'd want you to remember it will not always be this way."

"No, it won't. Not for my grandparents either." She gave him a warm stare. "Are you well? Been eating enough?"

"Yes to both questions. I eat at the tavern on the corner. The food is nothing like yours, but I can tolerate it."

"I've brought you a gift. I made bread this morning, and there is blackberry jam and butter."

His eyes glowed and he pulled her inside by the elbow. "I have something for you too. Come and see. Tell me if you like it."

Mercy raised her brows, intrigued by his wish to give her a present. She knew it would not be anything like what Lord Glenmont had given—no jewel, not bits of gold or silver. But something precious. Something from his heart worked by his own hands.

He opened a cupboard and placed his hands around a wooden box, turned and held it out to her. Her eyes widened. Fine polished wood with a rich cedar scent, the box was the prettiest she had seen. He carved her initial on top with vines and leaves wrapping around it.

"You made this with your own hands? I'm breathless."

"I needed something to do when I couldn't sleep. Do you like it?"

She set the box on a table and opened the lid. "It is lovely. Why would you make something like this for me?"

"Because I have feelings for you." He moved close.

She shut the lid. "Have I an admirer still?"

"You tease me, Mercy. I think of you night and day."

She looked up with misty eyes. "You think of my cooking, Caleb Treymayne."

He had laughter in his eyes. "That too."

What happened to her ability to speak? He placed his hands on her arms and drew her close. There it was, that wonderful feeling he gave her. It rose in her chest, ran through her limbs, and caused her heart to flutter. His lips drew close, and she shivered. "I should go."

"So soon?"

"It's getting late."

"You came all this way to bring me bread, jam, and butter? I see in your eyes, there's some other reason. What is it?"

"Well...there is a rumor..."

"About me?"

"They say you are keeping a woman."

He laughed. "And you believe it?"

"Do you have another woman?"

"I only have you to think of." He traced her jaw with his fingertip.

She moved his hand away. "It's been known to happen that men seek comfort from another kind of woman."

"What kind of man do you take me for?"

"I take you for a good man."

"Then why doubt?"

An awkward feeling she already took this too far bubbled over. "Are the rumors true? You must tell me."

"Why, so you can rescue me from the jaws of gossips and prudes? Let me tell you something, Mercy. I have never been nor will I be with a prostitute."

Humiliated, Mercy felt her face flush. By the look in his eyes, she knew she had offended him. "I'm sorry, Caleb. I was told…"

"A lie."

"Well, it troubled me greatly. In my heart, I did not believe it. I needed to hear it from your own lips it weren't true so I could end the talk once and for all."

A wryly smile crept over his lips as he looked past her. He leaned into her ear. "Is she the harlot they speak of standing at the door behind you?"

Mercy spun around. Her eyes met those of a middle-aged woman. Wisps of gray hair escaped the dingy coif. Her frock hugged her shoulders and her skirts were wide at the hips in typical Dutch fashion but taut over her plump frame. Under her arm, she carried a clay jug.

"I've brought you some cider, Mr. Treymayne," she said. Her accent was so smooth she came close to being English. "De water in de city is poorly they say." She set it firmly on the table with sighs of exhaustion. "Who's this lady?"

Mercy's embarrassment could not be measured. She gave the woman a sorry look and glanced at Caleb. He stood watching her, waiting to see what she would do. Before her was no harlot, but a woman bent by hard work. Mercy inwardly rebuked her stupidity. How could she have considered for an inkling those girls were right? How could she have been so bold to arrive at Caleb's flat and question him? The box sat on the table and her guilt worsened, spreading like a weight on her chest.

"My name is Mercy McCrea. I'm an acquaintance of Caleb's."

She heard him mock the word *acquaintance* under his breath.

The woman's brown eyes, deep-set within a Romanesque face, looked at Mercy. "You're as pretty as he said. Come to see me, *ja?*"

"Alice…" began Caleb.

Alice glared. "You don't have to tell me why she's here. I got sneers in the marketplace to know."

Mercy hardly knew what to say. "If anyone has judged you unfairly, I'm sorry for it."

Alice raised her chin proudly. "I'm a laundress. Mr. Treymayne hired me. There's nothing between us." Then she let out a cackling laugh. "I'm old enough to be his *moeder.*"

Mercy held her hand out. "Be assured, I'll put those cackling hens in their places."

Alice set the jug on the table and lifted her chin. "I can do *dat* myself."

Caleb grinned and Mercy knew how bewildered she must have looked.

"Ah, I see you finished de box," said Alice. "It's pretty." Smiling she walked over to it and touched the lid. "If you don't want it, *Engels* miss, I'll take it."

"Oh, I do love it," Mercy said. "I was about to leave and take it home with me."

Alice grinned. "So now *dat* you met me, do you trust me with Mr. Treymayne?"

"Why…yes."

"Good." Alice threw her hands on her knees and laughed so hard she toppled back against the table. Recovering, she faced Mercy. "Well, we've cleared all *dat* up, haven't we?" Smiling, she hiked her skirts above her heels and skipped out.

"Are you happy now, Mercy, now that you've seen Alice for yourself?" said Caleb.

"I'm sorry, Caleb."

He picked up the jug and poured cider into a mug. "Let me tell you about Alice. She lives across the street in a rundown boarding house and makes a living washing for other people. She married a merchant and he died last year, leaving her childless and alone. The people here are kind to her, and why anyone would accuse her of whoring, I'll never know."

"I'll be sure to stop it." Contrite, Mercy touched the sleeve of his doublet. "Perhaps Alice would like to come to a Separatist meeting."

"You think she would after what's been said about her?"

"If she did, hearts would be convicted."

"True her presence would make a point." He swallowed down a mouthful of cider.

A moment of silence fell between them. Sunlight shimmered through a window and alighted on Caleb's shoulders. Mercy watched him, how he kept his eyes on the light as it crossed the floor, how his hand gripped the handle of the mug. Desire for him to take her in his arms grew. She found herself wishing he would do it, wishing he would kiss her.

"I must go," she said. "I promised Dorothy I would help her...with some chores."

He picked up the box and handed it to her. "Do not forget my gift."

She took it, and when tears sprang into her eyes, she glanced at him wanting to flee the flat. Forward she went, and as she was about to pass him, he took her hand and drew her back. Mercy shivered when he closed the door and wrapped her in his arms. The sweep of his lips over hers brought her heels off the ground. "I have wanted to kiss you for a long time," he breathed.

She looked away. "Caleb Treymayne, why do you consume me so?"

"The same reason you do me. It's because we love each other."

She laid her head against his shoulder and they stood together in silence with their arms around each other. For the first time in her life, Mercy knew she was loved by a man. Martin had been infatuated with her. Lord Glenmont wanted her to fulfill his lustful desires. Caleb Treymayne? He was among the best of men, and not one to take advantage of her. A tender word, a soft kiss, a firm embrace, expressed his love.

The light weakened in the window. An orange glow flickered against the glass. At first, alarmed voices outside the door and downstairs were weak. Then they grew stronger. Feet stomped down the flight of stairs. Someone pounded on Caleb's door and shouted through it in Dutch. *"Brand! Brand!"*

Caleb drew her back, his eyes wide. Mercy gasped. "What are they yelling?"

He opened the door. "We have to get out." Smoke filled the hallway and twisted up to the ceiling. People ran by, handkerchiefs over their mouths, coughing and gagging.

"We have to go back inside, Caleb. Close the door," she said with urgency.

"And be trapped? Come here!" He picked Mercy up and headed toward the staircase. She buried her face against his chest, as fear clutched her throat.

"I've got you," Caleb cried above the din. "Do not let go."

He headed down. Flames reached the banister, blew back, flared again until the wood seared black. Intense heat wafted against their faces. Ash choked them, and the fire sucked the air from their lungs. Mercy cried out. Caleb heaved her up against him and ran up the stairs. He pushed through the door with his shoulder and set her down. Throwing open the window, he looked out. Mercy drew beside him. A crowd had gathered. Terror tensed on their faces. Alice motioned to Mercy with her hands to jump, her eyes looking misty and her face taut with worry. Men rushed to the canal, filling buckets in hopes of putting the fire out. A line formed and Mercy could hear the hiss the water brought, smell the dousing of flames.

"We're one flight up," Caleb said. "Come, take my hands and I'll lower you down."

Mercy held out her hands. He gripped them tight and helped her to the windowsill.

"Go on, Mercy. I'll not drop you—not until you are ready."

She swung her legs over and slipped down. "Caleb!" Terrified, she looked up at him.

"Hold tight!"

Some men rushed over to catch her. She hung straight down with at least eight feet left to go. If only she could reach the ground instead of dropping. Her heart raged against her chest, blood pounded in her temples. She kept her eyes on Caleb. "I'm afraid!"

"I'm letting go on the count of three," Caleb shouted down to her.

"Caleb!"

"One, two, three," and he released her hands.

Chapter 16

The stained hem of Mercy's gown fluttered against her legs. She leaned her head against Caleb's shoulder and listened to his hurried breathing as he carried her down the street. People raced by as bells in the church steeples sent out an alarm. The breeze smelled of smoke. So did his doublet and hair. Mercy prayed the water would conquer the fire. If not it would spread from building to building. Lives could be lost, homes destroyed, and people injured.

"Caleb," she spoke his name softly. "You can put me down."

He shouldered through a crowd. "I cannot unless you wish to be trampled."

She nestled her cheek against him. Saving her life, he risked his own, and when he jumped from the window, her heart flew into her throat. He had rushed back inside and helped others trapped in the hallway. The smoke had blinded their eyes and filled their lungs. She'd never forget the image of him coming out of the building carrying a child in his arms and a desperate mother grabbing her baby and thanking him.

"You were so brave," she said.

"No compliments, Mercy. I did what I had to do."

He headed across the street to the Bradford's front door. Dorothy rushed out. "Oh Caleb, I've been in great distress. Hurry and bring my friend inside."

Caleb carried Mercy through the door all the while looking down at the face set against his shoulder. She did not meet his eyes, only pressed her cheek firmer. Dorothy placed a pillow against the arm of the settee. "Bring her here, Caleb. Gently now." She looked at him. "The bells have been ringing."

Caleb stepped back. "I don't doubt by the day's end, I'll have no home to go back to."

"I went upstairs and from our bedroom window, I could see smoke rising above the rooftops. I feared, for I knew Mercy had gone in that direction."

"We are uninjured, Mrs. Bradford."

"Caleb lowered me from the window. He saved my life." Mercy's voice resounded with admiration and gratitude.

Dorothy sighed. "Thank you, Caleb. Is the fire out? Should we worry?"

"Let us pray it is."

"It was terrible," Mercy said. "It happened so fast—without any warning."

Mercy looked up into Caleb's face. Soot marred his cheeks and hands. Sweat covered his brow. His military training had come in handy. How many times had his life been in danger? If he had been hurt when he landed, he never showed it.

"I'll fetch water," Dorothy said. She returned with a bowl and towel, and two mugs of water. Caleb washed his face, and raked his fingers through his hair. He looked down at Mercy, and she met his eyes. "Thank you," she whispered sweetly.

At that moment, William Bradford hurried through the door and tossed his hat aside. He looked at Caleb. "Thank God, you've been spared. I hurried to your home as soon as I heard. But I could not find you."

"William." Dorothy's eyes shifted from her husband's to Mercy. He turned and looked down at a girl who looked strangely frail wrapped in his wife's shawl.

"I and others owe Caleb our lives." Mercy's heart drummed when she looked at Caleb. Her words seemed to embarrass him, but she believed he deserved the praise. "He lowered me from the window down to the street where some men caught me. The he rushed back in and helped others get out. He carried me through the crowded street home."

"You were there, Mercy...at Mr. Treymayne's quarters?" Bradford bent his brow. Did it seem inappropriate to him she had gone there alone? Would she have to explain?

She sat up. "Dorothy and I thought Caleb needed food. Men do not eat well when living alone."

Bradford nodded. "It is true." He put his arm around his wife.

Caleb put on his hat and stepped to the door. "I should be going now that Mercy is safe at home. I need to see whether or not the whole place has burned to the ground."

"It did not reach the roof, that much I know," Bradford said. "Leyden would have been in dire trouble if it had."

Mercy locked eyes with Caleb. "Caleb, your tools and my box. I hope they are not lost."

"They can be replaced, Mercy," Caleb said. "You cannot."

"I so loved the box." Her eyes smiled warmly. "Will you bring it to me if you can?"

He tipped his hat, and stepped out with William Bradford.

"I'll go with you, Caleb. Maybe I can help in some way."

"Thank you, William. I'm glad to have your company."

The two men left and Dorothy sat next to Mercy. "What an awful thing go through. Are you feeling better?"

"I'm a little shaken, but I'm fine. I smell of smoke. I must change."

Dorothy picked up the pitcher of water and headed up the staircase. "I've a new cake of soap you can have. I know I should not indulge, but I could not resist."

"There is no sin in a cake of soap. Surely the Lord does not object." Mercy hitched her skirts and climbed the steps behind her friend. Inside her humble chamber, she described the box. "Caleb carved my initial on the lid."

"Since the fire did not reach the upper floor, he will find it."

"That would make me happy." She tossed her skirts into a corner. At least her chemise was untouched. "I had to eat my words when I met Alice Lowell."

"The woman that's been talked about?"

"She is not at all what people say."

"I never believe gossip."

"Well, I learned my lesson. I should have never doubted Caleb."

As the sun set over Leyden, Mercy stood by the kitchen window and looked out onto the street. The bells stopped ringing and people moved about as before. Still the smell of charred wood mingled with the gentle breeze, and caused her heart to lift with thanksgiving no one had been killed by the smoke and blaze. Caleb and she had been spared. His bravery caused her to acknowledge her deep devotion for him. She drifted back to seeing him rush inside the building, unhindered by the heat and flames, the black smoke sucking the air out of all in its path. *Caleb. Caleb.*

Bradford had not returned home for his dinner, and young John Bradford fidgeted in his chair. "John is hungry," Mercy said. "Can I give him an apple slice?"

"I shan't wait any longer for William." Dorothy set a tray of bread slices on the table. "I'm sure he is deep in conversation and has lost track of time. Most likely he's taken Caleb with him to the tavern where the men often gather."

"Why the tavern?"

"To talk I suppose, about our leaving Holland."

"We women like our time together too. It is no different for men. Except our topics are different."

"Certainly they are. I am bothered they do not seek our opinion on this journey they plan." Dorothy filled pewter bowls with chunks of beef swimming in dark gravy, potatoes, carrots, and onions. "I worked hard on this. Tell me what you think?"

Drawing in the aroma, Mercy sat in one of Dorothy's kitchen chairs. She dipped in the spoon and placed it in her mouth. She closed her eyes. "This is excellent."

"You think so?"

"Yes indeed. You like it too, little one?" Mercy said to the child, and tickled his cheek. He giggled and she handed him a piece of bread. "Try it with this. Your mama has done well."

Hungry, she went on to finish the meal. When she set the spoon down, she said, "Perhaps the men are discussing the fire. If Caleb lost his tools, he will be in need of their help."

Dorothy spread butter over the bread. "Don't worry, Mercy. William will speak to the elders and they will find him a place to lodge. If he has lost his tools, we'll all gather what we can spare."

Little John climbed down from his chair, leaving only a bit of crust behind. He held his hand out to his mother. "Yes, my darling. You can give it to the birds. Here, go throw it out into the yard."

The curls on young John's head fell forward when he grasped the crust. "Mum, watch me," he said with an innocent lilt. Away went the bread, and Dorothy clapped her hands. She praised her boy and said to Mercy, "Did you hear? He calls me Mum now."

Mercy swore that moment would never pass from her mind. The child in a dark blue doublet and breeches, his flaxen hair caressing rosy cheeks, his hand clutching the bread as he swung open the door and tossed it out. What would become of the child in years to come? Would he grow into a man like his father and be kind like his mother? Would he live to be one of the builders of a new world?

Young John Bradford turned and looked at them with a proud lift of his head. "You are dear, my John. Now go play. You have an hour until bedtime."

Mercy turned. "I admire you. You are so caring."

"A mother must be."

"No wonder your neighbors love you so much."

"I love them too. I'll miss them when we leave, especially Esmee Anderson and her children. She is as bubbly as a pool of soap, always smiling and having a kind word to say. I'm amazed how she handles ten children."

"I hope there will always be people in the world like you and Esmee. Your price is far above rubies."

"You know I think the same of you," Dorothy said. "We've become good friends."

"One could say we are as close as sisters," Mercy replied.

Dorothy pulled the crust from her slice of bread, looking thoughtful. "It may be far into the future, but near the end of the age, the world will grow darker and hearts cold. We must guard against it and keep our love for God and his children burning within us."

Whenever Dorothy grew meditative, Mercy listened. Her wisdom and spiritual knowledge impressed Mercy. As Dorothy continued to speak on the subject of the end of days, Mercy too grew reflective. She stared at the red embers under Dorothy's iron kettle. "To think the world will grow worse than it is already is sad. But it may be far into the future after we are long gone."

"Think on this, Mercy. The men are sitting in that smoky inn and have no idea you and I are sharing such thoughts. Their minds are preoccupied with the present."

"Yes, I know. And William has missed a wonderful meal."

Dorothy smiled. "I will keep it warm for him."

"I wish I could be at that meeting."

"I as well. The idea of going to a foreign wilderness scares me a little, and it might do the men well to listen to us."

"It is easy for them to be courageous—for women not so much. Not in the same way."

Shaking her head, Dorothy said, "I do not wish to dwell on things that sadden me or cause me to fear. Instead, William and I lift up our eyes to the heavens, our dearest country, and quiet our spirits. He told me that, and I said he needs to write it down for young John to read when he is grown."

Dorothy's words softened Mercy's heart. "Dear me, Dorothy, those are words I welcome. Keep our eyes above, and our spirits will be quieted."

Dorothy stared forward. "In truth, I want to stay behind with my dear boy and my parents. Still, what I want does not matter. Leaving is the right course. You should know. You ran from England."

"Yet it was a short journey unlike the one to the New World. I had to do it in order to save my life. I had to rally courage and strength. I had to have faith all would be well once I got away. All will be well for you and William too. Before long, you'll see the second ship sailing in with her sails unfurred and billowing in the wind, bringing young John and your parents safely to you."

Dorothy agreed. "Yes, and he will be so grown. He has lived his short life in the city, so when he comes to Virginia, he will have fields to run in, fresh air to breath, and most of all freedom."

"Freedom from persecution surely. Let us hope, it remains that way."

Dorothy tilted her head. "What is it you mean, Mercy? Why would it not remain?"

"There will be others whose beliefs are different, some who remain with the Church of England. If the two cannot get along in England, how will they in the New World? In years to come, intolerance may rise again."

The thought of leaving everything behind and going to a strange land where plagues killed, where storms ravaged sea and land, where poverty led to starvation, and fever took the young and old, frightened Mercy. Yet, for the sake of her friend, she did not share all her fears. After voicing her concern that intolerance could rear its ugly head against the Separatists again, she regretted saying it. The color in Dorothy's face had gone.

"I have tried not to think that way," Dorothy told Mercy. "You speak of intolerance. Yet it is not the only thing to fear. We may not survive the voyage, not to say the first year there."

Mercy picked up Dorothy's hand. How thin and fragile it felt in hers—hers that kneaded bread with verve. Dorothy Bradford sat for hours sewing before her hearth, watching her little boy play on the floor before her. She ate enough to sustain a child. How long could her frailness sustain her in the wilderness of America?

"William will look after you, Dorothy." Going from the table, Mercy lifted the lid to the pot and stirred the stew. It would be enough for William Bradford and more.

Dorothy drew up. "Words do not take the dread away."

Mercy placed the lid back. "Would it if I told you I'm leaving too?"

"You are? It does comfort me." There, the color had returned to Dorothy's face. Her eyes glowed and her mouth curved into a pleasing smile. "With you with us, I'll have courage. But am I a bad mother for leaving my son behind? Am I abandoning him?"

Mercy set her arm across Dorothy's shoulders. "Oh, not at all. He's so small. The best place for him for a time is with his grandparents. You don't want him facing the hardships we will face. The voyage will be difficult, and we will have to work hard to establish a settlement."

"William says he cannot go without me. And I...cannot stay without him."

"He loves you."

"And I him. So I must be by my husband's side." Dorothy sniffed and wiped her eyes. "I do not know why I'm so timid. I was afraid when we left England. Yet it turned out all right."

"And it will again."

Mercy smiled at her friend, still feeling concerned. Hoping to distract Dorothy from dwelling on the trials that would come, she looked up at the ceiling. "Come, Dorothy. Let us go see what mischief your tot has gotten into. I hear the pitter-patter of little feet up stairs."

Chapter 17

Along the street above the canal, Caleb walked beside Bradford. As they drew closer to Caleb's dwelling the smell of smoke lingered in the air. The building remained standing. Only the first floor flat where the fire started suffered damage. The quick townsmen brigade had put out the flames before it could get hopelessly out of control.

Bradford offered to help the suffering family find temporary lodgings. The mother spoke in Dutch, pushing back limp strands of hair from her teary eyes. Her children clung to her skirts. She reached down and ran a loving hand over their hair.

"She has lost everything," Bradford said to Caleb, having knowledge of the language. "Fortunately, her brother and his family live in the neighborhood and she and her children will lodge with them."

She set a tin bucket down on the street. Caleb watched her sort through the contents—a delft dish, a pewter cup. She wiped them off as tears fell from her eyes. "My favorite," she said in broken English, then grasped Caleb's hand and kissed it.

Baffled Caleb pulled away. "I don't understand."

"She thanks you for saving her little girl," Bradford said. "Ah, here's her brother."

Caleb gave her a short bow, and stepped aside for the woman's bevy of children. After she left, Caleb and Bradford went inside and up the staircase. Caleb stepped slowly. The boards creaked. He lifted his hand from the sooty banister and wiped it against his doublet.

"Her husband is a seaman," he told Bradford. "What a shock he'll have when he returns home."

"Indeed. But at least his wife and children are alive, praise God."

"I only knew this family in passing. I've been too busy to know anyone. Besides, I cannot speak the language, yet I know the woman is attentive and loving to her children."

Bradford climbed the stairs behind Caleb. "The few among the many."

"You worry about the children don't you?" Caleb looked at Bradford and saw the change in his expression.

"About the voyage, you mean. All the parents are troubled."

"You have a lot on your shoulders, William. You have your business, wife and child to think of. If you need help with the organization of this thing, feel free to ask. I'll do what I can."

Bradford put his hand on Caleb's shoulder. "I take the planning of our weighty voyage gladly. I've thought deeply on what we are about to do, and believe it will be of great importance. So, I've decided to keep notes and documents, and write our story for future generations."

"It is wise you do so. Otherwise, the story will eventually be lost. We will be forgotten."

They reached the landing and hallway. Bradford waited by Caleb's door. "Your quarters seem to be intact."

"Yes, and I'm glad for Mercy's sake." He showed Bradford the box.

"This is a fine piece of work. You must admire her greatly to have made such an item. Now that I see all is well, I must be going." Bradford tipped his hat.

"William." Caleb stepped to the doorway and Bradford turned. "Thank you."

Bradford smiled and headed down the staircase. Caleb set the box on a table near the door and looked around. Such a shabby dwelling, but thank God, he had one—thank God the woman he loved lived.

Relieved to find his tools were where he had left them, Caleb shut his door. As he walked away, a cry for help stopped him. It came two doors down—a young girl's voice, full of fear and pain. He headed down the hallway as the cries continued, and as he stepped over the threshold, he saw a man so red in the face he could have burst. A girl with wide eyes rose from behind a stuffed chair. She hurried forward out of the man's reach, her stringy hair falling over her face.

The man seized the girl and shook her. Caleb could make out his Dutch, how he called her a thief.

"Stop!" Caleb ran forward and grasped the man's arm. He pushed him back and held the girl by her wrist. The man tottered and stared. He spoke, spittle oozing from his lips. "English, man. You know it?"

The man nodded. "She's looting."

He looked at the girl. "Is this true, girl?" Caleb drew her closer. Her eyes were wide with fright.

"Thief! You must be one too if you defend her."

"I'm one of the tenants here, you fool. If the girl has stolen, ask her why she is stealing, and tell her either she returns what she has taken or you'll call the authorities. The idea of prison will dampen her strong will."

The man repeated in Dutch what Caleb said. The girl frowned, twisted away from Caleb's hold, and balled her fists. "I know some English," she spat.

"Enough to know you could go to prison?" said Caleb.

She reached inside her skirt and pulled out a small *stokbrood*, a kind of onion baguette. "I'm hungry." She handed it back to the man. "That is why I took it." Casting down her eyes, she hung her head.

His anger faded, and he looked at her with pity. "You could have asked for it. I would have given it to you." The man glanced at the bread, and handed it back. "Well go on, take it, but don't come back here. If you do, I'll send for the law."

She pressed the bread to her breast and rushed out.

Caleb went after her. "Wait, girl." She halted and turned. "What's your name?"

Clutching the bread as if her life depended on it, she blinked her eyes. "Evi Vos."

Caleb set his hands over his hips. "Ah. I know enough Dutch to know your last name means *fox*. Where I come from foxes are known to be thieves."

"I spoke the truth, sir. Hunger made me take de bread."

"I do not doubt you. Where is your family—your parents? You shouldn't be roaming the streets like this."

"I'm orphaned, sir."

Indeed, she looked the part. Her clothes were dirty and in tatters, the seams of her sleeves pulling apart, the hem of her dress frayed like the feathers of a bird. She spoke with caution as if she feared everything and everyone. Her face and hands were filthy, her nails broken and crusted. Yet there was a trace of beauty in her young face behind all that smut and grime. Mercy could do wonders to clean up this waif. All she needed was food, a bath, and clean clothes.

He stepped toward her. "How old are you, Evi?"

"Almost fifteen years, sir. I cannot be sure."

"Where did you learn to speak English?"

"De nuns taught me at de orphanage in Amsterdam. I don't speak it well."

"You speak it well enough for us to have a conversation." He motioned with his hand for her to come inside. "Don't worry. I'll leave the door open. You've nothing to be afraid of."

Evi's large eyes searched the flat from the threshold. She stepped in with caution, and Caleb sat at the table thinking it might put her more at ease. He wanted to talk to her, find out more about her plight. "You're without a home and family, Evi?"

She shook her head. "I've no one but myself, and sleep where I can. I stole rather than beg."

"It must be hard living on the streets, especially for one as young as you."

Her eyes glistened with tears. "I sometimes wish I could go back to da orphanage, even though I was treated badly there. At least I had a roof over my head and food to eat. Porridge mostly, but my belly had something in it."

"I know people that can help if you are willing."

She flung her arms down, holding the bread and stomping her feet. "I won't do wrong. I won't sell my body."

Caleb held up his hand. "Be calm, Evi. I'm not suggesting you do. I'm a Christian, one of the Separatists. Our church can help you." He surprised himself he so easily declared who he was and what he believed. His heart enlarged at the words, as did his compassion for this young castoff.

Evi titled her head and looked at Caleb with interest. "You're one of de English Christians?"

"I am—not originally though. I've been in Holland a short while. You might say I did not find them. They found me."

Crinkling her nose, Evi sniffed the air. "Your quarters smell of de fire. You are glad it did not burn?"

"Yes, and thankful no one was injured or killed. You took advantage people were out of the building, didn't you?"

Evi lowered her eyes. "Ja, I thought it'd be easy. I was wrong."

"Indeed you were, child."

She stood forward, her eyes bright. "I'll clean for you for some food."

Caleb smiled at Evi's enthusiasm. "First things first. Over there is a basin and pitcher of water. Wash your face and hands. Then you may have something to eat other than moldy crust. I suppose you didn't notice the green stuff on the side of it."

Evi frowned and turned the baguette over. She set it down and rubbed her cheeks with the water. When she dried her face in a towel, she turned to him.

"Ah, much better. Here have some of this. A friend made it." He took out his knife and sliced off a chunk of bread. She clutched it and ate like a starved wolf cub. "Does it taste like smoke?" Caleb asked.

Evi shook her head and continued chewing.

"You may have some jam and butter."

Her eyes darted over to the small ceramic pots. After she spread the butter and poured the jam onto the bread, she finished it off. Her eyes begged for more and he placed a thicker slice in her palm. In the street below, the town crier called out all was well and the hour. The sun dipped below a hazy horizon and darkness fell. Caleb lit the only taper he could find, a stub he kept in a box. The tiny flame brightened the table he set it on. Evi watched it. By her heart-shaped face and lanky height, she looked younger than fifteen. She had a tiny frame, possibly due to the hard life she lived.

Caleb's window stood open and a cool breeze scented with the flowing waters of the canal blew through them. His thoughts drifted to Mercy and he found himself missing her, remembering he had kissed her. He tried to imagine what kind of look would be on her face when seeing Evi for the first time. Would she and the others believe him when he tells how he came to find this poor child, or would they question his story? It mattered not. God knew and that was more important than people's opinions.

"It's too late to take you to Mercy." He handed Evi a mug of water. "Drink. I hope it doesn't taste like smoke."

Evi drank and said, "It does a little, but I do not care."

Caleb smiled. "Mercy will like your easy ways."

"Who is Mercy?" Evi wiped her mouth with the back of her hand. "Is she your lady?"

"She's the one I love."

"Where is she? She should be living here with you."

"It is not our way. She won't live with me until we are wed."

"What if she lost her home? Would you bring her here? Would you ask her to live with you?"

"Didn't the nuns teach you about the sacrament of matrimony and God's moral laws?"

Evi shrugged. "They did, but I forgot some. There are Dutch people who do not obey the commandments. I'm guilty too—I stole."

"You did because you were starving. If there ever is a time like that again, ask for bread. There are people who would give it."

"Like you?" She looked thoughtful. "You have no wife and no children. I'm sad for you." She finished her water and yawned.

Caleb pulled off his boots, and tossed a blanket over his cot. "You sleep here. Tomorrow I'll find a place for you. It isn't the best, but it's all I have to offer."

"It is better than sleeping on de streets."

Evi stretched out and covered herself. Her lashes fluttered and she fell fast asleep. Caleb looked down at her and noticed the weariness in her face. He knew the pangs of hunger and the feeling of having no parents. He had slept rough in the King's Navy, and upon his journey home, he found shelter in barns and shacks. Evi was a child old enough to be his daughter. No child should have to live this way. He needed to find a home where she could be fed and sheltered, treated kindly, kept clean and taught how to be a proper young woman, even if it meant she would be a servant.

He settled into a chair under the open window and put his feet up on the sill. He studied the moon through it. Its light shimmered across rooftops and window glass. Stars stood out and he saw one shoot across the ebony sky. He listened to the child's even breathing. His last thought as he fell asleep was *Jesus of Nazareth passeth by*.

Woke to the peal of church bells, Caleb stretched his arms and stood. When he saw the blanket neatly folded on the cot, he figured Evi had run off. He drew on his boots and when he stood, she popped her head up from under his table.

"I spilled de tea." Her face turned ruddy with shame and she lowered her eyes.

"I do not drink it enough to care," Caleb said. "So don't worry. Besides it would have tasted awful." He leaned down to her and made her laugh.

"I cut de bread, sir." She arranged slices in a row on the table.

"Thank you, Evi. I'm glad to see you did not run away."

"You're a kind man. You did not touch or hurt me. You promised to find me a place among the English."

Hungry, Caleb bit into the bread. The crust stale, it tasted bitter with a hint of smoke. "I'll keep my word." He handed her a slice. He wanted to smile, as she chewed the crust slow and ladylike, knowing how hungry she must be.

"You'll have to work hard to earn your employer's trust, Evi. Otherwise, you'll be back where you began. You understand?"

Evi nodded. "Ja, sir." She bent her brows and flung out her arms. "I will die on de streets if I don't change. Or I'll end up in jail." Her gaze turned serious. "De men will chase me and hurt me, like they've done. I want to be like your lady. I want to be good and kind."

"I see those qualities in you already."

"I want to be pretty too, sir. Your lady—is she pretty?"

"Oh, she is extremely pretty."

Evi lifted her arm toward her nose. "I smell bad, sir."

Caleb smiled. "Well, that will change."

"I can't remember ever having a bath. Since I left the orphanage, I've used the canal to wash my face and hands."

"And a poor job you've done of it. You've got a smug on your chin."

Evi gasped and rubbed her chin briskly.

After finishing the last of the bread, Caleb slapped on his wide-brimmed hat. "Come along, Evi." He stepped out into the hallway. She followed behind him, her steps slow, her eyes watchful.

"Where are we going?"

"Where most people go on a Sunday morning."

She skirted back into the flat. "Oh, not I. They'd not want me there."

"Nonsense."

She shook out the front of her tattered dress. "My clothes." She pushed back her hair. "My hair. I'm poor and dirty."

"How you look does not matter. There's a comb over there. Run it through those tangles and hurry."

Evi looked where the comb lay.

"Well, go on. Comb that mop of yours. Do you want help or not?"

Evi's face flushed and she bent her brows. "*Ja*, I want help."

"Good, and hearing the Gospel won't hurt you either."

"The Gospel, sir?"

"Yes, Evi. You know, the Bible. Didn't they share it with you at the orphanage?"

"I don't know. They read to us in Latin."

"This will be in English. Comb your hair. We'll be late."

With a skip, Evi picked up the comb, and dragged it through her matted hair, pulling at the knots. She set it back down and waited. "Do I look better, sir?"

"I suppose it's the best you can do for now. Come along, and close the door behind you."

Caleb walked into the service with the bedraggled waif trailing behind him. Evi hung close, her eyes darting around at the people. A few heads turned and quickly focused back to Pastor Robinson as he preached the Sower and the Seed. Mercy sat next to Dorothy Bradford, pulled the string of her coif forward, and fixed her eyes on the man she had fallen in love with. Strange to see a slip of a girl clinging to him. She'd seen shabby street urchins before, but this one looked frightened to the point of tears. How thin and tiny she looked in her rags, her uncovered head a mass of ill kept hair. Her cheeks were sunken. Dark circles were under her eyes.

Caleb took a seat and the girl ease beside him. The congregation stirred and Pastor Robinson stopped speaking. "We're glad to have you with us, Mr. Treymayne."

Caleb stood and while holding his hat in his two hands thanked him. "Forgive me for being late, Reverend. I did not mean to disrupt your sermon."

"Who is this young lady you've brought with you today?"

Caleb heard Evi whisper *lady* and smiled. "May I introduce Evi Vos to our fellowship?"

Mercy met Caleb's glance. He gave her a quick wink and looked back at Pastor Robinson. "Evi is orphaned, sir, and has been living on the streets. She is in need of our help."

Robinson leaned forward, his expression kind and welcoming as he looked at the waif seated among the people. "Our hearts are always open to helping someone in need."

Mercy looked at Evi. The child blinked and her blue eyes watered. "Dunk u, sir," she replied barely above a whisper.

Upon the final amen, Caleb took Evi's hand and walked over to Mercy.

"You are recovered from yesterday?" he asked, his tone warm.

"I'm well."

He leaned to her ear and whispered, "More than well, you look pretty like you do every day."

"Hush," she scolded. Mercy's eyes drifted over to Evi. "Where did you find her?"

"At the flat or at least in that proximity. She was hungry and homeless. I thought someone in the fellowship could give her a position."

"Does she speak English?"

"She does." He moved Evi around in front of Mercy. "Evi, this is Mercy." He leaned down and whispered, "She is the woman I spoke of."

Evi made a wobbly curtsey. "Pleased to meet you."

"Why you barely have an accent."

"I was schooled in English."

"Please call me Mercy."

Evi's eyes widened. "I don't know if it is proper."

Caleb grinned from one corner of his mouth. "So the nuns did teach you manners."

Mercy turned to Caleb. "Surely someone will give her work. I'll speak to Martin. He might know whether Dr. Fuller needs help. With all the children he and Bridget have, Evi would be a great help." She raised her hand to Martin and he strode over.

"Martin, do you think Dr. Fuller would give Evi a position?"

Martin glanced at Evi. A small but quick smile, Mercy knew well. His was the kind of look he once gave her. "You mean this girl? You ask him, Mercy."

"Would you, Martin? He might be more apt to agree if the request comes from you."

"It is a splendid idea," Caleb said. "She cannot stay with me."

Martin stared at Evi. "No, sir, I suppose she cannot. Why would you need a servant? It's not as if you have a wife and children and a house that needs…."

Caleb set his hand over Martin's shoulder. "I understand your point, Martin."

"Well, if she does not object, I'll speak to the doctor on her behalf."

Evi clasped her hands. "I don't object."

Martin bounded off to where Dr. Fuller and his wife Bridget stood and began speaking to them. Mercy drew closer to Caleb. "I hope they agree."

"Here comes Martin. Perhaps he'll have some news."

"He's coming to tell me I must leave," Evi said." They have nothing for me." Evi was indeed frightened; her tiny frame shivered as if a blast of winter wind whipped around her.

"It isn't true, Evi," Mercy said. "These are good people. They will not reject you. I know for a fact." She drew out her handkerchief and wiped Evi's eyes. "Keep this. I have others."

"Cannot I go home with you?" Evi pleaded.

"It's not up to me. I live with the Bradford's."

Hanging her head, Evi took a step back. "No one wants to take in someone like me." A small cry escaped her lips and she turned away. She made it to the door but bumped into Martin as he made his way across the room. His arms went around her and she stared into his face. Weak and half-starved, her knees gave in beneath her. Martin caught her as she fell, and laid her gently on the floor. He shot a beseeching look at Mercy. At the same time, those remaining in the room gathered around.

Mercy went down on her knees and pillowed Evi's head on her lap. She tapped the girl's cheeks until her eyelashes fluttered. With a little moan, Evi crept closer into Mercy's arms. Dr. Fuller came through the crowd and picked up Evi's wrist. "She's alright. Just a little faint, poor child." He looked at Mercy. "Martin spoke to me, and I'm afraid I cannot take on another servant." He looked up at the intent faces. "Surely there are others among us that can."

"Yes, poor child." Dorothy's hair lined her lace coif. Her face glowed with compassion. If ever there were a gentlewoman amongst the English in Holland, it had to be Dorothy Bradford. She bent down beside Mercy. "She has fainted from hunger, don't you think Dr. Fuller?"

"There is no doubt about it."

She looked up at William Bradford as he drew near. "My father and mother will help this child. Can we not take her home with us?"

Bradford hesitate a moment. "Yes, of course. They could use another housemaid, especially to help with young John."

Again, Mercy tapped Evi's cheeks. "Wake, Evi. You're to go with the Bradfords."

Blinking her eyes, Evi sat up. She pushed her heavy dark hair back from off her face and looked at Dorothy.

"You'll need a bath and clean clothes, Evi Vos," said Dorothy.

Martin helped Evi to her feet. She brushed down the front of her tattered dress as if she could whisk away the tears and dirt. "I washed my face and hands last night. I combed my hair this morning. I could not wash my clothes."

"No doubt and they are certainly the only ones you own."

"I have nothing else."

"Besides something new to wear, you'll need a scrubbing."

Evi swallowed. "A bath?"

"Indeed yes. My mother will take you in as a housemaid if you are willing to do as she ask, work hard, and go to church."

Mercy watched Evi's eyes enlarged. "Oh, I'm willing to take a bath every day if she wants me to. And I'll work hard and go to church, I promise."

"You'll also watch over my son when the time comes."

"I will watch him like a sheepdog guards her sheep." She put her hands on her chest and bowed her head, the mass of curls tumbling forward. "I say it with all my heart."

Mercy could not miss the pleased look on Caleb's face. He held his hand down to her and she took it like a bride taking the hand of her beloved—with eager fingers entwining his. He drew her up beside him and she leaned into his arm. "Your waif has found a home. If it had not been for you, Caleb, where would she be now? It saddens me to think of it."

He picked up his hat. "I'd say God had his hand in it. I must go speak with William." He strode over to the men going into Pastor Robinson's study.

Dorothy put Mercy's arm through hers. "How long will you wait, Mercy?"

"I'm patient."

"But for how long? A woman should not have to wait forever, you know."

Mercy kept her eyes on the study door. "Forever is a long time. I'll not have to wait long." She spoke when Caleb walked out with the other gentlemen and their eyes met.

"Walk home with William and I and Evi. I've asked Caleb to sup with us."

"Let me prepare the food, Dorothy." Mercy being eager to please Caleb made a few suggestions. "A roasted chicken and parsnips, or a meat pie with greens? We have plenty of apples for a cream pie."

"I'd never say no to you on that account. All of us enjoy a good meal, and I'm not ashamed to admit you are a better cook than I will ever be." She glanced at Evi, who stood meekly by, and smiled. "But I can do the cleaning up, if you follow my meaning."

When Caleb and Bradford left the study, and the congregation parted, Mercy and Caleb and the Bradford's walked home together with the splendor of the morning about them, and Evi Vos skipping lightly in the rear.

Chapter 18

It was a cool and quiet Friday, when a coach drew up outside the Bradford house. Mercy set her sewing down and looked out from behind the curtains in the front room window. Dorothy's prosperous parents had arrived after spending the better part of the day traveling from Amsterdam. Dorothy sent her mother Katherine May a letter concerning Evi, and another to her father regarding a pair of fine sitting room chairs Caleb had made. Henry May was after all, noted for having a keen eye for fine craftsmanship, and was a collector of woodcarvings. Katherine sent a reply they would come immediately.

Dapple-gray horses pawed the bricks in the street as the footman opened the coach door. Henry May stepped out first and held his hand out to his wife. Mercy admired the summer gown Katherine wore. Pale rose in color, the linen cloth shimmered in the sunlight as she made her way up the walk.

For a moment, Mercy thought of the gowns given to her by Lady Glenmont. They were similar to what Katherine wore, soft against her skin, and so light, they whispered across the floor like the feathers of a bird. Today, she wore the simple dress of a Separatist woman. A dark green bodice hugged her waist and buttoned down the front. A beige scalloped collar lay across her shoulders. Her dark brown skirt hung above her ankles. She pulled at the strings of her apron and took it off. She must look her best—without flour and spices smearing the front of her.

An elder woman, Katherine retained the genteel demeanor of a well brought up lady. Instead of aging bent and wrinkled, she possessed a soft beauty that came with growing old gracefully. Her manner of dress was simple, but not severe like the garb of the lower classes of Puritan women. Dorothy told Mercy how her mother sent her a new gown made of fawn linen with a long collar trimmed in Belgium lace. She accepted the gift but had not worn it until today.

At the gate, Katherine lifted her head and looked at Mercy. It may have been against propriety, but Katherine waved from the street. "Hello there, Mercy," she called. "We've finally arrived."

Mercy rushed from the window and opened the door, her eyes fixed on Katherine May as she walked up regally to the door. Mr. May lagged behind giving instructions to the footman on the care of their bags.

"Good day, Mrs. May. Was your journey tolerable?"

Katherine fanned her hand in front of her face. "Warm, Mercy. Terribly warm inside that coach. And please call me Katherine at home." She leaned in with an impish smile. "I made Henry sit across from me so not to make it warmer. He argued, but I won out in the end."

Mercy's smile grew. "His steps are lively. I see he's done with the footman."

"Ha, the footman is done with Henry. The whole way here, he complained."

Henry May took Katherine's arm. "What is that you say, my dear?"

"A beautiful day is it not?"

"It is a perfect day. Why are you standing out here in the bright sun talking to Mercy when you could be inside where it is cool and enjoy our daughter's greetings?"

Katherine crossed the threshold. Henry May touched his wife's elbow. "Come, dear wife. I wish to see my grandson."

"All right, Henry." Katherine turned to Mercy. "Where are my daughter and her boy? Don't tell me they are away. I will be so disappointed if they are."

"Be at ease," Mercy said. "Dorothy is upstairs. I will call her down."

"We've brought the most wonderful toy for little John. Wait until you see it."

Bringing the couple into the sitting room, Mercy walked to the bottom of the staircase and called to Dorothy. Upstairs, the tapping of Dorothy's shoes rushed across the floor. She hurried down the staircase with young John bouncing down a step at a time behind his mother.

Mercy smiled as the proud grandpapa held his hands out to young John Bradford. "Little man. Come greet your Grandpapa."

Among many a Puritan, affection was the last thing to be expressed. Such was not the case with the Mays. Katherine embraced her daughter. Her father kissed her cheek, and they both made over small John Bradford as if he were a prince. The child looked up with large blue eyes and threw his arms around them. Henry May pulled something from his pocket, and Mercy watched on with delight.

"For you, my lad," said Henry May. "A top made of the finest maple. You like it?"

The child fisted the gift and nodded.

"Thank your Grandpapa, John," Dorothy said.

Holding out his hand, he looked like a miniature of William Bradford—the same eyes, the same shaped mouth. He and his grandpapa shook hands, and Henry May smiled at the show of politeness from his grandson.

Evi stood at the door with her hands over her apron. Hardly did Mercy recognize the girl from Sundays ago. She had so changed. Gone were the tattered clothes and messy hair. Instead, she wore a simple serving girl's dress of soft brown with a broad white collar that fell over her shoulders. A white linen coif covered her hair and framed her face. She had gained flesh upon her bones, her figure filled out, and a glow was in her eyes Mercy could only interpret as happiness.

Mercy hurried over to Evi and took up her hands. "My, you're looking well."

Evi smiled. "My mistress has made me thus."

"There is no need for you to delay. Come inside."

Mercy waited until Evi passed her. Across the street, a man clad in drab gray met her eyes. He crossed his arms and leaned against the wall behind him, the reddish stones contrasting against his figure. His hawkish face met the shadows. His tight lips curled, and a shudder rushed through her breast, as if a sudden gust of artic wind struck her. He looked familiar—disturbingly familiar. Could he be the man whose footsteps came up behind her the other day in the marketplace? Hobnails on cobblestone blended with the voices of housewives and servants buying goods and debating prices. At a stand where an elderly woman sold cabbages, Mercy paused to see if he'd pass her. Shadows, like the one the man stood beneath, swept alongside her, and when she shifted her glance from the cabbages to the crowd, he had vanished. Eventually, she counted the incident as nothing. Now to see whom she believed to be the same man made her dread she'd been discovered.

Her hand gripped the doorframe. She sank back from a sudden and mortal sense of danger. The man drew away from the wall and looked as if he meant to come forward. The May's coach pulled away, and so did the man. She left the entrance with her nerves taut and quivering and closed the door. Could the man be searching for her on behalf of Lord Glenmont, or was he a bounder whose eyes had marked her? Whoever he was, she feared him. She shut the door and pressed her back against it, her eyes upon a ray of sunlight striking against the wall.

The others had gone into the sitting room, and she heard them speaking happily one to another. She slipped away and stepped into the kitchen. The back door stood open and the scent of a wet garden newly sprinkled with dew mingled with the musky aromas of sage, lemongrass, and thyme. Instead of stepping out into the garden to sit in the cool grass and draw in the soothing scents that calmed body and soul, she slowly closed the door. She needed to busy her hands.

She found her apron and tied it to her waist. Pouring cream into a dish, she set it down for the Bradford's cat and tried to reason out her suspicions. She gathered a handful of mint and dressed a tray of teacakes with it. She worked her fingers nimbly, thinking it would calm her beating heart and shake off the worrisome feelings. Perhaps the man was a womanizing libertine—nothing more.

Evi walked in and lifted the tray of teacakes from the table and left. Whatever Evi said or did, Mercy missed. Her mind remained distracted by the man in dark clothing. Wiping her hands clean on her apron, she walked nervously to the window and looked outside. Not a soul stood on the front walk or across the way. Only shadows from the trees crossed the ground, while a full moon crept above them.

Stars glimmered in a clear ebony sky, and a southern breeze flowed warm and placid through the open windows of the sitting room. Separatist leaders with their wives had supped together, the men engaged in serious conversation at the table with their cups filled with cider. The women sat together near the hearth speaking of womanly things.

Mercy picked up a shirt from her wicker basket, and ran stitches through the hem. Made for Caleb, she glanced beyond the open dining room door and met his eyes. She smiled and slowly drew the thread through the muslin. Caleb's gaze turned elsewhere, his face intent as he leaned one arm over the back of his chair, with the other laying across the table. She hadn't had a moment to tell him about the stranger who peered at her from across the street. As she pulled on the thread, she wondered if she should mention him at all.

Inwardly that anxious disturbing feeling she'd been watched held on. She drew the thread tight, pricked her finger, and set it in her mouth. She tasted blood. Tears burned in the corners of her eyes, and she blinked them back. No one noticed. It wasn't uncommon to prick one's finger while sewing. Why just a moment before, Mary Brewster had jabbed the point of a knitting needle against the top of her hand. It caused no great injury, and the conversation went on as usual.

"Our journey to the New World will not be an easy one." Mary Brewster spoke in response to the fears the women were voicing. "With a fair wind and a calm sea, we will reach Virginia in quick time. Others will be there waiting for us on the shore." Mary set her hands on her lap and looked contemplative. "Just think of the welcome we shall have. A feast I should imagine. Our fears will pass quickly."

"I welcome your vision, Mrs. Brewster," Mercy said. "You have seen joy come out of suffering, I hear."

"Glory to God, yes." Mary Brewster went on with her knitting. "It is hard to believe so much time has passed since the English authorities came to Leyden to arrest my husband."

Mercy had not yet heard of this. She drove her needle into the fabric and frowned. "On the King's orders?"

"Yes."

"How could His Majesty do such a thing to a man whose mission is to live for Christ? I do not understand persecution, although it has gone on since the first century."

"He published books critical of the King and the Anglican Church by the Scottish minister David Calderwood. He was teaching at the University, and they protected him when he went into hiding, he and Reverend Calderwood."

"And he escaped arrest?"

"He did. The brave man he is, he handed himself over to the Dutch authority, but they refused to send my beloved husband to his death, and told King James they had arrested the wrong man, and let him go. God bless them."

"Has this occurred often with other members?"

"Not as yet, but if we do not leave soon the Crown will hunt our leaders down when given opportunity. We must be wise as serpents and harmless of doves to prevent it."

Mercy pondered this, and realized how dangerous life had become in Leyden for the Separatists. Caleb may have been right that Lord Glenmont had forgotten her by now, but who was to say. If he knew she lived in Holland among the Separatists, he could use his authority to seek her out. She pushed the idea from her mind, and the image of the man in gray. Instead, she turned to the wives sitting with her. What would they do if their husbands were arrested and separated from them? Her heart ached at the thought. For how would they and their children survive such a tragedy?

"You have men of courage and you are praying wives." Katherine said. "Wouldn't you say, Dorothy?"

"Indeed I would, Mother."

"And you, Mercy. Is there so much to fear?"

"The unknown can be frightening, but when such journeys are over, one wonders why." Crossing the Atlantic would be different from crossing the Channel in time and distance. Yet, Mercy recalled how deep her anxious heart drummed when fleeing Ipswich and sailing over that sea to Holland among brawny sailors and a few passengers whose business was secretive.

Katherine smiled. "Henry and I plan to come on the next ship with young John. I'm actually looking forward to it. I've always loved an adventure."

"At least we will have a settlement built by then, and you'll have a roof over your heads the moment you land, Mother. William says we will not be settling among the strangers."

"You can stay behind with us if you wish." Katherine handed young John a wooden block with an R painted on one side and a rabbit on the other. "William will have all in place by then."

Dorothy shook her head. "I must go with my husband," she said, looking down at the piece of lace she'd been handling. "You understand, don't you, Mother?"

"Of course I do, my dear. The voyage in itself would be hard on the boy, and then once you've arrived there'd be other hardships. It is best."

"Best for my son that is certain, Mother. I'd rather he stay with you and be safe and sound then with us, and when you and Father do come to our settlement, we will have houses built and plenty of food to eat, things John likes."

Katherine May smiled. Mercy looked at the child playing on the floor. He stacked blocks as high as the table leg. The next one caused it to all tumble into a heap. All should leave their young ones behind until a proper settlement had been readied. Several nights she had dreamt of the crossing, of harsh winds and raging seas. Of storms, pushing waves into mountains to overtake a lowly boat made of wood and pitch. She kept her fears to herself day after day, but as she listened to the men speaking of the voyage, of building humble dwellings of wood in a strange land, the hopes of planting and harvesting, her apprehensions were rising. What were the chances of a child surviving such hard conditions let alone their parents?

The wives talked over each other.

"None of us have been to the New World. We only have the word of those who have in order to know what to expect."

"Our men have no experience of the hardships and challenges that await us, and we will be bound for seven years to the merchants. We call ourselves Pilgrims. But perhaps we should add *indentured servants*."

"Do not think so bleakly," said Mary Brewster. "We've been delayed for too long and have grown impatient. My husband says we must go, that it is God's will. Our children are growing up Dutch. We must take this journey for their sakes."

Katherine sighed. "Dear sisters. You forget the voyage from England to Holland was not so grueling. The sea might be at its calmest and the winds fair this time of year."

"I do not worry," said Dorothy. "A voyage in summer will be pleasant."

"Our men will look after us and the children."

"What of the Indians?"

"Yes, I have read about them," said Mary Brewster. "If they have good hearts, they will not harm us."

Dorothy cocked her head. "I do hope you are right, Mary. I have read they could teach us many things about the land."

"And there are other settlers along the Hudson. We will have neighbors."

Bridget Robinson had been silent throughout the conversation. She sat in one of Dorothy's favorite spindle-backed chairs listening. Finally, she spoke up, and when her mouth opened, each woman turned their eyes to listen, for she was after all their pastor's wife. "All great and honorable actions are accompanied with great difficulties, ladies. God has enabled us to overcome them with courage. We women have it in abundance when it is needed of us. The difficulties you will face will be many. But they will not be invincible."

Mary Brewster nodded. "No they will not be. I look upon our leaving as a great adventure. We must think on the good that will come."

Dorothy smiled. "I have thought how exciting it will be to see a whale for the first time and dolphins too."

"I will be happy to leave Holland," said one of the other wives. "The truce between Holland and Spain is due to end next year. We will at least leave in peace…"

Mercy pondered this. Here they had lived in a city that bustled and moved with such speed that the wilderness of America moved in a slower, quieter pace. She preferred to think the best of it, and not to dwell on the chatter she had heard in the marketplaces of grievous diseases, fortune seekers who'd go to any length to grow rich, and the Starving Times of Jamestown.

Katherine May cleared her throat. "What else say you, Mercy?"

She paused. She hadn't expected anyone would care for her opinion. "Me, ma'am?"

"Yes, you have said so little. What are your thoughts on the matter? The wives have voiced their concerns. We have yet to hear yours."

Mercy set her sewing on her lap. "Mine are unimportant, ma'am."

"Truly they are."

"I suppose my concerns are unfounded."

"In what way, pray?"

"I do not know the future."

"And none can."

"It would help if these questions could be answered, but how can they? It is best to do as you said, Mrs. Brewster. We mustn't think so bleakly."

"Yet you are doubtful of our choice?" asked Mary Brewster.

"I am."

"You are welcomed to come live with us and make the journey next year," said Katherine May. "Unless you have other plans."

"It is a kind offer. But I have decided I shall go."

Katherine May smiled. "It depends on another?"

"It might." Mercy answered shyly.

Mercy leaned forward and picked up Caleb's shirt. The muslin felt smooth and warm in her hands and she imagined it against his skin. She sat near the window and glanced through it. People were strolling along the walkways, the Dutch in their brightly colored clothes.

The heat grew stifling in the house. Mercy stood and walked past the dining room door with her heart in her throat. Beyond it, she could hear the men speaking in low and serious tones. Caleb's voice caused a warm ripple over her skin. The door sat ajar, and she caught a glimpse of him seated in a chair, still with one arm over the back, the other on the table. She wished she could enter and pull him away, have him to herself, and he to listen to her worries, her fears, and her need for comfort.

She stepped out the back door and crossed a grassy knoll where the moonlight shone over leaf and blade. There she sat upon the grass with her head resting in her arms. She had not cried in a long time—not since the deaths of her grandparents and uncle. Her world had changed. Like the breaking of a butterfly from a chrysalis, she went from suffocating doubt to liberating faith. She loved her Redeemer, and strove to please her God instead of herself. Riches no longer mattered. Love did.

Her fondness for Holland with its canals and fields of tulips, lush grass and windmills, the kindly people, and freedom, seemed immediate. Gone was crowded Ipswich. Gone was the hard labor at the inn, and the licentious Lord Glenmont whose touch cast a dark foreboding through her veins. She whispered while looking up at the night sky. "Thou has sent me a protector."

The breeze murmured softly through the trees and quivered the leaves. A sparrow hawk cried above and she raised her head to see it. The bird swooped and dove to a branch. It spread its wings and plumped its breast. It hadn't a care in the world. What worry did it have for food or shelter?

She looked at the spangled sky. A shooting star shot across the zenith and she sighed. If only Caleb had followed her out and sat next to her, he too would have seen it. Footsteps crunched over the gravel path and drew near. Breathless, Mercy drew up her legs and focused on the figure coming toward her. Moonlight outlined his figure and touched upon his hair, causing her heart to quiver at the sight of him. What she had not spoken aloud, spoke within her. His comeliness not only reflected in his face, the strong arms and broad shoulders, but inside. Caleb Treymayne allowed her to see a side of him most had not. When he looked at her, his eyes were love lit, like the slow burning flame of a candle. When he spoke, his words were guarded, yet truthful.

He paused before her and looked down. Then he shifted on his booted feet and lowered himself beside her. "Are you all right, Mercy?"

She yanked at the folds of her dress. "I needed air. It is warm in the house."

"Warm inside and out. Warm within," and he laid his hand over his chest.

"I've not known anyone to speak as you do, Caleb."

"Too lofty a compliment for a man like me." He looked closer. "You've been crying."

She wiped her face. "How can you tell? It is too dark to see my tears."

"It is bright enough for me to see what you wish to hide, Mercy."

"I do not expect you to understand. Women cry to do ourselves good."

He paused. "I like the way the moonlight falls over your face, how it shines in your eyes."

Mercy glanced at the door. "We should not be alone."

"We have been before."

"Yes, but others do not think we should, and there are people in the house."

He nodded. "Ah, we might be tempted by one another. Is that it?"

She lowered her eyes. "We must keep our distance. I'm uneasy."

"With me?"

She shook her head. "With you? No. I am comfortable with you, except…"

"Tell me."

"I feel drawn to you…I want to be with you all the time."

Caleb frowned. "And that makes you uncomfortable?"

She smiled and shook her head. "Yes, in a pleasant kind of way." She looked him fully in the eyes. Her answer made them soften in the moonlight. "Will you protect me? Will you keep me safe?"

"On my life's blood I will."

"But I would not want you to spill your blood," she said surprised.

A corner of his mouth lifted. "A perfectly female reply."

"Perhaps, but only because I want you to live, and live long. You see, I've decided to leave with the others."

"I dare not think, for it would be arrogant, you've made that decision because of me."

"It is a very good reason." She pressed her lips, wishing he'd tell her they would go to the city hall and marry. "Would you rather I stay behind?" she said, anticipating his answer.

Caleb looked at the ground and pulled at the grass. "You should know how I feel." He stood abruptly and paced. Then he stopped and looked down at her. "I wish you'd take that cap off."

Mercy widened her eyes. "It would be vain if I did—they tell me."

"Why do you care what people think? A woman's hair is her glory and should not be hidden." He reached down and pulled her up. "I want to hold it in my hands, and see it fall over your shoulders. Why is that so wrong? I'm not even sure what color your hair is."

"Brown." When she made no move to take off the coif, he nodded and strode toward the door. She could tell by his stride, he was frustrated.

"Wait," she said, and he turned. "Have you nothing else to say?"

"I have, but I'll keep it for another time."

"What other time is there than now?" She wanted to shout, release all she was thinking and feeling. Caleb opened his mouth to speak, but hesitated. She slipped off her coif and dropped it. Then she shook out her hair. "There you see. It is ordinary. Dull. Lifeless. Brown."

He brought a tendril over her shoulder and lifted it to his lips. "Not to me. I once saw a jasper stone set in gold, the same color of your hair." Suddenly, all emotion broke over him. Caleb went down on his knees and kissed her hands. "I cannot be silent any longer. I love and want you. I have many faults, and I am a poor man. I have so little to offer you, save my heart. Day and night, I long for you. This love burns within me. I'm consumed by it and in agony. Don't you see it when I look at you?"

"Yes, Caleb. I do...I've seen it from the start."

"You know what I'm asking, don't you?"

"I have some idea," she said coyly. "I will not know for sure unless you tell me."

He pressed her hands to his lips once more. "Be my wife."

Mercy set her hand on his jaw, a gesture that brought him to his feet. "I will have no other but you."

A light passed the kitchen window. Mercy drew apart from Caleb and stepped to the flagstones in front of the door. She held a finger to her lips, and set her coif on her head. "You must go."

"Whose permission should I ask in order to wed you?" He stepped nearer, hat in hand.

She smiled, her joy bubbling over. "William's, since I've lived under his roof."

"First thing tomorrow morning." Smiling, Caleb set his hat on, and stepped through the back gate. Mercy watched him leave with a pounding of her heart, drawing in a breath at the way the moonlight alighted over him and how he left a shadow behind that quickly blended into the dark.

Slipping inside the house, she almost bumped into Evi, who held a candle in her hand and looked at Mercy with doe eyes. "They asked about you, Mercy."

"I needed a breath of fresh air."

"They've all gone home. The others have gone to bed. I'm to sleep on the palette over there."

"I wish you a good sleep, Evi." She headed for the door leading out to the hallway, and turned. "Speak the truth. Did you see me with Mr. Treymayne outside?"

A shy flush passed over Evi's face. "Just a glimpse. He loves you, doesn't he?"

Mercy smiled. "He does, and I love him."

"Will you wed?"

"Yes, but you are not to say anything until it is announced. Alright?"

Evi nodded and handed the candlestick to Mercy. "Good night, Mercy. God give you sweet dreams."

"To you as well, Evi. I doubt I shall be able to sleep much though. I'll be thinking of Caleb all night."

PART THREE

And there at the river, by Ahava, I proclaimed a fast, that we might humble ourselves before our God, and seek of him a right way for us, and for our children, and for all our substance.

Ezra 8:21

Jon Robinson's declaration

Chapter 19

There would be no satin gown, no lace, no flowers or ceremony. Mercy came to Caleb in her best clothes made of soft blue linen with a bleached kerchief fastened to her bosom with a pin. She gathered her hair brown to bronze into a loose knot at the nap of her neck and wore her Sunday cap. Caleb arrived before the noon hour, and when he saw her, he swept off his hat and sighed. He became the only one in the room to Mercy. Her heart pounded, captivated by his clean-shaven face and large brown eyes. He wore a black doublet, breeches, and boots, and from under his hat, his hair looked like woven flax.

One of Leyden's magistrates stepped beside Mercy and the documents for their civil marriage were signed by all parties, followed by a light dinner hosted by Reverend Robinson and his wife. Bidding all a good night, Mercy and Caleb went out into the cool evening and walked to his flat along the canal.

Twilight poured through the windows in silvery bands and magenta hazes. The hot July weather was fragrant with the saltiness of the English Channel. By dark, the seagulls settled, and the nighthawks came out to hunt prey. Mercy glanced at the simple covering of white linen and the pillows stuffed with feathers against the bolster of his bed. She turned to the bundle she carried from the Bradford's house and smiled. Casting off her gown, she loosened the ties to her shift and crawled in next to him. A tear fell from her eye, and onto his skin. He turned and ran his finger down the path the tear took.

"Why are you crying?"

"It is nothing." She stroked his cheek.

He kissed her hand. "Tell me."

"I was thinking of the day we met."

"The best day of my life next to wedding you. God willing, we have years ahead of us."

"I hope so."

"I know so. We have a house to build, and children to bring up."

She drew out of his arms. "Could it be a forlorn hope?"

"Not to me. You're afraid?"

"The more I think about the voyage, the more troubled I become."

"I thought you were ready by now."

"You're finding it hard to ease my mind, aren't you?"

"A little." Caleb caressed her shoulder.

Mercy nuzzled into him. "You are my protector."

"I'd lay my life down for you."

She sat up. "I will pray no harm comes to us. Only good."

"We don't know what the future holds, but I like your optimism."

"Then you must agree nothing shall part us until we are very old and die."

"I agree."

She settled into his arms. "Here I lay teary, when I should be happy and desiring of you. I've hidden my worries and now they are rising to the surface and engulfing me. I'm sorry." She fell back against her pillow and let out a long breath.

Caleb sat up on his elbow. "God has a plan for us. Plans to prosper us and not harm us. Plans to give us hope and a future. How many days that future is, only He knows. It does not mean we will not face hardships. But we will endure."

"Yes, my love. We will endure." She turned to him. "I should change the way I'm thinking. Instead, I should dream of seeing seabirds, whales and dolphins. The sea at sunset and the stars at night. A new land that is unspoiled by cities and towns, and making friends with the people there." She looked into his eyes. "We will make friends with them, will we not?"

He smiled at her. "That is what we all hope for."

Laying her hand across his bare chest, she let him gather her into his arms. They were silent, listening to the clanging of a ship's bell carried on the wind.

For seven days, Mercy woke to a wren singing outside the window. She opened the sash and looked out at a misty sky, at a bronze sun blanketed by haze. It would be a warm day. She busied packing the brass-hinged trunk Uncle Silas had given her. Before closing the lid, she drew in the heady scent of cedar. It reminded her of the sitting room in Ipswich, when Grandpapa laid out a fire in the hearth, always with at least one cedar log on Christmas Eve. Her heart thumped and her eyes pooled. She missed Grandpapa and Nan, and Uncle Silas. What would they think of her now being joyfully married, stronger in her faith, and setting out on an adventure into an unknown future?

She shut the lid and called Caleb. He strode into the room, and dusted off the knees of his breeches. He had been repairing a board in the floor that had come loose. Neither he nor Mercy wished to leave without the flat being in the condition Caleb had found it.

Hoisting the trunk, his knees buckled. "What have you in here, dear wife? Bricks?" He smiled teasingly.

"You know I do not. A few books and plate have made it heavy I suppose." She gave him a coy look. "Do you want me to remove them?"

"Not if what you've packed makes you happy."

"I've been choosey. We've been asked to only bring what we can fit in a trunk and leave the rest behind." She counted the items on her fingers. "Our Bible. The box you made me. Two pewter plates, forks, spoons, cups, your razor, bed linen…"

"And my satchel of tools."

She smiled. "Yes and your satchel of tools."

Caleb lifted the trunk and positioned it onto his back. Mercy squeezed the muscle in his arm, and took one last look at the room they had shared. Before they headed out the door, she seared in her mind their wedding bed where they were first together under the flicker of golden candlelight, where his embraces set her afire, and his kisses melted butter on her lips.

They left the small flat swept clean, with a jug of beer left on the table for the landlord. Together they headed down the stairs and out to a cobbled street. The people passing by were never to be seen again. The houses and shops would fade in Mercy's memory. The tall windmills, the fields of tulips, grazing cattle and sheep of the countryside would turn into pictures, still and silent in the distant past.

As she rounded the corner with Caleb, the home that had taken her in stood a ways off.

Mullioned windows sparkled in the morning light. Mercy gazed at the Bradford's door. It looked lonely to her, the rooms empty of furniture and plate, a loving couple…and a child, whose pattering and laughter, had left it. Even the tabby Mercy had cuddled was nowhere to be seen. She looked toward the window that faced the street where the cat had lounged in the sunshine.

"Do not linger, wife. It'll only make you sad."

"I think I will miss that dear kitten more than I've missed Jasper," she said. "I'm glad Katherine took him. Young John Bradford loved that cat."

"There'll be cats on board." Caleb walked forward. Mercy hurried to catch up.

"What do you mean?"

"Ships use cats to keep the rats down."

"Rats?" She shivered. "I hope not. I do not like rats or mice. You're teasing me, aren't you?"

"It is no lie, my love." They walked side-by-side, drawing closer to the Bradford's empty house. "When you came over, weren't there any on the ship you sailed in?"

"I did not see any," Mercy said.

"There was a large grey cat in the hold of the ship I was on. He kept to himself in corners and in the shadows. When a rat scurried across the floor, he'd leap at it and bury his claws into it. The poor creature would squeal until a bite on the neck silenced him."

"Oh, Caleb. Such a grim story. I hope I do not see such a thing."

He smiled. "Would you rather see a rat live? They spread disease and eat ship's provisions. They are sly creatures. Better to have the cat catch and destroy them."

She nodded. "You're right. I just don't want to see one…ever again. Parts of Ipswich had plenty of them."

Caleb laughed. "Have you ever heard the story of the cat that rolled himself in flour in order to catch mice after other attempts failed? When the old rat suspected him, he told the others to be cautious, and to keep their distance."

Mercy's smile widened. "And the moral is, don't make the same mistake twice."

Caleb looked ahead. "So wise you are, Mercy. It's a good story."

"From your childhood?"

One corner of his mouth lifted into a smile. "Aye, it was. My mother told it to me."

"You've never said much about your parents. You told me you had no siblings, something we share in common…and regret."

"I wish I could find a stronger word. They tried, but it was not God's will. Father worked me hard and made me a man. He expected much from me. My mother was tolerant. I've wondered if they had lived, would they have been proud."

"You know they would be. You served the King, and you came to serve Christ. Most of all, you are a good husband…and one day a good father."

"Have no doubt on that score, Mercy."

Caleb set their trunk down and walked up to the workman. "Excuse us, sir. My wife and I are friends of the Bradfords. Mr. Bradford said we could put our trunk on your wagon. Is that agreeable to you?"

"Mr. Bradford told me you'd be by." The man shook his head. "Your trunk looks too heavy to carry down to the canal."

"I'll lend you a hand."

"*Dank u*," the man said.

"It's a lot of lifting for one man."

"I'm use to it, sir." The workman looked at Mercy. In broken English he said, "Mistress, are you afraid of horses?"

She smiled. "I'm not afraid of any horse unless it bites."

"No biting. She's gentle as a lamb." He drew from his pocket an apple. "I've an apple. Would you hold *da* bridle and give it to her?"

Mercy took the apple from the man and walked to the front of the wagon. The horse bobbed its head and she brushed her hand down its velvety nose. Holding the apple in the flat of her palm, she spoke softly to the animal, until her eyes shifted to see the man in gray skulking down the street toward them. Her fingers slipped beneath the bridle and she gripped it hard. She kept her eyes on the man, and when he approached Caleb, she moved closer into the horse's neck.

"Good day, sir." The raspy voice matched his hawkish face and mean eyes. "Leaving town? Or are those chairs for sale?"

Caleb handed up another chair to the workman. "Do I know you, sir?"

"No, I'm just passing by. It isn't often I get the chance to speak to another Englishman."

"How did you know I was English since we've never met? Certainly not by looks alone."

"You are not dressed in the style of the Dutch. Do you need an extra hand?"

"I think we have it, sir. Thank you just the same." Caleb turned away, but the man stood where he was, arms crossed.

"It is good to meet another Englishman," the man said. "Your name?"

"Caleb Treymayne."

"I'm not familiar with anyone of that surname."

Caleb nodded and went on working.

"I'll give a good price for those chairs." The man in gray studied one of the spindle legs. "Nice craftsmanship."

Lifting the last one into the wagon, Caleb ran his hand along it. He was proud of his work, and pleased Dorothy Bradford refused to sell the chairs along with her other furniture.

"Sorry. The chairs are not mine to sell."

The man looked past him and caught Mercy's eyes. Through his parted lips, his breath heaved, and his eyes took on a look of satisfaction—riveted as if he had found something that would bring him gain. For a moment, she stared at him in return, her eyes widening and sensing the color had gone from her face. She shot him a proud look, a look that said she suspected who and what he was. He made no move toward her, but lifted his hat with a grin.

"Ah, that lady must be your wife," he said to Caleb. "Has she a name?"

Caleb set his hands over his hips. "She has. Mrs. Treymayne."

This fellow removed his hat and bowed like a court courtier, all the while keeping his eyes fastened upon her. "Charmed, Mrs. Treymayne. One so fair must have a first name that is as pretty as her face."

Caleb frowned. "A forward comment for a stranger."

"Oh, no offense. It has been some time since my eyes beheld a lady from my own country. I'm from Ipswich. Are you familiar with the town, Mrs. Treymayne?"

"Most people from Suffolk are, sir," she replied.

"Ah, then you might also be familiar with the *Blue Heron Inn*."

Mercy's chest tightened. She brought her hand down from the horse's bridle and flexed it. Not only did the question disturb her, but the look in his eyes did as well. She raised her chin, a feeling of defiance rushing over her, that she would answer his questions and catch him at his own game.

"I can see my husband is cautious of me answering your questions, sir, but yes, I am from Ipswich and I am familiar with the inn you speak of. I am curious why you want to know your reasons for asking me these questions. It is out of the ordinary my husband and I should meet another person from Ipswich. Why not tell me how that has come about."

"Coincidence, Mrs. Treymayne."

She gave him a look that caused his grin to fade. "Perhaps."

The man in gray glanced at Caleb. He was still loading the wagon, and so the man stepped a bit closer to Mercy. "Please spare your suspicions," he said softly. "For it is not unlikely I should meet you. Ipswich is not so large that I do not know people and places you might be acquainted with." He tapped his chin. "Before I left, I was familiar with a seamstress. She made this suit for me, and suggested I make for Holland. I am in trade, and will prosper better here than there."

"What kind of trade?"

"Oh this and that."

Caleb came around the wagon. "Mercy. Say no more to this man."

A knowing look spread over the stranger's face when he heard her name. He bowed. "I apologize. I did not mean to delay you and your wife. I am quite the gabber. I go on and on."

"I would ask you not to bother my wife, sir. Move on."

With a swing of his arm, the man in gray moved away. Mercy jerked away and looked at Caleb. He jumped down from the wagon and slammed the gate shut. Mercy bit her lip. It would have been better if she had not allowed her old ways to rise and converse with the man. Looking at the expression on Caleb's face caused her to realize she had said too much.

The workman climbed into his seat and picked up the reins. Caleb pushed back the brim of his hat and held his hand out to Mercy to climb up.

"Have you seen that man before?" he asked when she sat down beside him.

"Once," Mercy said. "I saw him from the door. He was standing across the street the day the Mays arrived. I have an ill feeling about him. Are my misgivings needless?"

"He seemed too interested in you. I should go after him…question him and…"

Mercy gripped his arm. "Please don't. I don't want you to leave me."

Caleb brushed her cheek with his thumb. "Perhaps we are overly suspicious."

"Yes," she said, savoring his calm caress. "Maybe we're nervous and don't need to be."

"Let's forget about the stranger. We've people waiting for us."

In front of Pastor Robinson's dwelling and the building that had been their meeting place, the people had gathered. Here they would begin their journey to Delfshaven. The driver drew off his hat, set it against his chest, and wished them Godspeed. Caleb put his arms around Mercy's waist, each facing the profound preacher. Robinson stepped forward into the crowd with his Bible tucked beneath his arm. He drew his congregation forward to speak to them. What words would he share to console the women and sure up the bravery of the men? Anxious, Mercy fixed her eyes on his solemn face. It reflected what was stirring in his heart. Heavy lines were in the corners of his eyes, and his hair had grown grayer since she first met him. His wife stood beside him, and he bid her to sit on a cask nearby. He cleared his throat, opened his Bible, and read from the Book of Ezra.

"'And there at the river, by Ahava, I proclaimed a fast, that we might humble ourselves before our God, and seek of him a right way for us, and for our children, and for all our substance'." Robinson went on near the close of his sermon. "We are soon to part. The Lord knows if I should live to see your faces again. But whether the Lord has appointed it or not, I charged you before God and his blessed angels, to follow me no further then I followed Christ."

Caleb squeezed Mercy when she drew in a shuddering breath. The exhortation given to them by Robinson brought tears to her eyes, and she gripped her husband's hands at her waist. They would go on without their pastor, encouraged to embrace truth from other instruments, to weigh it against scripture, for he told them he was confident the Lord had more light to break forth to them. Heads bowed at these humbling words, and with an abundance of tears. They spent the night with little sleep, and when the time came for them to depart, they left Leyden, the city that had been their resting place. Together with their fellow pilgrims, Mercy and Caleb lifted their eyes to the heavens, their dearest country, and quieted their spirits.

Chapter 20

Sunlight stole over the boats on the Vliet River and fell across Mercy's knees like a golden robe. The river's surface rippled from the trails of wild ducks and geese, and mirrored the variegated clouds drifting across the sky. Others of her fellow sojourners traveled by foot and wagon carrying their possessions, and their hopes of reaching the unknown shores of America. The rows of houses were soon gone, and the river opened up to a vast landscape rich with meadows of wildflowers, and fields where sheep and milking cows grazed.

Mercy's eyes searched the miles. Will the New World look as heavenly? Will the grass grow as green? She closed her eyes and imagined rivers abundant with fish. They'd been told settlers caught trout the length of a man's arm, and deer foraged in herds. The breeze blew against her face, and she pictured cool forests deep in wild fern and rhododendron.

She reached for Caleb's hand. He squeezed her fingers, and she scooted closer until his arm went around her back and glided to her waist. Silence bred silence as they travelled far from Leyden on to Delfshaven. Mercy's heart rested in that silence, both humbled and comforted by it, for the time of leaving they had spoken of for so long had finally come.

Once they reached the scenic town of Delfshaven, the sun sunk low and a warm night fell. A myriad of stars shone so thick constellations could barely be marked. Caleb pointed to the North Star. "By it sailors navigate."

Mercy watched it sparkle against black velvet. "And we'll see it as we cross the ocean?"

"As long as the sky is clear, yes."

"God's handiwork is marvelous," she sighed. "To think He placed that star there for guidance. It makes me feel hopeful our voyage will not be so difficult."

Deeper shadows crossed the placid water, interrupted by bands of moonlight passing over quiet ripples. Boats painted in colorful hues were moored for the night, and fishermen sat on the docks repairing nets and smoking clay pipes. They lifted their caps and Mercy waved.

"The Dutch have been so welcoming to the Separatists," she said. "Do you think some English will miss them?"

"Perhaps," said Caleb.

"I will miss Evi." She then nudged his shoulder. "You might miss Alice?"

He gave her a humored look. "Alice? Should I?"

Mercy smiled and nodded. "It might do our hearts well from time to time to think of those we knew here, and to hold fast their memories. I shall miss my grandparents and Uncle Silas, no matter how far from England's shores I may be."

Morning arrived in Delfshaven with a fair wind. Mercy gazed up at the tall masts of the *Speedwell*. A feeling of awe overtook her to see the ship that would take them to Southampton to join the *Mayflower*. Caleb stood beside her. The muscles in his face twitched and he folded his arms. "She looks battered and scared," he said to a sailor coiling a rope.

"The *Speedwell* has seen her share of battle, sir."

"The one with Spain, I presume."

"Aye, under the name *Swiftsure*, all sixty tons of h'r."

"Is not the mast too tall for such a small vessel?"

"Haven't you any knowledge of ships, sir?"

"I was in the King's Navy."

"Master Reinolds knows every inch of this ship. He knows when a vessel is seaworthy and when it's not. Consider your doubts private, so not to offend him."

Unfolding his arms, Caleb drew Mercy closer to him as ruff-necked sailors squeezed past. He continued to eye the masts. Mercy admired his attitude, if not his keen observation on matters of construction, from the smallest chair to a sailing ship like the *Speedwell.* Yet a flash of concern shone in his eyes.

"Is there something wrong with the ship?" she whispered in his ear.

"I'm no shipbuilder to tell, my love."

"No, but you've sailed before."

"The main mast looks too large to me. But who am I to know if it makes a difference?"

His eyes were fixed on the mast, then to the furled sails. Mercy she set her arm in his. "Is she seaworthy?"

He looked down at her and smiled. "I'm sure she is. Forget what I said."

The sky filled with squawking gulls and brilliant sunshine. The whoosh of the tide against the fishing boats, and the murmur of merchants, sailors, and passengers were borne to Mercy's ears. She knew she'd not hear such sounds for a long time, except for the push of the ocean and rushing of the wind. Then the rumble of carriage wheels overtook the clatter. When it stopped, a footman opened the carriage door, set the step down and extended his hand. A lady came forth, followed by a gentleman in dark blue. Mercy's eyes drifted from the man back to the woman. Her voluminous sleeves were white and full like the wings of a swan. Blue ribbons cinched the sleeves at her elbows. She wore a tall hat decorated with a lavender plume. Elegantly dressed, and walking regally, the pair had to be part of the company of pilgrim strangers. She set her hand over her commonplace jacket, her fingertips brushing over the leather ties. There had been a time when she envied such women and longed to wear expensive silks and satins.

When she had been Lady Irene's companion, the clothes she had to wear, though fine, were uncomfortable. She pulled and tugged at the stomachers, stretched the stockings when they sagged, and on warm days dreaded all the heavy folds that caused her to sweat beneath them. She had gone from tatters to satins, only to cast off the latter and return to simple clothes made of soft wool and linen.

The gentleman lent his arm to the lady. Intrigued, Mercy watched them and wondered who they were and where had they come from. Together they walked over to a sailor seated at a table with the passenger book, quill, and ink. The sailor looked up and spoke. "Name?"

"Christopher Martin and my wife Mary."

"You are assigned to the gun deck."

The gentleman stiffened and in a raised voice asked the weary sailor, "Do you not know who I am? Look in your little book and it will tell you. I am the assigned governor of this vessel."

"You are Christopher Martin and this lady is your wife. I understand."

Christopher Martin's voice carried so far that others turned their heads. "My wife and I are to have private quarters aboard this vessel. It should be written down in your book."

"There are no private quarters to be had, sir."

"Listen here, you. I represent the financial backers of this venture." He looked with contempt at the people who gathered around him. With a flourish of his cuff, he scorned them. "You people stand too close. Back away. You are not worthy to wipe my shoes."

"Christopher," his wife scolded. "These are to be our companions for a long time."

"Wife, they are not our companions. They are subservient to us. Therefore, I as their governor shall speak to them in the manner befitting my station."

Murmurs of disapproval passed through the crowd. "Your wife is right. No need to insult the people, sir," said the first mate. "Again, you are quartered in the gun deck.

"But how shall we have any privacy?"

"You won't."

"How shall we wash or dine, or…"

"Please move on. Master Reinolds wants everyone aboard." The sailor picked up a quill and wrote in his book. Then he waved the gentleman and wife off. Mr. Martin's faced turned red. His lady's lips trembled and she set her handkerchief against them. Looking defeated, the ship's governor drew his wife away.

The *Speedwell's* bell clanged for passengers to board. It were a woeful sight, one that wrenched Mercy's heart to see such sad and mournful partings, to hear sobs, heavy sighs, and prayers that did sound among the people. Children whimpered or stood at gaze. Wives and daughters drew into the arms of their men. Dutch strangers stood as spectators, and many could not refrain from calling out sorrowful farewells. Tears ran down Mercy's cheeks. She clutched Caleb's arm and he aided her up the gangplank.

"Such sorrow in parting," she breathed.

"I have not known such sorrow," he replied.

"Yet it is sweet to see such unfeigned love. I feel fearful and in awe all at the same time."

The moment Mercy set her feet on the deck of the *Speedwell* Martin sprang up the gangplank behind her. He smiled and jumped from the planks threshold to the deck. "I made it, Mercy. Ah, what a day for sailing, eh? And this ship, she's a beauty is she not?" As he was speaking, Evi rushed up the gangplank clutching her skirts above her ankles. She called out, "Martin! Martin Flagg! Wait!"

Martin heaved the sack he carried onto the deck and turned. "Go to her, Martin," said Mercy.

He stepped over to the brink of the gangplank and drew off his cap. After a word, Evi leaned up, kissed his cheek, and hurried away weeping. Martin stepped back with his face flushed. He shifted on his feet and whispered, "She embarrassed me. I hope no one saw, but in this crowd..."

"Does it matter, Martin? Was it not kind she bid you farewell?"

He nodded. "I daresay if I'd been alone with her, I would have kissed her. Funny how dear she has become to me."

"She'll come with the Mays when they sail. Until then, keep your hopes for her in your heart."

Martin lifted his sack and swung it over his shoulder. "When she does join us, I'll wed her. You were right when you told me you were not the one for me." He glanced at Caleb. "Pardon me, sir."

Caleb kept his eyes on the crowd. "You need no pardon."

Mercy set her hand on Martin's arm. "I was wrong on one account," she said. "Temperance Glasken. Remember her?"

Martin tapped his chin with his finger. "Temperance Gaskin. I wonder what happened to her. Probably went into service, I suppose."

"Or wedded and forgot all about you," Mercy said playfully.

Martin smiled and stepped toward the gangway. He looked over at Mercy and winked, then disappeared below deck with his sack of meager belongings.

"The tide doth not wait," they heard. "Visitors ashore."

The sailor she and Caleb had first spoken to drew up beside them. "That's Master Reinolds. Remember what I told you...praising his ship goes a long way with the man."

The master of the ship had hair that brushed along the collar of his doublet a shade darker than the sails. His face looked weatherworn, yet his bearing was strong and youthful as he stood on the deck calling out orders.

193

Pastor Robinson knelt with his tattered Bible in his hands. Mercy and Caleb joined him together with the others, their heads bowed and their hands folded. Mercy's limbs trembled beneath the folds of her garments, and a quivering of the heart caused her to shut her eyes more firmly. What lay ahead still frightened her, but she overpowered the sensation of fear with a Psalm gracing her lips. Once Robinson commended all into God's hands and blessed the people, they rose and took their leave one of another, knowing it might be the last.

The crowd moved like a current, and Mercy spotted Dorothy and William Bradford bidding tearful farewells to Dorothy's parents. The most poignant of the parting was with their son John. Mercy's heart ached for Dorothy and the wee boy. The young mother lovingly caressed her son's hair, kissed his forehead and cheek. Katherine May held the boy's hand, and after she and Mr. May said their goodbyes to Dorothy and William with kisses and tears, they walked down the gangplank to the dockside. The toddler reached out his arms to his mother and cried. Bradford drew Dorothy away.

Mercy started forward. "I must go to her."

Caleb drew her back and spoke softly in her ear. "I know your heart is heavy for Dorothy. But there is nothing any of us can do. It is between her and William."

"Others are bringing their children. Why didn't he want to bring John?"

"God alone sees what is ahead, and it could be a saving grace for the child for all we know."

She drew away from him so affected she leaned on the rail of the ship to catch her breath. Below the Mays climbed inside their carriage with their small grandson. The driver moved the horses on and the carriage blended into the crowd of Dutch onlookers. Mercy turned and wiped her eyes.

"Look, Mercy," Caleb said. "William has his arm around Dorothy and is speaking to her softly. She's dried her tears and…there you see she has a smile on her face. You must let them be."

Mercy set her hands on the breast of his doublet and looked into his eyes. "If our home is built before the Bradford's, promise me they can stay with us."

Caleb stroked her cheek. "Of course, my love. They were kind to give you a roof over your head. Should we do any less?"

Below a commotion rose and the pair looked over. Three men shouldered their way through the crowd. Their clothes were English and one had a blood red insignia on the right breast of his doublet. Mercy gripped the rail. From a distance, she could make out a pair of wyverns holding a crest crisscrossed with a red sash, a picture of pursuit and danger.

She turned to Caleb. "One wears a coat of arms…"

He frowned. "You recognize it?"

Amid the noise that rendered her uneasy, Mercy gasped and drew back after the man stomped up the gangplank. "It is Lord Glenmont's coat of arms."

Caleb pulled her to him. "Stay close to me."

Mercy's breath heaved. It was too late to go down into the gun deck. The three men had boarded. A sailor approached them. The leader shoved him aside, a lanky fellow with shallow skin, dusky brown hair, and thick bushy eyebrows. He set his legs wide and thrust his hands over his hips. "Where is the Master of this pitiful hulk?"

Mercy stiffened. She held her breath in those seconds. Heavy boots stomped over the deck. The lead man came within a foot of her. He narrowed his eyes and looked her up and down. "This one fits the description of that thief," he said to the man beside him. "You agree?"

Mercy lowered her eyes and squeezed Caleb's hand. A sudden lifting of the wind blew over her face. A gull flew down between the shrouds, perched onto a footrope, and opened its wings. It screeched at Lord Glenmont's creature. Looking up at the bird, the leader set his hand over the hilt of his blade. "I demand the master to come forward at once," he shouted.

Reinolds stepped in. "I'm Master of this vessel. What's your business?"

"I'm here to take into custody a thief."

"You're a long way from England, and will not find a thief aboard my ship."

The man laughed and looked at his cohorts. His arrogant sneer distorted his face. The wind blew strong. His lank brown hair drifted over a raised scar. "You see this?" he said, pointing to the insignia on his doublet.

"What of it?" said Reinolds.

"This is Lord Glenmont's coat of arms."

195

"It means nothing to me. Leave my ship or I'll have you thrown off."

Caleb had enough and stepped beside Reinolds. "There are more of us than you to help you obey the Master's order."

"Ha! A group of peaceful Separatists against us?" The man pointed at Mercy. "That woman fits the description of the thief. Bring her forward."

People gasped. "It isn't true what he says," Caleb told them. "You must all stand by her."

William Bradford stepped forward. "I can vouch for this woman. She has been with us many months, and is a dear friend to my wife."

"One common man's word does not acquit her. I say she is a thief. I'm to take her back to England for trial, and most likely a hanging."

Caleb stiffened and swore under his breath. He leapt forward. Reinolds stopped him. "Stay beside your wife, man." He then turned to Mercy's accuser. "English law does not apply on my ship while in Dutch waters. What proof do you have of her guilt?"

"This." He thrust a writ of arrest in front of Reinolds and Caleb. "Signed by his lordship. It is a warrant...if you can read it."

Reinolds grabbed the writ and looked it over. "This isn't a legal warrant." He thrust it back in the leader's face.

Mercy stepped up beside Caleb and asked if she could speak. Caleb forbade her, but she assured him the truth would keep her free. She explained the series of events briefly to Master Reinolds, and to the others standing near. Martin had sprung up to the top deck and pushed through the crowd.

"I am a witness to her innocence. Here me." He stood on the break of the deck and voiced his testimony. "On my life's blood, she is innocent of these accusations. Master Reinolds, these men have been sent only to do her harm. Cast them off the ship, or there are those of us who will."

Mercy's eyes lit up as she listened to Martin. Never had she heard him speak so bravely, so forcefully.

Lord Glenmont's man frowned and stomped forward. "Give her over. We'll see what the authorities have to say."

"The only authority aboard this vessel is Master Reinolds." Caleb placed his boots firmly on his deck. "It is my duty to protect my wife. Leave or I'll throw you into the canal."

"You dare threaten me? We are not leaving until you hand that woman over."

Caleb swept off his hat and handed it to Mercy. "Hold my hat, my darling." Turning, he took the man by the shoulders. "To avoid causing you injury—test out the water."

The man's eyes widened and his jaw dropped. He looked to his men for help. "Don't just stand there. Help me!" He struggled, attempting to pry loose Caleb's hands. "Let go of me!"

"As you wish." Caleb flung his hands open and let go. The man fell backward overboard into the murky water. People hurried to look over. He came up gasping, shaking his fists and cursing.

Reinolds laughed. Many of the Separatists stared in amazement. Many of the crew however, laughed and jaunted at the other cohorts. "Who's next?" one guffawed. Their eyes widened and with swift turns, hurried back down the gangplank. Mercy ran to Caleb and threw her arms around him.

"Raise the gangplank," ordered Reinolds. He looked at the group of gapping men and women. "Ladies, gentlemen, we are now under way."

Smiles and a round of cheers went through the group. The sails tumbled down and swelled in the wind. As the ship drifted forward, a farewell volley of small shot and three pieces of ordnance fired. The passengers gathered along the bulwark and waved to those staying behind.

Mercy cradled her head against Caleb's shoulder. Soon the shoreline of Holland faded into a slender blue line.

Standing at the bulwark, they looked toward Southampton, England to a ship called the *Mayflower*.

Chapter 21

Pushed by a robust wind the *Speedwell* sailed into Solent Strait. The fresh wind blew against Mercy's face as she gazed at the shoreline. Before her were misty lowlands, lapping tides, and flocks of seabirds. The Strait smelled sweet, a mix of the rivers Test and Itchen and the salt sea. A pale moon hung above the horizon and when she lifted her eyes to see it, she sighed. Night would soon come. The stars would stand out against the ebony sky, and Caleb would point out the Northern Star to her. The sun was near to setting and the scents of summer were heavy in the breeze. The closer they sailed toward Southampton Harbor the greater the scents grew. Wood fires, fields of tall grass, the fish markets, all touched her with melancholy, a sudden missing of Grandpapa Jonah and Nan Patience. She recalled the smells of Ipswich. Coal and wood. The markets and river. Then a peculiar fitful feeling one gets before some momentous event overtook her. It arrived from a deeper thought—leaving and never returning.

The *Mayflower* anchored in the harbor, held her attention. An impressive merchant vessel with three tall masts and a high aft-castle, her sails were rolled. Along the yardarms, seagulls perched and exercised their wings. The ship's square rigging added strength to the vessel with bastion-like structures fore-and-aft. Her symbol of a white mayflower shone clearly against a green pallet of carved leaves.

Caleb took her hand. "There's our sister ship."

Mercy sighed. "Look at her. She's beautiful."

"As sweet a craft as ever I saw. She's trim and smooth. *Mayflower* will be a refuge for anything the sea will throw at us."

Softly Mercy smiled, and then shifted her gaze from the symbol to other Separatist who had borne out their persecution in England. They hailed the *Speedwell* in joyful welcome. "The people must be the rest of our company. How happy they are to see us." She turned her head to Caleb. "We will all go to meet them?"

"I would think so," said Caleb. "There's work to do, but many will go ashore."

"I wish we had the provisions for me to celebrate our leaving. I can make a feast fit for the King, you know."

Caleb nudged her chin. "Yes, I do know. Remember your cooking made you even more attractive to me when we first met." He kissed her cheek.

"So you married me for my cooking, Caleb Treymayne?"

"Better to be wed and be well fed, then to be single and starving." He laughed, and she shoved his shoulder.

"Is that so? I shant cook for you again until you are deeply in love with me," she teased.

"Then I have no worries, for I am as you want me." Caleb stood behind her and circled his arms around her waist. "And what would you make for this feast we can imagine?"

"I'd lay out a long table abundant with roast goose, breads, sweet cakes, and fruits. We'd have barrels of ale, spiced puddings sweet with raisins, and toffee apples."

Caleb sighed into her neck. "I pray we have a feast like yours after our first harvest."

Mercy leaned her head against him. She reveled in his affection, the way he set his chin on top of her head, and rocked her. He was her champion, her lover and greatest friend. If their lives had not converged Mercy would not have found solace and happiness. She shut her eyes feeling the warmth of his body against her, thanking God they had gone down similar paths that brought them together.

The breeze stroked Mercy's face. The urge to pull off her cap and allow her hair to tumble down her back brought a smile to her face. How wonderful it would feel to have it blow back from her shoulders in the wind. She drew in a lungful of air and laid her head back against Caleb's shoulder. She set her hands over his. Some people would be shocked if she did remove her head covering. Should it matter what they thought? There was no law against it. Coifs and slouch hats were worn to keep hair clean and to show modesty. There were those who would say it was vain for a woman to wear her hair loose and uncovered. Others would not care. She had done it once before…alone with Caleb.

Mercy turned to him and drew off her steeple crowned hat, revealing the white cap beneath. "What would you say if I took off my cap?"

He set his forehead against hers. "What I said the night when I hoped you would."

She lowered her eyes. "Yes. I remember." Then she lifted her eyes and met his in a long gaze. "The air is so sweet here. I want to feel the wind through my hair. May I?"

Instead of answering, Caleb drew the coif from her head. Her locks fell in gentle twists along her shoulders, caught the sunlight as the breeze caused wisps to rise around her shoulders and face. 'Twas a glorious feeling—the caress of the sea breeze through each strand. She turned back to the rail and looked out at the scene of ships and land, birds and rock faces. Although they were to leave this place and never see it again, the moment made her feel hopeful—and happy.

The breeze ruffled through Mercy's hair and she lifted her face to the sun. She leaned on the bulwark to study their sister ship anchored in the harbor.

"She's larger than the *Speedwell*." Mercy's eyes followed along the lines of the ship, the neat and solid hull, the graceful curve of the beak, and the height of the fore, main, and mizzenmasts. "*Mayflower* is a beautiful ship and swift I imagine."

"She has thirty-six men and fourteen officers."

"By her size, I can see why so many crewmen are needed."

"Master Reinolds said they are seasoned sailors."

She turned to him. "Are you going with William?"

"I am."

"I wish I were going with you. I'd like to hear the conversation between you men."

He kissed her cheek. "I'd like to take you."

"We only have one boat and so many to fit in it. I should like to meet the other wives though."

"I'll ask, but don't get your hopes high. It will depend on how soon we are to set sail."

"I have a feeling the *Mayflower* is special. Perhaps her name will go down in history, and our descendants will know all about her."

The ship's ladder was let down and a boat bumped against the hull. William Bradford, Reinolds, and others started down. Caleb let Mercy go, and as he stepped away he said, "Use your pen, my love, to make sure they do."

He climbed down the rope and boarded, then rowed off toward the *Mayflower*. Mercy watched them reach the quay. Dorothy Bradford drew beside Mercy. "The *Mayflower* gives me hope," she said.

"As it does me," Mercy replied. "Look how tall her masts are."

"Taller than the *Speedwell's*."

"I wager she is swifter too."

Dorothy gripped the railing. "Not too swift to where she might get ahead of us."

"*Speedwell* will keep up. We'll cross the ocean in no time." She turned to Dorothy. "I'm feeling anxious in a good way, wishing we could fly across the Atlantic like the seabirds and begin our settlement without weeks of sailing. Imagine—seeing America for the first time. The land will be green and abundant. We'll be able to drink the water there too. Best of all we will be free."

"A joy for some. For me, I will think of the miles I am apart from my little boy and miss him. But in a year's time, he will be with me. I have thought what fun he will have sailing on a large ship, all the things he will see and do. My father said he believes the ship will be the *Fortune*. I'm not worried, Mercy. Not anymore."

The children were playing games on deck, innocent of the dangers ahead, bringing much delight to those watching them. Mothers scolded a daughter or son if too close to the bulwarks or in the way of a sailor.

Dorothy brushed her fingers over Wrestling Brewster's head as he swaggered by. "Do you want children? I cannot recall if we ever spoke of it."

"I want as many as my arms can carry, and that will be a lot," Mercy said. "Caleb will make a wonderful father." She leaned her arms across the ship's rail. "I love him so much, my heart aches. Every time I look at him, it pounds."

"You are still in love?"

"I am deeply," Mercy answered.

"I've questioned whether men can love us as we love them."

"I believe they can."

"You've never doubted Caleb?"

"I've no reason to. He speaks of love, but more than that, he shows it. It is his way, and when the doors are closed to the world outside…"

Dorothy blushed. "Say no more, Mercy," she giggled.

A quick smile lifted the corner of Mercy's mouth. "Ah. You think Caleb and I should not show affection for one another in front of others." She cocked her head. "Yet it is only small gestures of affection."

Dorothy's eyes widened. "We are not as the Puritans who think when a husband puts his arms around his wife in public it is a sin. Such thinking is ridiculous."

The children chased Wrestling across the deck. Mercy smiled and Dorothy leaned in. "They are the result of love. Bless God to give us more." She lifted Mary Allerton into her arms. "See the big ship, Mary?"

The child nodded and pointed to the symbol on the stern.

"Yes, that is a mayflower. They bloom in the spring all over England." She bounced the child. "Isn't it nice our friends will sail on a ship named after a flower?"

The *Speedwell* drew alongside the *Mayflower,* so close Mercy could reach out and touch her bulwarks. People were arriving along the quay with their trunks and goods.

"Look." Dorothy pointed at a woman with child. "Now there is a brave woman."

The woman's stiff gait made Mercy think how uncomfortable she felt. How much more uncomfortable would she be in the lower deck on a cot with the sea rolling the ship? She had grown deeply compassionate for others since coming to the Leyden church. In Ipswich, she hardly gave expectant mothers a thought. For the most part, they were kept behind closed doors unseen by others. When a baby did come into the world, she'd hear sounds of joy coming from within the house—or there'd be silent sorrow.

Mercy's brows creased. "She looks close to her time. I'll worry for her. The voyage cannot go well for a woman so far along. By the looks of her, the babe might be born at sea."

"I do not think I would want to be in her position," Dorothy said. "Babies should be born in private."

"We will help her if she goes into labor. I doubt the ship's surgeon knows anything about birthing babies."

The crews of the *Mayflower* and *Speedwell* rushed up the shrouds, and readied the sails. Reinolds, Caleb, and the others were making their way back to the *Speedwell*. Would the voyage be more treacherous than expected, or would it be as calm and uneventful as Mercy hoped?

For seven days, the ships sailed under fair winds and through calm waters. Those aboard basked in the quiet, but on the fifth day of August a great wind beat down upon the sea and pushed mighty waves against the ships. Rain fell, and walks on deck were prohibited.

Mercy curled her knees up against her chest. She pressed her eyes shut when the ship shuddered. Unlike any sound she had ever heard, the wind moaned and made her shiver. A sailor ducked his head into the tween deck, steadied against a beam and grinned.

"The wind is frightening, ain't it?" He stepped in, and set down a ration of biscuits for the passengers. Then he leaned down to the children. "It's a sea monster. It rises out of the ocean and blows the wind against the ship. Pray to yur god it doesn't whip its tail around us and drag us to the bottom."

The children's eyes widened with fright. Little Mary Allerton turned into her mother's arms. The sailor laughed. "Stop at once." Mercy stood and faced him. "It is cruel of you to frighten the children."

"Ah, just a seaman's tail, Mrs. Treymayne."

Caleb moved Mercy back and faced the sailor. "That may be, but look at their faces. Leave them alone, or I'll speak to Master Reinolds."

The smirk on the seaman's face fell away. He tugged at his cap, turned, and left. Waves rose against the hull as if indeed a serpent of the sea coiled around the ship. Mercy looked through the bleak light at the others seated around her. Children were cradled in their mother's arms. Some slept, but turned restlessly with the shrieking wind. The *Speedwell* rocked, and many were sickened. Mercy gripped her blanket and drew close to Caleb.

Reinolds came down the companionway with a lantern. The light fell over his weatherworn face as he ducked beneath the beams. He looked tired, his face drawn into a frown. Men stood and he motioned to them to come near. Caleb drew Mercy out of his arms and joined them. They huddled together, and she leaned her ear to hear the *Speedwell's* master speak.

"I've given orders to come alongside the *Mayflower*," he said in a lowered voice.

The *Speedwell* creaked and water trickled down some of the timbers. "We see water coming through," said Caleb. "Is that the reason?"

"Aye. I'm sorry to say, but we must turn back." The ship heaved and the sound of weeping and panicked sighs increased. "You men must calm your women and children."

"The creaking of the timbers frightens them and the children. And the wind—it is so fierce."

"Atlantic gales are not uncommon."

"Enough to make us turn back?" William Bradford asked.

"It's necessary," Reinolds said. "If we do not…" He paused and shook his head. "I can say no more."

He turned his back and climbed the stairs, the filtered light fading over his doublet, his shadow disappearing from the walls of the deck. Mercy waited a moment, her thoughts deep. She sat down again, and hugged her knees to her chest. How much danger were they in? Cold wind seeped through the hull. She drew her cloak tighter and looked up at Caleb. He moved beside her and she leaned her head against his arm.

"You're brave, Mercy."

"No, Caleb. I'm afraid. I see the water coming through. I feel the damp and cold, and the way the ship moves…it has sickened me in body and mind."

He kissed her cheek and moved her closer. "All will be well, my love. It is better we turn back now than go on. Farther out to sea we could meet with disaster."

Mercy looked into his eyes and nodded. Tears blurred her vision, yet she held his gaze. "My heart is pounding. I do not want us to die in the sea." She quietly wept and he held her close.

He squeezed her into his embrace. "Try not to worry. We will make it back."

"When you were in the King's Navy, had you experienced anything like this?" She hoped his answer would give her the comfort she needed.

"As with any voyage there were dangers."

"Leaks? So many you thought the ship would break apart?"

The ship leaned to starboard. "Eat your ship's biscuit," he whispered. He need not say more. She understood.

Timbers moaned and the wind swept over the waves and whistled a doleful tune. She glanced at the faces of the women as they held their children on their laps and wrapped them in their arms. Fear swam in their eyes, etched in the curves of their mouths. The children nuzzled their faces into their mothers' chests as the ship heaved and groaned as if it were a living thing that battled the sea and wind.

Mary Brewster stood. She lifted her voice and began to sing. Others joined in, their voices weak under the strain of what might happen if the water kept flooding in.

"He that dwelleth in the secret place of the most High, shall abide under the shadow of the Almighty. I will say of the Lord, He is my refuge and my fortress: my God; in Him will I trust."

Amid the crashing of the sea and the throes of the ship, each voice rose higher to drown out the wind. As the *Speedwell* united with the *Mayflower,* their force caused seawater to belch through the smallest thread of a crack and spread over the floor of the gun deck. Still the Separatist sang, though their voices quaked with alarm.

Mercy hid her face in the breast of Caleb's doublet, and trembled at the image of being taken by the sea. As the others strove to lift their voices, she turned out of his arms. She raised her eyes and shut them, as the words flooded her soul.

Chapter 22

W ithin two days, the ships sailed into Dartmouth. The
    Mayflower anchored in the River Dart while repairs to the
Speedwell were underway in Bayard's Cove. Ships in the harbor
were laden with wool and cloth to export, others arriving with casks
of wine from Bordeaux. Grateful to see land, Mercy looked out
across the span of water to a village of gray stone houses and
whitewashed doors. Morning had come, and she imagined
housewives and servants were preparing breakfast for their families
or masters. It would be a long time before she could bake bread
again. She set it in her mind, that when the time came, she'd bake
loaves enough to fill the bellies of everyone in the settlement. She
resented the tasteless gruel given the passengers aboard. *It is only for
a little while*, she told herself as she walked along. *I can endure it.*

She found relief in the morning light as the sun touched her face.
She drew in a deep breath at the sight of the gulls whirling overhead.
All that time spent below deck in cramped quarters caused her body
to ache. Time passed slowly, yet her hopes did not fail. They would
make for the sea again.

The deck grew crowded, and although their journey had been
delayed, some spoke excitedly about the village and the peaceful
harbor they had come to. A boat was let down, and many set ashore.
Mercy remained behind waiting for her beloved. When he came up
on deck in a fine suit of clothes, she gazed at him with shining eyes.
Broad-shouldered, his face clean and shaven, his hair touching the
edge of his collar, her desire for him rose. The close quarters of the

ship made it impossible for a man and wife to be alone, to show affection, as they should. He drew on a pair of gloves and looked at her.

"It will do us well to walk the steep hills of the village."

"Are you anxious, my love?" Mercy said with a smile.

"Aye anxious to stretch my legs. Don't you wish to go ashore?" His tone was soft and honeyed, and made her think he had other ideas in mind.

She answered him quietly. "I do not know."

"Everyone is going. A few of the crew are staying behind. It will be lonely below decks with no one around."

"If we both stay behind, we…"

"We'd have a few moments alone."

"For a while anyway."

"Yes, for a while."

He stretched out his hand and Mercy took it. He drew her down the companionway to a quiet place deep in shadow. She sensed the strength of his arms, and felt them tighten around her. She looked into his eyes, his face looking somewhat younger than the day they left Holland.

"I've missed holding you like this," he whispered.

"I have missed it too."

"We cannot stay long."

"Someone is bound to come."

"If they do, remember there is no shame in a husband kissing his wife."

She lightly smiled. "Only if it were a small kiss, on the hand, or cheek. Your kisses possess me, Caleb. You know I would desire more of you."

He put his hands around her face, tilted it up to his and kissed her long and soft. Mercy's heart leaped. Her skin prickled all over, and her longing for him grew. He pulled her closer, his hands gently searching the curves of her body beneath the woolen folds that hid it. Then he moved his mouth from hers—and breathed.

Once the *Speedwell* was declared seaworthy, her sailors climbed the riggings and unfurled the sails. The land change from green and brown, to faded blue along the horizon. The *Mayflower* cut through the waves with its consort close behind. Dolphins and porpoises swam alongside. Mercy leaned against the bulwark and watched them rise out of the water and plunge back into the depths. She smiled, wondering if they were a sign of good to come, that they were there to guide and protect the ships across the sea.

Her hopes swelled with the waves. The sails were shelters, the breeze a touch from the Master's hand. However, below her was a dark cavern. Cold, damp, and suffocating. As she leaned into the wind, she dashed the bleakness from her mind, and basked in the sunlight and the scent of the sea air. She calculated how long it would take to reach the Hudson River—their intended destination. Perhaps a little more than a month? Perhaps less? With fair winds and calm seas, they'd arrive early enough to build homes, forage woodlands for berries and nuts, for the men to hunt deer and wild turkey.

Reinolds's gruff voice interrupted her daydream, and she turned to see him pounding over his poop deck like a nervous cat. His sharp demands were followed by nods and salutes from his crew. Mercy sensed something serious was about to happen.

"Into the wind, helmsman," he shouted.

Once more she and Caleb had their hopes dashed, for after they had sailed one hundred leagues from Land's End, Reinolds declared with a great degree of frustration, his ship was so leaky he must bear up or let her sink at sea. West southwest of the modest headland, he gave the order to turn. The seamen ran over the decks and up the shrouds to save the imperiled ship. The *Speedwell* plunged sharp with the *Mayflower* coming alongside her.

Passengers rushed up on deck. "Why are we turning?"

"What has happened? Are we in peril?"

Mercy reached for Caleb's hand. "They said she was seaworthy. How can this happen?"

"Be calm, Mercy." He took her by the elbow and moved her aside. "We are all disappointed," he whispered. "But we must bear this best we can." He pressed his lips hard. "If you wish to blame someone, blame Reinolds. He should have known whether the *Speedwell* was seaworthy." He cupped his hands over her cheeks. "But then, there may be a greater purpose to this delay."

William Bradford lingered on deck. Mercy watched him set his hands on the bulwark, his face sullen as the gray clouds that gathered above. Turning away from the sea, he walked over to Mercy and Caleb. "Much is amiss here," he said soberly.

Caleb looked at Mercy, then at William. "What are you suggesting, William?"

"Naught that I or anyone else can prove."

"You think this was planned?"

"Possibly. Why else after a refitting we have need to turn back a second time?"

"I hope to God it is not what you are suggesting. It will be on Reinolds's head if it is."

"God forgive him if it is true he means to abort the voyage."

"Why would he do such a thing?" Caleb frowned.

"Starving to death and dying in a foreign land might be in his mind. I'd say that is enough for some."

Mercy's eyes stung with the want to cry. "I should join Dorothy. Perhaps this is not for a woman's ears."

William stopped her. "Please stay, Mercy. Dorothy has gone over to Mrs. Brewster and they are in conversation. It is best for her. If she does ask what you think of all this, I believe you will be able to reassure her. You have done so many times before."

Mercy nodded. "Then let me ask, could this be a sign we should not go to America?"

"I do not believe it is."

"But God could be using it to tell us…"

"To give up?" Caleb said. "God has saved us from drowning a second time, my love. I'd say that is a sure sign His hand is with us."

William put his hand on Caleb's shoulder. "Amen. Those who wish to make the voyage will go on the *Mayflower*."

"Mercy and I will."

"As will Dorothy and I."

Caleb nodded in agreement. William Bradford strode away and joined his wife. Mercy looked at Caleb. She could not cry—no not in front of him or the others. Turning, she went to leave, go below and busy herself with needless tasks. Caleb grabbed her hand and moved her beside him.

"What can I do to make you feel better, my love."

"I am all right, Caleb. Let me go below."

"If the sky is clear tonight," Caleb said, his hand running along her arm, "I would enjoy seeing you in the moonlight. My heart would gladden to see you smile."

Mercy looked into his eyes where she saw his love for her brimming over. Her heart swelled and she put her arms around his neck, set her forehead against his. "I so love you, Caleb."

Other wives were making ready their departure from the ill-fated ship. Mercy listened to their sighs as she folded her cloak and set it aside. The children had gathered in the middle of the deck and looked up at her.

"Faring well, children?"

A few nodded, but the others were silent.

Mary Brewster drew Mercy aside. "It is the heave of this ship and the sounds that make them afraid," she whispered.

"Poor dears," Mercy replied.

"They must learn to be brave. Many more hardships undoubtedly are to follow."

Mercy swallowed. It pained her to think what the children might face. She pressed her lips hard with the want to speak out, to question God. "I hate to think they will suffer. They are too young, and should have happy lives."

"It is the wish of every mother aboard. When I look into my children's faces, I want to hold them tight to my bosom and shield them from every ill. But how can I?"

Mary Allerton sat nearby. "You cannot, and should not."

"Why?" said Mercy.

"We mustn't coddle the children. It will make them weak."

"Fear they will have, but we can comfort them. Surely comfort is not coddling, Mrs. Allerton."

"Obviously you have had a soft life, Mrs. Treymayne."

"Hardly." If only they knew the poverty she had lived in, the small dusty house, the days without food, and how she sweated in a hot kitchen in a raucous inn. Some would have thought a position in a lord's house would have set her on a high pedestal. She had never completely climbed one, and if she had tried, it would have toppled.

She turned away and sat on the floor of the deck. Disapproving eyes followed her, until Dorothy Bradford rose from her seat with her head held high. Her young face looked heavy, blotchy with weariness. "Did not Jesus say 'let the children come to me'? Is he not our example? Hasn't God called us His children and promised to comfort us in times of trouble? What Mercy said is true. We cannot allow the children to waste away from fear."

Mary Brewster's eyes lowered. Others nearby enough to hear Dorothy were silent and grave. Suddenly, the ship trembled fiercely and pitched to starboard. Many held onto posts and anything they could reach. The ship shifted again and rose on the turbulent waves of the sea. Timbers creaked and the children cried out. Others stared at the ceiling, fearful it might collapse and the walls break apart, for seawater poured through with such violence that women gathered their children into their arms shaken—including Mary Allerton.

The moment was great for Mercy as well. Anxiety shot through her, and she too looked above. Why hadn't the men descended from the upper deck? The women needed them. The children longed for their fathers. Mercy yearned for Caleb, for his bravery and comfort. She heard their boots pound over the planks above and from the doorway to the companionway, Caleb and the others made haste to their wives and children.

His hands met her shoulders. The ship settled. The sea calmed, but the shrill wind seeping through the ship was tortuous. Remember Allerton and her sister Mary were weeping. Mary Brewster followed Mercy's led, sat on the damp floor with her boy Love, and drew her older son Wrestling next to her. "It is a fine adventure we've been on, is it not, children?"

Wrestling shook his head. "I want to go home, Mama."

"I know, Wrestling. But you must be brave."

"Are we going to sink?"

"Have faith, my son."

Love Brewster looked up at his mother. "My stomach hurts. I'm hungry."

"Try to think of something else."

"I will try. Father is going to build us a fine house. I can think about that."

Remember looked at Mercy, her eyes tearful. "My father said he'll build a barn and a house."

Mercy set her hand on Remember's and squeezed it. "That is something else to think about. You'll have a garden and..."

"A cow?"

"Surely you will have a cow. And chickens and geese too."

Bartholomew Allerton the oldest of the boys, leaned in with Wrestling Brewster, young John Cooke, and five-year-old Sammie Fuller. "We are going to hunt and fish, Mrs. Treymayne. My father said so."

Mercy smiled. "I have no doubt you boys will make excellent hunters and fishermen." She called to the mastiff, and the beast lumbered over and lay down next to her. She ran her hand over her head.

Wrestling scooted forward. "Mr. Goodman's dogs are the best hunters."

"Indeed they are. Come sit next to Olive. She is not afraid. Neither is Mr. Goodman's spaniel Chester, and he is smaller."

Wrestling squared his shoulders. "Olive and Chester fear nothing." He plopped down next to the dog and put his hand on Olive's neck. Olive nuzzled her massive head into him. The boys began speaking all at once, of what game they would gather. The conversation and the presence of the dogs seemed to ease the children. Yet, every time the *Speedwell* shuddered, fear shone in their eyes. Again, the ship pitched hard, shook, and made a frightful noise.

"Did you see the dolphins earlier?" Mercy tried to distract the children from the danger surrounding the leaky vessel.

Love looked at her. "I saw gray ones."

"Perhaps they are swimming alongside us and helping us back to port."

"We're going back to England," Wrestling said. "My father told me."

"Your father is correct. This old girl has had enough of the sea. She needs a long rest."

Love whispered, "I have had enough of the sea and want to go home."

The leaks worsened. Still the *Speedwell's* timbers held together. Time passed and the waves grew less mountainous. The wind remained steady and pushed the ill-fated ship on. Mercy peered out a porthole. "The sky has cleared. I can see stars. The moon is shining." Mary Brewster and Dorothy drew beside Mercy and looked out the porthole. Hope brightened on their faces.

Caleb grasped her hand and drew her away. He took her topside, and as she stepped out onto the deck, she hurried to the rail. A full moon glowed above the horizon. Shards of light danced on the tips of waves. A moment ago, her heart pounded through her chest, the fear gripping. Now it beat steadily and calmly. The dolphins had returned, and appeared to guide the ship toward land. She leaned over, and Caleb flung his arms around her waist.

"Do not lean too far over, my love. You're liable to fall in."

Mercy laughed. "I have a firm hold on the rail and your embrace to keep me from falling. I cannot help but watch the dolphins."

He pressed her closer to him. "Then I must hold you tight."

Lantern lights along the English coast came into view. Mercy sighed. "It is true what you said earlier, Caleb." She turned into his arms. "God saved us a second time from the sea."

Chapter 23

Mercy woke at the strike of ship bells. She snuggled into Caleb's shoulder and sighed. The waves breaking outside the hull were settled, practically peaceful in comparison to the ocean. She heard no heavy winds, felt no trembling of the timbers. Rising, she rubbed her face with a dry cloth, no water being provided for bathing, and combed out her hair. She folded their blanket and laid it in the cedar trunk she inherited from Uncle Silas. Others stirred and rose from their slumber. She turned her eyes away from the far end of the tight quarters where chamber pots were placed behind a sheet of sailcloth. *Thanks to God, we are in quiet waters. No one seems to be sick this morn.*

Coming through the gloom, Reinhold's first mate ducked under a beam. "We've made it to the harbor. Bring up what you can carry. The rest the crew will unload over to the *Mayflower*. Those of you that have decided to stay behind, your goods will be left ashore."

A great hustle and noise of excitement commenced among the passengers to leave the leaking ship and have some brief chance of stretching their legs on shore. Caleb lifted their trunk and set it across his shoulders. Slipping her cloak over her shoulders, Mercy hurried to the companionway. The women were gathered and the first to go topside with the children. Men followed, carrying what they could. She stood back, not wishing to go up without her beloved. Though safe at the coast, Caleb was her sun and shield, and she could not be parted from his side.

214

Mr. Cushman stood aside as women went up the companionway steps. His face appeared ashen and his countenance grave. "How many of us are to continue?" Caleb asked.

"Nine. The rest have lost hope of making it across the ocean alive, and cannot go on."

"And you and your wife, sir?"

"My wife is anxious. I have a dutiful to protect her. We are staying behind in England until we can leave for Holland." He winched and set hand across his chest.

Stunned, Mercy drew beside him "What is it?"

"A bundle of lead as it were, is crushing my heart."

"I will get Dr. Fuller."

Mr. Cushman shook his head, and when Caleb made a swift turn to fetch Dr. Fuller, Cushman grabbed his arm. "There is no need. It is nothing fresh air and the feel of the sun will not remedy."

"A good broth too, sir," Mercy said. "There are inns ashore."

"Believe me, my wife and I will find one and sup there. I am famished for a hearty meal. I hear you are a superior cook, Mercy. It is my misfortune I will not be able to enjoy it."

She smiled and looked over the heads of the passengers for Mrs. Cushman. Knowing the stress of the venture plagued Mr. Cushman, Mercy worried.

"There will be another ship in a year or so," Caleb said. "Perhaps you can follow. We've had a hard time of it so far, and no one blames those remaining behind."

"Thank you, Caleb. It gives me comfort to know my brothers and sisters see what we must do. It could very well be the Lord has reduced our numbers in order for us to fulfill our mission. This vessel is as leaky as a sieve. It is a miracle we made it back."

Cushman reached for his wife's hand when she approached. Together they went up the steps. Mercy watched them with knitted brows. Surely, Mrs. Cushman knew her husband's ailment. Perhaps this was the true reason they were staying behind.

Another tearful parting fell upon the people, and like Gideon's army, their numbers were divided. Up on deck, a soft breeze blew through the ship's shrouds. The sky was blue, cloudless. With Caleb's arm around her, Mercy heard murmurings.

"We are too many for the work that needs to be done."

"Our lives have been spared."

"Aye from starvation and disease."

"And a brutal winter no doubt."

Mercy pressed closer to Caleb's side. "Some have lost faith in the voyage."

"Do their words make you uneasy, my love?"

"A little, but that is only because what I see in their faces. Until they reach Holland, if they can at all, they will be in danger of persecution."

"What do you see in my face?"

Mercy bit her lip. "Sadness. The voyage has been hampered and there is confusion over what is God's will. How can we ever know for certain, until the voyage is over and we look back at what we've overcome?" She squeezed deeper into his arm and set her head on his shoulder. The *Speedwell* rocked gently as a swan upon the water—but not as calm as one, not as beautiful.

The boat, in which they were to depart the *Speedwell,* and be taken over to the *Mayflower,* swayed in the gentle harbor waves. Descending the *Speedwell's* wooden ladder attached to the hull, Caleb looked up at Mercy and motioned with his hand for her to come down.

"Remind you of anything?" He smiled up at her.

"We did this once before," she called to him. "The fire."

"Yes, so come down slowly. No need to jump this time."

He took a step up close to her heels. Once they reached the last few rungs, Caleb sprang into the boat and held out his arms to her. She felt them grasp her waist. He lifted her in his arms and sat her down. Then he turned to aid other women once Bradford helped Dorothy into the little vessel. Dorothy showed no fear, not a tear in her eye, nor had she suggested she and William return to Leyden. She had to be missing her son, but she held on to her husband's hopes and visions without complaint. Caleb too had hopes and dreams for the New World. Mercy could not disappoint him, or cause him to question their leaving.

The oarsmen glided the boat to the side of the *Mayflower*. Mercy looked up at the rope ladder hanging from the bulwark. Looking more treacherous than the attached ladder of the *Speedwell*, she swallowed and bit her lower lip. Could she make it up to the deck without slipping? If she did slip, her face would turn red as her cloak lining, and the sailors would laugh. She drew in a breath, stood, and with Caleb's help, she grabbed hold and placed her foot into the first rung. The climb was no easy feat, and once she reached the top, the hands of two men of her company grabbed hold and lifted her over. She sighed with relief when her feet touched the deck.

When the others were aboard, Caleb heaved a breath and looked at Mercy. "You could climb the tower of London if you had to, my love. Surefooted you are."

Mercy laughed. "I'd never attempt anything like the Tower. I was a bit nervous, Caleb."

"Wouldn't you like to stay up on deck a while and watch the sunset?"

"Oh, I would indeed." The sun was nigh to setting, and the sky deepening in color. "It is a pretty color red along the horizon," Mercy quietly said.

"The sky is clear for now, but it won't last."

She turned to him, surprised at his prediction. "Oh, I pray it will."

He gave her a quick smile. "I've been wrong before. Let's hope for clear skies as we cross."

"Yes and fair winds. And that we do not have to turn back ever again."

He put his arm across her shoulders. "Can you smell the grass on the hills?"

"I can. Even though we will never return to England, I won't forget." Mercy drew her hood over her head. Her gaze drifted to the cobbled road across from the quay. September breezes blew and the chilly air passed through her cloak. Autumn had arrived early in England, yet there trees only held a hint of color. Mercy shivered and Caleb held her tight. His hand pressed against her waist and she hoped he had not noticed a change. The laces to her waistcoat were cinched a bit closer. Provisions had run low since leaving Southampton, and she ate less to save more. She asked Caleb if the leaders intended on resupplying the voyage. He did not know, but assured her they would not starve.

"Then we must be careful," she told him. "I can bear hunger—but the children...I do not think I can bear seeing them go hungry."

"All of us will be sure they do not."

"You are truly a good man, Caleb."

Caleb let her go, stood to the side and sighed. "You speak too kindly of me."

"I am your wife. I have every right to speak kindly of you." She faced him and set her finger against his lips. The sun warmed his

217

face and droplets started on his brow. She brushed with the back of her hand the soft hair from hers, and then set her palm against his chest. She felt the calm breathing stir and the beating of his heart. He looked into her eyes and she gave him a sympathetic look.

"Dear girl," he whispered with a sad smile. "I am homesick for you."

As the ship lay at anchor, Mercy and the other women watched their men depart to do business ashore. The air was clean and sweet smelling that day, and the master of the ship had a sailor order the passengers out from the gun deck for a *good airing*. From the ship's railing, Mercy waved to Caleb. She smiled when he lifted his hat to her. Her eyes drew away from him at the sudden sound of horses beating over a rise of chalky hills. They appeared as black silhouettes against a magenta horizon as they made their way down the winding road. She had no concern as to the identity of the riders, until she saw them gallop out to where the longboat came ashore. Lumbering behind them, a coach slowed to a halt. A man alighted from it, dressed in a rust-colored doublet, matching breeches, and high boots.

Mercy gasped. She could not believe what her eyes beheld. She stared hard and fear rushed over her like the cold snap of an artic gale. Her hands trembled and she gripped them together. She stepped back. Had he seen her?

"'Tis time for our meal," said Mrs. Brewster. "We must all go below."

"I hope we are having beef," said Wrestling. "Gravy and potatoes."

His mother laughed. "Not this time, my son."

Mercy turned and pressed her hands on the rail behind her. Her heart thumped as she looked at the boy. She hurried to the companionway and entered the gun deck with the others. Perhaps she was safe here where she could not be spotted.

The women handed out trenchers of pea soup. Dorothy Bradford sat on a pallet holding a fair-haired child on her lap. Lamplight shown on their faces like candlelight on a dark night. Through it, Mercy could see the dusky rings under Dorothy's eyes. She glanced around the room. Despite their hardships, there were smiling faces, children in the arms of compassionate folk as they gave thanks and partook of their humble food. What she must do broke over her. She needed to keep the others from suffering because of her.

Dorothy looked up. "What is it, Mercy? Is something the matter?"

Mercy ran her hands up and down her arms. Fear rushed over her, captured her in an unyielding embrace. Her pulse raced and she could feel her heart beating through her gown. Looking worried, Dorothy set the child aside and stood. "By the expression on your face, there is something wrong."

Master Jones ducked under the beam. Mercy turned and it distressed her to see his face looking so grim. She drew up to him.

"Mistress Treymayne," he said, "the constable of this district has called over to me demanding I bring you out."

"Did he say why, sir?" She knew why.

"He carries a warrant."

How was it possible a repeat of what happened in Holland was about to take place? Why hadn't Lord Glenmont given up on her by now? For the sake of all her friends, she had to go with Master Jones and face the fire. She looked around and met their eyes. She could see there was no escaping some doubt in her innocence. If only Caleb had stayed aboard and defended her.

Mary Brewster stood forward. "Master Jones. Mercy has broken no law other than she scorned a man's unwelcomed advances. We all witnessed how he hounded her, and we stand beside her. She is innocent, and you, sir, must protect her, for her husband is not present."

Jones nodded. "Yes, I know. He has gone ashore. Still I am under His Majesty's law in these waters and want no trouble. I'll do what I can to keep the constable from coming aboard."

Mercy lifted her eyes to Master Jones and saw the concern in his eyes. No longer could she allow this to continue. For the sake of her friends and her husband, she had to face what seemed to be the inevitable. She would face her accuser. "I will speak to this man."

"Mrs. Treymayne, I'll…"

"Please, sir. Allow me to pass. I'll cause no trouble."

"You think I haven't had to deal with people like this before?"

"I've no doubt you have, sir."

"I'll send word back I have no one by the name McCrea aboard."

"My wedded name is known to them. Send me over for the sake of the others."

"There will be no delay to sail. You understand?"

219

Mercy nodded and headed to the upper deck with Master Jones. He ordered his first mate Robert Coppin, to call out across the span of water for them to return the boat. Mercy waited at the bulwarks, her hair beneath the hood of her cloak and her eyes fixed on the shore. The coach rolled back from the movement of the horses. Black in color, the seal blood red, the look of it sent a shiver down her spine, but not as much as the sight of Lord Glenmont. What possessed a man to the point of obsession? Was it pride, or something deeper—a canker rooted in the soul?

Her eyes drifted over to Caleb. Armed men stood in front of him, William Bradford, Martin Flagg, Myles Standish, and three of Jones's crew. Caleb moved forward with Captain Standish, and by the gestures of his hands, she knew he did his best to persuade the constable to leave in peace. When the constable threw his hands over his hips and his men raised their muskets, Mercy narrowed her eyes and fisted her hands. Sweat beaded at her temples, and she yanked the coif from her hair. It fell over her shoulders, blew back in the breezed from her ruddy cheeks.

Glenmont has gone too far with this folly. He brings armed men with him and they stand at the ready in front of my husband and friends. I will not cower to him and his pursuit of me.

The boat reached the ship, and Jones helped Mercy grab hold of the ladder and climb down. Her hands shook as she gripped the coarse rungs. "The Lord is my refuge," she whispered. "He is my strength."

A soldier waited for her, and when she reached the boat, he aided her aboard. He would not look her in the eye, but sat in the stern with knitted brows as the oarsmen shoved away. Dorothy and Mary Brewster leaned over the bulwark and called down to her.

"Do not go, Mercy."

"Listen to Dorothy, Mercy."

"Yes. You must stay with us."

She lifted her face to them, the light striking her eyes. She smiled, and then turned to face the shoreline. Sailors pulled hard on the oars and soon the boat skidded over the rocky beach. The hands that reached for her where Caleb's. His arm went tightly around her waist and she walked with him toward the constable and his men. As for her friends. Their faces were grave, brows bent, and their cheeks ruddy with the pumping of their racing hearts. Caleb's face was like chiseled stone—hard and unmovable, determined. His eyes were riveted on Lord Glenmont as he stepped forward with Mercy held firmly against him.

Chapter 24

In silence, away from the tide and the rocky beach, Mercy held Caleb's hand and paused in front of the constable. His name was not revealed to her, as she looked at him composed and speechless. She waited for him to speak, and lowered her eyes when he looked at her with doubtful eyes.

"You are Mercy McCrea?" he asked. His voice was lowered and he spoke amiable for a man of his position with a warrant in his hand.

"I was, sir. I am now Mercy Treymayne. This man is my husband."

Caleb held Mercy closer. "Do not shackle my wife, sir. She has done nothing to deserve it."

For a moment, the constable eyed them both. "You will vouch she will not flee?"

"How can she being among so many if you mean to take her."

The constable looked humored. "You'd be surprised. Some women are like grease. They slip out of your fingers before you can hold on to anything else."

As he spoke, Mercy lifted her eyes. "Sir, I will not run. But I beg you to let my husband come with me."

"He may," said the constable. "But you'll be shut away in the goal, if the magistrate is not ready to…receive you, ma'am."

"This must be over swiftly," cried Caleb. "We are to sail."

The constable rubbed his chin. "I cannot promise anything, but I will try. Most likely the magistrate is at the inn enjoying his daily cups of port." He turned to one of his officers. "Go find him," he said. "Tell him it is an urgent case that must be dealt with immediately."

Mercy gave the man a grateful smile, though the heart within her sank. The constable took her kindly by the arm and the others followed. "We'll make a quick end to this," Caleb said. His eyes were set on Glenmont, and that evil fiend exchanged glare for glare as he leaned against the door of his coach with a look of satisfaction on his face. Mercy glanced at him once. Then turned her eyes away.

Elegantly dressed, Glenmont stepped away from the door of his coach. "You have done well. Name your reward and I shall give it."

The constable frowned. "I seek no reward from you, my lord. Do not offer it."

Glenmont laughed. "I shan't. Only a fool would refuse money." His arrogance not only resonated in the tone of his voice, but in his demeanor and posture. It shown on his face and his eyes were aflame with pride—pride that said he believed he had captured his quarry at last.

"Ah, Mercy, we meet again." To mock Mercy, Glenmont bowed and lifted his hat. "I suppose you are wondering how I found you. You've been like a cat in the dark."

She stared at the ground wishing it would suck her down.

Caleb took a step forward. "Do not speak to her."

Glenmont raised his brows. "And what is she to you?"

"She is my wife."

"How unfortunate. You'll regret ever laying eyes upon a thief let alone marrying one."

"Mercy is no thief. You deceived her, threatened her." Caleb turned to the constable. "Sir, my wife is innocent. I beg of you to listen before you do anything."

The constable's eyes clouded over with concern. "I have no choice but to take her, Mr. Treymayne. If I do not, I myself will be accused of a crime, and I have a wife and child at home. If she is innocent, you have nothing to fear. Our magistrate is a just man."

Caleb grabbed Mercy with a little cry. He held her against him so tight she gasped and tears came into her eyes. "Mercy...my love..."

"I'm not afraid," she said. "Tell me that you love me, and let me go."

He drew her closer, pressed his lips upon her bowed head, and repeated his love for her until one of the constable's officers pulled them apart. "I want this to be over. I want peace."

Hard as she knew it was for him, Caleb let go. As they led her away, she looked back over her shoulder. His eyes stayed fixed upon her with a resolute gaze. He spoke to the others, crammed on his hat and followed. Lord Glenmont withdrew inside his carriage.

An hour later in a dank and dark courtroom, Mercy stood before a magistrate's bench. Misty sunlight seeped through the only window in the room. Caleb, William Bradford, and Martin waited in the seats nearby. She looked at Caleb. Anger tightened the muscles in his face. His jaw twitched. He set his arms over his knees and clenched his hands. Her heart stretched out to him. He'd been so brave, and now he faced the chance of losing her. She saw beads of sweat on his forehead and knew his pulse beat as loudly and hard as hers. She wished she could bring him to her side, hold her, and give her courage to face a hearing before a magistrate loyal to the King.

When her eyes shifted to William Bradford, she saw compassion in his eyes. He met her glance and nodded, almost unnoticeably, and she understood if he could speak words of comfort and prayers he would. Reverend Brewster would have been there as well, but the King pursued his life and he was wise to stay aboard the *Mayflower*. Dorothy too, and Mary Brewster. It was best, Mercy thought. She did not want Dorothy to weep or Mary Brewster to speak her mind forwardly.

The room smelled of the unwashed and the heavily perfumed. The light seemed yellow tinted as if some mire had found its way into it. People in the rear seats murmured. Lord Glenmont stared at Mercy, and brushed his finger over his mustache. For the briefest moment, she looked at him. She turned her eyes away and stared forward—at the judgment seat.

At last, the magistrate entered. To Mercy, he looked cold, insensitive to her plight, one apt to deal out swift merciless judgment. Would she hear the words *you'll hang by the neck until dead*? Or would prison await her? Her limbs trembled. She gripped her gown. Then lowered her head. The floor under her feet was worn. How many others had stood there before her?

"Who stands as a witness for this woman?" Already the magistrate sounded bored.

"I do, if it pleases Your Honor."

The magistrate looked at William Bradford. "And you are?"

"William Bradford, Your Honor, one of the pilgrims on the *Mayflower*."

The magistrate's eyes shifted to Mercy. "What better place to hide than among a group of peaceful Christians, Mercy McCrea."

"I can vouch for her, and so can this man." When Bradford said his name, Martin stood with his hat in hand and bowed. "Martin Flagg has known her many years. Her husband sits beside me, Your Honor," said Bradford.

The magistrate's eyebrows arched. "Her husband, are you? Stand when I speak to you, sir."

Caleb stood. "Yes, my lord. I am her husband Caleb Treymayne."

"Naturally you believe your wife."

"She gave me no reason not to, my lord." Then he looked at Lord Glenmont. "But this man gives me every reason to believe he is a liar."

"You will withhold such words. Lord Glenmont is not on trial here." The magistrate cleared his throat. "Sit down, sir. You will not speak to defend her, being her husband, for you are bias as any good husband would be."

Bradford then spoke up. "Then I will speak, Your Honor. Mercy McCrea is a godly woman falsely accused. She committed no crime, and has been with us in Holland."

"After fleeing England," spat Lord Glenmont.

The magistrate held up his hand. "We will get to you in a moment, Lord Glenmont. Let this man speak. How do you know this woman would not have attempted thievery? Have you ever known her to commit a crime?"

"We know her to be truthful, trustworthy, and faithful to the Lord's commandments. She will not lie. She told us her story, that his lordship pursued her, and when he did not have his way, he accused her of attempting to steal as a way of punishing her."

The magistrate puffed out his cheeks and acknowledged Lord Glenmont. "What say you, Lord Glenmont? This man says the woman is trustworthy. Have you proof she is not?"

"She is no more godly a person than a harlot on the street, my lord magistrate. I so testify, she was about to steal from my lady wife when I caught her. The necklace was in her hand."

"That is no proof of her trying to steal it."

"I believe it is, and she should hang for it."

"I see no reason for a hanging, my lord. There is no crime in holding a necklace in one's hand."

"Then prison!"

Mercy collapsed against the railing and cried. "Please, my lord, you must believe in my innocence. I would not lie."

The magistrate swished a beringed hand at her. "Calm yourself, woman. Stand up straight and plead your defense."

Rallying her courage and standing straight, Mercy went on. "I confess I did hold a necklace belonging to Lady Glenmont in my hand, but not in order to steal it. I admired it, certainly, but I would not take anything I did not own, especially from her ladyship who had been kind to me. I was her lady's maid, my lord. All I was doing was making her room ready for when she would return home. Lord Glenmont walked into the room. He said he would let me go if I…"

"Yes, go on."

"If I gave my body to him." She hung her head.

"And what did you do? Did you give it to him?"

"I did not, my lord. I fought to keep my virtue."

"Say on if you have more."

She raised her eyes. "He locked me in. A servant let me out, and I fled. I was frightened, my lord. I hurried as fast as I could to my grandparents and told them everything."

"And where are they?"

"They are dead, my lord."

"Well, Ipswich is a long way from here even if they weren't. Go on."

"They convinced me to flee to Holland, to my Uncle Silas."

She went on to tell her story of how Silas took her in, how she met the Separatists and Caleb. Now she had hopes of leaving England for the New World, to begin a new life, a family and home with her beloved. Caleb heaved a breath, and when she glanced at him and saw how he struggle to refrain from speaking, she said, "Is it not enough punishment for me to see my husband's distress, my lord? Would it not be enough for us to leave England forever?"

The magistrate turned his eyes back to Glenmont. "We of the upper class often take liberties with those below us. It is an unfortunate fact that cannot be ignored. Perhaps you have mistaken this woman's actions and have had your pride hurt?"

"My pride is intact. She is a liar."

Caleb set his feet firm and stood. "You attempted to take her innocence. What was she to do, allow you to take it? No, my Lord Glenmont, you are the guilty party here, for you sought revenge. And for what, sir? To satisfy your wounded vanity."

The magistrate pounded his podium. "Be silent and sit down."

His lordship's mouth jerked. "Yes, sit down, you heretic. I'm not accustomed to being challenged."

"And I'm not accustomed to having a bully falsely accuse my wife and threaten her life."

Bradford, ever calm, placed his hand on Caleb's shoulder.

Caleb gritted his teeth. "You've made a mistake, my lord."

His lordship's color mounted and he laid his hand over the hilt of his rapier. "I'll have justice before the day is over."

Caleb's face flushed. Bradford held him back, urged him to be calm.

"The court must come to order," said the magistrate. The atmosphere grew intense, and Mercy felt her knees weaken. A change came over the magistrate's face as he lifted a paper and unfolded it. He read it, and then set it down. His eyes latched onto Mercy.

"I have here an affidavit signed by his lordship, of the thing you are accused of doing, being he found you in Lady Glenmont's bedroom stealing some of her possessions, and when he confronted you, you attacked him in an attempt to murder him. It says," and he adjusted his spectacles, "you picked up a letter opener and plunged it at him. How do you plead?"

Her eyes widened. "I'm innocent of such a charge."

"Did you not set violent hands upon a lord high in His Majesty's favor?"

"Violent hands no, only hands meant to protect myself from the violence he threw upon me."

The magistrate frowned and Lord Glenmont swore beneath is breath. "Included in this document are statements from his butler and two footmen, who say you fled. That you have admitted to."

"It is true, my lord, I fled."

"You made no attempt to clear your name?"

Mercy lowered her eyes. "No, my lord. I was afraid."

The magistrate asked Lord Glenmont to stand and speak. With a flourish of his lace cuffs, his lordship repeated what he had written. His expression grew grave with each word. His voice deliberately trembling. "I feared my beloved wife would have returned home to find me dead on the floor in a pool of blood. What could I have done, but locked this girl in until a constable arrived? My dear lady was shaken after she returned home to find her companion, whom I had chosen for her, a girl we thought to be honest and trustworthy, had attempted to plunge a letter opener into my breast."

The longer he spoke, the more it appeared the magistrate believed him. He leaned forward after his lordship returned to his seat. "Now that I have heard both sides, I have a tendency to believe his lordship. Therefore…"

Caleb cried out and Mercy hung her head. "Is this English justice?"

"Sit down, sir," the magistrate said with a firmness that silenced the room. "I have the authority to pass sentence on offenders of this type and rebels and heretics. Do you wish to be next in line for disrupting this court?"

With tearful eyes, Mercy turned to her husband. She wished she could throw herself into his arms. She kept her eyes on Caleb's anxious face and angry eyes. He looked at her helpless to do anything, to fight for her, to rescue her from an uncertain fate. He lowered to his seat looking defeated, while tears slipped down her cheeks. It was over—her life and the dreams she had of Caleb and their new life together in a new world.

Bradford's face was drawn, his eyes distraught. Martin lowered his head and clasped his hands. The magistrate continued. "Mercy Treymayne, I hereby find you guilty of thievery and the willful attempted assault of Lord Glenmont. Therefore, you shall be put in the local goal until I decide what to do with you. I need to mull over this case more closely."

Suddenly, the hall doors flung open. Heads turned and gasps went around the room. A lady in a dark blue cloak marched inside with a woman behind her. The hood concealed her face, until she stopped and with gloved hands lowered it to her shoulders. Mercy fastened her eyes on her as her pulse raced. Lord Glenmont's face turned scarlet from his hairline to the collar of his doublet.

The magistrate blinked. "Who may you be, my lady?"

The gracious lady raised her chin. "Lady Glenmont."

The magistrate's jaw fell open. "My lady, forgive me. I should have realized…"

"That I am his lordship's wife? How could you?" She turned on her satin heels and smiled at Mercy. "I have come to speak on behalf of this girl, who is most seriously accused of an act she did not commit."

"My lady, you are welcome to speak in my courtroom. You say this girl is innocent?"

"I do." Her ladyship stepped forward. She stood in front of the magistrate's bench and turned so the crowd could hear her speak. "She is telling the truth. She is innocent of all the charges set against her."

"And how do you know this, my lady?" asked the magistrate.

"I can so testify to it. So can my servant who stands behind me."

Penance came forward when the magistrate gestured to her with his hand. She spread her skirts and made a short dip from her knees. She knew all there was to know about his lordship's ways. It shown in her expression, one that said she would stand up for Mercy without fear of punishment.

"Your name?"

"Penance Firth, my lord."

"Take a seat. I'll call you if I must." The magistrate waved his hand. "Prithee continue, my lady."

"Mercy McCrea is no criminal. Firstly, she did not steal from me. Every jewel and every belonging of mine is where I left them. She had been my companion for some time, and I trusted her implicitly. I've been deeply saddened to have lost her as well as concerned for her life. When I learned of Lord Glenmont's plan to pursue her here, I had to follow. Mercy is not in the wrong. Rather Lord Glenmont is in his attempt to pressure her to give her virtue to him."

"I see, and the other charge?"

"On my word, she made no attempt to murder Lord Glenmont— a known womanizer." A few of the aristocrats in the audience frowned and whispered to each other. The rest of the audience murmured. "Oh yes. A wife knows."

"And as Lord Glenmont's wife, you would lay the blame on him? Can you prove her innocence in this matter?"

"I can by my testimony. May I go on?"

"Please. Continue."

"I stood at a window in the hall facing my bedroom balcony. I had returned home. The moon was bright and I paused to look out at it. His lordship did not expect me until much later, but I had a craving for Mercy's sweet cocoa and left my host early. Her sweet cocoa helps me sleep, my lord."

With this, her ladyship smiled and quiet laughter slipped through the magistrate's lips. "My wife makes a fine cocoa too. Seems to be all the rage…" He stopped short and shook his head. "Oh, what am I about?" Returning to matters at hand, he leaned forward. "So you arrived home earlier than expected. What is it you saw from the window?"

"I saw his lordship grab Mercy and attempt to ravish her. My housekeeper was away so I called for Penance my cook. I told her to go to Mercy and tell her to flee. I found my husband perfectly hale, without a scratch on his person, dead drunk in a chair. I took the key from his pocket and gave it to Penance. I also found, as I told you, my jewels in their proper place. Therefore, you see, Mercy McCrea did only what any woman would have done." Lady Irene turned her eyes to Lord Glenmont. "She defended her virtue against a libertine."

Lord Glenmont looked unmoved, but his eyes were hateful. "If you believe my wife over me, my lord, I cannot say I blame you. She speaks convincingly."

The magistrate tapped the bench with his fingertips. "And with the truth, Lord Glenmont."

"Yes, according to how she saw things."

"It is a serious crime to falsely accuse a person, even if one is a lord of the realm. You have time to retract your accusations, or I'll have her ladyship's servant give testimony. On that score, her ladyship as a witness is enough to convince me you were deep in your cups and saw things, as they were not. Mistress Treymayne, you are free to go."

Mercy sunk forward. Caleb hurried to her and caught her in his arms. Lord Glenmont stormed out to the cobblestones where his dreary carriage waited. Mercy hurried over to Lady Irene. She stopped quickly before her and curtsied. "My lady, how can I thank you?"

Lady Irene raised Mercy up. "There is no need to thank me. I know what I saw, Mercy. I could not stand by and see my husband destroy another person's life. Simon decided to join me when I told him I was lonely for the house I inherited from my father here in Plymouth. People talk in this town, and when we heard the

Mayflower had arrived, Simon suspected you aboard. Those are the only details I have." Lady Irene's gaze fell on Caleb. "And who is this handsome gentleman at your side."

"My husband Caleb Treymayne."

He stepped forward and bowed. "At your service, my lady."

"And these gentlemen are our good friends William Bradford and Martin Flagg."

Bradford and Martin bowed.

"I've heard your name before, Mr. Bradford. You are among the Separatists, I believe."

"Yes, my lady, I am. Our fellowship will rejoice you arrived at the last moment and saved our sister."

"And you, Mr. Flagg. I recall Mercy mentioning you to me in a very favorable light."

Martin shifted on his feet and turned his hat in his hands. He glanced at Mercy and she smiled.

"I hear you are soon to sail aboard the *Mayflower*," said Lady Irene. "You should hurry back. You must be anxious to sail."

As they were leaving, Mercy hugged Penance. "Thank you for all you have done for me," she said. "I will never forget you."

Penance stepped back and wiped her eyes with the corner of her apron. With a little sigh, she hurried out. "She has a sensitive soul," Lady Irene said. "Your embrace meant much to her."

"If appropriate, my lady, I would have embraced you as well."

"There is no law that says you cannot, dear child." Lady Irene held out her arms to Mercy. "I wish you well on your journey and your future."

Outside the courtroom door, Glenmont looked out his coach window. "The sea will exact judgment on you all. As for you, Irene, I'll see to it you haven't a penny to your name."

An imperious look rose on Lady Irene's face and she laughed. "Simon, have you forgotten my father left me an enormous inheritance and that the country house is mine? I have no need of your money—or you for that matter."

She whirled away to her own private coach, climbed in with Penance and waved farewell to Mercy. A frigid wind swept over the land, raking the fields and causing the townsfolk to shutter their windows. Grey hurrying clouds drifted across the sky. Fog moved in from the sea, and a misty rain began to fall. Mercy drew her hood over her head. She lifted her face, allowing the drizzle to wash over her. She felt happy to be alive—happy to be free of Lord Glenmont.

Pronounced innocent the past was behind her and Caleb. They made their way down the dirt road with hope in their hearts, even though the weather had turned dismal.

"I will hurry ahead," said William Bradford. "I must tell the others the good news." With an energy Mercy had not seen in William since leaving Holland, he hurried down a slope to the beach where others were waiting.

Mercy stood on the precipice above the sea, and turned at the rumbling of coach wheels. It stopped shortly ahead of them, and Lord Glenmont's footman opened the coach door for him to exit the dark interior. His lordship's face blistered with anger. He slammed the door shut and pushed the footman aside with a vigor that set people gapping. The poor man stumbled back, his eyes wide, his face red with shame. Glenmont stormed toward Mercy. Caleb set her behind him.

Facing Caleb, Glenmont drew his rapier and pointed it beneath Caleb's chin. "Best you find a sword, scoundrel."

Caleb looked bewildered. He moved his head slowly side to side and pressed his brows together. "I won't fight you, my lord."

"Then I will slice your throat where you stand."

"Take care with your words, my lord. They may come back to trouble you." Caleb took Mercy by the arm and moved her beside Martin. "Take her to the ship." Martin nodded. Mercy begged him not to engage Lord Glenmont, but Caleb held a finger to her lips. He smiled. "No need to worry. I know what I'm doing."

"Please do not answer him, Caleb."

"I'll not kill him…wound his arrogance perhaps, but I'll not take his life." He set his hands on his hips. "It amazes me, my lord, how persistent you are to exact revenge. I suppose you have not read, or perhaps you have and you dismissed 'pride cometh before a fall'.

Like a spoiled child, Glenmont huffed. "Do not quote scripture at me, you dog. I'll show you how my pride wins me the day. Your death will bring me the pleasure of seeing your whore crushed. No woman will spurn me."

Caleb laughed. "You never grew out of your spoiled upbringing. You don't behave like a man but as a child. You may be accustomed to getting what you want, but you failed when it came to my wife. In the end, after all the trouble you've gone through to find her and persecute her, you lost, my lord. "

Glenmont circled his weapon. "Your loyalty to your wife is impressive."

"Unlike yours for your wife, my lord?"

"I've never had the need to be loyal. Will you fight?"

"If you come at me again and a sword is handed to me, I'll have no other choice."

The twisting of his lordship's face made him look the madman he was as he spat his fury into the unwelcomed wind. Glenmont's lips trembled and he called for his footman to supply Caleb a weapon. He raised his rapier, and with a flick of the tip, he nicked Caleb's cheek. Caleb's hand flew against the wound and Mercy cried out. Caleb narrowed his eyes and set his mouth hard. He had been pushed to the limit. His feet were firm and his body unmovable as blood oozed between his fingers.

Mercy touched the wound. "He's cut you. Come away, Caleb."

He looked down at her. "Back away with Martin."

"I cannot."

"You will." He turned her in front of Martin. "Move her away, Martin." Martin grabbed hold of Mercy's arm and she attempted to shake him off, but his grip was too firm.

"If you kill Lord Glenmont, you will hang," she cried. Martin pulled her further back. "If he kills you I will die too. Please come away."

Mercy felt faint and leaned against Martin. The thought of Glenmont running his sword through her beloved made her gasp for air and her heart pound. His lordship gritted his teeth and lunged at Caleb with a stab to his chest. Caleb, quick on his feet, leapt back, the rapier missing his him by mere inches. Glenmont rushed forward. He thrust, and Caleb blocked the blow and then with the strength Glenmont could not match, he beat back his lordship's blade with a fury. Glenmont twisted, and the more Caleb went at him, beating his blade against Glenmont's, the more his lordship weakened. Finally, he lost his footing and fell. Mud splashed over his lavish clothes and he looked up at Caleb in a daze. Caleb put his boot on his lordship's blade and called the footmen over.

"His lordship needs help getting up from the mud."

Glenmont clenched his teeth and scurried up. "Take your boot from my sword."

"Our disagreement is over, my lord." Caleb handed the blade back to his lordship's footmen.

"Return to your coach and be gone. Go back to your empty house and your empty life. Your pursuit of my wife is over, and thank God, she will never lay eyes on you again."

Beyond them, the magistrate accompanied by a group of men rushed toward them. The man's cloak blew around his legs in the wind, and he buffed out his cheeks as he walked in haste. "My Lord Glenmont. I'll have no more of this in my district."

Glenmont frowned, grabbed his rapier from his footman and sheathed it. He made a swift turn and stomped to his coach. Defeated, he climbed inside dirty than before, and the coach rolled off. Caleb put his arm over Mercy, and with Martin walking alongside them, they headed back down to the shore. She stopped and pressed her mouth hard. Caleb looked at her. "What is it?"

"I could have lost you. Do no fighting again." She smacked his shoulder and he laughed.

Martin skipped ahead. "I thought he was amazing."

Days had passed since Mercy's deliverance from Lord Glenmont's pursuit. The ocean was blue as blue could be during the day. In the evenings, it glowed with crimson red as the sun lowered. In the mornings, the rising sun spread upon it sheets of gold and turned to palest green to amethyst. At night the waters mirrored the stars and the wind laid low, the only sound the lapping of the waves against the hull of the *Mayflower*.

On the eleventh day of September, a harvest moon peeked above the horizon and ascended among a multitude of stars and constellations. The night was cool and the air sweet with the scent of salt water. Leaving the airless below, Mercy and Caleb strolled on deck. The sight of the moon and its lucent orange color charmed her.

"Is it not beautiful, Caleb?" she sighed. "And the sea air—oh, how I wish we could take it below. There is little fresh air blowing in through the portals to make a difference."

He stretched out his arm and pointed into the night sky. "Look at that line of light filtering down from the moon into the sea. Do you see it?"

"Yes, the water is illuminated by it." She fastened her eyes with intent on the ripples in the waves. "What is moving within it?"

"A mother whale and her calf. The light attracts them. The Vikings called it the Wale's Way. You see things when in the King's Navy." "And the stars. You know so much about them."

"My father taught me. He was a learned man, although he never went to university. He said to me, 'Caleb, God has written His Word across the Heavens.' Of course I was in awe of what he said."

"Show me something. What is that group of stars?" Mercy pointed.

"The Big Dipper, and above it is the North Star. Sailors use it to navigate." He turned her around and brought her to the other side of the ship. "Look there, it's what the Romans called the *Via Lactea*, the Milky Circle."

"Oh, it is the most striking thing I have ever seen. In Ipswich there is so much fog, you can barely make out the stars." She set her head against his arm. "I think I shall miss it for a very long time, but only because of Nan and Grandpapa. It is they I miss and Uncle Silas too. They were good to me more than I realized. Without them, there is not telling how my life would have been." She lifted her head to look at Caleb. "Did I tell you about the wonderful tops Grandpapa carved?" He nodded. "Every year, on the date of my birth, he would make me a new one and paint it a pretty color. He and Nan would tell me not to speak of it to anyone since the Puritans did not approve of celebrating birthdays. So I kept it a secret."

"I can carve tops," Caleb said. "Tell you this. I'll carry on your grandfather's craft and make the children aboard tops. It will give them something to do."

Mercy smiled, and in the moment, she believed the rest of the voyage would go on without incident or trouble. With the beauty of the sea, the glow of the moon and stars, and the sweet air, how could anything go wrong?

A hazy cluster twinkled in a cloud of purple and silvery magenta. Mercy absorbed the scene. Her heart filled with awe and a sense of tranquility. The further they sailed from England, the sweeter independence became. She would live in peace with the man she adored, build a home and raise a family. Never had she imagined such love as he drew his arm around her. Perhaps it was the romance of the night—or perhaps it was the natural course love meant to take.

Chapter 25

Mary Brewster rallied the children and ushered them up the companionway to the main deck. The sea air was reviving, and the children immediately chased each other about the deck like frolicking pups. Like a soothing balm, the air passed into their lungs, a sweet salty air that threw off weariness from being below in the cramped hold.

"Look how happy they are," said Mary Brewster to Mercy when she drew up beside her. "We can learn so much from them, and be as the Lord said we should be…as little children."

Mercy handed out broken pieces of ship's biscuit and an apple slice to each child. The provisions were low, and so the adults went without in order for the children to have enough to eat. "The voyage has not been easy for the children. They deserve to have fun. Some of the crew do not think so, and sneer at them. They are too young to understand why, and I wish Master Jones would tell the sailors to go easy on the children."

"He has. Let's hope they obey his orders, otherwise they will be dealt with."

One of the sailors, tall and strongly built with blunt features, stared at them with cruel eyes. Proud and profane, he strode toward the children. "You kids stop runnin' 'bout the deck," he shouted. Then he barred his teeth at them and growled.

"We are only playing a game, sir," said Love Brewster.

The man's shadow fell over Love. He bent down, nose-to-nose with the boy. "If you don't stop *playin' yur* game, I'll throw you all overboard."

The children ran back to their mothers frightened by his threat. The exception was Love. He stood straight as an arrow and looked the sailor in the eyes. Caleb did not like it. Bradford strode over to the sailor, and when he looked up from the rope he coiled, he threw back his shoulders and looked meanly at Bradford.

"You have no call to be contemptible with your language, or threaten our children. I'll report this to Master Jones."

The man brought his face closer to Bradford's, the corners of his eyes creasing with ire. "I'll do anything I want. You give me any trouble and I'll throw you overboard too."

When Caleb saw the crude deckhand was in a notion to strike Bradford, he stood forward and placed himself between the two men. Jones looked down from the helm and called out, "You there, I'll not have any more of that on my ship. If you don't leave these people alone, I'll have you clapped in irons."

"Aye, sir." The seaman shrugged and swaggered off.

Murmurs went around the deck, and the women kept their children close. "He frightens me, Caleb," Mercy said. "Only a cruel man would threaten children. And the way he spoke to William."

"He's all talk, Mercy. You heard Master Jones. If that man has any brains, he'll obey his orders or spend the rest of the voyage in irons."

"It is strange, but I feel sorry for him." Mercy looked at the man as he continued to coil a rope. Abruptly Caleb turned with her and walked toward the stern. Mercy looked at him. "Caleb?"

"I want him to take his wicked eyes off you."

"I do not fear him."

"Bravery is one of your virtues. Certainly not his. He's a coward to behave the way he has."

"He seems to hate all people. We must diligently quench it with kindness."

She took a step back and spoke to the seaman. "Sir, no doubt the voyage has put us all on edge. Perhaps you could sit with us this evening when we have our meal. I'm hoping the cook will allow me to prepare the soup tonight." She smiled as he stared with distain. "I imagine your mother made a fine soup, and it will remind you of her and how she raised you."

"You don't know a thing about me," he snapped back.

"That is true. However, I hope I'm right about your mother. Was she a good Christian woman?"

He paused with a twitch of his lip and narrowed his eyes. "Tried to be."

"She must have taught you as a lad to treat others as you would want them to treat you."

"I don't remember." He coiled the rope faster.

"Sir, you'll never know peace until you know the Prince of Peace. Won't you join us this evening? Come and hear us sing and read the scripture."

"Go away. I want nothin' to do with any of ya."

Mercy paused and drew in a breath. How she wished she could have touched his soul. Not even the mention of his mother could do it. What made him so calloused? Some deep pain? Some misfortunate or neglect? An absent parent or was it the loss of a love?

"Alright, I'll go, but try to think about what I said." She lifted her skirts and turned. Then she looked back at him from over her shoulder. "If you should change your mind…"

"I won't." He turned his back on her.

Caleb gave her a reproachful glare. "You're wasting your time, Mercy." He lifted her hand into his. "Still, I suppose what you did was out of compassion. I won't chide you for it."

"He is a broken man," she said, walking with him near the forecastle.

"From the moment I first saw you in Silas's barn, I knew you were the woman I had dreamed of. I've never met a more tender heart." He looked down at her, in awe of her kindness even for a cruel man.

The following morning broke with a fair wind. A cloudy sky streaked indigo and gray and warned of foul weather. For now, they were given sudden reprieve that brought sighs and words of praise. The passengers were allotted a gallon of beer a day, water being undrinkable and apt to cause dysentery. Mugs of it were handed out, and like Noah who planted a vineyard and was made happy by his wine, the Separatists' low spirits were lifted a little.

Mercy finished washing her face, and Caleb touched her shoulder. She turned and he tapped her cheek. "What is there to eat, my love? More ship's biscuit or porridge, I suppose."

She rubbed his jaw and smiled. "Ship's biscuit is better than nothing. Ah, but you need a shave, dear Caleb."

He ran his hand over his morning beard. "Indeed I do, but I'm thinking a beard will keep me warm."

She frowned. "Oh, do not hide your face from me. It is so handsome."

He put his arms around her and waited. She wished they could kiss long and soft in secret. She longed to feel the warmth of his hands, but on such a journey, it was not meant to be. "I'm off to see Master Jones," said Caleb. "I'm not the kind to sit idle."

He headed toward the companionway, and before going up the rungs, he looked over and smiled at her. Then he headed topside. Those close enough to see smiled, for it was not forbidden amongst the believers to show light gestures of affection. A light kiss upon a cheek. Hands held. A wife's head upon her husband's shoulder or laid against the breast of his doublet.

"It is true he loves you, Mercy," said Mary Brewster, as she pushed a needle through a torn garment. "It does me good to see husband and wife in love."

Mercy drew down next to Mary on one of the barrels against the wall. "Can I help?"

"I'm finished. It was but a small tear." Mary made a knot and broke the thread.

"Did you hear the news?"

"What news? Is it good?"

"I'm afraid not. That seaman who reviled us fell sick during the night. Elder Brewster tried to speak to him, but the man cursed him."

"Poor soul. He had his spirit crushed somehow."

"How can a man be so careless with the name of the Lord and curse a man of God?"

Strange how Mercy's heart ached. "If Dr. Fuller needs a nurse, I'll do it." She stood. "Perhaps I can speak to the man. Perhaps I can ease his suffering."

Mary Brewster frowned and closed her sewing basket. "And listen to the man's ravings and subject yourself to his violent behavior? You should stay away no matter how sick he is. Besides, the ship's surgeon Mr. Heale is caring for him."

Mercy lowered her eyes. "I understand, but if I can help…"

Dr. Fuller stood in the glare of one of the lanterns. He looked tired. Dark circles were beneath his eyes and his face was drawn and pale. "There is no need, Mercy. The man is dead."

Each man, woman, and child gathered on the main deck. Mercy marveled how loud the wind sounded and how silent grew the people. She looked at the faces of the crew. Some lowered their chins to their chests. Others stood relaxed. Master Jones had the look of a man accustomed to deaths and burials at sea—his expression stoic and stiff as the canvass above him. Unmoved by the event, he faced William Brewster.

"He was as heathen a man as you'd ever find and would not wish a prayer to be spoken over him, Reverend, but speak in brief, sir, for the benefit of the others."

"It is not our way to speak words over the dead, but to be reverently silent."

"Well, he would have preferred it that way, godless as he lived."

"We are hardly godless as you well know, sir. We are saddened by his passing and shall stand beside him while his body is given to the sea."

"Even though the man cursed your people daily?" Master Jones shook his head. "I as soon be done with him and let the fishes have him."

Jones turned back to the body. The wind raged through the sails and sent sprays of seawater over the ship. Silence fell among the people and the crew. "I commend the body of this seaman, loyal subject of His Majesty King James of England, Ireland, and Scotland, to the sea."

The crewmen set a stone at the feet of the dead man, folded the canvas around the body and tied it with cords. They lifted it onto a plank, raised it up and slid it into the sea. Mercy shut her eyes, but her ears heard the splash. She thought back to the day she tried to speak to the man, and sorrow, that he did not listen, or accept her invitation to join them, filled her.

"Elder Brewster has shown such kindness," she said to Caleb.

"Many showed kindness by being patient with the man. Yet it came to a point where we men could not tolerate him harassing our woman and children. Still, I am sorry he is dead."

"A year ago, I would not have cared. But now, my heart aches for the dead man. I wish he had found peace before he died. He left cursing us."

Along the horizon, gray clouds gathered, and the sea suddenly mounted. Mercy looked out at the waves and felt the great depth of the ocean around them. The wind grew stronger, and a northern gale sped toward the ship and fell upon it. She gripped her arms.

Caleb wrapped his arms around her. "You're cold. Do you want to go below?"

"As long as I can stay here and breathe the fresh air, I'll stay. I am cold though. Would you fetch my cloak for me?"

Gallantly, Caleb kissed her wrist. "Anything for my lady love."

The sky had yet to clear, and while the moment was somber, Mercy drew in the sea air deep into her lungs, knowing by the look of the sky she and Caleb would have to go below within the hour. She looked toward the forecastle when a sailor began singing a sea shanty. His lusty voice rose on the wind, and the words easy on the ears. She saw Dorothy sitting on the top of a barrel alone. William Bradford eased by, and Mercy stopped him.

"William. I am sorry for stopping you, but is Dorothy alright?"

"She is not feeling well."

"Is there anything I can do? I have a bit of peppermint cordial that would soothe her stomach."

"It isn't that." Bradford clutched his hands. "I wish I hadn't brought her with me. It would have been easier for her to stay behind in Holland with our son and her parents. I'm afraid she suffers for missing our boy and for my stubborn thinking. I hoped by now she would have grown use to the idea of young John coming to us next year. But she has grown quieter."

The first time Mercy heard Dorothy speak of leaving young John behind, Mercy knew Dorothy would terribly miss her son. What mother would not? To see her now established that sense. Dorothy had grown thin and pale, and as Bradford had said, she'd grown quieter.

"Would you like me to sit with her?" Mercy asked.

"I would appreciate it. I have done all I can think of." Bradford's eyes were sad and desperate. "I'll stay away for a time. I know the importance of women having company with each other."

"Caleb went below to fetch my cloak. Why not sit with him and play a game of checkers?" She then smiled in an attempt to cheer him. "But I must warn you, he is very good at winning."

"Good idea."

"Ask him to delay bringing it to me, will you? It will give me a chance to talk alone with Dorothy."

Bradford nodded and headed below. Men needed manly company as much as women needed womanly. Dorothy lifted her eyes when Mercy drew beside her, and held out her hands. "Oh, Mercy. I need your company."

Mercy wrapped her shawl over her shoulders. "Do you think we will ever feel warm again?"

"Or feel the caress of a hearth fire?" Dorothy sighed.

"Of course we will." A silence fell between them, then Mercy said, "I've neglected you, haven't I. Caleb keeps me occupied."

"You must spend as much time with your husband as you can. Savor every moment with him. Time passes quickly, and none of us knows how long our lives may be. William could lose me tomorrow—or I could lose William." Dorothy squeezed Mercy's hands. "If anything should happen to me, promise you will do all in your power to ensure he will not live the rest of his life alone."

Shocked to hear such dark words, Mercy gripped Dorothy Bradford's shoulders. "Do not say such things. You and William will live into old age, see many children and grandchildren."

"I am not afraid to die." When Mercy opened her mouth to speak, Dorothy shook her head. "I have distressed you. Let us talk of something else. I think Elizabeth Hopkins will deliver her baby soon. Won't it be a joyous moment to see a new life come into the world? I should like to hear a baby's cry. A lusty cry to drown out the wind and the moaning of the ship."

The mastiff shambled over and settled down at Dorothy's feet. "Olive is fond of you, Dorothy." Mercy reached over and patted Olive's head. "She knows you are downcast and wishes to comfort you. Poor Olive. There is naught for her to do. When she sleeps, perhaps she dreams as people do, and sees fields to run in. It won't be long before she and the spaniel are chasing rabbits." Mercy put her arm around the mastiff and pulled her closer. "I do love dogs."

"Where is the spaniel?"

"Hiding somewhere. He does not like the sound of the wind."

Dorothy lowered her head. "Perhaps I should hide too."

"And keep me from your company?" Mercy poked Dorothy's side. Dorothy laughed so softly Mercy bent to hear it. "If you hide, I shall seek you out. I cannot be without my best friend."

"I am such a coward." Dorothy looked at Mercy, and even in her downcast state, she managed to keep her smile. "You know that I am."

"I know nothing of the kind. Only a brave woman would think of her son's safety instead of her own feelings, and cross the ocean to a new land. You are purely unselfish. You see that do you not. You thought of your child before yourself."

"I miss him. I think of John every moment of the day. Yet, I know this voyage would have been too much for him, and what waits for us in the New World is unknown to us."

"You are a good mother, Dorothy. No one has the right to judge your decision. When you think of John, think of him being warm and well fed, going fishing with his grandfather, and tucked in at night by your mother. They are looking well after him. The time will go swiftly, and before you know it, they will join us in Virginia. By then you will have a comfortable house and a garden. In the end, all will be well."

"I know, still I cannot help it."

Mercy's heart ached to see her friend wiping her eyes. No words, no kind gestures eased her friend's suffering. She grasped Dorothy's hand and held it a moment. Then she lifted her eyes to the sky. "It looks like we will have a storm. Let's enjoy the fresh air while we have the chance."

"You stay, but I will go below and rest. I think that will do me more good than the sea air." Dorothy stood. A strange expression crept over her face, her cheeks turning pale, and her eyes haunted and hollow. "I've been watching the children aboard," she said. "Have you noticed how thin they have gotten? And their sweet faces seem so sallow, and their eyes dull. God help us, Mercy. God help us all."

The mastiff lifted her head, stood and whined as Dorothy headed below.

After Dorothy had gone, Mercy lingered on the main deck watching the approaching storm. She noticed the waves were growing higher. Heaps of white foam topped the swells and coated the hull. She looked up the masts to the billowing sails. Along the horizon, a narrow strip the color of coal settled along it. Pulling away, she looked toward the companionway. Dorothy would be all right, she told herself. She'd grow use to being just her and William for a time, use to the new land and a new home. Dorothy would always miss her boy, but their separation would be short lived. A smile crossed Mercy's face to imagine the Bradford's rejoicing when sails would be seen come up the Hudson reuniting them with young John Bradford.

"Mercy, what are you doing up here?" Caleb hurried to her.

"Waiting for you, my beloved, and my cloak."

He gave her a wry smile and put the cloak over her shoulders. "You told William to delay me. You don't have to explain. He told me why."

Jones leaned over the bulwark of the quarterdeck and looked down. "Go below," he ordered. "A storm approaches. Tell your friends to secure their belongings and settle in."

Caleb looked up. The sky turned dark with swirling clouds. *Mayflower's* bow lifted upon an enormous wave and plunged.

"And you, Mr. Treymayne, you are a scallywag for not keeping an eye on your wife. What if a huge wave broke over the ship and swept her into the sea? It would be the last you'd see of her."

Mercy felt the blood rush from her face. She looked out at the mounting waves, and back at Master Jones. She pushed away escaped strands of her hair against the wind. "My husband is no scallywag, Master Jones. Scallywags cause mischief, and he does not."

"True that may be, madam. My accusation was misdirected but he still needs to keep a sharp eye on you. Now please, go below. I'll not have any mishaps on my ship."

Caleb put his arm around Mercy's waist and drew her to the companionway. One by one, the passengers descended back into the belly of the ship enclosed in darkness, damp, and creaking timbers. As the wind grew stronger, a piece of rigging lashed in front of them. Caleb swung her out of its path. His arms were around her and he squeezed her tighter.

"Master Jones was quite wrong to scold you," she said with a little laugh. "You are, and always have been, there to rescue me."

"Think of the Psalm, Mercy. 'He would make haste for my deliverance from the stormy wind and tempest.'"

She smiled, and when they were about to go down the ladder the mastiff bumped into her legs. Mercy tried to snatch her by the collar. "Come, Olive. You cannot stay here."

The mastiff twisted and pulled. Mercy lost her balance and ended up sprawled out on the deck. She looked up at her husband and frowned. The mastiff nuzzled her nose against Mercy's shoulder, whined, and tried to lick her face.

"Do not laugh, Caleb Treymayne."

"I do not mean to." He held his hand down to her. "But you should have let me guide you down instead of you fooling around with the dog."

"She needs help too."

"She'll follow us and I'll help her. She's come and gone on her own so far."

Mercy rubbed Olive's ear. "You have, haven't you, Olive." She looked at Caleb. "How she climbs the ladder and leaps back down without injury is beyond me."

She grasped Caleb's hand and he lifted her. She gasped. "My ankle. I think I twisted it."

He swung her up into his arms. "How are you going to carry me down the ladder?" she said. "Put me down."

"Not when you are hurt," he said. He paused and looked into Mercy's eyes. "On my word, you are beautiful, in sun or rain, wind or calm. I want to kiss you so badly." His lips were close to hers. Mercy sighed. Caleb's cloak blew over them, hiding her against her beloved. His mouth touched hers gently, and then glided over hers— brief and warm. Then he set her down and stepped down the ladder. He lifted her down and carried her over to their space, where due to the storm only the sway of lantern light lit the gun deck. Some of the Separatist women gathered around and fussed over Mercy. Dorothy Bradford knelt beside her. "What happened?"

"I took a tumble. I'm alright."

Caleb's eyes widened. "No you are not alright." He looked at the women. "She's hurt her ankle."

"We'll take care of her, Mr. Treymayne," Mary Brewster said. With the look she gave him, Caleb stood back. With gentle hands, Mary drew off Mercy's shoe and examined the injured ankle. "Fortunate for you, it is not broken. Does it hurt much?"

"I can endure it," Mercy said.

"Still you must not walk on it for a while if you want it to heal. It could be sprained."

Mercy flexed her toes and frowned. "It will be hard for me to sit still. Look. I can wiggle my toes without it hurting."

"You will do as Mrs. Brewster says." Caleb turned to the older woman. "You're as good a physician as Dr. Fuller. I trust you with my wife."

Mary Brewster smiled. "There are some things women know best. Nursing is one of them."

At age fifty and one, Mary Brewster was a handsome woman and greatly respected. She was tall, slim, with soft brown eyes and milky-white skin. She was a woman of wit and wisdom, and the women sought her advice on everything from spiritual matters to child rearing. Her ways reminded Mercy of Nan—calm, wise, without prejudice. Thinking of her grandmother, Mercy knew Nan would have liked Mary Brewster, and oh how she wished she were there seated next to her, discussing with Mary how to best take care of Mercy's ankle.

"Mr. Treymayne, if you can find a cold compressed, it will help your wife." Mary Brewster folded a towel and set it under Mercy's ankle. "Dr. Fuller might have something with him we can use."

Caleb nodded and went in search of the good doctor.

Dorothy stood on the other side of the pallet. "Since you have things in hand, Mrs. Brewster, I have chores I must attend to."

Mercy followed Dorothy with her eyes as she drew away. The forlorn wife began folding her blankets, matching the edges perfectly and smoothing out the wrinkles. "I'm worried about Dorothy," Mercy said.

Mary Brewster looked over her shoulder. "It has been hard on her, leaving young John behind. We must all do our best to distract her."

The ship pitched and moaned. "A storm is upon us."

Mary Brewster pulled Wrestling onto her lap. The child turned his face into his mother's shoulder. Mary looked at Mercy. "'Twas kind of the Lord to give us tender arms to comfort those in distress."

The look on this dear mother's face brought a gentle smile to Mercy's lips. Arms to comfort those in distress were words she would never forget.

The ship rolled and rode on the crests of huge waves. The tempest plunged the *Mayflower* into deep watery caverns and back up again. The hours grew more desperate—dragged on and fear gripped the people.

"What if the storm sinks the ship?" Wrestling asked Caleb when he returned with a soaked clothe and a bucket of freezing seawater. The boy's brown eyes were searching for an answer.

"It won't." Caleb wrapped the compressed around Mercy's ankle. "The *Mayflower* will protect us against the sea. She does not leak like the other ship."

A peal of thunder rattled the timbers, and startled eyes flashed along with it. A chill ran up Mercy's spine and she clutched a blanket. She shivered and a silent prayer poured from her heart.

Caleb drew down beside her. He pulled her to him and whispered in her ear. "Try not to fear it, my love. I will not let you go."

She looked at him with watery eyes and wrapped her arms tighter around his waist. She could find no voice. The wind—the relentless, unforgiving wind—shoved against the tiny vessel as if something unearthly meant to break it in pieces.

Chapter 26

Long sleepless nights slowly passed as the *Mayflower* sailed through rough seas, high winds, and pelting rain. Each storm seemed more threatening than the last. Each wave lifted the ship as if it were a toy in the mounting sea. The air in the gun deck had a suffocating effect. Cold deepened as the winds howled. Every stitch of blanket and quilt were taken out of chests. Two-year-old Damaris Hopkins wept in her pregnant mother's arms. All the children were shivering, and it broke Mercy's heart to see them suffering.

"God, have mercy on us and bring us to land soon," she whispered in the crook of her husband's arm.

As the wind blew, it whistled in a menacing tone. She feared if the sea grew any rougher, if the wind icier, many would succumb in some way to its treachery and not make it to the New World. It was not enough to go up on deck to fill the lungs with the sea air. The wind ravaged those who dared. The bucking of the ship threw men's legs out from under them, and many a time waves were so great, seamen fell against the bulwarks close to being tossed overboard.

Could the journey grow any worse? If the ocean did not take them, disease and starvation would. They heard the stomp of boots approach. "You people stay below." John Clarke, ship's pilot, looked at them with pity and moved away.

"Wait, sir," said Caleb. "Is there no sign of a break in the storm?"

John Clarke turned and looked at him. "Not as yet, Mr. Treymayne. It won't be safe to go up on deck until there is. I suggest you people pray."

A fierce squall stirred the ocean waves and they crashed over the sides with such force the timbers groaned with a piercing noise in the gun deck. A sharp change in the moaning wind alarmed the female passengers, while the men put on brave faces. Mercy could not see above her, but in her mind, she knew strong crosswinds whirled the clouds as they dipped lower toward the sea threatening destruction.

William Bradford tried to calm the fearful souls. He smiled at them and spoke about the wonders of the New World. "Our ordeal will soon be over. The Lord will bring us to a new land. Think of the houses we shall build…"

They longed for it, but their faces stretched with terror and the women cried out when the wind buffeted the ship and the sea lifted it again and again upon its crests. A sharp renting sound grew louder with each gust of the gale. Mercy gasped and covered her ears. "The sails are tearing," she cried out.

Caleb grasped his wife's hands. "It's only the wind you hear." She looked at him with wide fearful eyes. "Come. Let me wrap my cloak around you." He set it over her and he held her close.

"You cannot say you could not hear it, Caleb."

"You mustn't dwell on it, Mercy."

"What if it is true the sails have torn?"

"There is other canvas, and the seamen know what to do. Try not to fear, my love."

"I cannot help but fear. The sounds are awful."

"Stay in my arms."

Mercy looked at Dorothy Bradford and saw her weeping. No longer could she hide her fears from Dorothy, and her desire to reassure her of their safety had vanished. She whispered, "God have mercy on us if the storm does not take us down."

Caleb turned her face to his. "Jones has no choice but to surrender the ship to the storm and sea. It will carry us over the waves. We must believe he knows what he is doing. We must trust God."

She took care to listen to Caleb. He had faced the fierceness of the oceans and its dull calmness. He never spoke of shipwrecks or worse. She repeated every word he spoke to her in her mind. But her fear of the storm mounted with the constant pitch of the ship. The sounds of sea and wind, of timbers moaning, quickened the beating of her heart. Silence fell over the people, until Mary Brewster began to sing. The others joined her. Their voices rose above the shriek of the wind.

"Let not the waterflood overflow me…neither let the deep swallow me up."

"You rule over the surging sea. When its waves mount up, you still them."

A minute later, they heard a sound like the crack of a lightning bolt when it strikes a tree. The whole of the ship trembled, and eyes shot open. Mercy gasped. Caleb jerked and tightened his arms around her. He too had grown afraid. Women muffled their cries. Children quaked and grew silent, their distress great. Men gathered wife and child to them, and William Brewster lifted his voice above the din of the storm.

"They cry unto the Lord in their trouble, and he bringeth them out of their distress. He turneth the storm to calm, so that the waves thereof are still."

Out of the shadows, Master Jones came through the companionway. His eyes were large and his face pale. His hand shook as he braced a beam. His clothes were soaked through. "Sirs." His breathing heaved. "I'm in need of a few able-bodied men."

Every man stood. Master Jones pointed out four including Caleb. Then he asked them to follow him. As Caleb was about to step away, Mercy grabbed his hand. He looked down into her worried face. "I'll be back shortly." He tucked their blanket around her. "Try to sleep."

She knew he meant to comfort her, but how could anyone sleep that night? She nodded to him and let him go. Then, watching him leave with the others, she pulled her knees up to her chest, and quietly allowed tears to fall from her eyes.

When Caleb witnessed the crack in the main beam, his heart sank. He'd seen this kind of thing before, not on a ship, but inside a house shabbily built. The owner neglected the beam, and soon it bowed and the crack grew deeper until it snapped and the ceiling collapsed.

Master Jones, a company of mariners, and pilgrim leaders stood together looking up at the damage. As if one man, they raised their arms and braced their hands against the beam to hold it up. They strained and pushed as the sea seeped through the cracks above them and poured down on their bodies. The water was ice cold and they shivered. Jones held a lantern high for all to see the great crack that zigzagged across the beam. His hand trembled and the lantern swayed. One seaman cried out. "We must turn back!"

Caleb felt the coarse edges of the crack, the splinters and fissures against his palms. "I've seen this before," he called out over the din of the storm. "We are in danger, Master Jones."

"Indeed we are, Mr. Treymayne. We can't turn back. We're more than halfway across the Atlantic."

"I agree. Turning back could mean our end, but we have a jack stored below."

"For the building of houses, not ships, sir. Mr. Bennett, speak up."

Soaking wet in his red cap and canvas breeches, *Mayflower's* carpenter kept his hand pressed against the beam. "I think we can sure it up, sir, and make it to land...if it will hold."

"How?"

"We can place a stout plank beneath it." He looked at Caleb. "Do you agree, Mr. Treymayne? You also are a carpenter by trade and said you've seen this before."

"And you have not?"

"Never in all my days of seafaring, no."

"Look at it. It's not only cracked it's bowed. We can use the jackscrew we brought with us. If we place it under the beam..."

"We can push the beam back into place," said the ship's carpenter.

"We'll make the crossing if it works. It's in the hold."

"Get it," Jones said to two of his seaman.

While they waited for them to return, John Howland and Caleb, the two huskiest men among them, and the ship's carpenter, set a plank under the beam. Caleb's heart pounded. Clearly, it would not hold, nor would it close the crack. Yet, he endeavored not to show his concern, but braced himself hard against the board. The others did the same, and just as it seemed the plank would hold—it snapped into pieces.

William Brewster clutched his hands and hung his head. "Lord God Almighty, help us."

"Keep up your prayers, Mr. Brewster," shouted Jones over the roar of the storm. "If the Almighty does not hear you and intervene, the beam will snap. When it does we will lose the main mast, and the ship could break apart."

Such words sucked the breath out of every man. Bradford groaned. "Dear God, hear us…The women and children. My dear wife."

Brewster squeezed Bradford's shoulder. "He will not resign us to the sea, William."

"And how do you know this, Mr. Brewster?" said Jones. "You people think everything that happens is the Almighty's will. Why not drowning? Mr. Flagg, go tell those men to hurry."

Martin hurried off. Caleb noticed a slight weakness in his gait, but dismissed it for the movement of the ship. Still, it did not leave his mind. He looked up at the cracked beam. "We must place another plank under the beam until we have the jackscrew."

"It will only break again," said John Howland.

"We must try," cried Caleb. "We cannot stand here and do nothing."

Heaving another beam in place, the men keep their hold firm. A wave pounded the hull and water poured through the rafters, soaking Caleb and the men beside him. The ship spun her head out of the wind and lay broadside to the crested swells. *Mayflower* struck an enormous wave. Cold trickling fear seized Caleb and the men. Seawater muffled the screams and cries of the women and children huddled in the gun deck. The fractured beam groaned. His chest tightened. He gripped the timber with all his strength. Wet and cold, he clenched his teeth. Brewster and Bradford sprang forward and held the timber up with the others. The men, their voices shaking for fear of the ship breaking apart, for the sea rushing in upon them and swallowing them into the murky depths, strained.

Martin rushed back in with the sailors. The others released their hold and stood back as they set the jackscrew under the beam, and balanced another timber on its flat lip. They cranked it upward. Caleb fixed his eyes on the crack. With each turn of the crank, the breach began to close. A cheer rose when the jack pushed the beam back into place and held.

The ship's carpenter smiled and smacked his hands. "That'll hold until we reach land and can spike a splint across and re-peg it to the upper deck."

As the others moved off, some silent, others speaking a word of praise and thanks, Caleb's heart swelled with the realization how precious their lives were, that they had been given a purpose and calling to fulfill. He turned to Bradford. "The Lord heard our cries, William. What a story we will have to tell our children and grandchildren."

Bradford's smiled deepened and a great humility shown on his face. "Aye, Caleb. We will. We will tell them that in moments of peril, He showed us His hand was as much with us, as it had been with the children of Israel as they crossed the Red Sea."

Together the men headed back to their women and children. Caleb ducked his head through the entrance and raised his eyes to see his wife seated with a gathering of women. Mercy looked at him, her eyes aglow. Even in the gloomy light, even in the crowded space, unwashed in her body and clothing, she was a beauty. Her hair slipped out from beneath the dingy cap she wore, and caught the lantern light above her, giving the wisps a bronzy radiance. He nodded to her all was well, and lay down on his palette and tried to sleep.

That evening, William Brewster gave a moving account to the people of their deliverance from the most violent of storms. None could deny it was a miracle they had brought the jackscrew aboard back in Holland. Indeed, the mighty hand of the Lord put it into the house builder's mind to do so. It stayed in Caleb's mind for days. He could not forget such an event, or the humbled looks on the faces of those aboard—including the seamen and the men under the command of Captain Myles Standish.

From the deep chambers of their hearts, the reality their lives had come within an inch of death, a blessed silence fell upon them. Hands joined. Wives set their heads upon their husband's shoulders. Children wondered—who in later years would grasp the gravity of what had occurred.

Still, as the days passed, relentless rain poured down on the small ship as it pitched in the mounting waves. The winds were fierce and the seas high. The ship could not bear a knot of sail. Jones ordered her to remain adrift with every thread of canvas furled.

A succession of strong westerly gales followed, and on one such day as the passengers were eating their portion of porridge there came such a cry, all looked up to the ceiling.

"Man overboard!" a seaman shouted.

Caleb stood with the other men. He hurried topside. The wind shoved against him. The rain and sea spray thrashed his face.

"Man overboard!" the crewmen shouted. "All hands!"

With the others, Caleb raced to the bulwark. He fought the wind and steadied his feet upon the deck. From the ship to the water, he saw a man holding on to the topsail halyards that hung overboard at length into the ocean. A head burst up from the waves. The man gasped, and went back down. Every able hand grabbed the halyards and pulled.

The sea and wind raged with no willingness to let go. The man sunk down several fathoms before coming up again, yet he held on until they heaved him to the brim of the water. Caleb could see his eyes, wide with terror and with pleas to save him. Waves rushed over him and he gulped for air. His face had gone gray, his lips blue. As the waves pushed him forward, mariners lowered a boathook and hooked the man's shirt.

"It is John Howland," shouted John Carver over the roar of wind, "my manservant. Hold on, John. We'll get you aboard in the name of God Almighty."

Dragged up to the bulwark, soaked and gasping for air, the men snatched at Howland's clothes and brought him over onto the deck. He stared at the crowd around him, glassy-eyed and still. Dr. Fuller bent over, tapped his checks. "Are you with us, John?" he asked the youth.

Howland looked around and smiled. "I am well, sir. Such a thing I'll never forget for as long as I live. I'll never look at life the same way after this."

"Thank God, you were able to hold on," said Carver. "I should scold you for being here during a storm, but I'll withhold my anger." Carver threw his arms around Howland and embraced him.

Dr. Fuller stood back. "He'll live if we get him below before he catches his death of cold."

Carver tried to lift him. Howland blinked his eyes. "I can walk on my own, sir."

Carver frowned. "Change out of those wet clothes, and rest until Dr. Fuller says you can get up. Understand?"

Howland nodded as some of the men lifted him from the deck and helped him below. Caleb gripped the halyards, awestruck by the event. He made an oath he would not allow Mercy to go topside unless it were fair. What good would it do since he had a strong-willed wife? He would most likely find her watching the sea and the whirl of clouds before a downpour.

The gun deck buzzed with the news of John Howland's death-defying rescue. Dr. Fuller asked Martin Flagg to help John change into dry clothes, and once done Mary Brewster brought to him a bowl of broth and a piece of ship's biscuit. Everyone gathered around.

"What happened, John?"

"Yes, how did you fall overboard?"

"And why would you be up there instead of down here out of the wind?"

"If you give me a moment," John Howland replied, "I'll tell you." He took a swallow of the broth. "A wave crashed over the side and swept me over into the sea. I plunged several fathoms and swam back to the surface. Wind and rain fought against me and the sea tried to drag me down. I held my breath until I thought my lungs would burst. I went under and something brushed against my body."

Young Wrestling gasped. "A shark or whale?"

"Nay, Wrestling. 'Twas the halyards. I grabbed hold. Save me! Oh Lord, spare my life, I cried, for I was terrified and thought to die. The next thing I knew, they lifted me straight out of the sea and onto the deck. I'm quite affected by it." Howland swallowed down another spoonful of broth. "My life will never be the same."

Mercy stood by his hammock. "Only the hand of God could have saved you, John."

Martin Flagg agreed. "It was indeed a miracle. But what a fool you were to be up there during a storm."

"I do not know what I was thinking, except my legs were stiff and my lungs done with the air in here." Howland's brows wrinkled and Mercy could see he searched for the reasons and regretted his choices. "Goes to prove, though a fool, God loves one still."

Caleb set his hand on Howland's shoulder. "Obey the rules from now on and stay below."

"To be sure, sir." Howland handed back the empty bowl to Mercy. "Thank you, Mrs. Treymayne. I'm warmer now."

"I am so happy for your deliverance, John, I feel like dancing."

Caleb lifted her into his arms and whirled her around. Mercy giggled, and when Caleb set her down, she tucked the loose strands of her hair into her cap.

Brewster stepped forward. "We must all use wisdom from now on. When there are storms, all must stay below. If there is fair weather, we may stretch our legs and take in the air. Never again shall any of us put ourselves, or our loved ones, at risk. Such a loss is beyond imagining. God gave us a brain, and so shall we use it."

John Carver rested his hand on his chest. "John's mishap is a lesson to us all. Think how much worse it could be if it were one of our small children. John is a lusty youth. Our children are not, and if it had been a child, or one of the women swept overboard—there is no doubt we would lose them."

Mercy looked over at Dorothy Bradford, and saw the color drain from her face.

Chapter 27

Elizabeth Hopkins scooted up on her elbows and bent forward. Her dark hair fell along her forehead in sweaty strands. Mary Brewster dabbed Elizabeth's head with a wet cloth and spoke softly. "It won't be long, Elizabeth. Your baby is coming fast."

Elizabeth turned her head and looked at Mercy. "Be sure Constance looks after Damaris."

"I will, Elizabeth."

"I do not want Damaris to see. She is too young."

"She won't. Constance is sitting with her on the other side of the deck."

"Where is my son?"

"Giles is with his father." Mercy smiled. "I saw Stephen a moment ago, and he looks quite nervous for you."

"He should be." Elizabeth blew out a breath.

"Have you seen a birth, Mercy?" Mary Brewster asked.

"This will be my first time."

"Do not let it frighten you and keep you from having babies. It is called labor for a reason. The joy that comes from it is wonderful."

Elizabeth clenched her teeth and grasped the sides of her cot. "Oh, I hate that all can hear my cries."

"They are praying for you and the child." Mary ran the cloth over Elizabeth's arms. Another contraction gripped the laboring mother. "Try not to think about what others are hearing. Concentrate on bringing the babe forth." She glanced at Mercy. "We will need hot water. Can you ask the ship's cook?"

"Yes, I will get it."

"Here take this." She handed Mercy a porcelain washbowl. "Fill it with whatever clean water you can find."

"But that is yours, Mary." Elizabeth struggled to rise.

Mary Brewster smiled. "You think I care? We are bringing your child into the world and have more need of it than I."

"But it is expensive Staffordshire."

Mary tucked the blanket around Elizabeth. "Hush. I'll not hear another word. You must think about the job you have to do and not my bowl. Go on, Mercy. Fetch water as quickly as you can."

Nodding, Mercy hurried away to the cook where he kept a kettle boiling on a low fire. He raised his brows when Mercy made her request. "A babe's to be born aboard our ship?" he said. "I never thought I'd see the day."

"We need clean water." Mercy held the washbowl out to him. "Please, sir."

The cook chuckled. "Not much of that aboard. Sure you can't use beer?"

"I'm sure," she said. "The water in your kettle has boiled, has it not?"

He nodded. "Aye. Take what you need."

She thanked him, and with the bowl filled, she hurried back careful not to spill a drop or slip. Down in the gun deck, the children sat silent and wide-eyed over Elizabeth's labor. Gentlemen looked nervous, and busied their hands with whatever chore they could find. Elizabeth's labor pains increased. She cried out in agony and the women gripped her hands and helped her rise up.

"It shan't be long," Mary Brewster said. "We must put up a sheet. This is not for the eyes of others."

"Still they'll hear my cries," said Elizabeth. "I'll frighten the children."

"They must learn what pains a woman faces when bringing a child into the world. It will make them appreciate their mothers." Mary secured the sheet.

"I never thought I'd have this child during our voyage." Elizabeth winched. "We should have been in the New World by now, safe and shielded in a warm house."

When Mercy saw Elizabeth's lips were growing pale, and that she shivered from the cold, she tucked the blanket closer. Elizabeth turned her eyes to Mercy. "Do not despair," she said. "Think of the day your child will tell his children the story of his birth."

Elizabeth struggled to smile. "What makes you sure it is a boy?"

Mercy shook her head and smiled back. "I am not sure. But we shall soon see."

Mary Brewster moved to the foot of the cot. "Now, you must do as I say, Elizabeth."

"I feel I'm going to split in two."

"You've done this before."

"This time it is worse."

"Draw your knees close to your chest. You remember how. Now, when you feel a pain, bear down. Mercy, help Elizabeth."

Mercy held Elizabeth up when she bore down. Struck by a sudden surge of pain, Elizabeth shut her eyes tight. Much water and blood gushed forth and when Mercy saw it, her heart thumped in her chest. Mary Brewster held a finger to her own lips. She realized what Mary meant. *Quiet now. Say nothing. 'Tis normal.*

Mary placed her hands near the child's head. "The head has crowned, Elizabeth. You are almost finished."

Elizabeth barred her teeth and pushed.

"The pain will pass. Your babe is about to be born."

Elizabeth fell back. "I cannot bare this agony."

Mercy put her arms around Elizabeth's shoulders and drew her up. "Hold on to me as hard as you can." Elizabeth reached for Mercy's hand and their fingers clasped.

"Again, Elizabeth, one more time should do it." Mary grabbed the muslin and set it between Elizabeth's legs. "That's right. Push hard."

Elizabeth bore down, her eyes closed tight. A moment later, the wail of a newborn filled the gun deck. Mercy gazed at the babe as Mary Brewster rubbed his little body clean. "You have a son," Mary Brewster cried. "A lusty boy. My, listen to that cry. You did well, Elizabeth."

Mercy saw the tiny head and the shock of black hair. Her heart swelled at the sight, and she wanted to cry. "He is beautiful, Elizabeth. I dare say he looks like you."

Elizabeth smiled. "I could not have done it without my friends. Thank you. Thank God."

The baby squirmed as Mary Brewster wrapped him tight. He quieted and she laid him in Elizabeth's arms. Then she drew back the sheet. There stood a nervous Stephen Hopkins, his face pale and sweaty, his eyes large and searching.

"Congratulations, Stephen, your wife has given you a healthy, yowling son," said Mary.

"A son? Is Elizabeth all right?"

"Yes, but this little lad has worn her out and she will need rest. I daresay he could shout out this weather."

"I wish to hold him," Stephen said. Elizabeth handed the child to his father. In the glow of lantern light, a small pink face with dark hair fit into Stephen Hopkins's hand. The infant's dark blue eyes blinked and his bow mouth opened and closed. His tiny pink tongue sought his mother's breast and he fidgeted with a soft whimper. Stephen slipped his finger into the baby's hand. At once, the babe's fist closed around it.

The birth cheered everyone. The passengers clapped their hands as Stephen Hopkins presented his son. The Hopkins children hurried forward to see their new brother.

"What will you name the child?" asked a passenger.

Stephen gazed into his son's face. "We will call him Oceanus— Oceanus Hopkins."

As Mercy watched Stephen hold the newborn, the longing for a child of her own passed through her. The only privacy she and Caleb had, had been in Holland—a newlywed life filled with passionate love. She laid her hand across her stomach and prayed what she suspected and hoped for she could soon tell him.

Mary Brewster drew the sheets closed once more. "A fresh shift for Mrs. Hopkins, Mercy, behind the pillows. We've more to do." As they pampered the new mother, Mary laid her hand on Mercy's arm. "You wish for your own, Mercy?"

"I do, Mary."

"It will happen in God's timing."

After all was set aright, Mercy rejoined Caleb. He held a piece of wood in his hand and smoothed it down. In the dim lantern light, he looked as hail as the day they left Holland. Her love for him swelled as she studied his face. He came into her life when she needed him most, and would be the only love she'd ever know. If she had not been approached by Charlton, gone to work in Lord Glenmont's kitchen, and fled when in danger, she would not have met him and been with him, leaving one world behind for another.

She sat next to him. "The Hopkins's baby is beautiful, is he not?"

"Indeed, he is. I've never been present at a birth. I cannot describe the feeling it gave me."

"To want a child of our own?"

He looked at her. "Yes, beloved. Hopefully to look like you."

She looked into his hands. "What are you making, my love?"

"A spinning top for Oceanus." A few of the children gathered near to watch. Caleb paused. "I'll make each of you a toy of your choice as long as you promise to be good and say your prayers at night."

"Can you carve a tipcat for me, sir?" asked Love Brewster.

"Easily."

"It is fascinating to see a spinning top form out of a stick of wood. Like when God formed Adam from the dust of the ground." Love shoved his brown hair from his forehead and kept his eyes fixed on Caleb's work.

Caleb smiled and pushed his knife through the wood. "Not quite, but I see your point. You think Oceanus will like it?'

"Yes, sir. Would you teach me how to carve?"

"I will. It may come in handy one day." Caleb finished the top and handed it to Love. "Give this to the child's mother," Caleb told him. All the little ones hurried over to the Hopkins.

"That was kind of you, Caleb." Mercy touched his hair with gentle fingertips.

He took her hand and drew her down beside him.

A few days of fair winds and clear skies lifted the spirits of the passengers and crew until stormy weather once again threatened the *Mayflower*. Cold and damp, rain and raging winds, tore at the masts and howled through the smallest opening. Seawater poured over the decks and through the hatchway, streamed down into the companionway and over the deck floors. Many of the passengers fell sick, heaved into the swab buckets, and lost their appetites. Mercy's peppermint cordial had run dry after she had administered it. She wished she had brought more, but how were she to know how desperate people would become?

Separatist leaders met with Master Jones and Dr. Heale ship's surgeon, when Dr. Fuller called them together. They included Mary Brewster and Mercy after seeing how they brought Elizabeth Hopkins through her labor. Dr. Fuller set his hands firmly on the table in Jones's quarters. "I'm afraid we have many sick, and one man is dying. He has lesions on his arms and legs, and swelling in the joints."

Jones sat in a chair made of tooled leather. "Mr. Heale. You're ship's surgeon. What do you think?"

"Scurvy perhaps, caused by a digestive issue. Broth would help him recover."

"Broth?" bulked Dr. Fuller. "He needs fresh fruit in order to recover. We have depleted our stock and…"

"Broth, sir, is all we can provide."

Master Jones tapped his finger on his table. "Then you don't agree with Dr. Fuller the man is dying?" Mercy believed this to be a test on Master Jones's part. Was the ship's doctor so lacking in knowledge of the seafarers disease to suggest simple broth would cure a man?

"How is anyone to know for certain, Master Jones? I've seen men recover and others die."

"We must have some fresh fruit stored for the crew." Jones stood. "I will have our boatswain ration it between the crew and passengers."

"That will mean less for our sailors, sir. I protest."

"And have more cases aboard, Dr. Heale?"

Heale turned to Fuller. "Why didn't your people bring adequate food stuffs? You of all people should have known you'd need fresh fruit."

Mary Brewster frowned. "Dr. Fuller is not to blame. We have had some lemon, and occasionally take the juice."

"Apparently our supply has not been enough for some, if it is scurvy." Fuller folded his arms. "However, it is only one illness. Let us hope it isn't something of a more serious nature."

"Such as?" Jones asked.

"Plague, sir."

Jones laughed. "Certainly not aboard *Mayflower*."

"It is not the fault of the ship, but passengers and negligent physicians." Mercy opened her mouth to speak up, but Heale stopped her with a harsh look and turned out of the cabin.

Dr. Fuller fixed his eyes on the deck floorboards, his brows pressed. Mercy drew up her shoulders. How dare Heale blame the good doctor for the ailments aboard? "It is not your fault, Dr. Fuller. You cannot blame yourself. The voyage has been hard. It is a wonder we aren't all sick. Mrs. Brewster and I will help, and listen to your instructions."

He looked at her as they left the cabin. "Then you trust me, do you?"

"We have no reason not to. We have not forgotten the time of the sweating disease in Holland. You labored day and night ministering to the sick and many recovered. Of course we trust you."

"Thank you, Mrs. Treymayne, Mrs. Brewster. Let us do all we can together." He stopped midway, and turned to Mary Brewster. "I would like you to speak to each of the women, find out what symptoms their families are having."

They moved on, Mary hurrying ahead of them. As they descended into the miserable quarters, Mercy asked Dr. Fuller who the dying man was. She gasped. "Martin?"

"Yes, poor lad."

"I spoke to him last night, and he seemed well."

"The man has been able to hide his ailments. I noticed this morning his lethargy, approached him and did an examination. Come, I will show you."

Back in the gun deck, Dr. Fuller drew beside Martin. He bent down and laid his hand on Martin's forehead. Then he checked his legs and arms by pressing against the muscles. Martin winced. "Does it hurt, Martin?"

Martin nodded. "It does, sir. And I've sores on them."

Mercy stood a few yards away, and watched Dr. Fuller draw up one of Martin's sleeves. Martin pushed the sleeve down. "I do not want Mercy to see."

"They are most serious." Fuller motioned to Mercy to draw closer. "I could use your help in applying a salve to these wounds. Are you willing to bear it?"

"I am." As she approached Martin's hampered space where stale odors reigned, she found Martin on his back, his breathing shallow. Sweat glistened on his forehead and his hands shook over the wool blanket that covered him.

"Let me show you what you are dealing with." Fuller raised the sleeve.

Martin moved back, his eyes wide open. "No, I do not want Mercy to see."

She sat on the side of his cot and picked up his hand. "Martin, there is nothing to be ashamed of. Do you remember the time you had a black eye? I was not repulsed. I shant be now. I want to help you."

"A black eye is nothing compared to this," he said.

263

"I know. Is there someone else you would want to nurse you?"

Martin shook his head and laid back. "No, but if Evi were here I'd want her to." He stared at the ceiling and frowned. "Then again, I'm glad she isn't. I wouldn't want her to see me like this. Not for the whole world would I."

"You just lie still, and let me have a look." Careful not to hurt him, Mercy raised the sleeve. For a moment, she stared at the red spots covering his skin. Her throat tightened from the lump forming in it. She swallowed and pushed back tears. Dr. Fuller moved her away.

"He's been a brother to me," she said to him, her eyes moist.

"You are sure you want to do this?" Dr. Fuller said. "He may not survive."

"I'm sure."

"You will be a comfort to the boy."

"What can be done to ease his pain?"

"I have nothing to give him. Try to make him comfortable. A fever is rising upon the poor lad. Be prepared for the worst."

She knitted her brows. "He'll pull through. I'll see to it. Would you find Caleb and tell him?"

Mercy thought of the days Martin walked her to and from the inn, and how troubled he was she was going to work for Lord Glenmont. He left with her for Holland, risked his own neck to get her away. In Leyden, he became Dr. Fuller's manservant. He had fallen in love with Evi, but not enough to remain with her. She dipped a cloth into a wooden bowl of water and wiped his face. Her hands were gentle and he opened his eyes. She filled a tin cup with a bit of stale beer and gave him to drink. Setting it to his lips, he took it down and gazed at Mercy.

"I wanted to see the New World, Mercy. I wanted to see you there safe and sound."

She squeezed his hand. "You will, Martin. You'll see."

"I think not...I think I may die. Will you hold my hand tighter?"

Wrapping her fingers around his, she wiped his brow with the other. "I'll not leave you."

Martin swallowed hard and blinked his eyes. "My body aches all over and I feel as if I'm on fire. Pray for me, Mercy."

"There now. Close your eyes and try to sleep."

Martin did as she said. The lids of his eyes were pale and streaked with blue veins. She turned and saw Caleb standing nearby. Sorrow shown in his eyes. He lifted her by the elbow and whispered,

"Are you sure, Mercy? You haven't seen death enough to steal yourself against it."

She jerked away. "But I have known it. I will not leave his side."

He held out his hands to her. "I'm only trying…"

"To make me change my mind. No, Caleb. I will not leave Martin to die alone in this wretched ship." Her face flooded with anger thinking that is what he was asking her to do, questioning whether she was strong enough to face Martin's suffering and end.

"Forgive me," Caleb said. "I wasn't asking you to leave him. I'll not leave either."

Mercy lowered down on the pallet and touched Martin's cheek. Caleb drew a cask up to it and sat down. He clutched his hands together, and Mercy could tell his heart ached as much as hers. Martin raised his eyes to hers. "Mercy, you've been good to me."

"Not always, Martin. I pained you. I hope you forgive me."

"There is nothing to forgive."

"You know I love you, don't you?"

"Yes, Mercy. You love me as if I were your brother. I expected nothing more, and that was enough for me."

Night fell and with it gross darkness. The lantern swinging above shed feeble light over the passengers, and the temperature plunged to unbearable degrees. Caleb laid a blanket over Mercy's shoulders. She huddled into it. "'Tis a cold night."

"You must stay warm."

Mercy forced the tears from her eyes. "It does not seem fair Martin should die. He is so young, and so good."

"A good lad should live to be an old man."

"But he won't…will he?"

"I do not know, nor will I say."

"I do not want him to go."

"I know, my love. I know."

"Stay me with me. Help me to be brave."

Through the night, they drifted in and out of sleep. When Martin moaned, Mercy would wake and grab hold of him. Would the sea ever settle? Would the sun ever shine again? Endless waves crashed over the sides of the ship and poured through the seams. The ship rolled violently. Moments of quiet became stranger than the woes of the people.

Dawn finally broke. Caleb took the cup from Mercy's hand and set her back, filled it and put it to Martin's lips. Then he gripped Martin's hand in a manner men would do when going into battle.

"All shall be well, Martin," he said.

Martin's eyes opened. "Take care of Mercy. I'll hold you to account."

Caleb smiled. "You and the Lord."

"Aye. Me and the Lord." Martin shut his eyes and opened them again. "I loved her, you know."

"I'm glad for it. If it weren't for you, I dare not think where she would have ended up."

Martin swallowed. "Kind words, Caleb."

"You deserve them."

"I'm not afraid to die. Heaven will be far better than the New World."

Strained by heartbreak, Mercy drew closer. Presently, Martin's mind wandered, and he talked of the Ipswich docks, the ships and people he knew. "Mercy, I cannot meet you today to walk you to the inn. You understand do you not?"

"Yes, Martin. It is all right."

"Jonah will be angry with me that I let you walk to Lord Glenmont's house all by yourself."

"He knew how stubborn I can be. Not to worry. It would have put you out of your way."

For a moment, he closed his eyes and breathed deeply as Mercy soothed his forehead. A ray of sunlight filtered through one of the gun ports that had come loose. Dawn fell across Martin's face. "Dr. Fuller needs me. I should rise and get to work." He struggled to get up. Caleb held him down gently with his hand.

"Dr. Fuller says you are to rest."

"Is it the Sabbath? I will see Evi. There is a storm outside, but I do not mind getting wet." Pale and shivering, and nigh gone, there came a knowing look in his eyes and a smile lifted his lips. Mercy knelt beside the pallet with Caleb. She wrung out a cloth and wiped the sweat off Martin's forehead. Martin turned and looked at her in a moment when his mind returned to the present.

"Do not cry for me, Mercy. Promise me you'll not forget me."

"I promise with all my heart." She held his fingers against her lips and kissed them. "Caleb and I will name our first son after you."

"Ah, that makes me happy, Mercy." A brightness shown on his face and he held her hand tighter. "Look, there is mother," he murmured. "She bids me to come home—oh and father too. Is the sun out today? It is so bright."

Then his hand in Mercy's sagged. His last breath eased from his lips and the light in his eyes vanished. Crushed, she laid her head against his chest and wept.

PART FOUR

'The lord is the help of my life.'

William Bradford

Chapter 28

Cape Cod Bay, Massachusetts, November 9, 1620

Mercy wished she could stay asleep lost in her dreams. Her mind snapped back to the memory of Martin and the grief in her heart. She shoved his loss from her mind and tried to think of other things, but it did no good. She hadn't left him, even now, as his body lie still and lifeless as the air around her. She had bathed him with the little water allotted to her. Then the women wrapped him in a canvas sheet and waited for the sailors to carry him away. Mercy wished not to see him slip into the cold Atlantic. Dear Martin. No stone to memorize him. No place for her to grieve. She whispered, "I will never forget you. I will remember you when I look out at the sea."

The children were playing on the floor with their wooden tops. Oceanus mewed in his mother's arms, and the loud creaking of the ship's timbers lessened. Sunlight streamed down the companionway and brought brightness to the bleak tween deck. The ship no longer rolled with the violent waves and wind. It rocked softly.

Mercy sat straight. "Caleb, the sun. It's coming down the companionway."

Caleb leaned over her. "The sky is as blue today, without a cloud in the sky."

"A good day for Martin."

"'Tis so, my love. Come, I'll take you topside to see it."

"Must I?"

"Don't you want to say goodbye to him?"

"I have already—repeatedly."

Two sailors stepped passed her and carried Martin's body away. Strange how no one looked on, not even the children. Was this something they had to become accustomed to more than normally? Mercy looked at Caleb's extended hand. She softly set hers within it, stood and followed the sailors. Others did as well. Then Martin's body was given to the sea.

Sunlight dazzled Mercy's eyes, and a frigid wind blew across her face. She stood at the bow of the *Mayflower* and watched the place where the body had gone move farther and farther away. Cold and damp, the air smelled earthy and sharp. "The wind has a different scent," she said to Caleb, "and the water is a different color."

"It smells like pine. Look at the gulls how they fly." He pointed to the tops of the masts.

She looked up. "What does it mean?"

"I'd venture to say we are near land."

She shut her eyes and drew in the air. Thank God, the voyage was ending.

"Land ho!" cried the seaman in the lookout.

Caleb grabbed Mercy's hand, and took her over to the opposite bulwarks with a dozens of other passengers. She stared at a broad strip of land as it came into view. 'Twas only a thin blue line, but land undoubtedly. Women broke into tears. Men hugged their wives and children.

"Land at last, Mr. Brewster," said Jones as they stood beside Caleb and Mercy. "But the storms threw us off course and your plans are not as they were. We will sail into the cove and anchor there."

"Where are we?" Caleb asked. He put his arm around Mercy.

"We are at the forty-seventh parallel above our original destination. We've missed the Hudson River by a few degrees."

Brewster stood forward. "Our agreement with the London Company is we do not settle north of the forty-first parallel."

"That I'm aware of, sir." Jones looked at the sky. "The wind may shift upon us, so do not get your hopes too high of reaching the Hudson in winter. We must sound our way in. The bottom is irregular. It may be fifty fathoms and then two, then twenty. We could tear the keel. Now you must excuse me. I have a crew to command."

Jones stepped away and shouted orders. For half the day, they continued this cautious progress along the coast. The leadsman's chant lulled everyone into a sleepy security. The water seemed safe enough, but the lookout shouted, "Breakers afore!"

Everyone turned and peered in the direction of his hand and saw white churning water. Mercy held on to Caleb's arm. Her heart quickened and she fixed her eyes ahead. "We've missed Virginia."

"Shoal water." Caleb held her close.

"Is it enough for us to sail through?"

"They have to be careful. It could pound out the bottom of the ship."

Mercy felt a lump grow in her throat. Hadn't they had enough hardship and? If they could not get through, and sail down to the Hudson, where would they end up?

The wind shifted. One moment the sails were flapping at an unusual calm and the next the wind filled them so that they bellied out and forced the ship back. The passengers sensed the crews' fears. After all those agonizing weeks, were they going to wreck here within sight of land? The movement of the ship made Mercy's head dizzy. She clung to Caleb, and he held her against him as tight as he did the day he carried her home from the fire. She set her hand on his chest, felt it rise and fall and his heart beat anxiously. Laying her head on his shoulder, she said, "Tell me truthfully. Are we doomed here?"

He gripped her hand in his and held it to his lips. "Master Jones and his crew want to live as much as we do, my love. He will find a way."

She drew back. He was always so sure, but this time his voice trembled and she believed he feared as well as the next man. She had not been with him when the beam cracked, and now imagined the anxiety he must have felt. Yet, he never told her. "You do not have to be strong for me, Caleb. We both know what we face."

Jones turned to the people. "Let us not make the attempt. I'm turning the ship back." He cupped his hand over his mouth and shouted, "Bout ship! Turn her into the wind."

"Can we not go around these shoals?" asked William Bradford.

Jones shook his head. "Only a non-mariner would ask such a question, sir. The wind is against us. The sea has become a blockade. We must turn back otherwise this ship will break apart and everyone aboard will die."

Caleb stepped forward. "We are all anxious to land. We cannot risk the lives of our women and children."

"Christopher Jones is master of this ship and knows what is best," said Brewster.

William said, "We can land in the cape and find a place to settle before winter sets in."

Jones looked at the men. "There is plenty of forestland. The harbor will be safest for now. I won't take this ship any farther."

As Jones stepped away, Caleb turned to Brewster. "Who knows the mind of the Lord, sir?"

"Not I. So we must trust in His providence."

That night the Separatist leaders met and talked for hours. When Caleb returned to Mercy, she drew him down beside her and set her head against his chest. "The first thing I will do is wash your doublet, my beloved."

He nudged her chin. "It is in need of a good washing, I admit. Aye and my body as well."

She could hear his heart beating through his doublet. It seemed faster than usual. "I can hear your heart. Are you worried?"

"Worry is commonplace, Mercy."

"And human. What did our leaders decide?"

"Mr. Clark, the Master's mate, told us there is a fine harbor on the other side of the cape."

"At least we will be safe there. I do not care where we land."

"Nor I, my love. I'm anxious to build a house for you."

She nestled against him. "But there is more troubling you."

"Some of us sense a mutiny against us among the crew. They are restless and disappointed in the voyage. They are not bound to land here and some are saying they'll turn around and go back to England."

"Jones would never allow it," Mercy said alarmed.

"I do not think he would, but we have got to do something. We cannot build a settlement without these men."

Artic cold swept through every seam, and the Separatists threw cloaks and blankets around their shivering bodies and drew their children into their arms. The seas were rough, fierce—constant and unrelenting. The little ship could not go on otherwise the raging waves would claim her, engulf her in its fury, and send her and all aboard to the frigid murky bottom.

Mercy pressed her lips against Caleb's. He had allowed his beard to grow during the voyage, and it felt soft against her smooth skin. She ran her fingers over his face. He took her hand and kissed her palm. Relieved they would stay put, and the sea would no longer imprison them in its unpredictable grasp, she wrapped her arms about his waist as the ship ran with the strength of the wind in her sails.

With no break in the cold or in the calming of the wind, the *Mayflower* escaped rough seas and a near shipwreck when Jones turned her. Put to anchor in the cape, the ship took on a stillness passengers had long missed. William Bradford came down the companionway. "Gentlemen, we are needed in the Master's quarters."

Murmurs went around, and the ladies and children were left alone. "Well," said Mary Brewster, "we are at last alone to speak of womanly things."

Rose Standish laid on a pallet, sick the entire voyage, nursed by young Pricilla Mullins. "I agree. We have been bottled up among the men for so long I'm to burst with wanting womanly conversation." Her confession brought a round of bright smiles to each face. "Why do you suppose Master Jones wishes to meet with our men?" she asked.

"Perhaps they need to discuss our alighting," said Dorothy.

Mercy glided a brush through her hair. "Then they are in conference, but not for any danger we are in."

"We will soon know." Mary Brewster took out her knitting needles and a ball of wool from her basket.

"Tell me, Mary," Mercy said, "what is the first dish you'll make in your new home?"

"It will depend on what my husband can hunt." Mary set her knitting down on her lap and sighed. "But I should love to roast a turkey."

"With chestnut stuffing," chimed in Elizabeth Hopkins.

"And peas swimming in butter," yearned Dorothy.

"What shall we plant in our gardens besides flowers?" Mary asked.

Mercy chimed in. "I should like to plant squash and onions. You can make hearty pasties with squash and onions."

"The men were sure to bring plenty of seeds for crops," Dorothy replied. "Next harvest we will have plenty. Every one of us ladies will have a house."

Mercy looked at the women around her. They had grown thin during the voyage, and she hoped the men would bring in enough deer and wild turkey to withstand the long winter. Among the women, Susanna White would bear her child anytime now. At least she had more flesh upon her than the rest. Smiling, she ran her hand over her belly. "I've no doubt we women will be having lots of babies."

Love Brewster drew beside his mother. "I'm hungry."

Mary rubbed her son's head and smiled. "When are you not, my son? You may have my portion of ship's biscuit."

Pricilla Mullins bit into her ration. "Mercy, we hear you are a fine cook. Would you teach me some specialties so I may please my future husband?"

"I would be pleased to, Pricilla," Mercy replied.

"My step-mother brought her book *The English Huswife*. It has tempting recipes in it."

"Mercy needs no cookbook," Dorothy said. "She is skilled, and her food is delicious. You'll learn much from her Pricilla, and I daresay John Alden will be glad for it."

Pricilla Mullins smiled shyly and lowered her eyes. Her flawless skin colored. "He may not stay. But I pray he does." The women teased her gently and spoke over each other giving the young girl advice.

"At least none of us will go without shoes," said Mary Brewster. "Your father has thought of every contingency, Pricilla."

"He was lucky he found room for all the shoes he brought." Pricilla stuck out hers and wiggled her feet. "He made these for me, and he has brought more than two hundred pairs including boots to fit us all out."

Mercy broke off a piece of ship's biscuit and put it in her mouth. It tasted bitter without anything to sweeten it. "Is it not splendid how the Lord put us together? We depend so much on our men to provide for us. It's only fitting we do the same in the ways of running a house. If there is one thing to plague a man it is a lazy wife, or a woman that does nothing but complain and make demands the live-long day." As she spoke, her voice rang true like a storyteller. She mimicked the kind of wife she spoke of, closing her eyes as if falling to sleep, and then eyeing the women as if searching for flaws. They laughed.

Mary Brewster continued her knitting. "You speak like a sage, Mercy."

Mercy shook her head. "I am no sage, Mary. I reserve wisdom to the aged."

"There is wisdom in most women that begins early in life," Mary said. "No earthly sage can compare their wisdom to ours."

Mercy stood and stretched. "The men must be engaged in some kind of business. I wonder what they are doing."

"I hope they will build us shelters soon and get us off this ship." Dorothy stood too, and stretched her back. "We will all die of scurvy if they do not."

"That is what the lemons are for." Mary Brewster scowled at Dorothy. "You'll not get scurvy as long as you drink the juice. Dr. Fuller says so."

"And why be so glum, Dorothy?" Mercy said. "Let us hear a story from Mary."

"Oh, my dear Mercy," said Mary. "I have enough stories to last the whole day. I shant tell you any that are sad. Those are aplenty. I will tell you the story of how I met Mr. Brewster and how I fell in love with him."

The women scooted forward. Before Mary could continue, a seaman ducked his head under the beams of the gun deck. "Come topside, if you please, ladies." He turned back up the companionway. The women gathered their children and one by one made their way up on deck. The men stood together. The crew and Master Jones among them.

"Each man among us has signed a compact in order to preserve our common good and for the furtherance and protection of our wives, children, friends and brethren," said William Brewster.

"Will you read it to us, husband?" said Mary Brewster.

"Indeed I will, good wife." He held the document closer to his eyes. "In the name of God, Amen."

Heads bowed. "Amen" all repeated.

"We, whose names are underwritten, the loyal subjects of our dread Sovereign Lord King James, by the Grace of God, of Great Britain, France, and Ireland, King, defender of the Faith, etc. Having undertaken for the Glory of God and advancements of the Christian faith and honor of our King and Country, a voyage to plant the first colony in the Northern parts of Virginia, do by these presents, solemnly and mutually in the presence of God and one another, covenant and combine ourselves together into a civil body politic; for our better ordering, and preservation and furtherance of the ends aforesaid; and by virtue hereof to enact, constitute, and frame, such just and equal laws, ordinances, acts, constitutions, and offices, from time to time, as shall be thought most meet and convenient for the general good of the colony; unto which we promise all due submission and obedience. In witness whereof we have hereunto subscribed our names at Cape Cod the eleventh of November, in the year of the reign of our Sovereign Lord King James, of England, France, and Ireland, the eighteenth, and of Scotland the fifty-fourth, 1620."

As Elder Brewster read, Mercy fixed her eyes on his face, and took in every word he spoke. Her heart grew within her. Her spirit rose to such a degree her breathing caught in her throat. To know each man pledged to protect the women and children, and build a new colony upon these desperate shores, regardless of their beliefs, was more than she had dreamt. Never in England had she seen such willingness among such differences come together for the good of all.

Separatist, Protestant, and crew rallied to begin the venture ashore and look out a place for habitation. They brought a shallop with them out of England and set the ship's carpenters to work to trim her after storm and rough sea bruised and shattered her parts. It provided great entertainment for the children, who by instruction of their mothers sat quietly out of the way.

"Look at her." Mr. Bennett clicked his tongue. "She's gonna be long in mending."

"Aye," said another. "I'd say a fortnight or more."

"That long?" Caleb asked. "Can I lend in my hand, sirs?"

Mercy stifled a giggle when the seaman shot Caleb a questioning look. "Shipbuilding and repairing is not the same as your trade. Not sure you are up to the task that awaits us."

"My husband is excellent at his trade, sirs," Mercy said.

"Aye no doubt," said the lead carpenter. "He'll have plenty of work to do building you a house, Mrs."

Caleb opened his mouth to argue. Mercy put her arm through his and moved him away. "Best you leave them to their work and go ashore with the others, my love."

"I'll give them credit for taking pride in their duty."

"If they need more help, you'll be the first they ask. You shall see."

"Aye, you are wise, Mercy. My pride is a bit sore." He looked out across the water to the yellow beach and the barren trees beyond it. "The sooner we find a place to build the better. Winter is upon us."

"Why must we stay on the ship?" she asked. "We cannot abide living in darkness below any long."

"It is safer until we know what we face on land."

"You think the Indians will be unwelcoming?"

He set his hand lovingly on her shoulder. "We will make friends if they will accept us."

"I hope so. I heard William speak of forming a confederacy with the tribe here."

"He has spoken of it, yes. It is as the apostle said that we should live peacefully with all men."

Pulling her hood over her head, she sat on a barrel near the children. Caleb moved uneasily on his feet. She knew him to be anxious to set his hands to work. As for Mercy, the pangs of hunger and the weakness in her body grew. She tried not to show it for fear he would worry, especially if he knew the secret she held until the right time came to tell him. She drew her cloak tighter when an unfamiliar sensation moved in her middle. Taking in a deep breath, she hugged her arms across her body. The feeling lingered, causing her heart to enlarge.

After several days exploring the land and suffering in the freezing temperatures, the men returned. Myles Standish put his hand on Caleb's shoulder. He was a tall man, stalwart with dark hair and eyes. Known for his courage as a skilled soldier, Mercy sensed a brutality in him. Indeed he would protect the colony, but she worried he would do it in such ways the Separatist would find disturbing. He walked on, and Mercy looked at Caleb bewildered.

"Myles looks concerned. What has happened?"

"I wish not to speak of it," he replied.

You think I cannot bear it, that I might fall apart?"

He looked back at her. "Yes."

She blinked. "Your answer is telling. What did you find on shore?"

"Another time."

Mercy pressed her lips and fisted her hands. Then she placed her right palm on his back. "Tell me gently if you are afraid of how I'll react."

"You've already faced a blow. Must I make it worse?"

"I must face what dangers lay ahead. Better now than not knowing at all."

"Why are you so persistent?"

"Because…I need to know. We all do. But if you think it best not to tell me, then I will not pressure you any further."

She drew back and picked up a cap she had been mending. Drawing the needle through the fabric, she grew silent, yet her mind wandered. If they had found a place to build the settlement, and all was well, he would have said so. Now she knew the opposite was true. They'd stay aboard the *Mayflower* and slowly starve or die from disease. Fear gripped her insides, but she kept her face calm and did not speak. Caleb pulled the tip of his knife from the board. He turned the blade in his hand and stared at it. Mercy tightened a thread and looked at him. His mouth was drawn down, his eyes staring forward. Despair sunk deep as a blade in his flesh.

Myles stood in the center of the gun deck. "Elder Brewster has asked me to tell you what we found on shore. I warn you, the news may not be pleasant to some of you."

Caleb looked up at Standish. "Are you sure it is wise with the children here?"

"Some are too young to understand, the rest need to know."

"Ah, the Puritan belief that children need exposure to hardship and death." He turned the knife in his hand. "I have no child, but if I did they would not know, and I would not have brought them on this voyage."

His jaw jerked and he struck the blade back into the plank between his feet. Mercy reached for Caleb's hand. He had held back his anxiety most of the voyage, and now it was catching up to him. What had he seen that troubled him so? What caused him to lash out at Myles? Those around them stared at the floor and were silent, except for Dorothy Bradford. Sympathy shown on her face, but none could understand him as well as Mercy. She squeezed his hand and whispered softly to him, "Rein in your anger, my love."

He pulled his hand from hers, snatched up the knife and sheaved it. "I am sorry for my outburst." He placed his arms across his knees. "I've come to think of you all as my family. I want none to suffer."

He ran his hands over his face. "Doesn't God see you have had enough?"

William Bradford spoke up. "You are our brother, Caleb. Whatever we may suffer, we will endure together."

Brewster joined Myles. "If anyone wishes to turn their hearing aside, take your cloaks and go to the upper deck. 'Tis cold, but you will be spared of what you fear. But I warn you, your thoughts may travel far beyond the truth."

No one moved. Myles Standish put his hands over his belt and proceeded to tell the people of their expeditions. Earlier they had marched about the space of a mile by the sea when they saw persons with a dog coming toward them. When they saw the English, they fled into the woods. Myles was prepared to engage them and see if there were more of them hiding in ambush. Night came on and they set out sentinels and rested quiet. In the morning, they followed the Indians' tracks until they met with a wide creek. The thickets were so dense they tore at their clothes. At length they found water and drank. "It was sweet to taste New England water," Myles said. "More pleasant than wine or beer."

A few passengers smiled, and all agreed fresh water made the land appealing. Myles went on to describe the Indian village they found. The inhabitance were dead, bones scattered, some in shallow places."

Mary Brewster's brow bent with sorrow. "The whole village?"

"I'd say so." His words struck fear into the hearts of the people.

"If there is plague here, we dare not settle in such a place," one man said.

"It happened a long time ago, and the village is many miles from the shore. We've nothing to fear."

"Is that true, Dr. Fuller?" asked Mercy.

"Myles is right. I do not believe there is danger of plague."

Myles went on. "The land is a goodly place. There are fields where we can plant crops in the spring, and trees for building our houses."

"Yet it is winter."

"Planting certainly will have to wait, but we can build."

"What of food, Myles?"

"This time of year the deer bed down and will be illusive. But there are fowl and fish to be caught." He paused and folded his arms. "We will face hardships here. I'll not say anything more."

"It does not sound too awful," said Elizabeth Hopkins as she rocked her newborn. "You say the plagued village is far, and you were not attacked by anyone. I think Caleb is wrong. We will do well here."

"You are ignorant of the dangers of this land," said her husband. "Be quiet, woman."

Caleb stood. "I did not say we could not settle here, Mrs. Hopkins. God knows we need to get off this boat. But from what I saw, and how it struck me in my heart, I was thinking of the women and children. My wife has settled me. Before God Almighty and all his angels every man in this company will protect and defend each woman and child even to the death."

"Surely there will be no need for our men to lay down their lives? Will there?"

Tense silence followed.

"Can any of you answer my question?" Elizabeth held her baby closer.

"Mrs. Hopkins, none know what the future will bring, let alone one day," said Brewster. "We must trust our lives into the hands of the Almighty."

"You Separatists. Can you not give a clearer answer than that? I am more afraid now than I ever was."

Mercy put her arm around Elizabeth's shoulders. She looked at Brewster, the man who led them, and asked if the women could have a few moments alone, so that they may discuss among themselves the things that needed to be done to comfort one another. He agreed when Mary Brewster, his devoted wife, agreed with Mercy. The men departed for the upper deck and the women were left with their children. One by one, they shared their thoughts, and as the time passed each settled into a sisterly mutuality having voiced their own kind of *Mayflower* Compact.

"So it is settled, ladies," said Mary Brewster. "As a whole, we will aid one another and encourage one another. When there is hunger, we will share our food. When there is sickness, we who are skilled will nurse the ill. We will pray together for the settlement, especially for our men for their lives and safety. We will obey the mandates of the Lord and break bread from house to house. We will comfort one another, as we do now whether saint of stranger. 'Tis no different than the women of the first century." She smiled and so did the others.

Mercy sat forward, her heart at ease. "The winter will be the hardest time for us. But when spring comes, we can all plant gardens. I think it would be wonderful if in the fall at the time of harvest, we gather out of our abundance and a have day of thanks with a feast."

Wrestling Brewster sat beside his mother. He'd been told to stay behind with the other children, while his brother Love being much older was allowed to leave with their father. He stood up with a determined look on his face. "Mrs. Treymayne?"

"Yes, Wrestling?"

"Be sure our feast is without ship's biscuits."

This brought on a round of smiles. "Out of the mouths of babes," laughed Mary.

Chapter 29

Mercy shivered. The cold bit at her skin and caused her eyes to water. She could not remember a time where she felt this cold. She grew sick of the salty air and ached for the taste of fresh water instead of stale beer. She tried to remember how a freshly picked apple tasted. She longed for bread instead of ship's biscuit, butter, savory greens, and tea sweetened with honey.

The wind blew high, capping the waves with white foam. The sky turned gray and stormy. The stretch of land drew out in an inky line, forbidding and barren. Seabirds dotted the beach. Some hovered above the sand, their wings motionless in the gusts, a boding sound rising from their throats.

Peering over the side, Mercy called down to Caleb. He sat in the stern of the shallop and met her eyes. "Bring us good news, Caleb."

He looked up at her and smiled. "God willing we shall, Mercy. Do not lean so far over the bulwark. You want to fall into the water?"

"No indeed not. Though I am in sore need of a bath."

He laughed. "The water is too cold for a bath. Too cold for both of us."

"But you would fish me out if I did fall in. Wouldn't you?"

"Indeed you know I would. At the risk of my own life, I'd do anything to save yours." He tipped his broad-brimmed hat back and his dark locks fell along his shoulders. She planted her feet firm on the deck, blew him a kiss and hoped he'd return with news that would gladden all hearts aboard. The boatmen plunged their oars into the water and rowed toward the shore. Winter had closed in. Game would have gone deep into the forests to shelter. What food could the men forage in this strange land? Would they find clams in the sand if they dug deep enough? Would fish be in plenty in such cold northern waters? So little aboard was left to sustain them. Meat had turned rancid. Barrels of flour and grain overran with weevils, and the stores of dried peas were gone. At least the forests were apt to give them timber to build their houses and warm their hearths.

Dorothy stepped beside her. "You think they will find a place for us?"

"I hope so. This is the third time they've tried."

"Houses take long to build. We'll be trapped on this hulk all that time."

"We should be thankful we made it this far. The men will hunt game."

"Or starve if they cannot find any."

"Why wouldn't they?"

"You heard what Captain Standish said. Deer will have fled deep into the forest and bedded. I imagine turkeys are equally illusive."

"That may be, but our men are capable."

The shallop sailed across the water and reached the shore. Mercy's eyes never left it, but watered when the men disembark and she saw Caleb plow his way through the surf and onto the sand. She and Dorothy were silent watching the men, silent and prayerful.

Dorothy shivered. She whispered, "William…"

"He'll be back, Dorothy. So will Caleb. I cannot think otherwise, though my heart is trembling."

"There are savages hiding in the forest." Dorothy eyes narrowed, as if she were searching the woodlands. "They peer out at our men from behind the trees and bushes. They are lying in wait for them. Heaven above, I'm glad we did not bring John with us."

Mercy did not immediately reply. When they first arrived into the Cape, the men had faced a barrage of arrows and retreated. Jones and Elder Brewster agreed to remove to the other side of the Bay for safety.

"Captain Standish and his men are skilled fighters. You've nothing to fear, Dorothy. Besides, if there are any Indians, we will make peace with them. They'll be our friends and…"

With her hands clutching in and out, Dorothy Bradford turned on Mercy. "Our men faced them already. Praise God not a single arrow struck. Don't forget, the Virginia tribes did not make peace with the Jamestown settlers. Why would they make peace with us?"

"Dorothy, war came from both sides."

"The colonists were starving."

"It was a long time ago."

"What happened to the people of Roanoke?"

"I do not know, Dorothy. Don't assume."

Dorothy's eyes shifted to the shoreline. "Mercy...they will kill our men and take us for wives. They will raise the children to be Indian..." She could not go on. Her body began to shake violently and fear filled her eyes.

Mercy placed her hands on Dorothy's shoulders. She had not spoken in this way for weeks, and now the suffering she assumed she and the others would face had resurfaced.

"Let us go below, Dorothy. The wind is strong and the cold is going through our cloaks."

"I want to wait for William."

"It will be hours before he returns. Come, we will read together."

"I'm not in the mood for reading."

"Then we can go through our belongings and decide what we need to take first."

"We won't be taking anything for some time. It has already been weeks since we landed. It will be more weeks we will stay on this wretched ship. Once they find a place for us, it will be more weeks, maybe months before we have a roof over our heads."

"Let's go below and watch the children play. It will do us good. I think I heard Olive whining for you. You know she has become very attached."

Dorothy nodded. "I love that beast and the spaniel too."

"Then let's go see them. We cannot stay up here in this cold."

"If anything happens to me, I want you to have my clothes and..."

"What is this talk? Why so dark? Nothing is going to happen to you. Have faith, Dorothy. We have a wonderful life ahead of us with our husbands. All will be well."

Dorothy sniffed and lowered her eyes. "You do not understand. I am ashamed."

"Ashamed of what?"

"I miss my house in Holland. I miss my son and parents."

"You are not alone in this. Many of us left loved ones behind."

"And they show no sorrow for it. Not like me."

"In a year, young John will be bouncing on your knees."

"You heard what Elder Brewster said. None of us know what the future holds."

"That is true. But before any future voyages take place, our houses will be filled with laughter and bountiful tables, and all before the year is over."

"And the days will be long."

"Time will go by swiftly."

"I do not think so, Mercy."

Mercy paused. She looked across the water to the shore. The men were not to be seen. "Whether our days are slow or swift, we will grow old with our men, and see our children grow and give us grandchildren. We will set them on our laps before our fires and tell them the story of our voyage and the hope God put into our hearts, and we will tell them of the Indians we befriended. You'll see."

"Stop trying to comfort me," Dorothy said, gripping the rail of the ship. "You see no trouble for us, do you? You spoke this way in Holland about our voyage, and it has been misery upon misery. The only thing you have seen is blue skies and a calming sea."

"That is not true. I have feared the storms as much as any other woman. If I do not dream of a better life, I fear I will sink into despair. I've never liked the feeling of despair."

"Your optimism is not reality." Dorothy looked out across the water to the land. "It may be your undoing."

"I do not understand you. I speak of having faith."

"Your faith is misguided, Mercy. Faith is not thinking only of the better, but believing when the worse comes, you can endure it."

"I thought it was trusting in God," Mercy said.

"It is that too."

"But I cannot speak of things as you want me to do. I cannot speak so bleakly."

"'Tis better to know what to expect in order to have courage. If you continue ignoring the hardships we have had, and are going to face that strange land, you will not be able to survive."

Shocked by Dorothy's confrontation, Mercy looked away. Could Dorothy be correct? Had she lived in a dream world of her own liking? Was her faith misguided? "I am sorry if I have been an annoyance to you, Dorothy. I thought I was a comfort to you, but I see I was wrong. I will not speak of my hopes with you again…that is if you will do the same regarding your fears."

Dorothy's eyes widened. "A breach has grown between us."

Such words caused a pang to pass through Mercy. She and Dorothy had been close all this time. "We should not allow our differences to cause any kind of breach. I love you as if you were my own sister."

Master Jones approached them. "I'm sure the men will find a suitable place today, ladies. For now, go below. The wind is too brisk for such fair skin."

Dorothy said, "Please, let me stay a little longer. I wish to pray and be alone with God."

Jones shifted on his feet. He was not a believer and failed to understand such things. He scratched his beard. "As long as you are below within a few moments, ma'am, you may stay. I would not want you falling sick and your husband blaming me."

Dorothy shook her head. "I won't fall sick. I never do, do I, Mercy?"

"I think you should listen," Mercy said. "And if you will permit me to say, you have, like the rest, of us grown weak from these horrible conditions." She felt tears burn her eyes. "It's a wonder more of us haven't died like Martin..." Her throat tightened and she wanted to cry. Not now, not in from of Master Jones who was looking at her.

Jones gave Dorothy and Mercy a short bow and walked across the deck to his cabin. Mercy hurried away and went below. The light shone dim from the lantern attached to the beam in the ceiling. Her stomach ached with hunger. When she looked into the eyes of the children, her heart lurched in her chest. They must find food and build warm shelters soon else, the children would perish. Scurvy and starvation crept upon them like sludge over the hull of the *Mayflower*.

She sat down in the place where she and Caleb slept and laid her head in her arms. *Dorothy is right. My faith is misplaced. I am wretched.*

She drew her hands to her breast and held them there a moment. She thought of Caleb. She shut her eyes and saw him in her mind. In a dark blue doublet, leather breeches, his broad-brimmed hat shadowing his face. Had her hope of making a quilt for their bed made of the same color blue, stitched together with white thread, been a sign of weakness? She dreamed of sewing linen pillowcases stuffed with soft down goose feathers, that their windows would overlook the harbor, catch the morning sun and soften in the evening light.

She had not voiced what deep inner thoughts she had, thoughts that she did her best to shove aside. The opposite of her dreams would crush them. Disease had already come upon them. Death had already visited them. There would be more, from the eldest to the youngest babe. They had no food. No clean water to drink. No way to bathe. For eight weeks, she had gone without washing her body or hair. For eight weeks, she had eaten ship's biscuit and spoilt food. She lost Martin, and now it seemed she had lost her best friend. Yes, Dorothy was right. What good was there amid this misery?

Above her, boots pounded over the deck. The ship's bell rang. She froze. Others around her paused to listen. Mary Brewster said. "Why are they ringing the ship's bell?"

"The last time was when Mr. Howland fell overboard."

Mercy waited and listened.

"It could be the men are returning."

"Oh, pray to God none have been hurt."

Startled, Mercy stood with the others and sped up the ladder to the deck. *Caleb. Oh, please let it be Caleb has come back.*

As the pilgrims gathered on the deck, Jones shouted orders. He turned to them. "Pray to your god for Dorothy Bradford. She had fallen overboard."

Mercy shoved her way through the crowd. Women were crying. Two of the eldest men were seeking a way to save the hapless woman. Two drew off their coats and pulled off their shoes. Jones reached them and held them back. "Unless you are good swimmers and can bear the icy water, you must stay where you are. Otherwise, you'll make your wives widows this day. My sailors will do the job."

Fear raced through Mercy. She looked down and saw Dorothy face down in the water. Her body lay beneath the waves, for her woolen clothes pulled her down. Her skirts flared out as if she were dressed in an old-fashioned farthingale. Her cap floated away on a wave. Her hair spread out in the water. Gasps and cries of despair rose from the Separatists. Some went down on bended knees. Others turned into each other's arms.

"Take the children below," ordered Master Jones. "This is not for their eyes."

Immediately the women drew their children away and took them back to the tween deck. Mercy trembled from the blow of seeing Dorothy's listless body floating in the murky waves. The pain seized her heart. She gripped the fabric at her breast. A seaman climbed down the ship's ladder and slipped into the water. Another threw a rope over the side. The one in the water caught it and swam with it to Dorothy's body where he tied it beneath her arms. He held up his hand to the sailor above, and when word was given, Dorothy Bradford was hauled upward. Two seamen brought Dorothy over the bulwark. They laid her down upon the deck and stood back.

In anguish and shock, Mercy fixed her eyes on her dear friend's face. All color had seeped away as if she'd been drained by the sea. Her once rosy cheeks were as white as her linen collar. Her lips blue and sealed. Empty eyes stared from a frightened face. Yet, how still she looked, with the sea on her lashes turning icy, her head bare of her cap, her hair crossing over her forehead and neck.

Mercy hastened to remove her cloak and cover Dorothy. She went down on her knees and pulled it up to Dorothy's chin. She tapped her cheeks. "Dorothy. Dorothy, it is I, Mercy. Do not leave us. Come to, Dorothy."

"That will do no good." Jones put his hand on Mercy's shoulder. "Mrs. Bradford is gone."

She looked up at Jones. "Do something."

"There is nothing I or anyone else can do."

"How could this have happened?" she cried.

"Whales have been playing in the harbor. Perhaps she leaned over to watch them and lost her balance." Jones spoke in a sober tone.

"I just left her."

"One of my seaman said he saw her go over, and sounded the alarm. I'm deeply sorry for Mr. Bradford."

"How shall we tell him?" Mercy looked at Mary Brewster, whose face was tense with sorrow. She drew down beside Mercy.

"We must take her below," said Mary. "Prithee, is there a place where we may lay her?" she asked Jones.

"Since there is sickness already in your quarters, she must be kept here, up on deck." Jones signaled his sailors and they lifted Dorothy's body.

Mercy stood up. "In the open, sir?"

"There is no better place, ma'am. When the men return they can bury her."

Mercy swallowed and sighed. "Not back in the water?"

"Not unless, Mr. Bradford wills it." He turned to go, then looked back. "I suggest you wrap her well."

Stifling her tears, Mercy placed her hand over her mouth. She looked down at the lifeless body of her friend, grieved to have lost her, heartbroken over their last words to each other. She turned to Mary and sought comfort. Mary Brewster took her into her arms.

"We will attend to her body—you and I, and watch over her until the men return."

Grieved, Mercy nodded.

"Find other clothes for her in her chest and a sheet to wrap her in."

Mercy returned to the tween deck and took from Dorothy's trunk her last set of clothes, a linsey-wool gray frock, a white chemise, a pair of wool stockings, and a collar made of Holland lace. The women stood around the body, hiding her from view while Dorothy's soaked garments were removed. The wool was heavy with water, and no doubt caused her to struggle, eventually dragging her down.

Mary Brewster dried Dorothy's her hair in her apron. "William must have loved her hair."

Crewmen and passengers were stunned into silence. The women wept silently. Men stared and frowned at the deck. Below, Oceanus, quieted at his mother's breast, and raised a fist.

Chapter 30

Nigh to sunset, the shallop bumped against the hull. Wives who were well enough waited on the deck for their husbands. Mercy looked down from the bulwarks to see Caleb seated in the stern. The sky was thick with winter clouds. A flurry of snowflakes fell and the ropes along the rigging were glazed with ice. She drew her hood over her head and gathered it close. Her heart quivered when she saw William Bradford. Poor William. How could anyone tell him Dorothy was gone? He looked anxious to board as he managed to stand inside the little boat. Bradford looked up and hailed Mercy.

"It does our hearts well, Mercy, to see such fair faces looking down on us. Bring Dorothy over."

Mercy stepped back. She could not answer. Taking in a breath, she moved back to the bulwarks and fixed her eyes on her husband.

"Go before me, Caleb," she heard William Bradford say. "Your wife appears more anxious to welcome you than mine." Of course, Dorothy could not be seen. She was not beside Mercy waiting for her beloved. Instead, her body was laid out near the forecastle wrapped in a linen shroud.

Caleb reached for the rope ladder. He seemed different, his face careworn, and his hair lank about his shoulders. The expedition ashore must have been difficult. His doublet was tattered and stained, his boots splattered with mud and sand. She hurried to him and embraced him.

"An embrace to crush my ribs, dear wife?" He smiled as he set her back. William Bradford came over the bulwark and greeted Mercy. "Happy to have him back, Mercy?"

She nodded. "Yes, William."

"Where is my wife? I hope she isn't so sick she cannot greet me."

Saved from answering, Master Jones drew William aside. Mercy looked on as Jones spoke, and William placing his hands on his hips and staring at the deck listened. His face grew taut as he shifted on his feet.

"What is he telling William?" Caleb asked Mercy. "Where's Dorothy?"

She looked at him a moment. "Dorothy," she finally said in a whisper. To speak her friend's name, to remember the paleness of her face after drowning, brought on a wave of emotion. Her hands trembled and she clutched his doublet to pull him closer. "She fell overboard and…Dorothy has drowned and is dead."

Caleb stiffened. She set her head against his arm. They looked toward the forecastle. The roaring of the sea became so loud, Mercy could hear nothing else, only watch Jones's mouth move with horrible words. William's countenance fell sharply. His head sank toward his chest, toward his broken heart. Everyone gathered close. William pulled off his hat and followed Master Jones.

"We must go to him." Caleb strode across the deck. Mercy followed. William stood transfixed at the foot of Dorothy's body. "How?"

"She fell overboard," said Jones. "My crewmen tried to save her, but it was too late. We…"

William raised his hand. "It is all I need to know, sir."

Brewster approached William and laid one trembling hand on his arm. "Dorothy was a brave woman. Bear your grief as she would have you, William."

"I should not have made her come." He looked back at the men around him. "Help me lower her into the shallop so I can bury her on shore. She will not go into the water."

Mercy started forward. "No, Mercy." Caleb held her back. "You must let him alone."

She turned and through her tears said, "How many of us will die in this wilderness? Already we have lost Martin, Edward Thompson, and Jasper More. Now Dorothy. The children are sick. Everyone is worn out, most are coughing…"

"Mercy…"

"We're hungry," she said through her tears.

"I know we are."

"Months at sea, and now months still on this hapless ship."

"We cannot go ashore to live, not in this weather, my love. I wish I knew what to say, what to do to comfort you."

"I think we shall all go mad." She pressed her fingertips against her temples.

Caleb grabbed her hands and brought them down. "Stop," he said in a gentle voice.

She tried to calm the racing thoughts. She looked into his eyes— eyes that spoke of love—deep, tender, protective love. She grasped the front of his doublet. "I'm sorry, Caleb. I want to sit by a home fire again. I want to cook for you, mend for you, and sleep beneath a warm quilt with you." They looked over at the sailors lifting Dorothy's body. Mercy trembled and she started crying harder. "I want Dorothy back."

Caleb's eyes grew deeply mournful. He grabbed her and held her tight.

Caleb and Mercy went up to the forecastle that night while the stars were bright and abundant. The breeze quivered the edges of her hood. She wept. He held her close. The warmth of his body evaded her cloak and flowed into her. A sudden rush of tenderness seized her, and for a moment, she felt lonely for him, although she was in his arms.

A bird, of what kind Mercy did not know, cried out. She saw its wings sweep across the face of a full moon and disappear into the darkness. She had not seen the moon in days, and traced it with her eyes. Round and orange as an autumn pumpkin, it spread its light across the water in the bay.

Courage revived in her, but grief resided in her heart over Dorothy's drowning and the loss of Martin. She wept for William Bradford and admired how he grieved in private, going on with his work to settle the people.

God only knew what the future held for her and Caleb. All she could do was put her trust in Him they would survive. She would not ask for riches or the best house in the settlement. She would not ask for her beauty to linger. All she wanted was she and Caleb to live happy by their fireside and to be warm on winter nights, to be healthy and live into old age together. If it was not to be, she knew they would go to a better home and never see sorrow, sickness, or death again. Yet, she prayed the New World and all its dangers would not take him before her.

"Caleb."

"Yes, sweet wife?"

She leaned against him and pushed aside her hood. She wore no cap and she allowed her hair to fall forward over her shoulder. The wind lifted it and Caleb ran his hand down its length. "Are you still sad, my love," he asked, squeezing her shoulder.

"I am, but not to worry. Life goes on." She looked into his eyes through a mist of tears and saw the moonlight caught within them. "We have hope, do we not?"

"Yes." He wiped the tears from her cheeks. "Touch my two hands." He released her and held them up for her. She ran her fingers over his palms. "They've seen little work since we've left Holland, and I've lost my calluses. Still, these hands will build you a fine house in the new colony. I'll build furniture to your liking, and a bed with posts touching the ceiling." He nudged her chin. "You'll have to stuff the mattress."

"Ah, woman's work you think?" She draped her arms around his waist. "I'll have goose down for our mattress, not straw."

He bowed. "As you wish, Mistress Treymayne, but we only have two geese aboard and I doubt they will give up their feathers any time soon."

Mercy laughed. "I'll wait for the other ships with hopes they will bring more. I have had another wish, which has happened. Do you want to know what it is?"

"I know you'll tell me whether I want to hear it or not."

Playful, she turned around and folded her arms. "I will not."

He turned her back. "Oh, no, Mercy, tell me. I have a feeling it is something important, something about you and me."

She paused, watched his eyes grow with anticipation. Reaching up she ran her fingers through his hair and gazed lovingly at him. Through the breeze came a soft cry, a mew so soft it seemed heaven sent.

"Listen. Do you hear? Susanna White's baby is crying."

"I hear him." Caleb smiled. "He's the first child born in the New World."

"There will be others." Mercy placed her hand against his cheek, and turned his head so he would look into her eyes. "Now, listen carefully, Caleb Treymayne, for you shall not want to miss what I am about to say. I am with child."

His eyes widened. "What…did you say?"

"Dearest, Caleb. Listen carefully." She leaned into him. "You and I are going to have a baby in the New World."

Caleb lifted her in his arms and swung her around. His eyes lit up and he set Mercy on the deck of the *Mayflower*. Tenderly he placed his hands around her face and kissed her lips.

Mercy laughed. "I take it you are happy."

"Yes, my girl. What man wouldn't be?"

"I'm glad." She put her arms around his neck and embraced him. "Last night, I had a dream," she said. "I was standing on the poop deck looking down at the smiling faces of the people. I could make out each one. The breeze was warm and the sun alighted over us. I felt something warm slip into my hand…your hand, Caleb. Then I woke to your voice calling me to rise and come see the dolphins."

The End

'What could now sustain them but the Spirit of God and His grace? May not and ought not the children of these fathers rightly say, 'Our fathers were Englishmen, which came over this great ocean, and were ready to perish in this wilderness; but they cried unto the Lord, and He heard their voice and looked on their adversity.'

William Bradford: 'Of Plymouth Plantation'.

1630 ~ 1651

ACCOUNTS FROM WILLIAM BRADFORD'S 'OF PLYMOUTH PLANTATION' THAT I WROTE INTO THE STORY.

- The *Mayflower's* course to the New World, her voyage and the missing of the Hudson.

- The *Speedwell* being unseaworthy.

- The Spiteful Seaman: It is recorded he badgered the Separatists and threatened to throw them overboard. He was the first person to die on the *Mayflower*, of what condition it is unknown. Although he behaved badly toward the Pilgrims, they were saddened by his passing.

- The Birth of Oceanus to Elizabeth and Stephen Hopkins: My account is certainly fictionalized, but his birth was a major event that gave the Separatists hope. He was the only child born on the *Mayflower* during its historic voyage. A boy, Peregrine White, was born on board, after arriving in America, as the ship lay at anchor. Oceanus did not survive long and died in 1621.

- The Broken Beam: When this occurred, it threatened to break the ship apart. The men shored it up with a 'great screw'. The foresight to bringing the jackscrew saved their lives from drowning in a raucous sea.

- The Near Drowning and Rescue of John Holland: From Bradford's account, it sure seemed a miracle that John survived. It appears he might have been thrown overboard by either wind or the pitch of the ship. The halyards saved him from being swept away from the *Mayflower* and enabled the sailors to pluck him out of the sea.

- The many shoes Mr. Mullins brought on board the *Mayflower*.

- The signing of the Mayflower Compact.

- The Drowning of Dorothy Bradford: Dorothy's death remains a mystery to this day. Why she went overboard while the *Mayflower* was anchored in Plymouth Harbor gave rise to various theories. Bradford did not record anything other than his wife had gone overboard and drown. As I researched her tragic end, I grieved for this wife and mother, who had given up so much to follow her husband to the unknown.

EXTRAS

The English Huswife: mentioned by Priscilla Mullins, was a book of English cookery and remedies by Gervase Markham, published in 1615. It was a bestseller in its time, going through nine editions, and at least two other reprints by 1683. *Huswife* is the correct spelling of the time.

Tipcats: Wrestling Brewster asks Caleb if he'd carve him a tipcat. Puritan children played a game using two sticks, one large used like a bat, and one small with carved pointed ends called the 'cat'. A cat was tossed into the air and hit with the large stick toward the other players. Whoever caught the 'cat' was up next.

Ship's biscuit : Called hardtack later in the 19th century. Made of flour and water. The dough was rolled out and cut into squares or rounds, and then baked. Ship's biscuit could last for ages and kept seaman from starving.

Pottage: A thick soup or stew made of boiled vegetables, grains. Meat or fish was added if available. Pottage was a stable dish for many centuries, a dish more often eaten by the poor.

Apple Custard Pie: From the 17th century cookbook of Clara van Molle of Antwerp made of a flour crust, apples, custard, cinnamon, and sugar. You can find the recipe on the Allemansend Re-enactment YouTube channel.

DUTCH TO ENGLISH
Moeder = Mother
Engels = English
De = The
Je = Yes
Dat = That
Brand = Fire
Dunk u = Thank you
Skokbood = onion baquette
Boven = upstairs

THE SEPARATISTS IN 'MERCY'S REFUGE'

William Bradford:
Born around 1590 in Austerfield, England. He married Dorothy
May in Amsterdam in 1613. They traveled on _Mayflower_
together, leaving behind their son, John, with Dorothy's parents.
After Dorothy's death, Bradford married Alice (Carpenter)
Southworth in 1623 and had three children with her. Bradford
served as Governor of Plymouth Colony for thirty-one terms, and
wrote 'Of Plymouth Plantation'. He died in 1657.

> _Dorothy (May) Bradford:_ Born in 1597 Cambridgeshire,
> England, the daughter of Henry and Katherine May. She
> married William Bradford in 1613 when she was sixteen. She
> fell off the deck of Mayflower and drowned December 7,
> 1620.

> _Son, John Bradford:_ John came to America later, married
> Martha Bourne, took up residence in Duxbury and later
> moved to Norwich, Connecticut where he died about 1676,
> having had no children.

> _Henry and Katherine May,_ Dorothy Bradford's parents:
> Henry May was a Separatist elder in the Henry Ainsworth
> church congregation in Amsterdam. They took over the care
> of young John Bradford when Dorothy and William set sail
> for America. A year later, they arrived in Plymouth aboard
> the _Fortune._

Pastor John Robinson:
Born in 1571, and led the congregation in Holland. He was a
celebrated preacher of the Gospel. He married Bridget White in
1603/4 and they had seven children. He died March 1, 1625.

> _Bridget (White) Robinson_: Born in 1579, Lincolnshire,
> England. She married John Robinson in 1604. The had
> seven children. She died in 1643.

William Brewster:
Born 1566. An elder in Leyden. William was involved with printing religious materials forcing him to go into hiding from English authorities. He was the highest-ranking Separatist church official on *Mayflower*. He married Mary in 1592. They had five surviving children. He died in Duxbury in 1644.

> *Mary Brewster:* born around 1569 and died on April 17, 1627 in Plymouth. She married William Brewster about 1592 and had their first son Jonathan in Scrooby a year later. A second child, a daughter Patience, was born around 1600. By 1606, the Separatists began meeting at Scrooby Manor, the Bradford's home. Persecution mounted, and the meetings became secretive. She gave birth to a daughter at this time, and named her Fear. The Brewsters fled to Holland with the other members of the congregation. Five women survived the first winter. Mary was one of them. By the first Thanksgiving in 1621, she was among four who survived.

> *Son, Love Brewster:* Born in 1611 in Leyden, Holland. He was nine when he sailed on the *Mayflower* with his parents. Love married Sarah Collier in 1634, after her family came to America in 1633. They had four children. He died between 1650 and 1651. Sarah survived him for about forty more years, dying on 26 April 1691.

> *Son, Wrestling Brewster*: Born in 1614 in Leyden, Holland. He was six years of age when on the *Mayflower*. Died between 1627 and 1644. He was alive in 1627 at Plymouth, where he is listed in the household of his father William. He is not listed in the will or estate inventory of his father in 1644. Historians surmise he must have died in the interim years.

Mary (Norris) Allerton:

Mary was from Newbury, England. She married Isaac Allerton in Leyden in 1611. Mary gave birth to a stillborn son in Plymouth Harbor on 22 December 1620. She died in February 1621, leaving her husband and children to carry on without her.

> *Son, Bartholomew*: Born 1613. He was seven when he went with his parents aboard the *Speedwell* and *Mayflower*. When

grown, he returned to England and became a minister in Bramfield, Suffolk. His first wife was Margaret, and his second was Sarah Fairfax. He had at least four children, and died in 1658.

Daughter, Remember: Born 1615. Remember was about six on the *Mayflower*. She married Moses Maverick in 1635 and had seven children. She died between 1652 and 1656.

Daughter, Mary: Born 1616. Mary was four when aboard the *Mayflower*. She married Thomas Cushman in 1636 and had eight children. She is known as the last surviving *Mayflower* passenger, and passed this life in 1699 at age 83.

Christopher Martin, his wife Mary:

Born 1580, and married Mary Prower a widow, February 1606/7 In 1611, he was appointed a churchwarden, but on Easter 1612, he refused to kneel at communion, a common Puritan infraction. In 1617 he was appointed as a purchasing agent and then governor of the *Speedwell*. He did not appeal to the Separatists, and John Carver was the governor aboard the *Mayflower*.

John Howland:

He came on the *Mayflower* in 1620 as a manservant of Governor John Carver. He was one of the signers of the *Mayflower* Compact. According to records, he was between eighteen and twenty-one years old in 1620.

John Carver:

John Carver was sent along with Robert Cushman to the Virginia Company in England to negotiate and organize their venture of leaving Holland for the New World. Carver joined the Pilgrims on the *Mayflower* with his wife Katherine. He was acting governor on the ship, and was elected governor of the Colony. He served in that office until his sudden death from heatstroke in April 1621. His wife Katherine died a few weeks later, purportedly of a broken heart.

Dr. Samuel Fuller:

Born January 1580 in Norfolk, England. He left behind his wife Bridget when he sailed on the *Mayflower*. Bridget came later on the Anne in 1623. Dr. Fuller died in 1633.

Susanna White: (mentioned) wife of William White: William died during the first winter. Susanna later married Edward Winslow, who was widowed during the first winter. Theirs was the first marriage in Plymouth Colony. They had five children. She died between 1654 and 1675.

John Goodman: (mentioned) Owner of the mastiff and spaniel: John is mentioned in Bradford's missive. There is no mention of a wife or children. He died in 1621.

Robert Cushman: Born 1577 in Kent, England. He was instrumental in the planning of the voyage to the New World.

OTHERS ABOARD THE MAYFLOWER IN 'MERCY'S REFUGE'

Captain Myles Standish and wife Rose:

Myles was born between 1584 and 1587 in England. *Standish served in Queen Elizabeth's army. He assigned for a time in Holland. There he met* John Robinson and the Separatists in Leyden. The Separatists hired Myles to lead their militia, to establish and coordinate the Colony's defense against both foreign (French, Spanish, Dutch) and domestic (Native American) threats. His wife Rose died the first winter in Plymouth. He later married and had seven children.

Stephen Hopkins:

Stephen sailed on the ship *Sea Venture* on a voyage to Jamestown, Virginia in 1609 as a minister's clerk. The ship wrecked in Bermuda and he was stranded for ten months. He was sentenced to death when he participated in a mutiny, but after much pleading, his sentence was commuted and he returned to England. He married Elizabeth Fisher in 1617. Considered an expert on the native Indians, he was an important negotiator. He and Elizabeth had seven children. Stephen had three by his first wife who died before he returned to England. Stephen died in 1644, and made out a will, asking to be buried near his wife, and naming his surviving children.

Elizabeth Hopkins: Born around 1585. She married Stephen Hopkins in 1617/18. She gave birth to their second child,

Oceanus, aboard the *Mayflower*, and was one of four women who survived to the first Thanksgiving. Stephen and Elizabeth had five more children while living in Plymouth. She died sometime between 1638 and 1644 in Plymouth.

Their children are mentioned in Chapter 27 ~ Damaris, Giles, and Constance.

Priscilla Mullins:

Born around 1602 in Surry, England. She came on the *Mayflower* with her father William, her brother Joseph, and mother or stepmother Alice. Her family all died the first winter. By 1623, she married John Alden, a cooper aboard the Mayflower, and went on to have ten children. John and Priscilla founded the town of Duxbury in Massachusetts in 1624.

MASTERS AND CREW

John Reinolds: Master of the *Speedwell*.

You will find his surname spelled Reynolds on some websites. I used this spelling as it was in William Bradford's 'Of Plymouth Plantation'.

Christopher Jones:

Master of the *Mayflower*. Jones was a veteran of the European cargo business. His ship often transported wine to England. By June 1620, he had been hired for the Pilgrims. The *Mayflower* left Plymouth, Massachusetts in April 1621.

John Clarke:

Ship's pilot.

Doctor Giles Heale:

The surgeon aboard the *Mayflower*. He survived the first winter and returned to London on the *Mayflower* in April 1621, where he began his medical practice and worked as a surgeon until his death in 1653.

Mr. Bennett:

The *Mayflower's* carpenter. His name is not listed in any

document. The name 'Bennett' is from my own imagination. A name always puts a face to a character. He played a major role in the voyage, regarding the main beam and the shallop.

Robert Coppin:

Master's Mate aboard the *Mayflower*. Not much is known about Coppin, except that he claimed to have made the crossing once before.

The seaman who cursed the Separatists: Historians are not certain to the identity of this sailor. When I read William Bradford's account of this man, I felt a strange compassion for him and wondered what had made him so bitter toward Christians.

OTHER BOOKS BY RITA GERLACH

Historical

The Rebel's Pledge
Thorns in Eden and The Everlasting Mountains
Surrender the Wind

The Daughters of the Potomac Series

Book 1: Before the Scarlet Dawn
Book 2: Beside Two Rivers
Book 3: Beyond the Valley

Historical ~ Edwardian / Golden Age

After the Rain

Historical Romance Novellas in the Following Collections from Barbour Publishing.

The Victorian Christmas Brides ~ The Holly and the Ivy
The Runaway Brides ~ From This Day Forward
The Erie Canal Brides ~ Wedding of the Waters
Lessons on Love ~ A Song in the Night
Homefront Heroines ~ Moonlight Serenade

Current Novel in Progress: *Wait Until Morning (a WWI historical romance).*

Website: ritagerlach@wordpress.com

2 1982 03150 6243

CPSIA information can be obtained
at www.ICGtesting.com
Printed in the USA
LVHW030129271120
672777LV00004B/1054

9 798684 517587